WHAT PEOPLE ARE SA

THE SNAKE AND T

'Profoundly rich and transporting... This beautiful book plunged me into another world. From the first page I knew I was in the hands of a seriously good storyteller – every scene vivid, brimming full of life. Robert Southam writes with passion and poise and humour, touching on the darkest reaches of the human soul, but always quick to soar with joy and relish for the world's good things. He is one of those generous writers who makes the reader feel more alive.'
Dr Andrea Ashworth, book reviewer and bestselling author

'Set against the brutality of the Pinochet régime in Chile, Robert Southam's vertiginous tale of the flight of two lovers from across the racial and class divide follows the fortunes of Julieta and Mawi as they criss-cross through that country, Bolivia and Peru and then on to London, keeping just ahead of their pursuers. *En route* we get to see the devastation wrought on individuals and communities, especially indigenous ones, by unbridled capitalism and its militaristic allies. Southam manages the pace of the novel skilfully, combining hairpin-bend plot twists with detailed, almost ethnographic descriptions of the communities through which the couple pass. The author writes with a tingling, heart-pounding tenderness of the lovers' growing awareness of and feelings for each other as they resist oppression and uncertainty together. The narrative and the detailed scenes through which it develops make this a compelling and emotional experience.'
Paul Simon, *The Morning Star*

The Snake and the Condor

The Snake and the Condor

Robert Southam

Winchester, UK
Washington, USA

First published by Roundfire Books, 2015
Roundfire Books is an imprint of John Hunt Publishing Ltd., Laurel House, Station Approach, Alresford, Hants, SO24 9JH, UK
office1@jhpbooks.net
www.johnhuntpublishing.com
www.roundfire-books.com

For distributor details and how to order please visit the 'Ordering' section on our website.

ISBN: 978 1 78279 731 9
Library of Congress Control Number: 201495956

A CIP catalogue record for this book is available from the British Library.

Design: Stuart Davies

Printed and bound by CPI Group (UK) Ltd, Croydon, CR0 4YY, UK

By the same author:

Aïsha's Jihad

published by fm Oxford

ISBN 978-0-9545038-2-6

also available on cassette read by the author

ISBN 978-0-9545038-3-3

This book is for all those who welcomed me into their homes and hearts in Peru, Bolivia and Chile: the Mapuche community on the shores of the lagoon in Araucanía with whom I rode on horseback along the Pacific coast; Fortunata and her Quechua family on the island of Amantaní in the middle of Lake Titicaca; the Boras Indians in their houses on stilts in the shallows of the River Amazon. Also for the miners of Potosí who led me on hands and knees deep into the Bolivian earth; for the weavers' co-operative at Cuzco; and for Rosa and Adelina, my intrepid guides through the shanty-towns of Lima.

1

The outskirts of Santiago had been harrowing enough, with their plywood shanties, barefoot children and mothers in rags collecting fallen cabbage-leaves from the costermongers' barrows, and rotten pawpaws and apples thrown by the venders into the gutter. In Lima, from the back of the cab on its way south from the centre, the view might have been out of Hieronymus Bosch or the younger Brueghel: a vision of hell. Barely clothed men, women and children, their faces, arms and legs covered in sores, lay weakened from hunger in the ruins of houses they had neither the means nor the energy to rebuild after the earthquakes that periodically and without warning shake Lima to pieces. Those who were less ill and a little stronger had managed to dislodge paving-stones from what had once been a pavement to provide material for the reconstruction work they would never finish. The collapsed houses were no longer recognized as homes by the council, the taxi-driver told his fare, the shanties were not officially listed, no rates were paid and no refuse collected. The traveller peered out at the mountains of rubbish on the streets and remains of pavements, towering higher than the few buildings left standing. Rats kept an eye open for dogs as they feasted on the refuse side by side with men, women and children who were collecting it to burn. The emaciated mongrels lived on the streets where they were born, the driver went on, colouring in those details of privation that his client hadn't yet seen for himself; when they grew too weak to catch rats, they would die in the gutter, to be eaten by those who were still just alive, or bundled into plastic bags by no less starving human beings and taken away to be cooked for supper over fires of acrid refuse. Old men and women, weak from disease and hunger, were publicly robbed by gangs of children of the little food they had managed to buy. The same gangs would raid the colourful tin-plated buses as soon as the doors opened at a stop and strip passengers at knifepoint of their valuables. The unlocked doors or boots of cars that were still moving were opened and the contents snatched; locked cars had their wing-mirrors torn off, so that they could be sold for a few coins to garages and scrap merchants; those that pulled up promptly lost their wheels.

The taxi slowed down. 'This is as far as I'm going,' said the driver. 'It's getting too dangerous. Even the buses don't come as far as this. Are you sure you don't want me to take you back to the centre?'

The traveller hesitated. A part of him longed to get away from this world of Brueghel and Bosch but he had a mission to accomplish. He paid the *mestizo* his ten-*sol* fare, which would have been more than twenty times the amount in Europe or North America, and gave him an extra two *soles* for his care and concern. The driver shook his passenger's hand, unlocked the door to let him out, turned his much-dented 1980s black Mercedes round and headed back towards the centre.

The stranger in his casual but smart new clothes, with his pristine canvas bag and oddly shaped black case, was conscious of being watched by hundreds of pairs of eyes as he stood beside the road wondering what to do next. The eyes were averted a split second before they met his, but he knew they would be fixed on him again as soon as he looked away. Indecision was fatal, he thought. He noticed two barefoot eleven- or twelve-year-old boys in what was left of a doorway a little way off. He walked over to them purposefully and asked if they knew Father Lorencio.

'*¿El comedor?*' asked one of the boys.

The stranger didn't know if Lorencio worked in a soup kitchen or not but anything was better than standing around in this unsafe place with its overpowering stench of refuse and diesel fumes. He nodded.

The boy waved in what seemed to be the direction of the Pacific Ocean.

'I'll give you ten *soles* each if you take me there.'

The two boys' eyes grew wider. 'Let's see the money,' said the bolder of the two.

The traveller managed to get two ten-*sol* notes out of his purse without taking the purse from his pocket and letting the boys see the larger-denomination notes it also held.

The boys led the way across the thoroughfare and up a sandy dirt road on to what the traveller guessed were dunes. Here he had a view westwards for two or three kilometres of hundreds of tightly packed cardboard shelters. Behind them, beyond the dunes, he could see the mist that always hangs over the Pacific coast during autumn and winter. There was no one about: the cardboard-city-dwellers were either inside their shanties or searching for food and fuel back in Bosch-and-Brueghel-Land. There were no piles of rubbish. The only smell was of the sea.

'Can we carry your bags?' asked the boy who did the talking.

The traveller had been warned: let go of your bags in Peru and you would never see them again. 'No thanks. It's kind of you but I'm paying you to lead the way, not carry my luggage.'

The boys walked on, treading over sharp stones in bare soles that must have been as thick as leather. Their shorts and T-shirts were torn and their arms and legs as thin as sticks, but their black hair was silky and thick in spite of their undernourishment, and their skin was like polished mahogany.

As he followed them along the dirt road, the traveller became aware of different categories of shanty. One- and two-star dwellings were made entirely of cardboard: cardboard walls and a cardboard roof, with a cardboard flap for a door. Three-star shanties had plywood instead of cardboard walls. Four stars were for plywood walls with a rusty corrugated-metal roof, five for plywood walls, a corrugated roof, a hinged door and window openings cut out of the plywood, with clear plastic squares for glass. Many of the shanties were painted in vivid colours – lime-green, canary yellow, scarlet, azure – with paint obtained from goodness knows where.

The traveller had been walking for fifteen or twenty minutes. The rhythm, and the pleasant warmth of the sun, had lulled him into a sense of semi-security, so that he was no longer thinking only about his two guides, the poverty around him and the possible dangers he faced. His mind was replaying the events of the day. It was now late afternoon – early afternoon in Spanish-speaking countries, where things only get started again at five or five thirty after lunch and the siesta. Less than six hours ago he was still two and a half thousand kilometres away, at Santiago in Chile. Eight hours ago he hadn't even heard of Father Lorencio and had no plan to come to Lima. Then there was the flight north with all the way a view from his window seat of the highest peaks of the Andes. And Jorge Chávez Airport with its crowds of thieves and unsafe taxi-drivers.

The three walkers had come to a crossing of the ways. The two boys turned left and the traveller followed them. Hundreds – thousands – more shanties stretched into the distance. His chief guide waved towards a five-star construction fifty metres ahead that had all the appearance with its high walls and its transverse windows close to the corrugated roof of a public shower-room or lavatory.

The traveller stopped, seized with fear. The boys had never heard of Father Lorencio and there was no *comedor*. They had brought him to this remote spot where their gang had its headquarters. The guide would whistle and another dozen boys would appear from among the shanties, armed with knives. They would march him into the shower-room, stab him a hundred times and make off with his money, passport and luggage.

2

All my love is here:
as the rocks are to the sea,
so is my love to their memory.

The words are in Spanish, engraved boldly along the top edge of a wall ten metres tall by thirty wide. Under them, in letters a fraction of the size, are the names of tens of thousands of *desaparecidos*, those who disappeared in Chile between 1973 and the 1990s: vanished men and women, boys and girls, whose reappearance after ten, twenty, thirty years remains a dim hope in the dreams of mothers, fathers, sisters, wives. The wall, as fresh as the memory of those it commemorates, stands in the main cemetery, the Cementerio General, of Santiago.

The traveller with his canvas bag and black case stood in front of the wall, at a distance that allowed him to survey it from end to end while still being able to read the names of all those sons, daughters, brothers, husbands for whom a light over the door is always left on at night. He was in his late fifties and wore casual straw-coloured trousers, a pale green smock and a straw sun-hat. The hair that covered half his neck and ears was more brown than grey, and he had the figure of a much younger man, but the loose skin and tissue on his face and neck, which suggested a dramatic loss of body mass, and the furrows and pockets made by the sag, had added the years back on. He read the words above the lists of names and translated them without hesitation into English, his lips moving voicelessly as he did so.

Out of a corner of his eye he noticed a man in green overalls watching him from the grass verge of the path leading from the wall to the main part of the cemetery. He was holding a rake: the month was April, the season autumn, and his job was to fight a losing battle against the falling leaves. The visitor continued to run his eyes down the columns of names.

'Have you come to bury your cat or dog?' The man in green had approached and was addressing the stranger in educated Spanish. The visitor looked round and saw a pair of large, black, intelligent eyes in a delicately structured face, thin, elegant hands and a shiny, tanned head with a rim of white hair. The gardener was pointing at the case in the stranger's hand, which was a little the shape of a small coffin.

Bafflement. Then it clicked. He laughed and held the case up for a moment to consider its shape. 'No cat or dog. And no machine-gun either.'

The gardener cast a quick glance at the backs of the group photographing the wall. The visitor caught a hint of alarm in his eyes. No one looked round: tourists probably, with a dozen words of Spanish between them.

'Have you always worked here?' asked the visitor.

'For nearly thirty years.'

'A steadfast gardener. And yet you seem… It doesn't matter.'

The gardener edged the stranger away from the wall. 'You're obviously a well-educated man,' he said quietly. 'I don't get much intelligent conversation. It's like manna from heaven. The other gardeners are decent enough fellows but our exchanges start and stop with the weather.'

The visitor was puzzled. 'If it's intelligent conversation you need, why— ?'

'Because I have no choice.'

The gardener took him by the arm and led him slowly away from the group and along the path.

'I can trust you,' he said. 'You're not Chilean. In Chile today friends grass on friends, parents on their own children, children on parents.'

'What have you done wrong?'

'Nothing. Just the reverse. I supported Allende for the presidency in the early seventies. You may not be a Communist yourself, *señor*, but then you have probably never known the injustice and inequality that grow like weeds in Chile. Allende would have rooted them out after his massive election victory.'

'Allende was a hero all over the world,' the visitor assured him.

The gardener brandished his rake as if to attack the leaves falling like injustices and inequalities just after he had raked the grass clean. He used it to point at a bed of brightly coloured flowers. 'If the University Chancellor hadn't liked my work, and if he hadn't also been a relative of our military despot and usurper, I would be feeding the roots of those chrysanthemums over there from below, instead of watering them from above.'

'What work? Your work as a gardener?'

'At thirty I was already Head of the Department of Botany at Santiago University.'

The visitor would have been surprised if his articulate companion had always been a gardener but the violent change of fortune shocked him. 'All that's in the past, isn't it?' he said after a pause. 'Why aren't you back at the University?'

The ex-academic shook his head. 'Today's régime would like the world to think that it's all in the past. That's why they put up the wall you were looking at: for the eyes of the world. Not for Chileans. Fewer than ten per cent of the names are on that wall. It would have to be fifteen or twenty times the size to include everyone. And the list is still growing.'

The path was no longer bordered by flowers and cypresses now but by tombs: vast, grandiose, marble sepulchres that defied anyone to say that death is a leveller. The occupants of these palaces of the dead had taken their status with them into eternity.

'Chile has always been in the stranglehold of a small landowning élite,' the professor went on. 'Ninety-eight per cent of the land in the hands of two per cent of the population. Who was the first to dare attempt a radical redistribution of land, do you think?'

'Salvador Allende?'

'Exactly. For the landowners of Chile Allende was Satan. They were ready to hang, draw, quarter, crucify and garrotte him. One of their tribe, a creature by the name of Pinochet, did the job for them, with a great deal of help from the United States. Do you know how?'

'He bombed the presidential palace and peppered your elected President with machine-gun bullets.'

'You know our history as well as I do, *señor*. For twenty years the usurper defied the world and held Chile in his coils. Why, do you suppose? How?'

'Thanks to the army, presumably. That's how it usually is.'

'The landowners have always been cunning enough to send one or two sons into the forces. As a result, all the senior officers belong to the landowning élite... It's all in the past, you say, my friend. Why then, do you imagine, was Pinochet never brought to justice when he was extradited to Chile a few years ago?'

'Because the important posts in the new government are also held by landowners,' suggested the visitor, who was now fully drawn into the professor's catechism.

'Precisely. If any lawyer declared his intention of indicting the tyrant for crimes against humanity, he would be found in a ditch a few days later with his throat cut. Look at these tombs! This is where Chile's landowners reside when they die. The rest of us are cremated, if we haven't already been thrown down a disused mine-shaft by the secret police. We have to content ourselves with cubicles.'

The two men came to a crossroads and turned left on to a path that took them between rows of what to a child's mind might be apartment blocks for dolls: row upon row, storey upon storey of squares smaller than the doors of left-luggage lockers, each with a name-tag like a post-office box, many of them with a posy of plastic flowers wired to the handle.

'When an earthquake strikes this part of Santiago, the tombs collapse and the rotting corpses of the rich are disgorged like infected food on to the grass and paths and among the laurels and cypresses. The tombs are rebuilt by the landowning families, their decaying relatives are laid in fresh coffins, and everything returns to normal – that is to say to corruption and social injustice.'

The professor emphasized his last few words by lunging with his rake, hoping perhaps to spear corruption and injustice as they slithered across the grass like vipers.

'You're taking a bit of a risk telling all this to a stranger,' said the visitor. 'I could be working for the CIA.'

That hint of alarm again in the professor's eyes. Then he shrugged and gave a bitter laugh. 'Would it matter if they cut my throat? I've wasted my life. I could have made my name internationally as a botanist. What better place to work than this part of South America, with Amazonia and the Galapagos on my doorstep? Thousands of species still undiscovered: I could have given my name to a flower or tree.'

'Why didn't you go abroad?'

'Because my place was in Chile,' the professor replied fiercely, 'helping other sympathizers escape the fangs of that cunning monster.'

'Then you haven't wasted your life. You've helped save the lives of others. In any case, it's never too late to start again. I... I know from personal ...'

The glazed look disappeared from the professor's eyes as he returned from what could have been to what was, and looked into his companion's face. 'I'm sorry, *señor*. I need to get these things off my chest sometimes. I've led you half a kilometre from the wall. You were looking for a name.'

The ten-minute walk had brought the two men to the main gate of the cemetery.

'I don't know if I'll find it on the wall,' said the visitor. 'I'm trying to trace a Mapuche from Araucanía. He would be almost forty now. I can't remember his full name. It was long and unpronounceable. I would recognize it if I saw it. He called himself Mawi.'

The professor paused for a moment, then said: 'You can save yourself the trouble of reading through all those lists. You won't find his name there. The story made headlines in the underground press in Chile and in the main newspapers in the rest of South America. Everyone who was reading those papers twenty years ago will remember Mawi.'

'How do I find him?'

'There's a priest who knows the story better than anyone. He used to live in Santiago but he escaped to Peru just before DINA, the secret police, came knocking on his door.'

'Where is he now?'

'He went to work in a shanty-town in Lima: El Salvador. Lorencio is his name: Father Lorencio.'

The visitor shook the gardener-professor warmly by the hand, promised to invite him to dinner to hear his own story next time he was in Santiago, and walked briskly through the main gate. He stopped for a moment to glance up at Aconcagua, the highest mountain in the Andes, towering seven thousand metres above Santiago, white against the azure sky, then hailed a taxi. Half an hour later he was at the Lan Chile counter at Arturo Merino Benítez Airport buying a ticket to Lima. Another two hours and his aircraft was taxiing to the runway for the four-hour flight to the Peruvian capital.

3

The traveller was bracing himself for fight, flight or surrender to the inevitable, when the door of the cabin opened and a man in his sixties or seventies appeared, wearing a chef's blue-and-white-striped apron over his green corduroy trousers and check shirt, with a white hat perched on a head covered in dense grey stubble. He was tall and strong-looking, ruggedly handsome, with the physique of a scrum forward in spite of his years. He didn't seem a man who expected allowances to be made for his age. He carried an aura of benevolence and authority, and the traveller's fears at once evaporated.

'*¡Hola, los gorriones!*' he called out to the boys. 'Have you brought a visitor?'

'*¡Buenas tardes, padre!*' the two sparrows called back in unison.

They reached up to be embraced, so he bent down and kissed them on both cheeks.

'The gentleman is paying us ten *soles* each for bringing him here,' the boy who did the talking told him.

'Ten *soles*!' The *padre*'s astonishment was genuine. 'That's ten times the going rate. It's more than you've ever earned in a week. You didn't even carry his luggage.'

'The gentleman didn't want us to.'

The *padre* gave the boys glasses of water, the traveller paid their wages and the more articulate of the two girded himself for the half-hour walk back to the main road.

The second boy spoke to the stranger for the first time. 'You're a good man,' he told him quietly. 'We are your friends.' He ran off to join his companion, who was already on his way.

The *padre* smiled, stretched out a thin arm and crushed the visitor's hand in his. 'Welcome to the Ritz!' he said.

Inside the cabin the visitor saw a four-ring cooker fuelled by a cylinder of butane, iron cooking-pots lined up on a wooden pallet on the earth floor and ranging from fifteen-litre giants to four-litre standards, two old oil-drums filled with water, one of them presumably for washing up, and on the ground in a corner of the room several dozen litres of bottled water.

The chef was at the cooker, stirring a mountain of rice over all four flames in a frying-pan the best part of a metre wide. 'Will you have lunch with us?' he said. 'I don't know who you are but there's a place at the table for you. The price is two *soles*: paella without the prawns but with plenty of rice and a few pieces of chicken and fish.'

As the visitor's eyes adjusted from the bright light outside to the shade of the cabin, he became aware of a wooden table stretching the length of the far wall, and of two rows of smiling faces watching him as he stood blinking like an owl dazzled by sunlight.

'*¡Buenas tardes!*' he said, taking off his hat and smiling himself.

'*¡Buenas tardes!*' the *padre*'s guests chorused back.

He stepped towards the table and at once there was a double domino effect as both ranks of shanty-dwellers shuffled up their benches to make space for the newcomer. He decided to have his back to the wall, so that he could see the chef, and sat down on the end of the far bench among smiles of welcome and curiosity and eyes that perhaps owed their brightness to life on the sharp edge between starvation and survival. The faces had the east Asian look of indigenous Americans, like those of the two boys who had brought him here: dark brown skin, high cheek-bones, round eyes set far apart, a large mouth and an eagle nose. The age range must have been from twenty to fifty but even those who were little more than children were already showing the first signs of wear: a puckering of the skin, a few grey hairs. Gappy mouths made all the faces look older: when you hadn't enough money for food, the visitor guessed, you saved your coins for what you considered essentials. Coca, yes, because it took the edge off your hunger and cost only a few *centavos*, but toothpaste, no. Coca-Cola, yes, the days you struck it rich: when all your teeth fell out, you wouldn't need to worry about toothpaste.

The *padre*'s flock were cheerful, clean and well turned out in spite of their penury. The visitor thought of the rich of his own country, with their ennui and their pose of sartorial informality – neglect might be a better word. The bigger your bank balance the more slovenly your appearance and the dirtier your fingernails and hair. The skin and clothes of these smiling and impoverished people smelt of soap – carbolic, perhaps, but at least they made the effort. They may have been wearing the cast-offs of the magnanimous rich who kept them in their poverty but they did so with flair: a piece of scarlet or emerald rag as a cravat to hide a hopelessly frayed shirt-collar; a hibiscus in a button-hole to cover the tear in a blouse. The one thing that let them down was their footwear, or lack of it. The visitor glanced down and at once there was a scuffling, like rodents scurrying for cover, as sockless toes retreated from holes in plimsolls and bare feet were pulled under the benches. There wasn't much you could do to hide bare feet and decaying footwear.

The *padre* was both chef and waiter. Within two minutes of the paella reaching its apotheosis, plates heaped with food were set in front of his famished guests. He brought a plate for himself and sat at the end of the bench opposite the newcomer. For a minute or more the only sounds were of forks on plates and food being chewed.

The paella was better than anything the traveller had tasted in the restaurants of Santiago, in spite of the *comedor*'s modest resources. The rice was cooked until the grains were separate but not dried out, the chicken was as tender as new-born veal, the fish crisp on the outside and *fondant* inside. The *padre* obviously believed the poor had the same right to good food as the rich.

'You must be Father Lorencio,' the visitor said across the table, to break the silence.

The elderly man laughed. 'I gave up that title years ago,' he said. 'I'm more of a grandfather now. Grandfather Lorencio.'

The visitor wanted to tell his host how surprised and grateful he felt. He had arrived expecting to have his throat cut. Instead, here he was enjoying a meal with a group of tranquil people who had welcomed and accepted him – a meal that would have cost him ten times as much in the centre and fifty times as much in his own country. He decided to keep his appreciation for later and said: 'Can you tell me about Mawi?'

Grandfather Lorencio paused before putting the next forkful of paella in his mouth, and the whole table paused with him.

'Damn! That was too abrupt,' thought the visitor. 'I should have waited till I was asked.'

But the bird had taken fright and flown. The smiles had vanished. The mist had blown in from the Pacific and settled over the table. Grandfather and grandchildren were subdued as they finished their paella.

The chef got up, filled a medium-size saucepan from one of the oil-drums and lit a gas-ring to heat the water for washing up. Two of the regular guests got up and started collecting the plates.

'We know about Mawi,' one of them said gently. 'We all know the story. He taught us that there's no shame in having a dark skin.'

'And that the future of South America lies in peace, not in violence,' said another of the grandchildren.

'Where is he now?' the visitor asked.

Before anyone could answer, the chef called out *'¡Postre!'* to announce the dessert and placed a bowl of oranges on the table.

The visitor's gentle companions ate their oranges and left the table. They dropped the peel into a bin, paid their two *soles*, smiled their farewells to the newcomer – *'¡Adios!' '¡Hasta luego!'* – and were gone.

'They're mostly migrants from the Andes,' the chef told him as he did the washing-up. 'They left for a better life in the city only to find even greater poverty. They haven't enough money to get back.'

He took off his hat and apron and plunged his arms into the second drum of cold water. They re-emerged with a litre bottle of Cristal lager clutched in each hand. He returned to the table with the two bottles and an opener, and sat down opposite the visitor.

'So you want to hear about Mawi,' he said, opening the bottles and pausing to look into his guest's face. 'I think I can guess who you are. You've flown all the way from England, haven't you, on the wings of your conscience?'

4

One of the best stands in Santiago for a *limpiabotas*, or shoeshine boy, was under the colonnades of the Plaza de la Constitución. The plaza was the stamping-ground of well-fleshed and suited politicians, civil servants and businessmen ever more obsessed as the years went by with having their already dazzling shoes shined to an even more brilliant finish, much as their wives went day after day to the nearby beauty salons to have their hair set and reset. A *limpiabotas* was guaranteed a steady stream of customers who seldom underpaid and often added a tip.

The down side was that stands on the Plaza de la Constitución were run by a mafia of *carabineros*, as the semi-military Chilean police are called, who supplemented their official income by demanding what they called rent from the *limpiabotas*. If anyone failed to pay up, they descended on him in civvies in their off-duty hours and beat him unconscious. Another disadvantage of being a *limpiabotas* in a fashionable area was that you needed expensive equipment: a varnished walnut rack with a handle for your polish, brushes and cloths, and a seat with a foot-rest made of the same varnished wood for your client. Most *limpiabotas* bought their equipment on hire purchase. What with this expense and the weekly instalments of protection money, they were left with just enough for food but nothing for accommodation, which was why many of them slept in the open air.

Pure indigenous faces are not so different from unmixed Hispanic ones in this part of South America, but a *limpiabotas* with a square enough head, a brown enough skin and a low enough fringe of black hair was likely to find himself the butt of constant racist abuse, even from politicians and civil servants, as well as physical attacks by gangs of Hispanic youths.

The twenty-one-year-old *limpiabotas* with brown skin and a black fringe who worked in one of the arcades of the Plaza de la

Constitución did so in spite of the risk of being beaten up by off-duty policemen and pimply louts with their bellies full of beer. He was driven by a passion too strong to be doused by risk or fear. Not revenge: he had learnt from the elders of his village a thousand kilometres away that revenge only fuelled the wheels of violence, which turned and turned generation after generation until the original grievance was long forgotten. Justice was what he had travelled to Santiago for alone at the age of fifteen: justice after the outrage that had destroyed his community; an acknowledgement of the wrong done; compensation for the survivors so that they could rebuild their village and their lives and husband the growth of a new community. His appeal must be made at the Ministry of the Interior, and he must make it not to an underling who wouldn't bother to pass it on to his superiors but directly to someone with real authority. The classical balustrades and columns of the Ministry of the Interior occupied one side of the Plaza de la Constitución. From his stand under one of the colonnades the young man could watch all the comings and goings and learn to distinguish between the top dogs and the dogsbodies, and between the faces carved out of rock and those with flesh-and-blood ears able to hear and listen. When he had found out names, and chosen his moment and his man, he would ask for two minutes of *Su Señoría's* valuable time and make his well-rehearsed appeal.

Lights were flashing and the steel gates of the Ministry opening. Instead of a Cadillac or a Mercedes with tinted windows sweeping smoothly and swiftly on to the Avenida Moneda, out burst a portly gentleman in a dark grey three-piece suit. The gates closed behind him and he turned towards the east side of the plaza, where the *limpiabotas* had just finished with a customer. The gentleman from the Ministry must have weighed something between a hundred and thirty and a hundred and fifty kilos and seemed to be struggling to stop his dignity slipping from a stride into a shamble or a waddle.

Bally shoes and a face carved out of jelly rather than rock, the *limpiabotas* noted as the gentleman reached the colonnade and stumbled perspiring into the confectioner's just behind the shoe-cleaning stand. Two minutes later he was out again, with a copy of *El Mercurio,* the mouthpiece of the military régime, in one hand, a bag of chocolate-coated marshmallows in the other, and a fat black cigar protruding from his mouth. He caught sight of the *limpiabotas'* varnished walnut seat and stepped towards it.

'Buenas tardes, señor,' said the young man, who was caught on the hop by the sudden decision of the gentleman to have his shoes shined. *'Sentase, por favor.'* He helped the customer up on to the seat and was relieved when it didn't collapse under his weight. The *señor* put the paper on his knee, opened the marsh-mallows, took the cigar from between his lips and poured the contents of the packet into his mouth. Half a minute of chewing, swallowing and smacking his lips, then a pair of reading-glasses was on his nose, the cigar back in his mouth and the Fascist newspaper open in hands like two bloated jellyfish. He banged his calfskin shoes down on the foot-rest, causing the whole structure to judder.

The *limpiabotas* got to work with his brushes and dusters. 'One of these shoes would feed me for more than two months,' he thought as he polished an already spotless mirror. A reflection of the customer's reading-glasses appeared for a moment in the shoe and caused the young man to glance up. The gentleman's eyes were just visible behind his suety eyelids, two diamonds secreted in pats of butter.

The *limpiabotas* was about to start on the other shoe when without warning the customer was on his feet, yanking the cigar from his mouth and the glasses from his nose. *'¡Julieta! ¡Cara!'* he shouted. *'¡Mi querida!'*

'¡Hola, Papa!' a young woman's voice called from further down the colonnade.

Six years ago the young man had stared in wonder at the

beautiful girls who passed. Santiago wasn't short of Hispanic beauties. Good-looking they may have been but not one of them had ever made his heart race. He was starting to worry about himself when he realized what was wrong: the more beautiful the young woman, the more she strutted, her head held high, conscious of her own good looks, holding the world in contempt. If he happened to catch the eye of one of the girls, her contempt would change from unsweetened lemon to curdled milk: no one was as despicable as a penniless Indian. The young man discovered he was looking for more than beauty in a girl: for humanity, a love of life, a coin or two and a few words for the beggar further down the arcade, a smile for a disabled child. There was more warmth in a tailor's dummy than in the girls who stalked by, and he had stopped looking at them.

'How about coffee and a cake at the O'Higgins?' boomed the father.

'We haven't time, Papa. We have to get home to dinner.'

'Oh!' The father sounded disappointed. He stepped down on to the pavement and set off to join his daughter.

'Papa, you haven't paid the young man who cleaned your shoes.'

'The young man who— ' Not 'bootblack', not '*roto*', not 'native', but 'the young man who cleaned your shoes'. The *limpiabotas* looked round and saw the girl for the first time, standing ten metres away, waiting for her father to join her.

The moment he set eyes on her, he knew that she was different from all those girls he used to moon at during his first months in Santiago. There was a looseness and energy in her movements, in the quick, graceful swing of her arm as she swept her dark hair from her face back over her shoulders, in the way she stepped lithely aside to let a mother with a push-chair past. Her smile was all at once generous and vulnerable. Unlike those haughty girls of six years ago, this young woman seemed quite unaware of her own beauty.

The young man stood open-mouthed, gazing at the girl entranced, spellbound, as if a long-worshipped goddess had just appeared to him in human form. His arms hung as limp as the cloth in his right hand. Every muscle in his body seemed to have liquefied. All his attention was concentrated on this kindler of his deepest longings: for home, for the lakes and mountains of his childhood, for the birdsong, the silence, the sunshine after heavy rain, the fragrance of acacia-trees, the giant blood-red campanulas.

He woke from his trance. The girl had gone. He saw her with her father crossing the square in the direction of the Ministry. They must be going for their car. He stuffed the cloth he was holding into the walnut rack, threw in the brushes that were still under the seat and took it into the sweet shop belonging to the couple with blond hair and blue eyes from a country the other side of the world called Switzerland, which like his homeland had blue lakes and snow-capped mountains. They had nothing against indigenous South Americans and looked after his equipment for him. He ran back for the seat and foot-rest.

'But I want my shoes cleaned,' brayed an indignant voice. Another suited gentleman, not as fat as the last.

'Sorry, sir. I'm packing up for the day.'

The young man left the sweet shop and reached the kerb just in time to see a black Mercedes lurching out of the Ministry gates. The windows were untinted and he recognized the girl and her father.

He hailed a black-and-yellow cab and jumped into the front. 'Follow that Mercedes!' he blurted.

'You what?' The driver turned for a leisurely look at his passenger. 'Now what would an impoverished slum-rat like you want with the driver of a Merc?'

'Customer left without paying for his brush and polish. I want my money.'

'A four-hundred-peso taxi ride for a hundred-peso shoeshine?

And how are you going to pay me, sonny?'

The passenger took a fistful of pesos from his pocket. 'Hurry! The lights have turned green. We'll lose them if you don't put your foot down.'

The gentleman with the Bally shoes wasn't the first customer to leave without paying. It wasn't the loss of a hundred pesos that spurred the young man on but the opportunity for an interview with someone who had to be more than a pen-pusher at the Ministry of the Interior. And yet the picture in his mind as the taxi tailed the Mercedes up the Avenida Bandera to the river, then right along Valdes Vergara and Providencia, was not of the fat man in the three-piece suit but of his willowy, wild-rose daughter. He wanted to be near her again, to lift the veil between them with a word of thanks, to touch her eyes with his and feel the warmth of her generous smile.

5

Julieta Reyes lived with her parents and the maid, Copihue, in a spacious five-bedroomed house in the smartest residential district in Santiago. The houses were well spaced, with large gardens between them, and each was a fortress against robbers, real or imaginary, with high surrounding walls and metal gates friezed with barbed or razor wire. Copihue was Julieta's close friend, to her father's annoyance, and described the house as a balance between feminine and masculine, between the lightness and light, the elegance and softer colours of Señora Reyes, and the substance, weight and deeper tones of the master. Julieta would have put it less tactfully: the parts of the house that were beautiful, simple and homely showed the artistry of her mother; the parts that were dark, heavy, grandiose and over-ornate were like an elephant trying to dance.

Home was like swimming in an ocean: a constant struggle not to be swamped by rollers from her father, an eternal battle for air and light. Her mother was an ally and a fellow-sufferer, but she sometimes seemed to have given up the struggle and left Julieta to carry the standard. Mealtimes were never family gatherings, a time for conversation and laughter. Julieta and her mother were simply a captive audience for Franco Reyes' lectures and diatribes. And the food always had to be what Julieta's father wanted, not what everyone liked.

He was storming on about something now, having been escorted home by his daughter in time for dinner, instead of arriving up to two hours late and reducing Copihue, who did most of the cooking, to tears: Argentina was the theme, in between forkfuls of *chorillana* and with his mouth full, so that bits of food flew like bullets across the table.

'I'm no friend of the Argentinians,' he was saying as he devoured the mountain of steak, onions, eggs and chips in front of him. 'I can't stand them: they're greedy. But what do the British want with a group of barren islands in the worst climate and stormiest seas in the world?' He poured more wine for himself.

'What do the Argentinians want with them?' said Julieta. She wasn't faintly interested in the Malvinas but challenged her father out of habit: it was her way of keeping her head above water. She knew it irritated him but she also knew he respected her for standing up to him. He wanted total control of his daughter but despised her when she showed signs of giving in to him.

Reyes ignored the question and turned his guns on the Peruvians: dirty, lazy people the Peruvians, but then what did anyone expect in a country overrun by Indians?

Julieta poured wine for her mother, since her father was too busy eating, drinking and talking to attend to anybody's needs but his own. The attack on Peru was aimed at his wife, who was half-Peruvian. Not only was she half-Peruvian but half of that half was Indian. Reyes had married her for her looks and her French half, all things French having glamour and snob value attached to them by urbane Chileans. When after several years of marriage the French appeal began to wear, it was the Peruvian he saw in her. Having a Peruvian wife attracted no kudos in Santiago society – just the reverse.

During a pause in the monologue, while Reyes shovelled more food into his mouth, the front-door chimed for everyone in the dining-room to hear.

'Have you seen Adolfo recently?' Reyes asked his daughter.

It was her father's promotion of this eligible army officer, destined for high rank, that riled Julieta more than anything else. 'If you're so sweet on Adolfo Cortez, marry him yourself,' she thought but hadn't dared say. Was he too unsubtle to realize that barging into this most intimate corner of her life was like pulling a plant up by the roots to see how well it was growing?

Promotion was turning to pressure and would soon lead to a showdown. It was her habit of surrendering to her father's will that Julieta was most afraid of.

'You know I only see him when you arrange meetings, Father.'

'Then we must arrange another meeting.'

Why be equivocal, Julieta asked herself. Why not just say no?

The door opened and Copihue came in to clear the dishes and serve the dessert. The weight crushing Julieta lifted and her spirits picked up. Copihue always had this effect on her with her cheerful smile and the twinkle in her eye and, when they were alone together, her never quite disrespectful comments on the Reyes household. Copihue was a Mapuche, from Araucanía, one of the jewels of the South American landscape, a thousand kilometres south of Santiago. She took her name from the flowers that grow in that area, the giant campanulas that hang from their stems like drops of blood the size of fruit-bowls under the araucaria trees. Quite the wrong name for Julieta's friend! She should have been called Petunia, with her round face, her sunny smile and her delicate features.

'There's a young gentleman to see you, sir,' said Copihue.

'What's he want?'

'I'm not sure, sir. I told him you were having supper. There's no hurry, he says. He's happy to wait.'

'It's not Señor Adolfo, is it?'

'No, sir,' she replied with a fleeting glance at Julieta. She knew all about Señor Reyes' plans for Julieta and the major. She served the *sopaipillas* and left with the dirty plates.

Reyes' mouth watered as he dug his spoon into his favourite dessert of pumpkin cakes in syrup. He returned to his theme of South American Indians, this time ethnically cleansing the whole continent from the north of Colombia down to the south of Chile.

'They've been here for thousands of years,' Julieta's mother protested patiently, knowing she would be ignored. 'The Europeans took their land from them.' Being partly Indian herself, she felt a solidarity with other indigenous South Americans.

Julieta's father finished his meal, got to his feet, took out a revolver, removed the safety-catch and returned it to his pocket. Why her father imagined anyone outside the family would bother to assassinate him Julieta could never understand.

She exchanged smiles with her mother. 'I'll make the *tisanes*,' she said, and followed her father out of the dining-room.

As she crossed the hall to the kitchen, she had a glimpse of the caller, sitting calm and upright in his jeans, white shirt and black slip-ons on the chair outside her father's study with his back half turned to her. She recognized him: it was the good-looking boy who had polished her father's shoes and looked at her out of eyes like coffee creams in such innocent, unfeigned wonder. Julieta's heart warmed. She was curious too: why was he here?

She went into the kitchen and closed the door. 'What does he want?' she asked Copihue.

'He says he cleaned your father's shoes but wasn't paid.'

Was it Julieta's imagination or were there lights in Copihue's eyes? Had she taken a liking to the boy? Perhaps Julieta could help her friend get to know him. The poor thing had no life outside her workplace.

'A hundred pesos may not sound much to anyone with a good income,' said Copihue, 'but it's life or death when you're living hand to mouth.' She opened the kitchen door and went to finish clearing away in the dining-room.

'He's got pluck,' thought Julieta with a smile. She had seen displays of bravado among the sons of her father's colleagues, trying to impress her, but never the quiet courage this boy must have needed to bring him from the streets across the threshold of a *caballero*'s fortress.

After two or three minutes Julieta heard her father shouting. Moments later the young man pulled open the study door and marched unaccompanied across the hall. Julieta left the kitchen to try and stop him but before she could think of anything to say he had shut the front-door smartly behind him.

Her father emerged from his study, muttering to himself.

'Did you give him his money?' she asked.

'He didn't want it.'

'What did he want?'

'He's a Mapuche, like the maid. He wanted what he calls justice for his friends and relatives.'

'What are you going to do?'

'Report him. Have him arrested as a potential troublemaker.'

'He hasn't done anything.'

'He will.'

He marched into the downstairs lavatory and banged the door shut. A massive explosion of wind was followed by grunting and half a minute of noisy splashing.

Julieta felt such indignation and revulsion against her father that she had to run upstairs to her bedroom to stop herself shouting at him through the lavatory door. It was one thing to try and push her down the aisle with Adolfo Cortez, stifling and infuriating her, but when he decided to have a pure-hearted Mapuche boy thrown into prison to be bullied and tortured for a wrong he hadn't done and had no intention of doing, her father's tyranny took on a new dimension. For years Julieta had listened to priests and nuns at school banging on about the importance of the family. If family meant supporting close relatives in their cruelty towards people who were unrelated, she wanted none of it. She would redefine family on her own terms.

Julieta must help the Mapuche. How? It was too late in the day to take a taxi to the centre. Her father would cross-question her about where she had been. Anyway, the boy might not clean shoes in the evening. Copihue? Copihue went to market every morning. She could make a detour to the Plaza de la Constitución and pass on a letter. Julieta went to her writing-table, grabbed a pen and tore a sheet of paper from a pad. What if the boy couldn't read? In any case, if they arrested him, a letter could be incriminating for the boy and for Copihue and herself. She stood in a quandary, pen in one hand, paper in the other.

An idea glimmered in Julieta's mind and, like a star, grew brighter the longer she considered it. She put down paper and pen and hurried downstairs to the key-rack in her father's study. She heard the lavatory being flushed. The labels tied to the keys were fading and she had to read each one carefully until she found the key she was looking for. The lavatory, gorged after the master's visit, was flushed a second time. The door opened just as she reached the kitchen, where Copihue was doing the washing-up. Julieta whispered to her and slipped her the key, having first removed the label.

Five minutes later Julieta's father was back in his study and she and her mother were sitting on the terrace outside the dining-room, sipping their *tisanes* and waiting for the sun to set and the moon to rise, for the honeysuckle to open its petals and the nightingale to begin his song.

6

'Whose side are we on in this row over the Malvinas?' a junior officer with a slightly German accent called out in the changing-room attached to the gym at army headquarters in central Santiago. 'Britain's or Argentina's?'

'On Chile's side,' Major Cortez replied quietly. The junior officers laughed, as subordinates always laugh at the quips of their superiors, even when they aren't funny.

Why was it that Germans exposed themselves so unselfconsciously in shower-rooms and changing-rooms, the major wondered as he tied and retied his tie in front of the small mirror so that the two ends were of equal length and the knot was neither too large nor too small. He was half-German himself but he had inherited his Chilean father's and grandfather's prudishness and distaste for physical display. He took his shower facing the wall and he kept his towel round his waist until his shirt was buttoned and he was ready to jump into his pants. The young Germans, on the other hand, showered facing outwards, then stood around stark naked in the changing-room talking at the tops of their voices. Tarts was what they were, the major decided as he ran a comb along his parting, then through his biscuit-coloured hair, out to wake the beast in their fellow-officers.

Things were looking rosy for Adolfo Cortez. He had only recently been awarded his major's stripe for tracking down and eliminating a group of insurgents in Araucanía – unarmed they may have been, but they would certainly have armed themselves if he hadn't eliminated them. Adolfo Cortez was the second youngest major in the Chilean army, the youngest being the lame-brained son of one of the President's flunkeys.

Major Cortez had originally planned a life in the arts. His father had been a musician from one of the oldest and most respected families in Chile, his mother and maternal grandfather exiles from Germany in 1945 who had fixed on the Cortez family as a way of reaching the upper échelons of Santiago society. Eduardo Cortez was forced to give up his career for a better-paid job in a bank. He took to drink, lost his job and died of cirrhosis at the age of forty-eight, when Adolfo was fifteen. The boy was taken in hand by his mother and German grandfather, and home became a training camp, a never-ending assault course. Adolfo was purged of his love of music and dance and, before he realized what was happening to him, found himself enlisted in the Chilean army.

Adolfo Cortez' career had been planned for him by his mother and grandfather all the way to retirement: at forty or so he would become a colonel; at fifty he would enter politics, for which under a military dictatorship his uniform and rank would be essential; at sixty he would become President of Chile. Adolfo Cortez' pedigree, education and influential friends and relatives would help pave his way to high office. A decorative wife would be found for him, to create the image of a man who was every Chilean woman's dream but only one lucky girl's reality.

Adolfo Cortez was submissive, like his father. He knew it but couldn't help it. He had no rebellious streak and had never once strayed from the course set for him by his mother and grandfather or resisted their indoctrination and drilling: at thirty-three he had just been promoted to the rank of major; a suitable wife was waiting in the wings.

Julieta was his: Cortez had no doubt of it. After all, she hadn't returned the ring he sent her. The way with Julieta, he reckoned, was to play it cool: to let her come to him like a fish to the hook. His letter and the ring were the bait. It was now a matter of being patient: waiting for a bite, for her gratitude. Cortez wasn't going to behave like an infatuated schoolboy. He was a soldier: he believed in rank. Just as a major must have the respect of junior officers, so a wife must show deference to her husband. He would take no further interest in her until she thanked him for the ring. He could afford to be stand-offish. Reyes was hell-bent on marrying his daughter to him. The girl would never disobey her overbearing father. Cortez hoped he wasn't marrying Reyes, with his table manners that would make a pig wince. He would feed his father-in-law on thin slices of ham with lettuce, and give him soda-water to drink: keep him at arm's length. As far as Julieta was concerned, she would be strictly ornamental: no more than a social and professional asset. They would sleep in separate beds; a family would be postponed till Julieta was past child-bearing age.

'What about the Reyes girl?' a fellow-major called out across the changing-room. 'Have you had her yet, Cortez? Is she good at it?'

'Marry a girl without laying her first?' Cortez replied. 'You must be joking. She might turn out to be a bloke.'

Roars of laughter from the young German officers. If only they knew, thought Cortez. The female body most of them lusted after he found ridiculous, with its bulges and curves, its porcine smoothness and ripe-apricot sponginess. Lay Julieta Reyes? He would rather lay some of his fellow-officers. Ugh! The thought of laying anyone made him shudder. If only they knew the squeamishness he felt about the human body, with its fluids and its odours. He couldn't even stand the sight of blood. A soldier squeamish about blood? The other officers would laugh him to scorn.

As he buttoned his tunic in front of the little mirror, Cortez saw a reflection of one of the German officers – Lieutenant Görisch, was it? – doing his stretching exercises naked in the far corner of the changing-room. He was surprised at the excitement he felt at the sight of this lean, fit, fair-skinned male body. It was the excitement of the artist still alive inside him, he told himself, of the discoverer of a contemporary Antinoüs to rival that slave, that second-century paragon of male beauty, adored by the

Roman emperor Hadrian. Sexual desire – was that what he felt? God forbid! No, but he had an urge to tear off his own clothes and wrestle with the German – wrestle with him until he broke one of his arms, then put pressure and counter-pressure on the broken arm so that the German screamed in agony.

Major Cortez took his brown leather shoulder-bag, went to the door marked *servicios* and locked it behind him. It was thanks to him that the lavatory flushed and no longer stank, that the basin was scrubbed every day, that there were clean towels and verbena-scented soap. The *servicios* were now like the ladies' room at the Hilton, the other officers joked: this was exactly how Cortez had intended it to be.

From his bag he took a red leatherette case, which he unzipped. With a small pair of scissors he trimmed first his fingernails, then his moustache. He filed his nails, then plucked a hair from each eyebrow with a pair of tweezers, and another from one of his nostrils, wincing as he did so. He zipped up the case, put it back in the bag, took out a compact and opened it. He drew the little brush across the cake of mascara and touched a soupçon on to his eyebrows, to strengthen their thin, weak line. Next time he went to the hairdresser he would have his hair dyed a deeper shade of brown, he decided: it irked him to have the same mousy hair his German-speaking grandfather had had before he turned white.

The major's manicured hand was suspended for a few moments, with the little brush held between his long, thin thumb and forefinger, as he studied his face in the mirror. How like the waiter at the officers' club he looked. The same age and features. He remembered a glimpse he had had of him through the swing-doors into the kitchen, attending to his appearance before serving the guests in the restaurant. Without the advantages of a distinguished family and a private education, of contacts in the government and army, perhaps he too would be a waiter preening himself with all the vainglory of a prince or prelate before each appearance in front of the guests on whom he had to fawn.

Major Cortez replaced the compact in the bag, slipped the strap over his shoulder, flushed the lavatory to make it seem he had just relieved his bowels or bladder, and stepped back into the changing-room, immaculate to the last detail, ready to play himself in close-up if need be.

7

The bus left the Plaza Italia and followed the Parque Balmaceda eastwards to the Museo de los Tajamares, where it stopped on the edge of Santiago's smartest residential district. It had no need to penetrate a district it didn't serve: the residents travelled by taxi, or in their own Cadillacs, Mercedes or BMWs, and would never dream of sitting on a bus with the down-at-heel hoi polloi, the *rotos*.

The Mapuche got off at Tajamares, left Providencia and turned up the Avenida Seminario, walking as casually as he could at first and keeping to the shadows as much as possible. The further he made his way from the lights, the cars and the passers-by of the Avenida Providencia, the darker the street became, with only an occasional lamp-post standing in a pool of pale light. He quickened his pace, stopping whenever he saw headlights or heard an engine, to stand with his back to a wall or crouch behind a parked car. The police patrolled these streets. What would an Indian be doing here at nearly midnight? Indians didn't live in this sort of area.

The Mapuche came to the high wall surrounding the garden at the side of the girl's house. He followed it to the iron gate at the front, which like the railings either side was fringed with barbed wire. He looked up at the house: not a light to be seen. Had they all gone to bed? He felt uneasy. A sign of life would have been reassuring: the maid, Copihue, cleaning the family silver under a lamp, or polishing the father's shoes. Was he being lured into a trap? He retraced his steps along the wall, his eyes peeled for anyone lurking in the shadows, and turned a corner into a street overhung with the branches of a locust-tree, where he wrapped himself in the darkness. He came to an old wooden gate, strong as the mahogany-tree from which it was made, with an old wrought-iron ring for a handle but a modern lock that seemed to be cut from the same brass as the key Copihue had given him. He took the key from his trouser pocket and slid it into the lock. It turned easily. He held the ring in both hands and eased the gate open a few centimetres, ready to sprint at the sound of a jangling alarm or snarling mastiff. Nothing. The gate moved without a creak. When it was half-open, he slipped through, pushing it to but not locking it, in case he needed to make a speedy exit. He put the key in his pocket.

A wave of scented air made the young man catch his breath. He had already noticed the orangy fragrance from the branches of flower-laden acacia above his head. The perfume he now breathed was more intoxicating: the moon emerged from behind a tail of cirrus cloud and he could make out a paved walk all the way along a wall under a trellis smothered in jasmine, honeysuckle and climbing roses. The house was at the far end of the walk, with rooms giving on to a terrace that stretched the width of the garden. The Mapuche became conscious of the sound of water, making him think for a moment of the brook that purled past the village and into the lake a few metres from his home: a fountain became visible in the middle of the garden, the water falling as a shower of sparkling moonlight.

The young man was relieved to see a light on in a first-floor window: he had had the impression of being watched through the dark eyes of the house; now his own eyes could see without being seen. But whose room was it? He might throw a clod of earth up only to have the window opened by the girl's bullfrog of a father.

'The Mapuche are rebels and troublemakers,' the *caballero* had bellowed. 'You have no right to complain of injustice.'

No right to complain that your grandfathers, and their fathers and grandfathers, drove us off land we had been peacefully cultivating for thousands of years? It was you who turned us into fighters. For four centuries we were better at it than you were, until a hundred years ago you weakened us with diseases you brought from your own unhealthy lands across the eastern ocean, massacred more than three-quarters of our people, burnt our homes and fields and drove the survivors like animals on to reservations. No right to complain of injustice? You have just murdered your President, Salvador Allende, who had promised to return our lands to us. You reversed his decision and, when my village marched peacefully on the streets of Temuco to protest, your soldiers opened fire and kept on firing till the blood flowed like flood-water in the gutters. No right to complain? What am I doing in this garden? It belongs to my enemies. If my people were as violent as yours, I would be here with a bomb to blow your house to pieces.

The young man was about to turn and go when the window opened and he saw the head of a girl in silhouette against the light inside. He recognized the shoulder-length hair and the quick, fluent movement of the arms. All his anger melted away and, what with the heady scent of jasmine and honeysuckle, the dazzle of the fountain, and now the image of the girl who had sent him the key to the garden-gate framed in the open casement, his knees felt close to buckling.

The girl coughed quietly. Because of the cooler air outside? Or was it a signal? The boy coughed quietly in reply.

'Come closer!' Her call was hardly more than a whisper.

He felt himself lifted, as if cupped in her graceful hands, and transported past the fountain and pool to the corner of the terrace under her window.

'What is your name?'

'Mawi.' The reply, like the question, was more breath than voice.

'Mawi,' she repeated, as if trying a fruit she had never tasted.

'It's short for Ñankomawizantu… Yours is Julieta.'

The head above him nodded.

'*Señorita,* with the light behind you, I can't see your face. Why don't you turn it off?'

'And I can't see yours... *señor*.' She disappeared from the window.

Mawi waited, and every second he waited felt longer than an hour spent under the arches, cleaning shoes. Had he offended her? Driven her from the window for good? Had it been indiscreet to use just her first name? Should he have asked her surname? Would she close the window on him?

The light was switched off. Mawi held his breath.

The head reappeared at the window as quietly and effortlessly as the moon floating out from behind a cloud, the face visible now, pale in the moonlight, the dark brown hair that fell about it deepened to jet by the night. The face was as perfect in form as the sun, the eyes were like two forest lakes at night, but what made it different from other beautiful faces Mawi had seen was not its symmetry or the blackness of the eyes against the pale skin, but their gentleness and sparkle, the tenderness and joy in the smile. Life and intelligence danced in this girl's face like the moonlight in the fountain.

'That's better, *señorita*. I can see you now.'

'And I can see you, Mawi. Did Copihue say why I asked you to come?'

'She said you wanted to warn me about something.'

'You came and saw my father yesterday. He told me what it was about. He said he was going to have you arrested.'

'What for?'

'For something you hadn't done and wouldn't think of doing.'

The sound of leaves being brushed to one side made Mawi look round for a moment, but he saw nothing.

'I wanted to warn you not to clean shoes in the Plaza de la Constitución.'

'Where else can I clean them? It's the best spot in town. I need the money to buy food.'

The sound of moving leaves again. Mawi glanced over his shoulder.

'Don't worry. It's only the cat.'

'Is it safe to talk like this?'

'My father sleeps the other side of the house.'

'Why are you doing this? Why are you warning me? He's your father.'

'I don't agree with everything my father says and does.'

'Why should you care what happens to me?'

Julieta paused, as if to consider which of several possible answers to give. 'I don't like to see innocent people suffer.'

'If I go back to the country, what happened in Temuco will be brushed under the rug and justice will never be done.'

'Copihue knows someone who helps people on the official blacklist. He has ears and eyes inside the Government and army. He finds safe houses for them, with free food and a bed. You wouldn't have to worry about money.'

Was Mawi walking into a trap? Was the garden behind him quietly filling with soldiers under orders to grab him, march him to an army bus, drive him to a disused mine or to a remote spot on the way to the coast, execute him and drop his body down a mineshaft, or into the quicksands, to join the thousands of other bodies of the *desaparecidos*? There was such frankness in the way she spoke, such nervousness, as if she were risking her own freedom and life, that Mawi was ashamed to imagine she could betray him.

'Trust me.' She had read his thoughts. She took a ring from her finger. 'Why didn't you let my father pay you for the work you did for him?'

'I don't want his money. I want justice for my people.'

'This is for you. It's a token of my good faith. Somebody sent it to me. I don't want it. Keep it if you like. If you need money, sell it.'

She threw the ring. Mawi caught it and looked at it. Twenty-four-carat gold, with Julieta's name carved on it. Sell it? Not if he were starving. He would wear it till his dying day. He slid it on to the ring-finger of his left hand.

Julieta rested her chin on the back of her hand, and her elbow on the window-ledge. 'I've never talked like this into the night with someone,' she said. 'Except my mother. My friends are home by ten – the children of my father's friends. They never stay to enjoy the moonlight and the jasmine and honeysuckle.'

'Not even the friend who gave you this ring?'

Julieta laughed. 'Especially not him. He was my father's choice of friend for me, not mine.'

To be the first to talk into the night with the girl who had filled his thoughts and heart for the past day and a half, even if it was on different floors, with locked doors and no stairs between them. Mawi wanted to shout for joy. 'I'd happily stay and talk all night,' he heard himself say. 'If I were a nightingale, I'd sing to you till dawn.'

Julieta gave a laugh of surprise. 'And if I were a nightingale, we could spend all night singing duets. But we must be practical. Do you want Copihue to talk to her friend?'

'If he helps me, what will I have to do in return?'

'Remember him in your prayers perhaps. Me too, if you think of it. Copihue's going to the Mercado Central at seven. She could see him on the way, then meet you at the market. In the part with all the fruit stalls?'

'And will I see you sometimes?'

'Copihue will tell me how to find you.'

Mawi heard a door open behind Julieta and caught a lightning moment of alarm in her eyes. He recognized the father's braying.

'I heard your voice as I was coming out of the bathroom. Who were you talking to?'

'I was talking to the cat, Papa,' Mawi heard Julieta reply without hesitation. 'She understands what I say. If she could speak Spanish, she would reply. We would have long conversations.'

'What nonsense! Talking to animals at your age. Why cats?

Horrible little creatures! Used to stone them to death when I was a boy.'

Mawi tiptoed to the edge of the terrace, where the house met the garden wall. Ducking, to avoid the moonlight, he made his way softly through a band of shadow to where the trellised walk began. He waited for his eyes to adjust to the gloom, then trod catlike under the overhanging jasmine, honeysuckle and eglantine towards the gate, taking care not to step on any twigs or leaves. The bottom of the garden was in deep shadow. He stopped to look back at the house. The father was framed in the window, straining like a guard-dog on its chain, peering into the darkness, seeing nothing.

There was a mewing at Mawi's feet. He bent down to run his fingers through the soft fur.

'Are you Julieta's?' he whispered. 'One of her chosen friends? Why would anyone want to hurt a friendly little thing like you? You and Julieta should come and live with the Mapuche. We treat animals with the same care we treat our fellow-humans.'

'Sssss!'

Mawi pushed a branch aside and looked up through a gap in the leaves at Julieta's window. She was waving with one hand, trying to attract his attention. As a child Mawi had learnt caution from the animals living about his settlement, the deer, the birds, the wolves and the wild cats, but now on impulse he sprang from the shadows out into the moonlight and ran without a sound across the grass and terrace to his place under Julieta's window.

'It was my father,' she whispered. 'He's gone to bed now. Is that agreed then? The fruit market between seven and eight?'

'Agreed. I'd better go. What if your father steals back and listens at the door?'

'We were going to talk all night.'

'Not if it gets you into trouble.'

'Good night, then.'

'Good night, *señorita*.'

Mawi managed two or three steps back but couldn't turn or take his eyes off Julieta.

'Mawi!' she called to him.

He stopped.

'Don't call me *señorita*. My name's Julieta.'

'Good night, Julieta.'

Mawi raised his hand to blow a kiss but something stopped him: not the thought of offending Julieta – she might even return his kiss – but of crossing the limits of class and race that every day for the past three years had been a little more sharply etched into his mind by well-heeled Hispanic customers like Julieta's father, each one bringing a barb or a nail to fence him into an image of himself as landless and contemptible.

He was about to set off across the moonlit terrace, past the sparkling fountain, but he thought better of it this time and kept close to the wall, out of the light. He reached the gate and looked back. Julieta was still at her window. He stood with one hand on the iron ring, without the heart to turn it while he could still see her. The moon vanished behind a cloud and Julieta disappeared from view. Mawi opened the gate and let himself out, locking it quietly and putting the key back in his pocket.

The past six years struggling to survive in a hostile city had been hard. The previous three years, living in his village in the aftermath of the massacre, had been harder still. Tonight, for the first time for nine years, his happy thoughts were not with his childhood past but in the present: here, now, tonight.

Mawi set off along the Avenida Seminario, keeping to the shadows at first, towards the park by the river where he slept under the bougainvillea. Then he thought: 'An impoverished slum-rat? Maybe I am, but I'm also the friend of the most beautiful girl in Santiago.' He stepped out from the shadows and walked unhurriedly and with his head held high along the outside edge of the pavement, from one pool of lamplight to the next.

8

A tall, dark, strong-looking man, ruggedly handsome, wearing farmers' clothes, took an egg-tray of two dozen eggs from the boot of his car in a village of thatched adobe huts high in the Andes overlooking Santiago, walked to the door of a hut smothered in pale blue clematis and knocked.

The door opened and the tired but still beautiful face of a woman in her late thirties or early forties looked up at him in surprise. She wore her hair in a single plait down her front. Her features were more Asiatic than Hispanic. Her black three-quarter length skirt and dark green llama-wool jumper were torn and threadbare, and she was barefoot.

'Eggs? We haven't enough money.' She gasped, as surprise turned to fear. 'I know who you are. You're the farmer who— '

'*Buenos días, señora.* Is your brother Fidel at home?'

'Fidel doesn't live here any more. He— '

A man appeared out of the shadows behind her. He must have been four or five years younger than the woman. His face had the same bone structure, and the same eyes. He had large, strong hands roughened and scarred by work. His white smock and dark blue jeans were torn and his moccasins were in holes. '*Buenos días*. I'm Fidel. What do you want?'

'I think you know why I'm here, Señor Fidel. The army are going to call at your home during the next few days. I advise you to leave at once and stay away for two or three months.'

Fidel advanced, pushing his sister aside. 'Who are you? How do you know this?'

'It's better I don't tell you who I am.'

'You're one of them, aren't you?' Fidel snarled. 'How else would you know?'

'If I were one of them, I wouldn't call to warn you. The walls have ears, Señor Fidel: best they shouldn't hear my name or how

I know. No more warnings, and hundreds would disappear.'

'I've got a living here as a carpenter. Do you expect me to walk out on my work?'

'If you don't walk out now, you'll be removed in an army lorry in a day or two.' The stranger handed the tray of eggs to Fidel's sister. 'Take these eggs, *señora*. Cook your brother the largest omelette he's ever eaten. Tonight an Indian called Tupac will call at the house. He will be your brother's guide across the mountains. Have you heard of the town of Tunuyán, sixty kilometres from here, Señor Fidel?'

'I know it,' his sister replied. 'It's in Argentina.'

'There's a family there called Qurihuarachina. They will provide a bed, food and safety until the hounds give up the chase.' He held his hand out to Fidel and wished him luck.

Fidel paused, then slowly took the tall, strange farmer's hand. '*Gracias, señor.*'

As the visitor made his way back to the car, he heard the sister's sobs and the door being closed softly behind him. He sighed. He knew Fidel's story and why he was living with his sister: the surprise rocket attack on his adobe home five years ago while he was working in a nearby village; his young wife and her brother blown to pieces.

The stranger started the engine and began the three-thousand-metre descent, winding slowly down the rutted, four-in-one dirt road in second, first through a stark landscape of grey rocks and débris, with just enough earth here and there for clumps of grass to take root, then through forests of towering araucaria trees, on his way now to a church and presbytery in the centre of Santiago. In his rear-view mirror he saw the giants of the Andes, snow-covered, six – nearly seven – thousand metres high. To the west, far below, vineyards, meadows, pastureland and orchards full of peach-trees stretched like a lawn, seen from this height, as far as the capital, visible only as a band of haze and tiny cubes. Beyond was the coastal cordillera and, behind a veil of sea mist, the

Pacific Ocean.

Among the mosaic of cubes stood the Church of Santo Domingo de Guzmán, built in 1633 and named after the thirteenth-century founder of the Dominican order and scourge of heresy and non-conformity. It was situated in the heart of Santiago's most exclusive residential area, kept in tiptop condition with donations from wealthy parishioners, and rebuilt without delay after each earthquake. The red carpet from the door to the altar was changed at the first sign of wear and tear, and the orchids and lilies were thrown out and replaced before they even began to wilt. The gold plate above the altar was the finest in Santiago – more sumptuous even than the chancel-screen and reredos in the Cathedral – and the silver candlesticks and brass censers were polished not once a week but every day by maids compelled by the parish families who employed them to volunteer for the work out of their few hours of free time.

The rector of Santo Domingo was in no way the pietist's idea of a model priest. Most of his congregation were as gold-plated as his altar-screen. He didn't live a life of poverty and self-denial, or run soup-kitchens for the hungry and destitute, or spend all his time in prayer. He had wealthy relatives. He ate and drank well. He drove his own car.

The *padre*'s congregation included senior army officers, politicians and civil servants, and owners of some of the largest estates in Chile. In his sermons the rector, who had a strong baritone voice and a gift for oratory, told his listeners what he knew they wanted to hear. He was true to the spirit of Santo Domingo de Guzmán, who threatened all heretics with damnation. The heresies the preacher inveighed against were not doctrinal but political, and his sermons were music to the ears of the thick-set, bull-necked colonels, generals and ministers who occupied the front stalls. Franco Reyes was one of the faithful, and he brought his wife and daughter and maid, Copihue, to mass at Santo Domingo every Sunday without fail.

The rector was not a typical priest to look at either. Dumpy, bald and pasty-faced were not for him. A quick change of costume in the vestry and he would have been right for a TV commercial selling luxury cars to the rich.

On the face of it, the Father of Santo Domingo was everything the Establishment could wish him to be and all that the top brass in his congregation were capable of seeing. To some of his more perceptive parishioners it must have seemed strange that a priest whose sermons were in the tradition of the grim-faced, unsmiling eponym of their church should himself be so cheerful by nature, always with a twinkle in his eye, more of a St Francis than a St Dominic. Strange too that their rector, who had been seen going in and out of expensive restaurants with generals and ministers, should seem perfectly at ease at the bedsides of the sick of his parish, or at the tables of the hungry, sharing the bread he brought them, or placing wafers on the tongues of the less privileged members of his flock, who attended mass not with the ministers and chiefs of staff at eleven after a large breakfast, but early on Sunday morning on an empty stomach, or without ostentation on a weekday, before or after twelve hours' grind.

Until eight years ago the rector had been no more than he seemed: an upwardly mobile clergyman shutting his mind against the chilling reality of the régime. Then something had happened to shake the foundations of his blinkered life.

One of his two dearest relatives had been – or was, perhaps, though hopes were fading – a dear friend, the closest he had had, a man of his own age, a virtual brother. Gentle, soft-spoken Fernando had been a supporter of Allende and a journalist. After the assassination and military coup he refused to go into hiding and went on writing pro-Communist articles. He was arrested at his friend's family home. Nothing had been heard of Fernando since.

'And there you are giving your blessing to the very men who arrested him,' the rector's forceful elder sister, Gabriela, had told him. 'You're a Christian, and a priest. You should be the voice of whatever conscience they still have, not their lackey. The early Christians were rebels. They were martyred in their thousands for their beliefs, but those who survived went on denouncing the Roman authorities who were persecuting them.'

Then came Constantine, the cleric thought as his sister reeled off the heroes and heroines of the Early Christian Resistance – the Roman Emperor Constantine who had the bright idea of making Christianity a state religion and ending its subversive influence. Believers were transformed into good citizens and became champions of convention and orthodoxy. And so they remained through the centuries, by and large, in countries and empires that called themselves Christian. But what was the Church to do when a state patently gave up all pretence of Christian values, violated human rights, revelled in an orgy of torture, rape and murder? Keep the bloodshed and screams out of sight and earshot, as most of the rector's fellow-priests did? Return to the rebellion and subversion of the early Christians?

'Violence only breeds violence,' he had answered his sister. 'As it is, thousands of innocent, peace-loving UP supporters are being arrested, tortured and liquidated simply for exercising their right to vote for Allende. Start blowing up police stations and barracks, and twice the number of people will be picked up and made the martyrs of state terrorism. Hatred is for the defeated, anger for the proud. What we need is the cunning of the fox.'

It was soon after Fernando's disappearance and Gabriela's harangue that the rector's regular dinners at restaurants with army officers and government officials began. One evening he found himself sitting opposite an up-and-coming officer, a young man with a troubled expression who couldn't look him in the eye. Over coffee and cognac in the plush *salón* the officer asked the priest under his breath when he would next be hearing confessions. The following Sunday, in the curtained privacy of the cubicle, the pious young man revealed that he had been commissioned to round up the late President's supporters in the mountains east of Santiago and engineer their disappearance. How was he to square his commission with the teachings of Christ and with the Sixth Commandment? The rector invited his confessant to return before each stage of the military operation with a list of the villages to be raided and the Allende supporters to be purged from them, so that they could pray together for the individual soul of each villager who would disappear. Obedience came easily to the officer: before each raid he would come to confession with the required list fastidiously copied in his careful hand and deliver his litany into the murk, unaware that his confessor was holding a microphone the other side of the grille and recording all the names. The rector would then absolve him, knowing that, if he didn't, the young man might refuse the assignment, which would then almost certainly go to an officer with fewer scruples and without the same zeal for confession.

'I'm sorry: Father won't be taking mass this evening. His sister's poorly and he's had to go to her.' The rector's cleaning-woman had learnt to double as door-keeper and telephonist.

About once a week during Gabriela's affliction the pastor would climb into his old Volkswagen and set off for the foothills of the Andes to visit his ailing sister, who lived a life of epicurean ease and enjoyed excellent health in spite of the *pisco* sours she kept on the go all day and the Peter Stuyvesants she chain-smoked. He would change into working clothes belonging to one of Gabriela's tenant farmers, leave his own car in the shade of the cedars next to his sister's Japanese four-wheel drive, stride down to the local garage and hire one of the second-hand cars that were for sale – a different one each time. He would then head for the scene of the next planned raid and warn the blacklisted villagers to go at once to another part of Chile, or abroad, and lie low till the danger was past.

The results of the priest's mission had a mathematical

simplicity. The lives of those who heeded his warning were spared. Those who dismissed him as an eccentric farmer with a taste for practical jokes were rounded up by the military, disappeared and were not seen again. Word spread among the late President Allende's supporters: if the tall, handsome farmer comes knocking on your door, do as he says, pack your bags and leave. Hundreds of lives were saved. More and more raids were abortive. The young officer confessed to fewer and fewer deportations. Sometimes he didn't come to confession for weeks. When he did come, his wrongdoings were trivial, fastidious, Pharisaic: eating a slice of ham on Friday, forgetting to cross himself at the required moment during mass.

The rector's visits to his infirm and debilitated sister had started nearly eight years ago but no one – not even his zealous army officer – appeared to have made the connection between the man of God and the absence of former Allende supporters from their villages when the soldiers called.

The priest in farmer's guise arrived back at the garage, paid for the car and walked up the drive through two acres of grounds to the large, comfortable eighteenth-century Spanish Colonial house, with its Roman tiles and carved oak balconies, where his wine-growing parents had lived and their children were born.

Gabriela, sister and mother in one, lavished affection on her younger brother, a Stuyvesant in one hand, a glass in the other, half-seas-over as usual, staggering slightly. She was wearing her pale green housecoat with the white peonies as big as cauliflowers, her white sandals and, as always, more jewellery than the Queen of Sheba: their mother's diamonds and emeralds in her ears, round her neck, on her wrists and fingers, as if she were about to welcome the President. She was in her early fifties but had the looks and figure of a much younger woman. She could have been in her thirties if it hadn't been for the nicotine-stained fingers and teeth, the gravelly voice, half an octave lower than her brother's, and the smell of cigarettes, which even her liberal use of Chanel Number Five couldn't erase.

'Not stay for a meal, Lorencio?' Gabriela protested strongly. 'There's avocado pear with prawns, sirloin steak, wine from Grandfather's estate. It's not enough to save other people's lives. You have your own to look after.'

'I'm expecting a visitor,' her brother explained gently. 'A homeless boy who may have been blacklisted. I must be there when he arrives.'

Copihue, the Reyes' maid, had called early that morning to ask for protection for the boy; Father Lorencio had told her to bring him to the rectory in the late evening. Copihue was more than just another member of his congregation. Her parents were among the many he had saved.

Gabriela's dismay wasn't faked. Her brother knew how lonely she was in spite of her brave front, and how important his visits were to her. He understood why she took so much trouble with her appearance and why she kept the house immaculate and full of flowers from the garden, why the light over the porch was kept on at night. His sister lived a life of fading hope and expectation, refusing to accept widowhood without proof. Losing Fernando had been bad enough for Lorencio; what it could have been like for Gabriela he could only imagine. Lorencio never talked about him in the past tense, mainly for his sister's sake. Sometimes the Santo Domingo in him told him they should face the terrible reality together, but then he heard the gentler voice of St Francis saying that even a false hope was better than no hope at all.

He hugged Gabriela. 'I'll be back as soon as I can. We'll have a long, leisurely meal on the verandah, and I'll bring my best wine from the cellar at Santo Domingo.'

In the car Lorencio put on a tape of Bach oratorios and now and again broke into song in a voice that had once sung with the Cathedral choir. As he drove he tried to think of a suitable refuge for the boy Copihue was bringing to Santo Domingo tonight. He was about to go through all the safe families a third time when a rush of paternal feeling swept them out of his mind. The boy would stay at the presbytery and be treated like a son. If he had no family in Santiago, he would welcome a father's affection and guidance. The rector wondered if the boy was a Christian. If not, as a priest he must help him find a friend in Christ.

The music ended. The dirt road turned to tarmac, carts drawn by horses, donkeys and oxen gave way to lorries and vans, peace and clean air to noise and fumes, rural dreams to urban reality. The closer he drew to Santiago, the more uneasy Father Lorencio felt. He must forestall rumour and spread the word that he was preparing a protégé for the priesthood. What if Franco Reyes saw the boy and recognized him? The rector's credibility as a supporter of the régime would start to crumble.

9

The Café O'Higgins, just off the Plaza de Armas in the centre of Santiago, was carpeted in red, furnished with red plush chairs and white wrought-iron tables with marble tops, and staffed by liveried waiters with stoops and greying hair. Most of the clients were stooped and greying too, or would be in a few years' time. The gentlemen were dressed as all self-respecting Chileans should be, in dark suits with freshly laundered and pressed white shirts, starched collars and sober ties. The ladies were decked in black lace, gold and diamonds inherited from their grandmothers and great-grandmothers. Tourists who stumbled unwittingly across the threshold of the O'Higgins received frosty service from the doddering waiters and never returned. Jeans and T-shirts were turned away peremptorily by the doorman.

'Quite right too,' thought Franco Reyes, as he sat sipping his coffee while he waited for Major Adolfo Cortez. 'Young people today are casual and undisciplined. It's the liberal influence.' He was perspiring under his dark grey, three-piece serge suit. The fresh, clean shirt Copihue had laid out for him only a few hours ago was already sodden with sweat.

The Café O'Higgins, named after the half-Irish father of Chilean independence, Bernardo O'Higgins, catered for the tastes of its élite clientèle, tastes fashioned by the wave of fugitives from Austria and Germany in 1945. No modest dollops of whipped cream on the meringues, *Kirschetorten* and *Apfelstrudel*. O'Higgins piled it on thirty centimetres high. Even a plain cup of coffee was what Chile's good food guide described as a ten-minute journey through milky-white cumuli of frothy *Sahne* to an epicure's heaven of best Brazilian arabica freshly made from newly ground beans. Some of those who had helped shape modern Chilean gastronomic tastes were still among O'Higgins' clients. Reyes eyed with curiosity the frail, fussy old men, sitting alone, calling tetchily for service, sipping seltzer to counteract the effects of all the whipped cream as fastidiously as they had once dipped their pens in inkwells a hundred times a day for six years and calmly signed to death several million of their fellow-Germans, including the flower of the medical, scientific, artistic and legal professions, all so as to purify their blood. Reyes studied the pallid, emaciated old men over his Everest of whipped cream, their blood so purified that it had turned to water – seltzer water without the fizz. Spanish colonials had been smarter when they cleansed Chile of its indigenous population: they had wiped out half of them with guns and disease but married the other half, so diluting Indian blood out of existence while enriching their own. Only the Mapuche had held out against the white invaders. Reyes couldn't help admiring them, even if he would have liked to see them exterminated.

The Café O'Higgins was one of Franco Reyes' favourite haunts. He felt at home in the affluent surroundings. His mouth watered at the portions. No hills for Reyes; he was a mountain man and liked to get his crampons into what he was eating.

'Adolfo!' he called across the room, and raised his free arm in greeting. He put down his cup and licked the wisps of cream from his upper lip.

Adolfo Cortez took off his officer's peaked cap and stepped and side-stepped and square-danced his way among the tables and chairs and up the two stairs to Franco Reyes' table.

Reyes sensed the young man's unease and attempted to dispel it. 'So glad you could come, dear boy!' he boomed. 'What will you have?'

'Lemon tea, sir.' Cortez sat down.

'Meringue?'

'No thank you, sir.'

'Looks after his health,' thought Reyes. 'Good thing too. Don't want him paralysed with a stroke fathering Julieta's first child.'

Reyes clapped to attract the waiter's attention and ordered his guest's tea and another coffee for himself. He would have liked a cream cake but couldn't very well order one for himself if Cortez wasn't having one.

'Haven't seen much of you recently,' he said. 'Field duty?'

'No, sir. HQ. Lists of names. Have to be sure we don't miss any of the bigger fish.'

'Clean-up?'

'Exactly.'

'Good egg.' Reyes took a file from the battered leather bag on the floor beside him and handed it to Cortez. 'Here are the government records you wanted. Allende's letters to his supporters in the Santiago area. He only wrote to the ringleaders. You've probably picked most of them up already.' He knocked back the rest of his coffee and spooned the cream at the bottom of the cup into his mouth. 'Could have sent a messenger. Then I thought: no, I'll give them to him in person. It'll be good to see the major again.' He beamed at the officer.

Cortez' face showed not a glimmer of a smile. In fact, Reyes caught a flicker of irritation as the young man took the file. 'Am I keeping him from his work?' he wondered. 'His desk and his officers' mess: is that where his world begins and ends? Won't be much of a life for Julieta.'

'Family well, sir?'

'That's better,' thought Reyes. 'He's remembered to ask.'

'Fit as a fiddle,' he said, licked his teaspoon and put it on the saucer. 'Julieta sends her greetings.'

'That sounds wrong,' he thought. 'Too formal. What else can I say? Julieta's panting for you? I'm not good at fibs. Greetings isn't a Julieta word. What on earth would she say?'

'Charming girl,' said Cortez.

'Charming girl? Charming posy on that old woman's hat. Charming cup of weak tea to keep him slim as a schoolgirl. He isn't exactly passionate, this future son-in-law of mine.'

The waiter arrived, creaking almost audibly, set the tea and coffee on the table, placed Reyes' empty cup on his tray, and departed stiffly.

Conversation was suspended while Reyes got to work with his spoon and Cortez sipped his unsweetened lemon tea.

Reyes began his next volley. 'Busy week ahead?'

'More paperwork, I expect, sir.'

'Come to dinner! Monday suit you?'

'I'm afraid I've got dinner with the CO on Monday, sir.'

'Tuesday?'

'Staff meeting.'

'Wednesday?'

'It would be a pleasure, sir,' said Cortez, after a moment's pause. 'Most kind of you.'

That flicker of irritation again. Good food. Good wine. A beautiful girl. What was irritating about that?

'Excellent. About nine? What do you like to eat?'

Cortez laughed. Thinly, thought Reyes, like lemon tea. 'I leave the menu to the excellent judgement of your wife and the cook, sir. The last two meals were delicious.'

Meals for dainty ladies. It came of always letting Nicole choose the menu. 'That's settled then. Any message for Julieta?'

'My greetings in return, sir. And my hopes for an early reply to the letter I enclosed with a small present some days ago.'

Reyes' eyes and whole face lit up and he stopped spooning cream into his mouth. 'You wrote a letter and sent a present? Splendid! I will pass your message on without fail.' Ill-mannered brat, not bothering to thank him or answer his letter! No wonder he was blowing cool. She got that from her Peruvian mother, not her father. He would have words with her.

Cortez finished his tea. 'Sorry not to stay longer, sir. Expected back at HQ.'

'I quite understand, dear boy. Get all those lists out of the way for next Wednesday. Then relax and enjoy a good meal, with bucketfuls of wine.'

'I'll try to, sir. Most kind.' And he was up, with undisguised relief, gliding down the steps, snaking his way through a bevy of white-haired Germans and out of the café.

Not exactly a bundle of fun, his future son-in-law, thought Reyes, spooning cream furiously into his mouth. Still, he would go a long way in the army. Probably end up as President of the Republic. A good match for Julieta, and useful to Reyes. But about as hot-blooded as a goldfish. Piqued at not hearing from that wretched girl. 'It's his diet,' he murmured to himself, disappearing inside the cloud of cream. 'He needs feeding up. I'll choose the menu this time. No delicate little fillets of sole on a thin bed of rice. I'll send Copihue down to the market for a few kilos of best steak. And I'll open a couple of bottles of good strong Chilean *pinot*: fourteen per cent. That'll put the colour in his cheeks. The fire in his blood.'

Reyes re-emerged from his dive into the coffee-cup, his nose tipped with white, hailed the creaking waiter and ordered the cream cake he had been longing for.

10

Father Lorencio couldn't make out his Mapuche protégé. The boy was taciturn. At first the priest thought he was hostile, perhaps because of what had happened to his people a hundred years ago: the massacres, the deliberate spreading of disease among them, the deportation of survivors from villages that had been theirs for thousands of years to reservations far from their homes. But the boy was keen to show his thanks to his protector: he did the washing-up, took the rubbish from the kitchen-bin to the dustbin, made his bed and left the room tidy, had cleaned the presbytery and redecorated the kitchen. None of this was compatible with hostility. Was he shy? His relaxed manner and the way he looked you straight in the eye suggested he wasn't. Was his Spanish poor? He seemed to understand everything Father Lorencio said to him and, on the few occasions he spoke, he did so fluently and without a fault.

On the fourth day of his Mapuche guest's Carthusian economy of words, Father Lorencio decided things had to move on and, to break the silence at lunch as they started on his speciality of chicken, prawn and egg *escabeche* with onions, peppers, herbs, spices, olives and cheese, Father Lorencio told his protégé the story of Jesus, having guessed the boy had only the haziest idea of what he called the Spanish gods.

'Not gods but God,' Father Lorencio explained. 'He first revealed himself four thousand years ago to the Jews, a nation who lived beyond the great sea that fills the middle of the world. They called him Jehovah. Two thousand years ago knowledge of him spread to other countries round the great sea. Today he is known and worshipped all over the world, and his name is God.'

To mark what he had decreed would be a new millennium, Father Lorencio went on, Jehovah had decided to father a son. He wanted the boy's mother to be a human, and his choice fell on a young Jewish woman called Mary. Jesus was born in a cowshed, warmed by the bodies and breath of cows and sheep. He grew up as a normal human boy. At the age of twelve or thirteen he learnt a trade.

When Jesus was a young man, his father Jehovah needed to speak to the Jewish people about an important matter, and he asked his son to act as go-between. The young man became a preacher and went about his country preaching his father's message, which was that the Jews were to love Jehovah, love and be gentle to one another, and even love and forgive their enemies, just as Jehovah loved his followers and forgave them their wrongs.

Jesus himself was comfortably off, being a carpenter, which was a well-paid trade, but this didn't stop him feeling the strongest possible compassion for the poor. He told them Jehovah preferred them to the rich, and he told the rich to look after the poor. As well as preaching, Jesus cured people of their illnesses and astonished those around him by turning water into wine, walking on water, transforming a handful of fishes and loaves of bread into a feast for five thousand, and bringing the dead back to life.

Jesus arrived in the capital of his country, where he was mistaken by the authorities for a rebel and put to death. After three days Jehovah learnt that his son was dead, brought him back to life and took him to live with him in his kingdom in the heavens. A few hundred years after Jesus' death, his return to life and journey to heaven, the Spaniards adopted Jehovah as the true god and also worshipped his son Jesus. Today, if you knelt in front of a Spanish priest, he would turn even poor-quality wine into Jesus' blood, which you could then drink, and pieces of bread no thicker than paper into his body for you to eat.

Father Lorencio felt pleased with his summary. He had told the story simply and clearly, so that his protégé would understand it. He glanced at the boy two or three times as they finished their *escabeche,* to see if he would at last break his silence.

The Mapuche got up thoughtfully, collected the plates, took them to the sink and washed them carefully.

What a model guest the boy was, thought Father Lorencio. The kitchen had never sparkled as it did now. The floor always used to be swept, certainly, but until last week the tiles had never been quite free of stains. Not a drop of oil or a burn on the cooker now, not a finger-mark on the fridge and, between meals, not a crumb on the stripped pine table. The sink was as clean and white as fresh snow, the window so transparent that the glass seemed to have disappeared from it. Father Lorencio's guest had even washed the walls and given them a coat of white paint. 'I have no money to offer you for the bed and meals,' he seemed to be saying to his protector, 'but I will pay you with my work.'

The boy put two clean plates and the carved gourd heaped with apples, oranges and papayas on the table, and sat down. He took a papaya but didn't cut it. After a long pause for thought he asked: 'Why does a priest have to turn wine into blood and bread into meat, *señor*? With all the killing the Spanish soldiers do, there should be more than enough human flesh for their priests to eat and human blood for them to drink.'

Was the boy joking? No, he seemed in dead earnest. Father Lorencio had had to field every kind of question during his conversions but this one was new to him. His first impulse was to defend the priesthood against cannibalism but he quickly realized this wasn't the point. The boy was right: instead of speaking out against the torture and killing, the Church just quailed and let it happen. He was about to say this to his protégé when a vivid image sprang to mind: the pulpit here at Santo Domingo; the parish priest speaking out, yes, but to endorse, not condemn, the brutality of the régime. Simon Peter had spoken out when he denied knowing Jesus. Judas Iscariot spoke out with an embrace to betray his master.

'Priests are men, and men are sometimes weak,' he told the

Mapuche at last. 'Their weakness is no reason to reject God and Jesus.'

'And Mary, the mother of Jesus... Now I know why the Spanish temple I walk past every day is called Holy Trinity. Trinity means three: Jesus, his father Jehovah, and his mother Mary.'

'No, no,' Father Lorencio corrected him. 'Jesus, his father, and the Holy Ghost.'

'The what?'

Another vivid image stopped Father Lorencio in his tracks: his sister, Gabriela, glass in hand, eyes bloodshot after a succession of *pisco* sours, her speech slurred, inveighing against the fundamental beliefs of the Christian Church. 'Did Christ ever say anything about a trinity? About a holy ghost? You know as well as I do, Lorencio, they were cooked up centuries later to try and put a stop to the ferocious quibbles and quarrels of malevolent Christian bishops.'

'What happened to Mary?' the boy asked. 'Didn't she go and live with Jesus and Jehovah in the kingdom in the sky?'

'Later she did,' Father Lorencio replied.

'Centuries later,' he heard his sister say. 'When the bishops at last realized their antifeminism was driving not only women away from the Church but also men who weren't misogynists. Mary was rescued from obscurity and bundled into heaven without delay before anyone could start questioning her virginity.'

'Why later?' the boy insisted.

'Mary had to finish her life on earth with her husband, Joseph the carpenter.'

His protégé was about to pick up a knife to cut his papaya, but his hand remained suspended above the plate. 'Mary had two husbands?' he asked, wide-eyed.

The story that a few minutes ago had seemed simple and unquestionable was turning into a maze, and Father Lorencio was in danger of losing his way. 'Mary wasn't God's wife,' he said with a hint of desperation. 'She was married to Joseph, the carpenter.'

'I have heard from my people that Spanish priests rage and roar against adultery, and that two hundred years ago their executioners strangled adulterers or burnt them alive.'

'Jesus forgave a woman taken in adultery but, yes, the Church has always regarded adultery as a sin.' What was the boy driving at?

The Mapuche picked up his knife. 'And yet your own god is an adulterer, *señor*.'

'What?' Father Lorencio could hardly believe his ears. A hundred and fifty years ago the boy would have been summarily garrotted by the Inquisition.

'Why couldn't Jehovah find an unmarried girl to bear his son, *señor*, instead of having sex with a carpenter's wife?' He sliced the papaya in two.

Coming from anyone but an untutored Indian, this would be the grossest blasphemy. 'God doesn't have sex,' he replied emphatically. 'Mary was a virgin when she gave birth to Jesus.'

The spoonful of orange pulp stopped just before it reached the boy's mouth and hung there like a stranded cable-car. 'A virgin? But how...?' He seemed to realize his questions were disconcerting his host and didn't finish the sentence. The spoon completed its journey and he started on the papaya absent-mindedly, puzzlement written all over his face. 'Thank you for your story, *señor*,' he said flatly when he had finished chewing.

'It's history. It's a true story.'

The boy finished his papaya, washed his plate and knife at the sink, added water to the old kettle and put it on the gas-ring, which he lit with a match.

'Would you like to hear a story from Araucanía?' he said as he sat down again at the table.

This would let Father Lorencio off the hook: he quietly sighed with relief. But unlocking the Mapuche's tongue might also open a Pandora's box. Too bad: they couldn't go on eating together in silence. He smiled and nodded.

'Like you we have a trinity,' the boy began slowly, collecting his thoughts. 'Our mother is the Earth. Thanks to her fertility the forests of Araucanía are thick with araucaria and eucalyptus trees more than a hundred metres high, and the glades are bordered with sweet-smelling acacia. Have you ever seen a rainbow shatter into a billion pieces, *señor*? The meadows of Araucanía are covered with the fragments of rainbows: camomile, larkspur and lucerne, poppies, cornflowers, anemones and a hundred other flowers and herbs fill them in the spring and summer. The flowers bring bees, and the bees make as many different kinds of honey as there are flowers in the meadows. Fields that once belonged to the Mapuche people swell with wheat, maize, maté and alfalfa. Orchards and vineyards seized from our grandfathers overflow with oranges and apples, grapes and wine for the invaders. Even with the little land that's left to us, our Earth Mother provides us with food and drink, medicine and clothes, and with wood to build our carts and the frames of our homes, and to make the fires that keep us warm.'

It was Father Lorencio's turn to stare wide-eyed, and his glass of cider hovered forgotten under his chin. He had been expecting a few hesitant words, instead of the tapestry his protégé was weaving in front of their eyes. Not only was the boy's tongue unlocked but he seemed inspired, as if his imaginary gods were speaking through him. When had God ever spoken through his servant Lorencio like this? Not in his sermons, certainly.

The Mapuche had much to thank their Mother for, the boy went on, but all that lives needs to drink and nothing of all she gave them – not a flower or a shrub or a tree – could grow without water. Second in the Mapuche trinity was the Rain God, who came from his home south of Araucanía, always hidden from view behind layers of cloud, and rained his love down on the Earth to make her fertile, so that the seeds inside her could become seedlings or grow into saplings.

With only the Earth Mother and the Rain God, Araucanía would be a thousand times colder than the lands in the far south, where there were no trees or flowers but only glaciers and icebergs, it would be perpetual night and not even lichen or moss would grow. Life was only possible thanks to the third member of the trinity: the Sun God. His golden face and his serenity as he flew across the sky, higher than the highest condors, sometimes made the Rain God jealous. In those moments he suffered at having to share his love for the Earth and at having to share her love with the Sun. He thundered and flashed furiously and tried to blot out the daylight with angry, black clouds. He at last went home to the mountains south of Araucanía and slept away his pain. While he slept, the Sun poured down his warmth on the Earth, so that the seedlings became plants and flowers and the saplings grew into trees.

The kettle was boiling. The young Mapuche got up and filled the two cups, which he brought to the table on their saucers.

Father Lorencio's training told him he must find the errors in what he had just heard. His first instinct was to challenge both the sex and the sexuality of the first member of his protégé's trinity but, before he could open his mouth, Gabriela's husky, thirty-a-day voice rang again in his head.

'Why shouldn't God be a woman? Women are more peace-loving and creative than men. How many armies of women soldiers have there been during the past three or four thousand years? Not a single one. How many men have ever given birth to a baby? I've read your early Christian saints: Paul, Augustine, Ambrose, Athanasius, Jerome. They hated all women and most men. If a woman wasn't a virgin, she must be a whore. But why shouldn't she be a mother? Why shouldn't God be a mother, producing fruit and flowers, humans and animals, as women produce babies?'

Father Lorencio's protégé sat down and took a sip of coffee. The rector sipped his own coffee and studied the Mapuche's face over his cup. What made this boy different from a Hispanic boy of the same age? The black eyes were the same, even if the fringe was lower and the cheek-bones were higher, but he was much too handsome to be Spanish, with none of the heavy, pasty look of the typical Hispanic male. And he was strong, healthy and fit, unlike the white-skinned, overweight youths of Santiago. The intelligence and sensitivity were beyond anything Father Lorencio had encountered in a young Spanish Chilean with ten years of primary and secondary education under his belt. And yet Lorencio the servant of God had been subconsciously regarding the boy as several rungs below South Americans of European origin in the social Darwinian scheme of things. Was it so hard to escape the prejudices of one's race and class? Father Lorencio's protégé deserved more respect than any Hispanic youth he knew. The boy had probably never been to school and yet he had the maturity and seriousness of a university scholar. A Christian priest should be thinking of ways of demolishing a pagan's erroneous ideas. Father Lorencio could think of nothing to say that wouldn't sound discordant and intrusive. He rejected what he had heard but realized the beliefs were sacred to the boy and inseparable from the land where he was born and which he loved. To destroy them would be as great a violation as bulldozing his house. He felt a surge of paternal affection for his protégé, who deserved a place at university and a professional career but had been forced to earn his living cleaning shoes.

'Would you like to hear how man and the animals began?' the boy asked.

Father Lorencio nodded. Better fairy-tales than a blank page.

'Many millions of years ago there were no birds, animals or insects on the earth and no fish in the sea,' the Mapuche began again, his tongue unloosed now. 'The only signs of life on land were grass and mosses and the odd tree, and in the water seaweed and algae. One day two pieces of seaweed that had been waving and wriggling for centuries broke away from their roots and were carried this way and that by the currents, wriggling as they went. After thousands of years they were transformed cell by cell into water-snakes, one male, one female. Before long the sea was teeming with wriggling water-snakes and they started to wriggle and slither their way on to dry land. Some of them made their way to the hot, wet regions that would one day be jungle, where they grew and grew until the biggest became anacondas. Others climbed into trees, where they draped themselves over branches and slowly turned the same colour as the leaves and stems. A third kind preferred dry, rocky places, where they grew fangs and became vipers.'

Millions of years passed. Many of the rock snakes had stopped sliding over stony ground, developed legs and were beginning to look like the jaguars and pumas that roam the mountains, forests and jungle today. Most of the tree snakes had grown bored with always hanging in the same tree and had sprouted wings, some of them huge and black and as strong as the boughs of trees.

Man had been an accident, a hybrid, the result of the union between a rock snake and a tree snake. Because many rock snakes developed into jaguars and tree snakes into condors, man kept features of all three creatures: the snake, the jaguar and the condor. Like the snake he is sometimes treacherous and deceitful, injuring others when they least expect it and poisoning their lives. Like the jaguar he is a hunter, even though he goes on hunting when his stomach is full. In his best moments, in love or in the act of creation, he is like the condor, soaring high above the earth.

'Man has the freedom and the wit to choose,' the Mapuche went on. 'The wise man chooses to leave behind the snake in himself, learns from the strength and control and hunting skill of the jaguar, and finds as many moments as he can to fly with the condor: when he plays music or makes beautiful things out of gold, silver, pottery, cloth... when he thinks beautiful thoughts... prays to the gods... in the love he feels for his family... in his journey from this world to join his ancestors...'

The Mapuche reached out for his cup with the delicacy of a cat probing with its paw, and quietly finished his coffee.

'Good story,' Father Lorencio said quietly. 'Well told.'

'It's a true story, *señor*,' the boy replied with a sly smile, purring now, his story told.

'You're asking me to believe what you've just told me?'

'Why not? You want me to believe that your god was father to Mary's son, Jesus, that Jesus' mother was a virgin, that he died and was brought back to life, that he could cure people's illnesses and was clever at tricks like walking on water and turning water into wine—'

'Tricks?' Father Lorencio got up abruptly, grabbed the two cups and saucers and took them to the sink, where he banged them down. 'Miracles!'

'Sorry: miracles. And you want me to believe that your priests are wizards who can turn bread and wine into flesh and blood.'

'They can! They can! And they're not wizards. The difference between your story and mine is that yours is fantasy and mine is true.'

The priest washed the cups and saucers and put them on the draining-board. When he turned, he caught a smile on the face of his guest. There was no irony in the smile. Wisdom rather. *The child is father of the man.* Where had he heard those words?

'Is the difference between our stories?' said the boy. 'Or between truth and truth?... Many hundreds of years ago, long before the Spaniards invaded this continent, the people of the Andes had worked out the exact distance between the earth and the other planets. They knew how to find their way on land and at sea by reading the stars. They could measure the height of mountains and they knew exactly how high to plant their crops, their fruit, vegetables and herbs. They understood how to build houses and temples that wouldn't fall down in earthquakes. That was one kind of knowledge. But they also knew that the Rain God thundered when he felt jealous of the Sun, that jaguars and condors had once been water-snakes, that man hatched out of an egg laid after the marriage between a rock snake and a tree snake. That was a different truth, to sing and dance and tell round the fire, not prove scientifically. The only untruth is when the parts grate against each other like wrong notes in a piece of music. How could a loving god forget to make the mother of his own son one of the family in his kingdom in the sky?'

'So the value of a religion is to be judged on how well it holds together as a piece of narrative?'

'A piece of what?'

'As a story.'

The boy thought for a moment. 'Why not? Stories help us understand the world. They help us find the light and accept the darkness. They teach us to fly with the condor. The better we understand, the better the story.'

'Religion is more than just a story. It also has a ritualistic side. When the Spaniards arrived four or five hundred years ago, they found Indians offering fourteen-year-old girls as sacrifices to their gods.You can't blame Spanish priests for wanting to stamp out barbaric practices.'

The Mapuche stood up and took several steps towards the priest, who was still standing with his back to the sink. The Indian's eyes were flashing. For a fraction of a second Father Lorencio thought the boy was going to seize a kitchen knife but he stopped short of the drawer at the end of the table.

'What barbaric practices?' the Mapuche said quietly and with perfect control. 'The people of the Andes offered animals as sacrifices, not humans. The Mapuche didn't even sacrifice animals to their gods – only the first fruits of the year. If you're looking for human sacrifice, you'll find it among your own priests. They strangled and burnt our people because we worshipped our own gods. They egged your soldiers on to burn our villages, rape our women, massacre our communities. Your police and army behave today as your soldiers have always done, and your priests say nothing.'

The thought of his sermons burnt like nitric acid in Father Lorencio's mind. Could he inadvertently have given his blessing to an outrage against the Mapuche people, perhaps against his protégé's own community, his own kin? The thought made him feel sick. He went back to his chair at the table and sat down.

The coals in the boy's eyes had cooled. 'The invaders from Europe worshipped two gods,' he went on. 'They told the people of this continent about a god of gentleness, love and forgiveness, but they forced this gentle god on them with the help of a god of hatred, massacre and torture. When your soldiers had destroyed their homes and temples and fields, the priests would tell them the story you have just told me. If they laughed or said "No thank you, we prefer our own gods," they would lay them on tables, tie their ankles and wrists, and stretch them till their bones snapped and their sinews split; lock their heads, feet and hands in wooden holes and lash them with whips spiked with nails, then sear their flesh with red-hot iron. To stop the pain they would scream that they accepted your god of love and gentleness. With time your god became familiar to them, like a step-parent seen across the table day after day. Deep down the memory is still there, of a real parent lost in early childhood.'

Father Lorencio said nothing. His mind and body were still sick with the thought of the lives his sermons may have cost.

'Your priests tell us your god is the god of the poor. You said so yourself. Why then did the Spaniards take the beautiful things we had made to honour our own gods – vessels, ornaments and statues in gold, silver and copper – and make fires to melt them, and turn the metal into money to make them rich? We were never rich ourselves. Our gold and silver were used to honour our gods. Nothing has changed. Today people from other continents take the gold and silver from under our land, and the food we grow, and they buy big houses and cars with what they have stolen and leave us to sleep in the streets.'

'It is true that Christians have sometimes forgotten their god,' Father Lorencio murmured. 'Human nature is weak.'

'Our gods make us strong, not weak,' replied the Mapuche. 'Every day we see the Sun's brightness and we feel his heat. We feel our Earth Mother holding the whole Mapuche nation in her arms and telling us to be strong. Where does your god live? At the other end of the sea in the middle of the world, where you can't see or hear him.'

'Our god doesn't live anywhere,' Father Lorencio protested, reviving, like an insect that has been trodden on but discovered that he's still alive. 'That is, he lives everywhere and nowhere. We can't see or hear him. He's our god, not an audiovisual entertainment. He moves in a mysterious way.'

The boy looked puzzled. 'If you can't see him and he doesn't speak to you, how do you know so much about him? How can you be sure he's a god of love and gentleness, not of hatred and cruelty?'

'Because he sent his son Jesus as his messenger. He sent him to die for us, so that we could be forgiven for our sins.'

'Forgiven for your sins? So that you can sin again and again? So that Hispanic soldiers can kill the people they call Indians, be forgiven, and kill more Indians? Forgiveness doesn't interest me.'

'You want revenge?'

'I want justice.'

Father Lorencio said nothing at first. His explanations rang hollow in his ears before he had even uttered them. Where did this boy get his knowledge and wisdom, his clarity of thought and command of Spanish?

'The basis of our faith is love,' Father Lorencio said quietly at last. 'Where there is love, justice and forgiveness will find their proper places.'

'Love?'

'Looking after our neighbours. And our family and friends. Feeling no hatred, even towards our enemies.'

The boy returned to his chair and sat down. 'But this is something the Mapuche have done for thousands of years, *señor*. We do it, instead of talking about it. How could our communities exist if we didn't? We look after our children and parents and grandparents. Perhaps we look after them better than the Spanish look after theirs. There were no quarrels in our village. If people disagreed about something, they talked without getting angry. It's the same everywhere in Araucanía. Everywhere in the Andes. In the days of the Inca Empire, conquered nations weren't hated, humiliated, tortured to death, made slaves, as they were when the savages arrived from across the eastern ocean. They were honoured as newcomers to the Empire, and their leaders joined the circle of the Sapa Inca's wise men. The result was not just more land and more people for the Incas but an empire without rebellion and civil war.'

The boy noticed Father Lorencio slumped in his chair the other side of the table.

'I'm sorry, *señor*. I've been talking too much. Shall I make you some more coffee?'

Father Lorencio sat up slowly, looked at his guest and smiled wearily. 'No thanks. I need a brandy. I'll get it.' He hauled himself to his feet and headed for the cupboard above the draining-board. 'You don't have to call me *señor*, you know.' He took a bottle and two glasses from the cupboard, poured brandy for himself and cider for his guest. 'I wanted you to talk. That's why I told you the story of Jesus. I was hoping it would loosen your tongue. We had hardly spoken to each other.'

'For the past five years, since I came to Santiago, my gods have been my only friends. I was afraid you would take them from me.'

Father Lorencio brought the glasses to the table and sat down.

'I know what I would like to call you, if you will let me,' said the Mapuche. 'I would like to call you Father, because you treat me like a son. You give me delicious food and a bed and talk to me as a father talks to his son.'

Father Lorencio took a sip of brandy. 'Of course, Mawi. Call me Father. Most people do.'

Father Lorencio thought of an amaryllis as he watched his protégé holding his glass in his long, thin, supple hands, the flower that stays silent and part of the greenery for weeks, then explodes overnight into a massive, exotic bloom. The rector should have been racking his brains for possible ways of bringing the boy into the Christian fold but for the first time in his twenty years as a priest he recoiled from the sacrilege of stealing a non-Christian from his faith. Mawi had been defending his gods against the true god of Christ and the Apostles but doing so with the conviction and passion of a seminarist about to receive holy orders. As he sipped his brandy, Father Lorencio watched his spiritual son over his glass and imagined he was looking at Jesus resting from his work as an apprentice in Joseph's workshop. Was it absurd to see Jesus in a boy who was anything but a Christian? No, Father Lorencio almost said aloud: this was exactly what Jesus Christ was talking about. He was asking us to see him even in a non-believer, in criminals and murderers, even in an army officer who had enough conscience left to confess before each planned outrage. This was what Christ meant by love and forgiveness, thought Father Lorencio. The condor soaring high above the earth: now there was an image for transcendence, for reaching beyond oneself to love and forgiveness. Were Jesus and Mawi talking about the same thing, one in words, the other with an image?

Father Lorencio must stop his reactionary sermons, even though he didn't believe a word of what he was saying, he thought later as he undressed for bed. A word spoken was like a signature on a cheque or at the end of a letter. To give support in words to something you knew to be wrong was like forging a signature. His signature may have condoned the very purges he was trying to foil.

Father Lorencio had never believed in punishing the body, as if God had sinned in creating it. Fasting and self-flagellation were morbid and against the spirit of Christ. God meant us to enjoy the nourishment he provided for us. And he didn't ask us to wear hair-shirts and pray to him on our knees on cold stone floors. Father Lorencio prayed on his back in bed. He prayed till he fell asleep, and he slept the better for his prayers.

Tonight his thoughts were with Mawi and his people, with the massacres and the seizing of their land. Father Lorencio prayed to God for an explanation. Was this the world he wanted for his children? Was he on the side of the thugs, bullies and killers? Why must innocent Indians be made social outcasts, tortured, driven from their homes, murdered? What was the divine purpose of such cruelty? He listened, waiting for an answer, and he fell asleep, still waiting.

11

The scene was set for Franco Reyes' dinner. The best silver had been polished by Copihue. The crested forks and spoons sparkled in the light of the candles, already lit, as did the steak knives, sharpened till they cut like razors. Two large silver bowls filled with passion-fruit and pomegranates reflected the room like mirrors but with the objects distorted almost beyond recognition: the lilies in the white porcelain urn on the mahogany pedestal in the corner enlarged so that they looked like wedding-dresses in a shop-window; Franco Reyes' mother, a brawny countrywoman refined two decades ago by Chile's leading painter into a duchess, tonight transformed into one of her own farm animals – sheep, pig and cow rolled into one – in her portrait ornately framed in silver between the two French windows; the crucifix on the far wall now with hairpin bends at its extremities and more like a swastika than a Latin cross. The five-branched candelabrum on the white tablecloth would have looked as much in place on a high altar as on a dinner-table. Two bottles of 1969 Tarapaca stood open in their silver holders. Copihue's poppy-seed rolls, which two hours ago had filled the house with the smell of baking bread, waited without scent or warmth in their silver basket. The only lightness and simplicity in all this silver glitter was in the set of Limoges fruit plates that had belonged to Nicole Reyes' French grandmother; they were piled discreetly on the rosewood side-table beside the door into the hall.

Julieta stood in the dining-room, out of view of the terrace, where her parents and the two guests, one of them obviously a North American, were standing sipping their *kirs* or *pisco* sours and filling the air with small talk. In English, for the benefit of her father's North American guest, most likely one of the many he invited to Santiago to help Chile's economy, so he said, furiously dismissing critics now in exile who preferred to call it making a gift of the country's natural resources to foreigners. Julieta's mother and Adolfo Cortez were managing pretty well. Her father was managing about as deftly as a beginner on the trumpet, his grammatical errors ringing out like wrong notes. There they stood waiting for the daughter of the house, her father preparing for his sacrifice to Hymen, the god of marriage, sharpening his knife like Abraham. And the daughter of the house wished she were ten thousand kilometres away, out of reach of her father's machinations.

Julieta heard the squeak of wheels from the hall, and the tap of her friend's shoes, loud enough to warn of her approach but too quiet to disturb. Copihue came in, her trolley laden with a silver tureen that must have weighed at least ten kilos. Julieta had often thought how much prettier and more elegant Copihue looked than most of her father's women guests, with the white blouse and three-quarter length black skirt she wore for waiting at table, her trim figure, black eyes, oval face and lustrous black shoulder-length hair gathered at the nape of the neck and fastened with a wooden Mapuche comb.

'Soup, on a night like this?' said Julieta.

'Your father chose the menu,' Copihue whispered. She examined the table to make sure nothing had been forgotten. 'Looks like a wedding feast.'

'Like a funeral supper, you mean, with me as the corpse.'

Copihue chuckled, her quiet laughter gentle as the patter of rain.

A trumpet call from the terrace: 'Do I hears my daughter voice? Come, daughter, come! Come in the terrace! We are waiting you.'

'I'll have to go out and face them.'

'Your mother's on your side. So am I. You look lovely in that dress.'

Julieta had wanted to wear her trouser suit – smart but sexless

– not dress feminine for Adolfo Cortez. But her father had made her change into this frilly thing she hated: black and red lace made her look at best like a flamenco dancer, at worst like one of the tarts on the Plaza Sotomayor near the port.

She took a deep breath and went outside, where her parents and the two guests were standing in a group and Julieta's father was tracing his Chilean lineage back to Valdivia's conquest in 1540.

'Gee! What a beautiful girl!' The North American was massive and copper-haired, a few years younger than his host, and he wore a copper-coloured summer suit.

'Is my daughter,' Julieta's father explained proudly, dabbing his forehead with a white handkerchief the size of a tea-towel. Julieta never understood why he persisted in wearing a dark grey three-piece suit even in hot weather. Far from giving him gravitas, it simply made him look absurd, like a snowman melting in the sun.

Cortez glanced over his shoulder at Julieta, with a proprietorial smirk, as if the North American had just complimented him on a filly he was about to ride.

Julieta's mother, Nicole, had an elegance and poise that set her apart from the three men present. Julieta wanted to be like her when she was forty-five: to have the style of an educated European and the dignity of an indigenous South American, with none of the loudness and gaucherie passed down the generations by the Conquistadores and colonials. Her mother's high cheekbones were those of an Andean but she had the fairer skin of a European. She was taller than most South American women – the same height as Julieta, but her platform shoes gave her an extra three centimetres – and had the figure of a dancer or fashion model. Her black hair was tied in a loose bun and she was wearing her three-quarter length burgundy skirt, a wide black belt, a white blouse and black evening shoes. Her long fingernails were painted red, she had rings on five or six of her fingers, and bangles on her wrists. She made Julieta think of a long bunch of sweet *muscat* grapes and, like an orchard or vineyard, she filled the air around her with the delicious lemony scent of her perfume.

'Your mother's so serene,' Copihue had often told Julieta. Julieta agreed but they both knew there was one person who regularly disturbed that serenity: Julieta's father. Her mother's normally calm face was troubled this evening by ripples of worry. Julieta could guess why. Her mother knew why this dinner had been arranged, even though her husband hadn't discussed his scheme with her. She would use all her wiles to thwart a plan that had everything to do with her husband's need to manipulate his family and nothing to do with their daughter's happiness. She knew Julieta felt little for Cortez and that whatever the major's qualities as a soldier, he didn't love Julieta and wouldn't make her happy. She had said as much to Julieta and, without actually inciting her to disobey her father, kept telling her to listen to her own heart, not to any plans her parents might have for her. Julieta knew what most worried her mother was that, however much she rebelled at first when her father tried to make her do something she didn't want to do, she had always given in in the end.

Julieta approached the group and made for the North American, holding out her hand to shake his. 'Good evening,' she said in English. 'My name is Julieta.'

'And mine is Herman Gorringe.' His hands were like steam-hammers but the handshake was gentle. 'Call me Herman.' He was smiling and affable, the same size as Julieta's father but made of muscle instead of fat. He could have been an ex-boxer or -wrestler. 'What a good accent you have! Genuine Brit.' His *genuine* rhymed with *wine*: the North American pronunciation. 'Where did you learn your English?'

'At school.'

Julieta took in the strong jaw and the nose that changed direction halfway – badly repaired after a break, she guessed, or not repaired at all. It didn't spoil his rugged good looks; in fact, it enhanced them. Even the mild pock-marking on the cheeks and the scar on the chin added to the rugged effect. Normally Julieta didn't like red hair, but this was pale copper, not strawberry, and matched his suit to a tee. *'Encantado,'* he drawled. 'Pardon my Texan!'

Julieta turned to Adolfo Cortez, who was wearing full-dress military uniform: khaki with red trimmings and gold épaulettes and a decoration below his left lapel like a row of flags – all the colours of the peacock. *'Buenas noches.'*

The major nodded his head stiffly but said nothing, then half-turned away.

Julieta felt stung. Was this the way army officers courted the girls they wanted to marry? He had the same prim expression as one of the nuns Julieta remembered from school, when one of the more boisterous pupils asked her a question. What had Major Adolfo Cortez got to reproach Julieta for? She couldn't even bring herself to shake his hand.

She turned back to Herman Gorringe. 'What brings you to Chile, Mr Gorringe?'

The question took the North American by surprise. He hesitated.

Julieta's father came quickly to the rescue. 'Mr Gorringe interested in Chile wine. No, Mr Gorringe? Import-export, no? We drink California, you drink Chile, no?' He guffawed.

Mr Gorringe liked this idea, which was obviously new to him, like the fact that Chile produced its own wine perhaps. 'Er... Yeah, that's right. Chile wine.' He beamed.

'And which are your favourite Chilean wines?' asked Julieta, who wasn't going to let him off the hook as easily as that.

The Texan hesitated again. 'Er... It's a little too early to say. We arrived in Chile just a couple of days ago.'

We? You, and who else?... Strange that Mr Gorringe didn't seem to know why he was in Chile, thought Julieta. Or perhaps he knew but didn't want to say.

'Are you staying long?'

'Just a few days. I have a little business in Peru. But I'll be back.'

Julieta's father stepped in to prevent more questions. 'So, is time for eat. I see maid bring plate for soup.' He led the way through the French windows into the dining-room, tripping as always on the sill as he went.

Julieta's mother looked pained, as she and Julieta followed. Hot soup on a hot night. Good cuisine was in her blood, as was a proper choice of menu, but her husband was becoming more of an autocrat every day and now tried to control household matters, about which he knew nothing.

Julieta's father stood at the head of the table, directing his family and guests to their places. How like the King of Spain he looked! Julieta had never noticed it before. Fatter and older, of course, but the same Roman nose and protruding eyes, the hair thinning in the same way on the crown and at the temples but curling abundantly at the back. All sat, the guests either side of the King, the family flanking them at the opposite end of the table, with Julieta next to Cortez, inevitably. Copihue, who had been waiting beside the tureen, served: first the ladies, then the guests, and finally the master.

'You know *caldillo de congrio*, Mr Gorringe?' asked Julieta's father, slurping his soup noisily and giving everyone the cue to start.

'Er... No, I can't say I do, Franco.' Herman Gorringe was sitting on his host's left, occupying the whole of one side of the table on account of his size.

'Is my favourite soup... What is *congrio* in English?'

'Conger eel, Papa.'

The question was addressed to the whole table but Julieta from her place opposite Gorringe, on Cortez' right, was first off the mark with the answer. She enjoyed translating for her father:

she didn't often get the chance to be in control.

'Congeree. *Gracias.* Congeree, onion, potato balls. Is very good, Mr Gorringe.'

Julieta's father launched into one of his stories, one Julieta and her mother hadn't heard before for a change. It dated from his days in the army, where meals were prepared in massive cauldrons,

'Large enough for feed *todo el batallón.*'

'The whole battalion,' Julieta prompted.

Her father and his regiment had been stationed on the coast in northern Chile, where they spent weekdays slaughtering striking miners and Sundays after mass fishing. One Sunday a group of soldiers caught a conger eel three metres long, thick as a man's leg.

Franco Reyes paused in his story, leant over to Cortez and gave him a broad, salacious wink. The major looked perplexed. Reyes went on with his story.

The soldiers had dragged the eel in their net to the kitchen. There they filled a cauldron with water, emptied their captive from the net into the cooking-pot, banged on the lid and lit the gas.

'El congrio empezó a agitarse.'

Julieta hesitated, wondering where her father's story would lead. 'The eel started to… thrash about.'

Another wink for Cortez, who had put his spoon down and was looking pale. Embarrassment brought a little colour back to his cheeks. He seemed uncertain whether to wink back or not. Reyes slurped his soup.

Soon the eel had been thrashing about so much that two men had to sit on the pot.

'Para sujetar la tapa.' More slurping.

'To keep the lid on.' Julieta's voice was faint now. She wished she had never offered to translate.

At last the water boiled and the eel expired. The soldiers

cooked it for several hours, then took the lid off the pot. The eel stared blindly at them out of the bubbling, frothy scum, its eyes having melted long since in the boiling water.

A black-skinned chunk of fish surfaced in Reyes' soup. He grabbed a fork from beside his plate, harpooned it and, using both fork and spoon, shovelled it into his mouth.

Adolfo Cortez was not the only member of the company to have turned green at the gills and given up on the first course. Julieta's mother was too appalled to move a muscle as she stared at her husband. Julieta was wondering whether to plead dyspepsia and disappear upstairs. Only Herman Gorringe was soldiering on, sipping his soup, with longer and longer pauses between sips.

'The congeree he have his revenge,' Franco Reyes continued, oblivious of the effect his story was having on his family and guests. 'All the people who eats him, they die. *La cólera*. Sixty-five soldiers killed by congeree.' He removed a piece of cartilage from between his teeth and draped it over the rim of his soup-plate. 'The ones who drink the soup, they are very ill. Four hundred soldiers very ill. Very ill but not die. I drink soup. Was best soup I ever drink. I not ill. I eat congeree. I not die.' He downed his last spoonful and glanced at Copihue, who was standing beside the tureen, ready to serve another round. 'More *caldillo* for all people?'

'No thank you, sir,' murmured Adolfo Cortez, who was staring back at a watery eye fixed on him from just below the surface of his broth.

Franco Reyes was the only one to want more but a look of desperation from his wife changed his mind. He nodded to Copihue.

Copihue cleared the plates and wheeled the trolley to the kitchen. Reyes grabbed one of the bottles of Tarapaca from in front of him, poured a generous amount into his glass, tasted it, nodded and handed the wine to Cortez, so that he could help himself and pass the bottle on. Cortez got up and, with one hand behind his back, poured wine for everyone.

Julieta's heart had warmed one or two degrees to Cortez during the meal. He had after all caught the full blast of her father's intemperance, been embarrassed by the winking and leering, sprayed with soup and perspiration and brought almost to the point of throwing up by the reminiscences. She relented another few degrees at the sight of the major folding away his tail feathers and dutifully playing the rôle of wine-waiter. Perhaps his aloofness was a front. Maybe he felt uncomfortable with women at dinner-parties.

Franco Reyes slurped his wine and held his glass out for Cortez to fill. The trolley-wheels clattered and squeaked again and Copihue returned with more silver. She took the lid off a large oval dish to reveal five slabs of best sirloin steak.

'How you like your steak?' Julieta's father asked Adolfo Cortez. 'Rare? *Sangrante, se dice en francés, ¿no?* Bleeding? Bloody?'

Cortez winced. 'No, no,' he replied faintly. 'Well done.'

Julieta's father was the only one to like his meat rare. Copihue served the master his hunk of barely cooked steak and trundled the groaning trolley back to the kitchen.

Franco Reyes started on his steak. Blood oozed from either side of his knife and from the holes made by the prongs of his fork. Sweat poured from his forehead and temples. 'Cut like butter,' he said.

His wife's face, normally calm and resigned, was stretched into her mother's habitual expression of Parisian contempt. 'Have you ordered vegetables to go with the steak?' she asked from the opposite end of the table. 'Or are we to eat it *brut*? *Nature*?'

'Maid bring French fried,' her husband replied.

'And a salad, I hope.'

A silence followed while Julieta and her mother and the

guests sat riveted by the spectacle at the head of the table, like onlookers in the jungle or at a zoo watching an anaconda devour its prey.

Herman Gorringe seemed to notice things had gone quiet and to decide the party needed an injection of good humour. 'Say, what a great evening!' he said loudly, glancing at Cortez, Julieta and her mother, whose expressions ranged from queasy bewilderment to embarrassment, shock and hostility. 'I feel honoured to pass the evening in your beautiful house, drinking this excellent wine and breathing in the exotic perfumes of your garden.'

No sooner had the Texan finished his encomium than Franco Reyes' steak, which was being attacked with manic energy, skidded off his plate and landed fair and square on the snowy linen table-mat in front of Adolfo Cortez, soaking it in blood and spattering red drops on his pristine white cotton shirt. There was an intake of breath from Julieta's mother, and a look like the blade of a guillotine. Julieta wished she could grow wings, fly out of the French windows and away from home and Santiago. Cortez studied his thin, elegant hands as if he had just noticed them for the first time.

'Copihue!' yelled Franco Reyes, fork-lifting the meat back on to his plate.

There was the sound of running. Copihue appeared in the doorway. She saw what had happened, hurried back to the kitchen, reappeared moments later and replaced the stained table-mat with a clean one. She went back for the trolley, which, like a goods train being shunted to and fro, clattered into motion once again. Copihue was back, the silver lid was off and the four slabs of steak reappeared like old friends, tanned after their extra spell under the grill. The steak was served from the trolley, the French fried potatoes from the hot-plate on the mahogany sideboard, and Copihue disappeared back to the kitchen.

Another silence as Julieta and her mother and the two guests got started on the main course. There was no salad but the steak was from one of the best herds just over the mountains in Argentina, and it cut and melted in the mouth like *pâté de foie gras,* with juices that had turned from red to the colour of caramel. The French fried were thin, crisp and light, with a slight taste of olive oil and salt. The wine was deep and strong, with the colour and after-taste of blackberries. Appetites returned and embarrassment and discomfort gave way to uneasy contentment.

Julieta's mother smiled up at Copihue to thank her for working her magic on an unpromising menu as she cleared the dirty plates and replaced them with five of the Limoges fruit plates, hand-painted, each rim a coronet of grapes, apples, apricots, peaches and cherries. Franco Reyes and his family and guests finished their meal with pomegranates and passion-fruit.

Adolfo Cortez cut primly into his pomegranate and started at the gush of seed and red pulp from inside. Reyes noticed, gave him one of his winks and whispered to him, loud enough for everyone to hear: 'Like blood, my friend, no? Blood and seed.' He gave Cortez' pomegranate a squeeze with his fat hand. Red pulp and white seed burst on to the plate. He slapped Cortez on the shoulder. The pinheads of red disappeared from the major's cheeks, his lips turned pale and he put down his knife. Julieta tried to remember from her first-aid course what to do when someone fainted. Franco Reyes shrugged and got up. Major Cortez was clearly not his idea of a soldier. 'We drink coffee on the terrace, no?' He went into the hall.

The others finished their fruit, got up and moved outside. On the terrace were two round white wrought-iron tables, one with two matching cushioned chairs, the other with three. Herman Gorringe was heading for the table with two chairs. Julieta felt drawn to this good-humoured hulk, and was also curious to find out his real reason for coming to Chile. She was about to join him when Adolfo Cortez, who had made a speedy recovery after his attack of the vapours, brushed past her, took Gorringe by the arm and sat down with him at the table for two.

So this was the man Julieta was supposed to marry! She had put his failure to greet her or say a word to her during dinner down to gaucherie, but it was clear now that his rudeness was deliberate. What had she done to deserve unpleasantness from a man who was supposed to be wooing her? One question led to another. Julieta had seen the looks her father had given the major during dinner. She knew her own father well enough to sense when he liked someone. The expression on his face when he talked to Cortez was one of amused contempt. If he didn't like the man, why did he want his daughter to marry him? What were her father's motives? The Cortez were one of the best-known families in Chile. The Government and army were full of members of the Cortez family. Adolfo Cortez was well connected. Was Franco Reyes prepared to give his daughter's life away to a man he despised because he came from a good family and would raise his own family's social standing and perhaps in turn bring him more political power? The thought had never occurred to Julieta in sharp outline till now. It hurt her and made her ashamed of her father.

She sat down next to her mother at the table for three. Her mother put her hand on Julieta's. Dear Mama! Her silent ally. If only they had been alone on the terrace, watching the moon rise above the trees, breathing in the scent of honeysuckle and listening to the song of the nightingale. An experience that had once been routine now felt like a memory of paradise.

A peal of laughter from the other table, where the two men had been engaged in earnest conversation. Julieta's curiosity was aroused. Cortez and Gorringe hadn't exchanged a word all evening. What could they now have to say to each other that was so important? Cortez was speaking in a murmur, so that the words were lost, but Gorringe found it harder to keep his voice down. Julieta concentrated all her attention on what he was saying.

'I learnt on the job, not in a military academy. Vietnam. You start tough. You ease up when they're all dead or done for. Ever thought of air strikes? Napalm?'

Napalm? The chemical that explodes out of bombs on to women and children working in the fields and burns them alive? Spoken casually, with a genial smile on the avuncular North American's face, as if he were planning a Christmas outing for orphans. Julieta shuddered.

'Scare the shit out of the natives, that's what you got to do.'

Natives? What natives?

'We got rid of ours more than a century ago. Except for the leftovers on the reservations. The USA is a cleaner place without them.'

Cortez signalled his approval with a mirthless, staccato laugh.

Julieta had had to read extracts from *Dr Jekyll and Mr Hyde* for her English classes at school. The affable Herman Gorringe of a few minutes ago had been transformed into his murderous alter ego, everyone's favourite uncle into a slyly grinning crocodile. Julieta took deep breaths to calm herself. She must make her excuses and get away from the terrace and these two creatures who were poisoning the air with their visions of mutilation and genocide.

'Commies are all bastards. If your hill-billies are Commies, that makes them bastards too. Mapuche: is that what you call them? You wiped out more than half of them a century ago. Why not finish the job off?'

Mawi. Her father's dinner-party, and her dread of it, hadn't given Julieta a moment to think about her friend all day. The thought of him now calmed her and sent a pleasant tingling through her body all the way to her fingers and toes. Her hand changed places with her mother's, so that Julieta was now squeezing her mother's hand. Mawi: her gentle, handsome friend, with his brown skin, like Copihue's, and the same big, black eyes. Julieta longed to protect him, to get him away from

Santiago, from this human jungle of greed and violence, where innocence and a simple heart were easy prey for eyes and jaws waiting in the long grass, to see him to the safety of the mountains, where the only eyes were those of the great birds circling overhead.

The two speakers her father had positioned outside the French windows hummed, crackled, then burst into life at a volume that sent Julieta's and her mother's hands rushing to their ears. The big band blaring out Franco Reyes' favourite tango would have made only half the noise playing live on the terrace.

Julieta's father tripped out of the house carrying a little silver bucket full of ice, and in it one of his bottles of vintage champagne. He placed it on the table in front of his wife and daughter and returned to the dining-room for a tray and five champagne glasses, which he set down next to the silver bucket.

'I like to propose toast,' he announced, but his words were drowned out by Jorge Silvestri and his Big Bandsmen. He tripped back into the house, turned down the volume, returned and started again. 'I like to propose toast.' He seized the bottle and pulled out the cork, which flew past his nose, over his head and into the pond surrounding the fountain behind him. Julieta's father tried to direct the gush of froth into the glasses. He finished pouring, handed glasses to Gorringe and Julieta's mother and took one for himself. 'I like to propose toast to two jungest members of this group: my belovely daughter Julieta, and Alfonso… er… Adolfo…' He paused to clear his throat. 'Adolfo Cortez. Their life lie before them. Brilliant military career wait the colonel… er, major. Happiness hang…' He paused to choose his words. 'Happiness hang like bunch of fat, ripe grape before their lip. Let them catch it and fill their mouth, belly and heart with sweet fruit! To Julieta and Major Adolfo Cortez!' He swigged his champagne.

'Bravo!' murmured his wife, coating the word with a thick layer of irony. She put her glass down without drinking from it.

'To Julieta and Adolfo!' boomed Gorringe, and drank.

Julieta looked at the high walls of the garden all around under the darkening sky. They suddenly seemed to her like the walls of a tomb. The sky was her gravestone, which her father and the smiling Gorringe were lowering on to her. If she didn't get up and out before the sky was dark, their work would be done, they would drag Julieta's mother powerless into the house, wall up the French windows and entomb Julieta in a living death with Adolfo Cortez.

Julieta was on her feet, not controlled now by her conscious will but driven by a primal instinct for survival. 'You were kind enough to send me a present, Major Cortez,' she heard herself begin. 'A gold ring. As you can see, I live a comfortable life – luxurious, even – and have no need of gold, so I have given your ring to one of the many poor of our country, whose poverty makes it possible for you and me to live as comfortably as we do.'

'You what?' exploded her father.

'Thank you for the toast, Papa. Like you, I wish Major Cortez a brilliant military career. And I share your concern for my own happiness. Now, if everyone will excuse me...'

'Excuse you?' blustered her father. 'Where are you going?'

'To my room. The eel soup doesn't seem to have agreed with me.'

'You're going nowhere. You're staying on this terrace.'

But Julieta was already through the French windows. Her father could follow if he wanted, but she was her own woman and free of his authority, for the present at least.

Julieta had acted spontaneously, without knowing what she would do next. Having spent the evening twisting and turning in her trap, she had been driven by desperation to tear herself out of it. During the moments it took her to get to the kitchen a clear-cut plan of action fell into place. She knew now what she was going to do and how she was going to do it.

'Leave the washing-up and come with me in a taxi,' she said to Copihue.

Copihue burst out laughing. 'Where to?' She was all sparkle and fun when she wasn't serving at table. Julieta told Copihue her plan, and the laughter subsided. 'Are you trying to get me sacked?' she said.

'You can tell my father you had to take me to hospital. I'll give you the medical details in the taxi. Papa won't understand them and Mama will know I've made them up.'

Ten minutes later they were in the back of a taxi, heading at 100 kph along the Avenida Providencia towards the Plaza Italia with a driver who was not over-respectful of traffic rules, overtaking on the inside and hardly slowing down for red lights, let alone stopping for them.

'You'll be back before they've noticed you're gone,' Julieta said quietly.

'If I don't die first.'

At the Plaza Italia the taxi turned left, squealed round a series of corners and screeched to a stop outside the Iglesia Santo Domingo de Guzmán.

'This can't be right,' Julieta said in surprise. 'This is where we come to mass.'

Copihue asked the driver to wait and got out with Julieta.

'The priest here is worse than the generals,' Julieta whispered when they were in front of a pair of oak doors twenty metres along the street from the church. 'Don't you listen to his sermons?'

'Trust me.' Copihue lifted the cotton pouch she was wearing round her neck from under her blouse, took out a large key and gave it to Julieta. 'This is the rectory for the church. The doors lead into a patio. Father's rooms are on the left. He sleeps soundly. Keep ringing the bell till you hear him coming downstairs. He may recognize you from mass. Say you're Copihue's friend, that you've got an urgent message and need to speak to his Mapuche guest alone.'

Copihue squeezed Julieta's hands in her own small, delicate ones and hurried back to the taxi.

Julieta hesitated, then slid the key quietly into the lock, turned it and took it out, used both hands to turn the iron ring, opened one of the oak doors less than half a metre and slipped inside. She peered into the darkness, listened, closed the door gently behind her, locked it and put the key in her shoulder-bag.

The patio was sixteenth-century, the same age as the church, as far as she could tell in the light of the moon and stars. All the windows had window-boxes overflowing with dark shapes that looked like camellias. The left side of the patio was completely dark. The right side was dark except for one window at the top in the corner. The window was open. There was a pool of light at the far end of the room, probably from a reading-lamp.

As Julieta looked up at the window, a wind instrument began to play softly in the room – some kind of flute, she guessed. At first she thought it was a tape but the music stopped for a moment, the passage was repeated several times, then the piece continued. Whoever was playing played well. Sensitively. Why disturb the priest when there was someone already awake? She found a pebble to throw up at the window. If whoever was up there seemed to pose a threat, she could always disappear into the shadows. Julieta was about to throw the little stone when the mode changed from major to minor and the music touched her heart. Strange that music could be both happy and sad at the same time, she thought, and that it was so much lighter-footed than language and could go straight to the heart and understanding. The world was a cold place, the music seemed to be telling Julieta, a frozen expanse without comfort or pity. Just when the piece seemed about to end in despair, minor changed back to major, like a warm breeze bringing relief and hope, thought Julieta, thawing the ice, melting hearts, promising life and growth, turning pain to joy, bitterness to love.

12

Mawi's belongings amounted to no more than he could carry in a small haversack, and yet they included two possessions dearer to him than a mansion full of silver and a fleet of Cadillacs ever were to a millionaire: the gold ring given him by Julieta and the wooden flute made for him by his father. His flute was more than a possession – more than a talisman, even. It had been his only companion for the last five years, the voice of home, of the forests and lakes of Araucanía and the birds that call from the branches and shallows, of his gods and ancestors, of his nation and the surviving members of his community.

For the past few evenings Mawi's music had been infused with two emotions new to it: the longing to see his friend of less than a week again, and the fear that he never would. How would Julieta ever get past her father, the railings and alarms that surrounded the house and in through the oak doors that guarded the presbytery? Was what happened a few nights ago now only a memory, no more substantial than a dream, a vision shorter than the life of a butterfly of what could have been in a fairer world? Expressing himself through music took the edge off Mawi's sharper feelings, calmed him, prepared him for whatever the days and weeks ahead would bring.

He began his piece again: the Mapuche love-song that was played at his parents' marriage and had perhaps been played for generations of family marriages.

The rap of stone against glass stopped Mawi in mid-bar. Father Lorencio? At this time of night? Why didn't he come upstairs and knock on the door? Mawi went to the window, leant out and called softly: 'Who's there?'

A girl's voice called back, too quiet to be recognizable: 'Me.'

Copihue?

'Come up!' Mawi called and went to the door. He heard a

single set of footsteps on the stone stairs, light and effortless. He waited for them to get to the landing, then reached down for the handle and key. A trap-door in Mawi's room led to an attic, where a skylight gave access to the roof. In an emergency he could escape on to the tiles and down one of the drainpipes into the street. He unlocked the door and opened it carefully, ready to shut and lock it again, faster than a snake can dart, if this was a trap set by Julieta's father. Standing in the doorway, like a poppy in her red and black silk and lace dress, was the answer to Mawi's prayers, a gift from the gods and ancestors he had honoured and who had protected him every day for the past five years.

'You were playing so beautifully,' Julieta said apologetically. 'I didn't want to interrupt.'

Mawi had just redecorated his room, as a way of repaying Father Lorencio's hospitality, but this didn't stop him feeling awkward. What would Julieta think of his humble accommodation after the grand surroundings she was used to? He couldn't even offer her anything to eat or drink.

Julieta seemed to sense the cause of Mawi's embarrassment. 'What a beautiful room!' she said, peering past Mawi's shoulder. 'All the old wood: the beams and floorboards. It's all so clean and fresh. Can I come in? My shoulder-bag's full of fruit and wine: leftovers from one of my father's binges.'

Mawi stepped aside, closed the door after Julieta and helped her unpack the contents of her bag on to the oak writing-table. There were purple peaches, black grapes and cherries, pomegranates, a bottle of red wine. Julieta had even brought glasses, plates, knives, spoons and a corkscrew. The bag seemed bottomless. Together they moved the table. Julieta sat on the bed on one side of the table. Mawi placed his only chair on the opposite side for himself. Julieta explained to him how the corkscrew worked. He opened the bottle, poured the deep red wine for them both and sat down.

Mawi watched Julieta's hands as she cut two pomegranates in half. How delicate they were: two flowers moving in a breeze. And her arms, circled with gold bangles, were like the slender branches of a willow-tree. He longed to touch and hold her hands and arms but was afraid she might fly away, like blossom in a wind.

Julieta put the two halves of a pomegranate on Mawi's plate, then raised her glass. 'Here's to a safer future for you, Mawi, and justice for your people.'

These words from someone Mawi cared nothing for would have turned indifference to friendship. A toast like this from the girl who filled his heart and thoughts was worth a hundred blessings from Pacha Mama herself. For a few moments he was back in the dream in which he had seen Julieta for the first time, under the arches of the Plaza de la Constitución, speechless with wonder, unable to move a muscle. He recovered and raised his own glass. Speaking quietly, so as not to let his strong feelings show, Mawi said: 'May your life, however long or short, be shaped by your dreams, not by the minds of those who try to control you. May your friends be the friends of your heart… Julieta… not of the schemes of those who say they care for you.'

Julieta clinked Mawi's glass and they sipped their wine. He had never drunk wine before. It had a taste as deep as its colour, of the berries and currants that were part of his daily diet at home in the mountains. What a pity to turn such a good drink into blood!

As Mawi put his glass down, Julieta took the hand that was holding it. 'You're wearing the ring I gave you.'

'Of course. I'll wear it as long as I live. If anyone tries to take it from me, they'll have to take the finger with it.'

Julieta kept hold of Mawi's hand until he slipped it free and took hold of hers. 'You're different from other Chilean girls,' he said. 'They despise me. You treat me like a friend.'

'I'm only Chilean on my father's side. My mother's half-

French and half-Peruvian. My Peruvian grandfather had a Spanish-speaking father and a Quechua mother. That makes part of me true South American, like you.'

Mawi let go Julieta's hand and they ate the pomegranates, cherries, grapes and peaches, and drank the wine. Together they took the plates, glasses and cutlery to the bathroom the other side of the landing to wash them.

Mawi rinsed the tableware at the wash-basin. Julieta took a plate to dry it with the tea-cloth she had brought from home. As she did so, her hair brushed against Mawi's face. He straightened up and they stood facing each other for a few seconds, holding their breath. Before they had time to think, they were locked in each other's arms, Mawi burying his face in Julieta's hair, which smelt of orange-blossom, brushing his lips over her eyes, forehead and cheeks, like a bee stroking the petals of a flower with its wings as it searches for nectar, and at last pressing his mouth against hers, the tip of his tongue light as a breath of wind on hers.

'Why so serious?' asked Julieta, when they at last drew apart and looked into each other's eyes. She was still holding the plate in one hand and the tea-cloth in the other.

'I don't want to turn you against your own father.'

'My father's turning himself against me.'

'You live among Chileans. I'm a Mapuche. Your friends won't want to know you.'

'Then they're not my friends.'

'My life has been very different from yours. I've never lived in a grand house. I grew up in the mountains a thousand kilometres south of here in a *ruka*: a hut made of reeds with an earth floor and wood fire and without any windows.'

'Rather happiness in a reed hut by a warm fire than misery in a mansion full of crystal, silver and cold marble.'

Mawi felt reassured. He kissed Julieta gently on the mouth.

'You're still serious.'

'I would like to take you to my home to meet my people, but most of them are gone: destroyed.'

'Destroyed by my people.' Julieta dropped the tea-towel and put her hand behind Mawi's neck. 'Time will heal your wounds. An end is also a new beginning. We have to make Chile a home for all our people.'

Mawi thought for a moment, then started to tingle with a feeling he hadn't felt for a long time. All that had kept him going for the past five years was his bitter quest for justice. He had been surviving joylessly, not living. Julieta had brought him a fruit whose taste he had forgotten: hope. As the feeling swelled inside him, so did his love for Julieta. It would have taken more than a single flute to sing his song of hope and love: he would need a choir and an orchestra. He kissed her with as much passion as gentleness, and placed his hands on her thighs.

Julieta resisted. 'Not here. Not now.'

Mawi let her go and stepped back. He felt awkward again and was about to apologize.

'Don't be angry. It's not that I don't want to. It's that… I've been brought up a strict Catholic.'

Mawi was puzzled. 'Your gods?'

'Yes.'

'The Spanish gods?'

It was Julieta's turn to look puzzled.

'Jehovah and Mary and their son Jesus the carpenter, and his stepfather Joseph?'

Julieta gave a laugh of surprise. 'Yes: the whole household.'

'But your gods are gods of love. Father Lorencio told me so.'

'Not love outside marriage.'

Mawi felt as if the new life he had started to construct in his mind was being shaken to pieces by an earthquake.

'What's the matter?' asked Julieta.

'The castle I was building for us both: what use is it the other side of a wall you can't climb?'

'All I'm saying is that love can only be consummated after marriage.'

What was Julieta trying to tell him?

She took his hand. 'It's not a question of possible and impossible but of what already is. All I want is for it to be seen and blessed by God. By my gods.' When Mawi still looked perplexed, she went on gently: 'There's a gate. Just open it and walk through.'

'You mean... if I asked you, you wouldn't refuse?' Mawi murmured, afraid of saying it too loud and scaring it away. Julieta was still holding his hand. 'But your parents. Would they allow it?' He felt he had to reach out and touch the jewelled casket of happiness the night had brought him, to make sure it wasn't an illusion.

'It's not their life. It's mine... My mother would be thrilled.'

'And your father?'

'Would have to choose between accepting you and losing me.'

The cold mist that had fallen on Mawi's hope and turned it into doubt and desolation started to lift. In his mind he asked Pacha Mama to forgive him for not trusting her goodwill towards him and offered two lines of a traditional Mapuche prayer for her blessing: for sunshine by day and rain at night, for orchards laden with fruit and rivers teeming with fish, for children who would honour their parents, gods and ancestors.

Julieta let go his hand. 'I suppose I'd better knock on Father Lorencio's door and ask for a bed for the night.'

Mawi felt a chill of fear: the fear of waking in the morning and finding this had all been a dream. 'You can sleep in my bed. Rosa, the maid, put clean sheets on this morning.'

'But Mawi, I've already told you—'

'I'll sleep on the floor.'

'On the floor! No!'

'I've spent more nights on floors and on bare earth than in beds.'

Mawi settled down under a blanket on the wooden floor, his face to the wall, while Julieta went to the bathroom to wash and change into her night things. He was half-asleep when she came back from the bathroom. She kissed him gently on the cheek, got into bed and switched off the light. Mawi couldn't remember ever feeling so full of hope and free of anxiety. Perhaps before the murder of Allende and the massacre at Temuco. Had he ever been so happy? He had lost dozens and found one, and yet this one, Julieta, had already filled the emptiness left in his heart by all those who had gone.

13

Father Lorencio had been lost in his thoughts, and racked by doubt, for the past few days, since his discussion with Mawi, which instead of leading to an easy conversion had shone the light under the floorboards and into the rafters of his own beliefs and raised questions it would have been more comfortable not to ask. Love and gentleness were at the heart of his faith but was this psychologically realistic? Was unbridled violence part of man's nature? If so, what value was there in a Church that looked at human nature with one eye shut? Perhaps the real problem, as Mawi had intuitively identified it, was that Christ's message had been meant for his own people, and meant not as a new faith but as a plea to them to find the patience and gentleness in themselves and as an urgent warning not to provoke the Romans with subversion and rebellion and bring about the possible destruction of Ancient Palestine.

Father Lorencio liked toast for his breakfast: two large pieces, hot-buttered then cut in half, which he ate with the home-made peach jam sent to him from a village the other side of Puente Alto by a family he had helped. 'If only I could save the lives of one or two coffee-growers and buy the occasional bag of beans under the counter at an affordable price before the rest gets taken from them and shipped off to Europe and North America,' he thought as he emptied a heaped teaspoonful of instant into his cup and poured on boiling water.

Where was Mawi? He was usually down by seven.

Mawi may have been right about habitat too. The Syrian Desert, between Babylon and the Mediterranean, without trees, mountains or colours, birdsong or the sound of the sea or of running water, without the smell of pines or orange-blossom, had been the obvious birthplace in the days of Abraham for an invisible, soundless, odourless god. But weren't the places of natural beauty in most other parts of the world – the forests, mountains, lakes and rivers – meant to be inhabited by gods, as those of Ancient Greece had been, and wouldn't we show more respect to our environment if they were? And didn't the absence of a natural, geographical home for the god inherited by the Christians from the Jews make him too available, so that violent men in every part of the world could more easily nail Christ's face to their standards and masts and fool themselves and their followers they were men of peace forced to take up arms to defend the ubiquitous, invisible god? Kings, emperors and adventurers, and theologians in their pay, had seized on the only two hints of anger in the story of Christ told by the Gospelists – if you accepted their authenticity, which Father Lorencio's sister Gabriela certainly did not – and used Christ's statement that he came sword in hand, and his overturning of the money-changers' tables in the Temple, to justify the orgiastic violence and genocide of religious wars, of the Crusades, of the massacres of the Cathars, and the barbarity of the Inquisition, all carried out in the name of God the Father and God the Son when the true motives were territorial or material greed and national or imperial ambition. Perhaps most terrible of all atrocities had been the persecution of the very people from whom the Son of God had sprung, founded on the false charge that it was they who had condemned him to death by crucifixion, and culminating in their genocide only forty years ago at the hands of the Germans, Austrians, Italians and French.

Father Lorencio was late today. He was normally up at six, at the breakfast table by six thirty, at his prayers by seven, behind his desk by eight, and confessing his old ladies' peccadillos at nine. It was already after seven and he was only just sitting down to breakfast. It had taken him a quarter of an hour to shave this morning, with long pauses between strokes as he spotted more areas of crumbling plaster or rotting wood in his faith. He would skip his hour of prayer today. Sustained prayer was impossible while the scaffolding was up round his spiritual house. His time was better spent at the kitchen table or behind his desk, drinking two or three cups of this instant muck, which was coffee only in name, and giving his mental energy to the battle inside his head.

Here was Mawi now.

The kitchen was on the Santo Domingo side of the presbytery and looked through a window with Venetian blinds on to the quadrangle south of the church. Steps led down through a glazed door into the dining-room, where large windows gave on to the patio and provided a clear view from the kitchen, especially in the morning sun, of the opposite side, where the guest-rooms were. One of these was Mawi's. He was emerging from the arch where a stone staircase led up to the first- and second-floor rooms.

'Good grief!' muttered Father Lorencio, unconsciously getting to his feet. 'He's got a girl with him. Now that's something I hadn't reckoned on. I thought I was living with a saint, and here he is turning the guest wing into a love-nest. Don't be a fool, Mawi! The sure way to get yourself caught, and me into trouble, is to take a girl into your confidence. She'll tell her friends, her friends will tell their parents, and instead of toast and peach jam for breakfast bright and early one morning we'll have the *carabineros* or the army banging on the gate.'

Mawi and his Eve were crossing the patio. 'I know that girl,' murmured Father Lorencio. 'The willowy figure, long black hair, madonna face, ebony eyes.' When he realized who it was, his heart began to pound. 'It's Reyes' daughter, in her party frock by the look of it. What's the girl's name? Julieta.' What if someone saw her coming to Santo Domingo and told Reyes? Of all the people who mustn't know about Mawi, her father came top of the list. The girl could let a careless word slip and Reyes would pick up the scent. Father Lorencio held on to the table to try and calm himself. 'Mawi, you're putting your head in the lion's mouth. My head too.' The table-top resounded with the throbbing of his hand, as if a party were in full swing in the cellar.

The French windows into the dining-room opened and the draught set the Venetian blinds in the kitchen shaking and rustling, so that the sun shining in between the slats seemed transformed into a strobe light.

'Good morning, Father,' Mawi called out when he saw Father Lorencio. He followed the girl up the steps into the kitchen. 'This is Julieta Reyes. You must know her, Father: she... she drinks blood in your temple. Julieta called last night to ask you for a bed but your light was out and she didn't want to disturb you. I was still awake, so she slept in my room. Julieta slept in the bed and I slept on the floor.'

Father Lorencio believed Mawi. The boy had a frank nature. It would take a mean spirit and suspicious mind to doubt him.

'Copihue lent me her key to the gate, Father,' said Julieta.

'Copihue?' Were the two girls allies? Father Lorencio heard the note of hope in his own voice.

'It's thanks to Julieta that you heard about me and offered me shelter,' said Mawi, in answer to his friend's thought.

Father Lorencio felt relief spread quickly from somewhere in his gut, relaxing his neck and shoulders as it went. He sank back on to his chair. 'Sit down and have some breakfast, both of you. There's fruit, fruit juice, toast and jam. And tea or coffee.'

Mawi and Julieta helped themselves and sat down.

'Why were you wanting a bed last night at the presbytery?' Father Lorencio asked Julieta.

'Father...' Mawi began before Julieta could reply. The priest knew he had something important or difficult to say. He recognized the tone of voice and hesitation. He had heard them ten thousand times in the confessional. 'Father... Julieta and I are going to get married. We want you to perform the ceremony.'

Father Lorencio's heart started to pound again and the tension returned to his neck and shoulders. 'Does your father know about this, Julieta?' he asked, sounding calm but with his heart in his mouth.

A look of alarm appeared on Julieta's face. 'No, no, no! My father wants Mawi arrested. That's why you're protecting him.'

'I know I'm hiding Mawi from your father,' said Father Lorencio. 'But don't you see? A marriage isn't legal unless it's recorded at the registry office. You have to show them your identity card. They'll want to know where your parents are. Your father could arrive as you step out of the registry office door.'

'By which time we'll be legally married.'

'What use will that be if Mawi's arrested on a trumped-up charge and thrown in gaol? Julieta, you're a clever girl. Mawi wouldn't fall for a simpleton. Talk your father round. If you can do that, Mawi will be out of danger.'

'Talk him round?' Julieta gave a dry laugh. 'My father's as pig-headed as I am.'

'He must have his weaknesses. Play on them.'

'Food. And wine.'

'Buy him a bottle of wine.'

'He already has a cellarful.'

'Take him out to dinner. When's his birthday?'

'Not for about nine months... If only it were so simple... I'll do my best.' Julieta finished the piece of toast and jam she was eating and drank up her coffee. She got up, went to Mawi, kissed him on the forehead, then turned to Father Lorencio. 'Thank you for breakfast, Father,' she said. 'And for the roof over my head. I'm going upstairs for my bag, then home. I'll be back as soon as I have an answer.' She gave Mawi a last kiss and disappeared down the steps and out on to the patio, leaving behind her a scent of orange-blossom.

Father Lorencio was grateful to his two young friends: they had shaken him out of his pensive mood. If you can't solve a problem, shelve it and come back to it. He would engage with the day without leaving half his mind in front of the shaving-mirror or on the breakfast table.

Mawi was already at the sink, doing the washing-up. 'I'll paint the last of the guest-rooms today, Father,' he said. 'I've done all but one.'

'You've slaved enough, my son. This may be your wedding-day. Why not make it a day of rest?' Father Lorencio opened the door from the kitchen on to the quadrangle and paused in the doorway. 'When did you first meet Julieta?'

'Last night,' replied Mawi, hanging the tea-cloth over the back of a chair in a band of sunshine to dry.

'Will this end as quickly as it began?' Father Lorencio wondered as he set off across the quadrangle to open up the church for his old ladies who every week with their frightened eyes begged to be told they would never die. 'Is their love no more than a shooting-star?'

In the vestry, while he buttoned himself into his black cassock, the thought occurred to him that a marriage between a leading Hispanic family and a Mapuche might stir a few influential Chileans into asking why indigenous people, who had inhabited the recently created state of Chile for thousands of years, were treated as outcasts in their own land.

Father Lorencio opened the main door of the church and heard the sound of Mawi's flute in the distance. He could tell from the way his protégé was playing that this was a hymn to the Mapuche gods to thank them for bringing him Julieta. The young man's love was no meteor, he decided; it was as steady as the four stars of the Southern Cross. What arrogance and insensitivity it would be to try and make him sing a different hymn. What right had priests to make converts? God assumed a myriad of shapes, went by as many names and asked to be worshipped in as many different ways.

14

The taxi dropped Julieta off three blocks from the house. She walked the five hundred metres to the garden wall and the shade of the locust-tree, feeling as conspicuous as a parrot in her party frills, opened the gate with the key Copihue had taken to Mawi, closed it quietly behind her and paused under the acacias, from where she had a clear view of the terrace and dining-room.

It was autumn but the sun was as hot as in midsummer, and the humidity stifling. She had been walking for only five or six minutes but her skin was damp already and she felt exhausted. It took an effort of will not to sink on to the grass in the filtered light under the trees, close her eyes, feel the cool breeze from the fountain on her face and breathe in the smell of acacia, jasmine and roses.

There was no sign of her father, who often worked at home in the morning if he had no meetings, so Julieta slipped from the trees to the trellised walk, followed the wall to the terrace and stepped quietly into the dining-room. She was steeling herself for the last lap into the hall and up the stairs when the door opened and a pair of arms appeared carrying a pile of plates.

Copihue gasped and nearly dropped the crockery when she saw Julieta. 'Your father's in his study,' she whispered. 'He doesn't know about the taxi ride. He thinks you've been in your room all this time.' She recovered from her shock but didn't quite manage a smile. Something seemed to be worrying her.

'I'm going up to change,' Julieta whispered back and slipped past Copihue and up the staircase.

Julieta peeled off her black and red dress, which was all but welded to her skin, and had a cold shower to cool down, wake up and brace herself for a confrontation with her father. She put on her favourite dress, a pale lemon one her mother had given her for her birthday in October, and her only pair of platform shoes, to give herself the psychological advantage of being taller than her father, and went downstairs.

Julieta had no wine, invitations to restaurants, meringues or *choux à la crème* to offer him. Why should she ingratiate herself to get what was hers by right: a life with the partner of her choice? She would apologize for walking out of the dinner-party, though even this went against the grain. If he refused to consent to the marriage, she would disappear with Mawi across the border into Argentina or to the safety of the mountains and forests of the Mapuche homeland a thousand kilometres south of Santiago.

Franco Reyes' study was the one room in the house that hadn't been touched by his wife's taste in furnishings and Impressionist's love of lightness and light. The desk was massive – 'bigger than the President's' Reyes had boasted to his family when he was appointed third in command at the Ministry of Internal Affairs – and the Spanish Colonial rococo dresser behind it, with its lion's feet and its frieze ornate as a ball of string that had tied itself in knots, was on the same colossal scale. The curtains were maroon velvet, the large rug was plum with a pattern, and the floor-tiles were brick-coloured. Together they absorbed most of the daylight, so that even at eleven in the morning Don Franco had to work by the light of the wrought-iron table lamp on his desk, with its faded parchment lampshade.

To Julieta's surprise, her father was in a good mood – or seemed to be. He wasn't stamping and storming, which was a relief. He sat presidentially at his immense desk behind a muddle of papers, smoking a Havana cigar and clutching a large cup of sweet, milky coffee. He appeared placatory, though it was difficult to know what he was thinking when he smiled and hooded his stainless steel eyes.

Julieta sat on the interviewee's armless, straight-backed chair, swallowed her pride and apologized for leaving the party so suddenly.

'You should have said you were unwell,' her father replied.

'Adolfo would have understood.'

'Adolfo?' thought Julieta. 'What does it matter what Adolfo Cortez does or doesn't understand?'

She came to the point and told her father she wasn't in love with Cortez and that there was someone else she wanted to marry.

Her father paused to take this in but seemed unfazed. 'Do I know him?' he asked.

'No. Just as Mama is partly Andean, so my future husband has Indian blood.'

Julieta thought she saw the knives in her father's eyes glint. She had to stop herself saying more, for fear of blurting out Mawi's name and giving away the fact that he was a Mapuche.

Her father's cigar had gone out. He tossed the butt into the large glass ashtray on the desk, took a leather cigar-case, silver lighter and silver cigar-cutter from his jacket pocket and five cigars from the cedar-wood box in front of him. He refilled the case with four of the cigars, cut and put the fifth in his mouth, then held the lighter for half a minute while he puffed at the cigar to get it going. The gold signet-ring on his little finger caught the light from the desk lamp as he cupped the lighter in his hand. 'My daughter…' he began.

'My daughter my foot!' thought Julieta. 'Why doesn't he throw his ashtray at me?'

Her father got to his feet and started to pace the room in his three-piece suit, puffing at his cigar. The window was closed and the study was thick with smoke. Julieta had to hold her breath for a few seconds to stop herself choking.

'My daughter… It's marvellous that you should be at the spring and early summer of your life. Marvellous! Splendid! Wine, women and song. Enjoy them to the full! Er… the wine and the song, that is, not the women.'

His laugh of embarrassment turned into a splutter as the cigar smoke made a detour up his nose.

'Marvellous! Sing! Dance! Get out into the fields and sow your wild oats! Yes, sow those oats! But in a moment of tranquillity between revelries take time to reflect. Relationships formed at social gatherings may seem intense but they have no roots. Love blooms for a day, then fades.'

'Revelries? Social gatherings?' thought Julieta. 'What revelries and social gatherings? You never allow me out of the house. Dance? Who with?'

'Marriage, on the other hand, is a sacrilege… er… sacrament… a contract for life. Take time! Slow down! Indians live a very different life from ours. Interesting to observe for a week or two, especially for an anthropologist. But to live with all one's life? And money. I don't know anything about your young man's circumstances but Indians are by and large very poor. As you know, I'm not altogether unfamiliar with poverty: we often had to tighten our belts when I was a boy. How would you survive, Julieta? Adolfo may not seem passionate – he may even appear cold – but that is because… because…'

Whatever Cortez lacked in warmth, thought Julieta, was made up for by the hot air being generated by her father, whose voice was cracking, and face melting, with pressure-cooked emotion.

' …Because… because he's… he's shy.'

He even managed a few crocodile tears, which oozed from the corners of his eyes and at once merged with the drops of perspiration that now covered his face.

Julieta's father had choreographed his speech so that the mention of Cortez brought him to a table in the far corner of the room where Julieta saw for the first time through the fog and half-light a large bunch of cellophane-wrapped flowers jammed into a crystal vase.

'Look, Julieta! Look at these beautiful flowers Adolfo brought for you.'

He shambled over to Julieta, who got to her feet to take the flowers, cellophane, vase and all, from him.

'Take time, Julieta. Don't rush into something you might regret.'

Her father's speech had irritated Julieta so much that she had been on the point of storming out of the study. The flowers defused her anger. She heard herself promise to do as her father asked, left the room quietly and went upstairs. She felt confused and needed to talk to her mother. She left the vase of flowers in her own bedroom, then walked along the passage to her mother's, where she found Copihue putting clean sheets on the bed.

'It's Thursday,' said Copihue. 'Had you forgotten? Your mother's out all day at her painting class.' She lowered her voice. 'I spoke to her last night and told her not to worry. She said she wanted you to be free and that she'd worry more if you had no will of your own.'

'I'll speak to her later. And to you. I'm going to my room for a bit. I don't think I'll come down for lunch.'

Julieta removed the cellophane from the flowers and trimmed the stems with her nail-scissors. She took two vases of her own from her built-in wardrobe and divided the mixed flowers between the three vessels. Mimosa, freesias and wild roses. How did Cortez know those were her favourite flowers? Had she let it slip? Their scent already filled her bedroom.

How humid it was today! Standing by the open window didn't help. She would lie down. She took off her dress, so as not to crumple it, put on her white cotton dressing-gown and stretched out on her single bed with its swan's down mattress. The heat had sapped all her energy; the flowers had undermined her sense of purpose.

Of all the rooms in the house, this was the one Julieta would miss most when she left home: this and her mother's bedroom, both of them with a view of the garden, the sound of the fountain, of the nightingale after dark and the scent of honey-suckle, of acacia, jasmine and roses. These were the two rooms where she had most often felt secure and at peace. Both were the antithesis of the study: white cotton curtains blowing in the breeze, off-white bedspreads and lampshades, bedside rugs with multi-coloured Quechua patterns. Julieta's bedroom was modelled on her mother's. Her mother had told her to find a style of her own but Julieta said she would rather have a room in a style she liked than in one that hadn't been found. She chose pale blue instead of pale green for her sheets and blankets, and Renoir instead of Monet for the reproductions on the walls, but otherwise the rooms were as alike as twin sisters: comfortable, beautiful, virginal.

Julieta drifted in and out of semi-consciousness. When she touched consciousness, she heard a calm, sensible voice speaking to her, one she couldn't quite recognize even though it sounded familiar. 'You love Mawi and feel nothing for Adolfo Cortez,' the voice was saying soothingly from somewhere in the room or inside her head, 'but marriage is a long haul and the first flush of love is soon gone. After that who would make the better husband? Would you rather live with an Indian for whom your love has become routine in a grass hut without windows, running water, flooring, central heating or electricity, and without any privacy, or with a man you can tolerate, even if you don't love him, in the large, comfortable house he has inherited from his grandfather right on the Pacific coast, where you're the envy of your friends, have your own space and have to see him for only a few hours every day?' The hot, damp air worked on Julieta's mind like ether, and she sank from doze into sleep.

When she woke, among scraps and tail-ends of partly remembered dreams, the sun had moved to the other side of the house and the bedroom was in deep shadow, but hotter and more humid than ever. Julieta's most vivid dream was that her mother had left home for ever. She felt feverish. Was she ill? Had she been poisoned by her father's *caldillo de congrio*? The lining of her stomach felt raw, as if it had been scrubbed with vinegar. Her emotions, like her energy and her will, had drained away. Love, the greatest joy of her life until a few hours ago, had lost its taste, been infected with bacteria, become an illusion, no more than a stimulation of the senses, the cynical exploitation of one human being by another. Julieta needed more than ever to see her mother, her wise mother. Was she back from her painting class?

In the passage Julieta met Copihue, on her way to the stairs with a tray and the remains of a meal. 'Your mother's back,' she told Julieta. 'She was tired and went straight to her room. Your father had supper alone.'

'I'm sure it didn't spoil his appetite.'

Copihue's face, which normally smiled so easily, remained pensive. 'I'll bring some ham and salad and fruit to your room,' she said. 'You haven't eaten all day.'

Julieta knocked on her mother's door. There was no reply. She went in. Her mother was in bed asleep. The bedside lamp was still on. She had fallen asleep over her book, as she often did on the terrace after a day of painting classes.

This room was as much a haven for her mother as its twin was for Julieta. The bed was single, like Julieta's, as her parents now had separate bedrooms. Red roses in a white vase on a mahogany side-table filled the room with their scent. A glass bowl full of black grapes covered in bloom stood on the rosewood bureau. Her mother's lightweight burgundy dressing-gown lay across the bed. The only thing that jarred and clashed in the room was the grandiose, ornate dressing-table that had been an early wedding anniversary present from Julieta's father.

How young Julieta's mother looked! Not just because of the soft light but because the tension had gone from her face. She looked as she must have looked when her adult life was just beginning, when marriage promised a paradise of love, laughter and the exchange of ideas, without discord, stress or disappointment. The window was wide open, the sun was setting, the honeysuckle was beginning to release its intoxicating night perfume and overpower the fragrance of the climbing roses, and the nightingale was starting his elegy for that moment in Nicole Reyes' life more than twenty years ago.

Julieta looked down at her mother's face and felt as she had felt when she was a little girl. Her mother filled her heart and thoughts. There wasn't a corner left even for Mawi. She would never marry, she used to tell her mother; she would live with her always.

The years rushed by and Julieta was twenty again. 'Tell me what to do, Mama,' she thought. 'If I marry Cortez, I will see you as often as I like. With Mawi, who knows? It may be difficult or impossible to come home. Don't wake, Mama, but tell me what to do.'

The look on her mother's face told Julieta nothing for the moment but she remembered what Copihue had said this morning: 'Your mother wants you to be free and would worry more if you had no will of your own.'

Julieta brushed her mother's temple with her lips, switched off the light, tiptoed to the door and closed it quietly behind her.

Copihue was on her way upstairs with Julieta's supper tray. Julieta opened her bedroom door for her and followed her in.

'Look at these flowers!' she said when she had shut the door. 'And smell them! Mimosa, freesias, and roses the colour of apricots. Just the flowers we both love. Cortez sent them.'

Copihue laughed incredulously as she put the tray on the walnut writing-table. 'Is that what you were told?' she said, keeping her voice down, even though the door was closed. 'Your father sent me out to buy them this morning.'

Julieta was too stunned to speak. Astonishment soon turned to anger. How could her own father deceive her like this? She felt an urge to run downstairs with the flowers and throw them in his face.

'That's not all,' Copihue went on. 'I'm not one to listen at doors. When I hear something that's not meant for me, I keep it to myself. This is the first time I'm repeating what I've heard. I'm doing it to help you.'

Copihue glanced at the door, stepped towards Julieta and spoke in little more than a whisper.

'Your father was on the phone. I was on my way from the dining-room to the kitchen. The study door was pushed to. I didn't stop to listen but I've got sharp ears. He was talking quietly but I clearly heard him say: "I want my daughter followed whenever she leaves the house." I missed the next part but then he said: "Grab him when she's not looking. Grab him and get rid of him." '

'Who was he talking to?'

'No idea. Police. Military.'

Julieta's anger turned to fear. Her hands became clammy, and somewhere in her abdomen there was a throbbing like toothache. She wasn't afraid of her father, who was more mouth than muscle, but of the thugs he obviously got to do his dirty work for him. She was afraid for Mawi. Her father apparently made no distinction between his family and their friends and his professional victims.

'What are we going to do?'

Copihue had a plan. Every morning at six she left the house to go to market. She wore her brightly coloured Andean skirt, shawl and headscarf and carried a large basket. Tomorrow Julieta would go in her place. There was enough food in the house, as there would be only three people and Julieta's mother had a small appetite. Julieta would walk to Providencia and take the number twenty bus to the Central Market. Once in the throng of the market, she would shake off anyone following her, jump in a taxi and go to Santo Domingo. There she would have to make her own plans to get Mawi and herself away from Santiago and out of harm's way,

'Keep the clothes. You may need them again.'

Julieta gave Copihue a hug. 'You're a good friend. You're my sister. I wish you were coming with us.'

'To play gooseberry?'

'To see the world and fall in love.'

'It wouldn't be fair on your mother to take her daughter and her maid from her at one go.' She sighed. 'It's true though. You don't see the world or meet many boys when you're a maid… I'll miss you, Julieta.'

Julieta gave her another hug. There were tears in Copihue's eyes as she left the room.

Julieta was angry at letting herself be duped by her father and at imagining for one moment that she could ever marry Cortez. Now she recognized the voice inside her head while she was dozing earlier in the day: it was the voice of Julieta robbed of will, deprived of personality, the obedient pawn of her father. The energy that had drained out of her when she saw marriage as no more than a wasteland filled her again and reminded her where her heart lay. The expression she had seen on her mother's face was no longer enigmatic: if you want to look as I look when I'm awake – anxious and careworn – it had been saying to Julieta, marry for comfort; if you want to look always as I look when I'm asleep – serene and younger than my years – marry for love.

Julieta ate her supper and packed as many belongings as she dared into her soft bag, which had to fit into Copihue's basket. She allowed herself two pairs of jeans and two pairs of trousers but only one dress, the lemon one her mother gave her, as she guessed leg cover would be more useful in the country. Julieta took off her bangles and put them in a drawer. She zipped up the bag, undressed and had a shower and, before getting into bed, knelt at the window for at least fifteen minutes – longer than usual – and prayed for Mawi and her own life with the boy she loved, for her mother, for a husband for Copihue, for a change of heart in her father, a wife for Cortez who would teach him to love, for Chile and a society without terror, police torture and mass murder by the army, a country where human rights were not abused, where love could grow between the people of the mountains and the people of the towns. The nightingale trilled, a world away from man's compulsion to pull up God's garden of love and fellowship by the roots, the honeysuckle added its aromatic music to the honey-and-fern fragrance of Copihue's mimosa and the ripe peach headiness of her freesias. 'I have prepared the environment for a heaven on earth,' God seemed to be saying to man. 'Now it's up to you to do the rest.'

Having slept most of the day, Julieta wasn't tired. She lay awake thinking of the change about to take place in her life. The safest way would be to do as the nuns had taught her at school, honour her father, marry Cortez, never be short of money or in danger from the army or police: to be a good daughter of Chile and Franco Reyes. This was not what Julieta's god wanted. How could she honour a father she didn't respect, and enjoy a privileged position in a society that oppressed its native population? How dull to pad your moral life with cotton wool and live without love, passion or risk! The thought of being tailed by armed thugs no longer made her afraid for Mawi and herself. The idea almost thrilled her, like the prospect of a ride on a roller-coaster. Together they would foil the lackeys of this police and military state.

Julieta dozed for what seemed like only five minutes but must have been nearer three or four hours. Copihue was gently shaking her shoulder. Julieta got up, washed her face in cold water and brushed her teeth. She put on a white blouse and her friend's colourful skirt. Copihue arranged Julieta's hair to look like her own, tied on the headscarf and wrapped the shawl round her twin's shoulders. They squeezed the bag into the basket and covered it with a towel.

At six Julieta went down to the kitchen, hugged her friend and sister and let herself out of the front-door. Goodbye, Copihue! Goodbye, Mama! Goodbye, childhood! Her father had lost his hold on her. She could no longer turn to her mother for comfort and advice. Julieta felt strong – alone but strong. She had an appetite for life.

Dawn, pink and grey above the trees and rooftops opposite, was edging out the blue-black sky behind. The street-lamps cut out. Under one of them two men, one with a moped, were watching Julieta and talking inaudibly. She could be followed on foot or on wheels, thought Julieta. She ignored them. A street-sweeper called out a greeting. She waved and called back. As she walked, she glanced into the wing-mirror of a parked car facing her way. There was no one following her. Not yet.

15

Father Lorencio and Mawi were having breakfast in the presbytery kitchen. After twenty-four hours there was still no sign of Julieta. What could have happened? The rector kept getting up and going down to the dining-room to look across the patio towards the gate. Then he would return to the kitchen and tell his protégé not to worry. Mawi went on eating his breakfast unperturbed. Perhaps he was expecting Julieta's father to agree to the marriage. Or had he resigned himself to being refused? Maybe he didn't care, so long as he had Julieta's love.

Father Lorencio sipped his coffee. Franco Reyes' answer had taken on a critical importance for him, as if his own future hung in the balance. 'So you have no objection to getting married in one of our Christian temples?' he asked Mawi, trying to drive away anxiety with banter. 'Under the eyes of the Spanish god?'

'Why should I, Father?'

'A god you did your best to demolish a few days ago?'

'I was only asking questions, Father.'

'A god of hatred and cruelty?'

'The Spanish god is also Julieta's god. Julieta wouldn't worship a god of hatred and cruelty.'

The church bell rang once. Father Lorencio looked at his watch. 'Half past seven.'

The gate from the street into the patio banged shut. Father Lorencio jumped to his feet and hurried into the dining-room. Mawi finished the piece of toast he was eating, sipped his coffee and got up.

From out of the porch came a young woman in a shawl and headscarf, carrying a basket.

'It's Copihue!' Father Lorencio heard the dismay in his own voice. 'I hope this isn't bad news.'

The girl came into the dining-room and ran up the steps into the kitchen. Father Lorencio followed at his own pace. The girl took off her headscarf.

'Julieta!' The two voices rang out in unison.

A moment later Julieta had her arms round Mawi's neck. When they had finished kissing, Mawi lowered her on to a chair, poured coffee for her, pulled his own chair over and sat down.

'Well?' asked Father Lorencio, looking down at Julieta.

'My father's consent? Never.'

The priest groaned and sank on to his chair.

Julieta was on her feet again. She grabbed Mawi's hand and pulled him up. 'Will you marry us, Father?'

'I've told you, Julieta. A marriage that isn't formalized in a registry office—'

'God doesn't work in a registry office. I want to be married in the sight of God. You can marry us, Father: you're a priest.'

The rector paused to take this in, then said: 'Your father won't recognize the marriage.'

'I don't recognize him as my father any more.'

Julieta repeated what he had been overheard saying on the telephone and told Mawi and Father Lorencio about Copihue's plan and her own escape from home in the borrowed clothes she was wearing.

'God help us!' thought Father Lorencio. 'The devils may be at the gate with guns this very moment. The sooner Mawi and Julieta are out of Santiago, the better for them both – and for me, and for all the Chileans who are being hunted down for voting Allende in as President and who need my protection.'

'My father's tentacles reach the length of the country,' said Julieta. 'Nowhere in Chile's safe. Not even Mawi's village. My father knows I'm engaged to an Indian. There are not many Indians left in Chile, apart from the Mapuche. Araucanía is where his men will start looking. We need to go abroad till they give up the search.'

'Have you both got passports?' asked Father Lorencio.

'My father's got mine,' replied Julieta.

'I've never had a passport,' said Mawi. 'No one in our village had one. We didn't recognize Spanish frontiers. It didn't stop us visiting Mapuche communities in Argentina. You have to know where to cross the mountains.'

'Can you get us passports, Father?' said Julieta.

Father Lorencio played the soft-hearted godfather, under siege from his godchildren. 'Secret marriages, hiding-places, false passports: just ask the priest,' he said. 'Preferably at seven o'clock in the morning, when he's having his breakfast. I'm a servant of God, Julieta, not a one-man mafia.'

Julieta left Mawi's side and put her hand on Father Lorencio's. 'You're a good man, Father, and a brave one. Copihue told me a bit about how you help people who are being hunted by the police and army. I thought you might know how to get hold of two passports.'

This seemed like a good idea to Father Lorencio. As soon as Mawi and Julieta had passports, they would be out of Santo Domingo, which was getting more dangerous every minute. He stopped acting the beleaguered godparent. 'I can get hold of the passports of two *desaperecidos,*' he said. 'They won't be an exact match: date of birth and so on. It shouldn't matter. Not even the pictures: people never look like their passport photos. Now finish your breakfast and come over to the church with me.'

Ten minutes later Mawi and Julieta followed the priest across the quadrangle and through the side door into the shadowy church. The air was heavy with incense, which always made Father Lorencio think of his grandmother's larder, with its smell of candied peel. He left the main doors locked and the electricity switched off but lit the candles. The soft, warm light fell on the fresh flowers, like giant blood-red bluebells, in a copper jug on a little table near the altar.

'Copihues,' said Mawi, when he saw them. 'They grow in the forests in my country.'

Father Lorencio watched Mawi as the young man knelt at Julieta's side. He had never seen such devotion on the faces of his Christian worshippers – devotion in Mawi's case not to God as defined by Christians but to higher powers. What was worship, after all, but the acceptance of man's powerlessness in the face of forces beyond his understanding or control: Jehovah, Nature, Thunder, the Sun? Or to a power without name: we all had a sense of the divine even if we couldn't put a name to it. The deeper the acceptance, the greater the worshipper's humility. Mawi might be thinking of Mother Earth or the Sun as he knelt before Father Lorencio but his surrender of self was total. Father Lorencio felt a sense of fulfilment as a priest he had never felt before. A priest's function was to clear a path between worshippers and the deity worshipped. He might be a Christian but if a worshipper was praying to the Sun he was as much a priest of the Sun as of God and Christ. Father Lorencio felt he had grown from being a Christian priest into one for all men and women of whatever religion or no religion at all.

The simple ceremony was completed. The young couple's eyes were dilated because of the dark church: four ebony pools reflecting the candlelight. The three made their way quietly back to the presbytery.

Father Lorencio went up to his study to use the phone, then returned to the kitchen, where Mawi and Julieta were holding each other in their arms and exchanging an almost questioning look, as if to ask, 'Why has nothing changed? We feel exactly as we did half an hour ago.'

'As soon as I've confessed my old ladies, I'll go for your passports,' Father Lorencio told his two protégés. 'It's only a short drive out of town. I'll do some shopping on the way and we'll have a little celebration at lunchtime.'

He showed Mawi and Julieta a heavy door leading from the kitchen down to the cellar.

'Don't stir from the presbytery,' he told them. 'Don't open the gate to anyone. If you hear people trying to force their way in, go down to the cellar. Bolt the door behind you with these two heavy bolts.'

'May I make a phone call, Father?' asked Julieta. 'I want to buy an air ticket to Mendoza, just across the border in Argentina, for a week from today.'

Father Lorencio's heart sank: were they planning to spend another week at Santo Domingo?

'Just one ticket?' he asked.

Julieta gave him a slight smile but didn't reply.

16

Franco Reyes stood in his study in front of the rococo dresser and behind his presidential desk, the telephone receiver hanging limply in his hand. The captain was at his wheel but the wheel was no longer connected to the rudder and spun uselessly when he tried to steer. Reyes' ship had been torpedoed by his own daughter.

Julieta's father rehearsed in his mind what he would do to the girl when he got his hands on her. There would be no more patience and gentle persuasion, no more waiting for her to come round to his choice of a husband for her. A builder would be hired to brick up her bedroom window, a locksmith to fit outside bolts and an outside lock on the door. Reyes would take away the light bulbs and starve her into submission. He would have her begging on her knees at the sealed keyhole for food, until she agreed to marry Cortez. And if she were still too stubborn to agree, he would let her starve to death.

Franco Reyes was in a quandary. What was he going to say to Cortez? His first instinct had been to jump on the phone and tell him the bird had flown – eloped with an Indian – but he soon realized Cortez would be lost for good. As it was, if he played his cards right, there was a good chance of saving the marriage. But what if Julieta didn't come back for weeks or months? He had to have an explanation for the major. Gone to stay with her aunt? Would a young bride-to-be rather spend six months with her aunt than see the man she was going to marry? Not much of a compliment to Cortez. He would lose interest. And what if she came back and told him she hadn't got an aunt?

The girl's degenerate mother was to blame. He should never have married that Peruvian *mestiza*. This wouldn't have happened with a pure-blooded Spanish-American wife. If he were a violent man, he would beat her half to death. As it was, he wouldn't speak to her till he got Julieta back. Until then he would consider himself not married but widowed: he would treat his wife as dead.

The telephone rang. Reyes picked up the receiver.

'*¿Señor Reyes? Buenos días.* Police headquarters here. Superintendent Garrote. We have one or two leads. Passenger by the name of Julieta Reyes on a flight to Mendoza in five days' time. She phoned to book a ticket, then posted a cheque. We've traced the cheque to your daughter's bank account.'

'Just one ticket? The boy must be one of the other passengers. Any with Indian names?'

'One.'

'That's him. Grab him! Mendoza? In Argentina?' Reyes pulled open a drawer and rummaged in the jumble of papers. 'She hasn't got her passport. I've got it here in front of me. Ha! She won't even get through the first gate.'

'Our dogs have picked up your daughter's scent. Near the Central Market. It stops suddenly. She may have got into a car. We'll work outwards from the market with the dogs, area by area. I'll let you know when we find something.'

At last the police had got something right, thought Reyes as he replaced the receiver. How could they have missed the girl as she walked out of the front-door? If he were Chief of Police, he would have the two men in question stripped and flogged.

The telephone call flicked Reyes' mind from the window-pane it had been banging against for the past twenty-four hours. Why hadn't he thought of it? All he had to do was lay all the blame on the boy.

He dialled army HQ and got through to Cortez. 'Prepare yourself for a shock!' he told the major. 'Julieta's been kidnapped. Abducted.' He waited for the news to sink in.

'Who's behind this?' Cortez asked after a few seconds. His voice was cold, quiet and controlled. 'Communist terrorists?'

'An Indian. Yes, probably a Communist and member of a

terrorist organization.'

'Have they asked for a ransom?'

'Not yet. They'll try and get her out of the country first. Don't worry! We've netted the Indian: flight to Argentina in five days' time. Julieta and her kidnapper both on the passenger list. The police will be at the gate to meet them.'

'I'll make sure there's a detachment at the airport to help the police.'

'Excellent,' thought Reyes when he had hung up. 'Cortez galloping to the rescue of his betrothed. That'll stir his blood, cure his anaemia. It'll be in all the papers. I'll bind and gag the girl, if necessary. March her to the altar at gunpoint.'

Reyes was back at the helm. His rudder was repaired. His appetite was restored. He became aware of the yelling hole in his stomach where breakfast should have been. He poured himself a glass of raspberry *chicha* from the bottle on the dresser and helped himself to a large piece of chocolate-coated marzipan.

17

Father Lorencio had celebrated evening mass, locked the church, tidied his files into the filing-cabinet, and was looking forward to a glass of *pinot* before supper, another with his food, and the rest of the evening reading in a comfortable armchair.

He spent ten minutes in the cellar trying to make sense of labels that were fading and half peeled from bottles fifteen or twenty years old and climbed back up to the kitchen with one his father had given him in 1969, a few months before he died, and told him to keep for at least ten years. He took a corkscrew from the table drawer and uncorked the wine. He poured his first glass and held it under his nose. 'Heaven on earth,' he thought. 'Why do some Christians concern themselves exclusively with life after death when there are so many good things, and so many things to make better, in this life?'

Father Lorencio felt a wave of relief as he sipped the heady, full-bodied wine with its after-taste of blackcurrants and Lombardy plums: his two young friends were on their way goodness knows where. They deliberately hadn't told him where they were making for, so that he wouldn't have to lie if anyone started asking questions. Bless their hearts! If only they knew! He would have no scruples about lying through his teeth to anyone wearing a uniform and carrying a gun. God be with them and protect them, wherever they were! It was a good marriage, he felt: Mawi would look after her, and she would stick by him through thick and thin. This didn't seem to be the rich girl's caprice he had been afraid of at first.

Father Lorencio had planned to re-read St Augustine and St Thomas Aquinas but his conversation with Mawi had changed his mind. He would read the books given him by his heathen sister. He had already dipped into them and been disturbed to discover that beliefs he had always considered uniquely

Christian were shared by the Ancient Greeks, the Phoenicians, Persians and Babylonians. Virgin birth was commonly ascribed to exceptional men as a way of exalting them to divinity or semi-divinity, as were resurrection and the power to work miracles, of which the transubstantiation of water into wine occurred again and again. The fulfilment of prophecy was as important to the Greeks, Persians and Babylonians as it was to the Jews. Descent to earth in the form of a dove was a favourite avatar among the gods of western Asia. Throughout the Ancient World bread and wine were believed to be the flesh and blood of the fertility gods: Greek worshippers of Bacchus had held a festival of bread and wine every year to ingest his body and blood and ensure their own fertility and the fertility of their crops. Was Mawi right? Was the Christian story founded on well-tried narrative techniques? If so, what made it special? Its greater compassion? Why then was Mary the mother of Jesus forgotten until her reinstatement centuries after his death?

Father Lorencio was on his way up to his study with his glass of wine to sit and enjoy the evening sun, when he heard a thunderous banging on the presbytery gate and the sound of dogs barking and men's voices shouting 'Open up!'

His first thought was to go on up to the study and wait there until the noise stopped and the men with their dogs went away. Father Lorencio's second thought, as the banging became more insistent, was to hide in the cellar, having bolted the thick oak door behind him with the two heavy bolts. What if they broke open the gate and found him in his study? He couldn't say he hadn't heard the banging. It would look suspicious. If they dynamited the cellar door and found him hiding among the bottles, his goose would be cooked. What was he afraid of? He had removed all trace of Mawi and Julieta. Best open the gate and let them in.

Fear was not so easy to reason away. Father Lorencio was shaking from head to toe. He breathed deeply to try and control his nerves. 'Help me, Lord, to look calm and serene,' he muttered, forcing himself not to hurry as he rose from his armchair. 'God knows I don't feel it.'

He went back downstairs, crossed the patio and opened the gate. He was almost knocked off his feet as at least half a dozen *carabineros* in green military uniforms, machine-guns in their hands, pushed past him with their dogs. The policemen looked like their Rockweilers: thick-set, small, muscular.

'Where are they?' one of the men shouted in Father Lorencio's face. He seemed to be in command: a barrel of a man with a receding chin and no neck.

'Where are who, my son?' Father Lorencio replied quietly, hoping that if he spoke softly his voice wouldn't tremble.

'You know who. Julieta Reyes and the Indian.'

'Julieta Reyes? Why should she be here? What Indian?'

'Don't mess me around, priest. You know who we mean.'

'I'm afraid I don't. But please come in and look round.'

'We will.'

They did. They didn't just look round. They charged with their dogs to the south side of the patio, up the stairs and into the bedrooms, where they overturned the beds, tables and chairs. They charged back downstairs, across the patio and into the dining-room, where they pulled open drawers and emptied knives and forks on to the floor, as if hoping to find the two fugitives among the cutlery. In the kitchen they turned out drawers and cupboards, breaking cups, plates and glasses as they did so. Upstairs, in Father Lorencio's study, they pulled open the drawers of the desk, threw the papers on the floor, broke open a locked drawer, opened the filing-cabinet and strewed the papers across the room. They worked together, like a pack of wild animals, one room at a time.

Father Lorencio followed, waiting till they had turned over a room before going in himself to survey the devastation. He was still shaking, but with anger now, anger he knew he must contain if he wasn't to be beaten up or killed. 'Do your damnedest, you swine!' he thought. 'Ransack my study! Read all my papers! Take away my files! Church records are all you'll find, because I'm not fool enough to commit anything incriminating to index-card or paper.'

'What's through that door?' demanded the chief vandal, the barrel with no chin or neck. He and his Rockweilers, four-legged and two-, were back in the kitchen, and Father Lorencio had followed them in.

'The wine cellar,' he replied quietly. 'There may be a few bottles. I never go down there.' 'Act shifty,' he told himself. 'Make him think that's where they're hiding. Delay him. Keep him waiting as long as possible. Give Mawi and Julieta a head start.' 'May I ask what you're looking for? I may be able to help you find it.'

'Open the door!'

'The key doesn't seem to be in its usual place after your search. I'll have to look for it.'

Father Lorencio had spotted the key among the broken glass and crockery on the floor but he pretended not to see it. He looked at the keys on the key-rack, took several and tried them. They didn't fit. He went up to his study, accompanied by three of the thugs, and rummaged on the floor among the contents of his desk and filing-cabinet, a Rockweiler panting near his ear. The only keys were little aluminium ones for suitcases, not at all suitable for cellar doors. Back downstairs to the kitchen.

'Yes, I thought I recognized you,' thought Father Lorencio as he looked at the youngest of the *carabineros*, whose face was caught by a shaft of reflected light from one of the church windows. 'You're Jesús María Salvador,' he said. 'You've been to confession here at Santo Domingo.'

The *carabinero* looked embarrassed.

'Win support!' thought Father Lorencio. 'Divide the pack! Break the hold of that barrel of a cur!'

'Cut the small talk!' barked the sergeant. 'Where's the key?'

'I've looked everywhere,' said the rector. 'I'd suggest forcing the door but I know you wouldn't want to damage any more church property.'

The *cabo* moved towards the door, followed by his men.

'What's that on the floor with the smashed plates and glasses?' said the priest. 'Yes, that's it.'

He picked it up. The sergeant snatched it from him and opened the door. His men followed him down the steps. They were so sure of finding the fugitives in the cellar that for a minute they seemed to have forgotten all about Father Lorencio. Even the dogs had caught the imagined whiff of their quarry and disappeared snorting and salivating into the bowels of the presbytery.

Just enough time to make a run for it, thought Father Lorencio. No, he decided: they would soon be on his heels, and if they caught him he would be done for.

A good, brave man was what Julieta had called him. Good? Father Lorencio's fingers itched to ease the door shut behind the *carabineros*, lock it, throw away the key, jump in his car and head for the border. Brave? However easy it would be to do this, and however much he thrilled at the idea, his legs refused to move from his spot beside the kitchen table. 'A fox wouldn't miss the chance,' he told himself, 'but brave Lorencio hasn't the nerve.'

He heard the scrape of boots on the stone stairs and the sound of panting, slavering dogs, and saw the bus he had just missed vanishing into the distance.

'Our dogs have followed Julieta Reyes' scent to your gate,' barked the chief *carabinero*. 'Where is she?'

'Have you tried her home?' replied the rector in a voice calm as a mill-pond in spite of his agitation. 'She's certainly not at Santo Domingo. Why are you looking for her? What has she done wrong?'

'When was she last here?'

'She comes to confession every Sunday. She was here before mass last Sunday.'

'What did she confess?'

Father Lorencio feigned the shocked clergyman. 'I can't divulge what I hear *sub sigillo*.' 'You could beat me unconscious, vicious thug that you are,' he thought. 'I still wouldn't betray a word of what I hear in confession. I've never even repeated what my mass-murdering army officer tells me.'

'What did she confess?'

Jesús María Salvador sprang to the priest's defence. '*¡No, cabo! Eso no se hace*.' Two or three of the others murmured their agreement.

'Thank you, my son,' Father Lorencio said in his thoughts. He told himself: 'It pays to recognize your confessants.'

The *cabo* dropped the question and moved on to others, which he fired off in quick succession. Which gate did Julieta use when she came to Santo Domingo? Normally the church gate but it was locked last time, so she used the presbytery gate. Who else had been in the presbytery during the last week, apart from the rector? Only the maid and a trainee priest from Puerto Montt. Trainee priest? At Santo Domingo for a week: the rector had been instructing him in the teachings of St Augustine and Thomas Aquinas. Where did the trainee priest stay when he was at Santo Domingo? In a room on the top floor the other side of the patio. Where was he now? Back at Puerto Montt, presumably. With Señorita Reyes? With—? The rector feigned astonishment.

'How do you account for the fact that Señorita Reyes' trail leads from the gate up to your trainee priest's room?'

This time Father Lorencio's astonishment was genuine. It was no surprise that Julieta had gone up to Mawi's room. What astounded him was the skill of the dogs following her two-day-old trail.

'Julieta Reyes and—' The rector conjured up a name for his trainee priest. 'Julieta Reyes and Pedro? How could they have known each other?'

'I'm asking you.'

Father Lorencio paused for a second, then said, 'So far as I know, they never met.'

'You're lying.'

Father Lorencio sighed. 'If you don't believe my answers, why ask the questions?'

'We have ways of getting the answers we want. You'll come with us to police headquarters.'

'What are you charging me with?'

The question remained unanswered. Father Lorencio asked if he could pack a few belongings but was refused. He was led from the kitchen to the gate.

'Can I at least lock the gate behind me?' he said. 'There's no one else to look after the presbytery.'

He locked the gate. The key was confiscated. He was escorted to a khaki armour-plated bus, a relic from the last outbreak of hostilities with Argentina probably, and took a seat on a slatted wooden bench, flanked by drooling dogs and uniformed thugs. The engine exploded into what was left of its life and the bus juddered off past the west front of the Church of Santo Domingo de Guzmán.

The charabanc lurched and swerved, and the prisoner, his captors and their dogs slid up and down the benches or the floor and were thrown from one side of the bus to the other.

At last they arrived at a high gate made of iron bars. A light started to flash and the gate slid open. The bus drove in. Father Lorencio was ordered out and led, stiff and bruised, among high brick walls topped with barbed wire to a steel door, which slid open automatically. There was a corridor with four more steel doors, each with a grille at the top. They stopped at one of the doors. The *carabinero* unlocked it. Father Lorencio walked in. The door crashed shut behind him.

Less than an hour ago Father Lorencio had been about to sit

down and drink a glass of one of Chile's outstanding wines in the evening sun in his study, whose west window looked out on to the patio. Now he found himself without wine, sunshine, books or freedom in a windowless police cell, where the furniture, bolted to the floor, consisted of a slatted wooden bench similar to the one he had sat on in the bus and an iron bedstead with a stained mattress and nothing to cover it.

18

Mawi's was a land of turquoise and emerald lakes, of eddying, trout-filled rivers splashing and cascading over rocks washed smooth by time, of araucaria and cedar forests, and mountain-sides silvered with rustling, shimmering birches. Where the land was cultivated, the fields produced tall, thick crops of wheat and barley, the fruit-trees strained under the weight of firm, green apples the size of grapefruit, oranges heavy with juice, and rose-fleshed peaches yielding just a hair's breadth to the touch, and the air was filled at harvest-time with scents that must be a foretaste of the delights waiting for us when we go to join our ancestors.

That the desert he and Julieta had been travelling through for the past six hours, first by moonlight, now under the scorching sun, should be part of the same country as his native land seemed absurd to Mawi. This was a lunar landscape, one without trees or bushes or plants, with no grass, no scent, and with only brownish yellow or grey for colour. No one but the invaders from the northern hemisphere, giants devouring everything in their path, could have called this sterile waste by the same name – Chile – as the fertile land, blessed by the gods, that they seized from the Mapuche. Why did the savages want this god-forsaken land? Not out of a love for dirt and débris but from an appetite for the minerals buried underneath. So insanely greedy were they to mine nitrates for their gunpowder, copper for their shells and gold to finance their wars, that they fought among themselves for these regions of dust and sand, Chilean against Bolivian Spaniards, Peruvians against Chileans. The Chileans, being greedier than their neighbours, had seized the most dirt and become the richest of the three nations.

Mawi and Julieta had been on a bus for more than twenty-four hours, travelling north from Santiago through ever drier and less fertile land towards Arica, two and a half thousand kilometres from the capital and within walking distance of the Peruvian frontier. The first few hours of the journey could almost have been through Mawi's homeland, except that the trees were fewer and smaller, the grass and leaves less green and the apples, oranges and peaches half the size of those that grew in Araucanía. The next few hours were along the coast, with the Pacific invisible to the west behind a wall of fog, and a sterile landscape of rock and rubble to the east broken only occasionally by a river valley where a dribble of water provided just enough irrigation for a few vines and olive-trees as it trickled under the road bridge towards the ocean. Then for hundreds of kilometres cactuses and tufts of oat-grass were the only spots of green in a landscape of sand, dust and rubble. After that, nothing: the Atacama Desert, the only absolute desert in the world.

The wealth of this barren region lay underground. Mines flourished where no cactus could grow: craters gaping like wounds left in a corpse by the beaks and claws of vultures. Mawi had heard about the Atacama mines from *limpiabotas* who had worked in them. Till today he had thought they were exaggerating. He could see for himself that the towns which had grown up round the mines were unnatural places to live, stark, soulless, many hours by road from vegetation and water, built at low cost on the orders of the mine-owners for the men who sweated and strained for them: terraces of stables made of unpainted plywood or unplastered breeze-blocks and roofed with corrugated metal – rows of molars in the corpse's skull. A bag of apples might not be worth a pile of gold, and yet the men and women who grew them lived in little whitewashed houses that smiled. No one cared if these men lived in what Christians called Hell, Mawi guessed, provided the mine-owners could gorge themselves on the metals buried in the earth.

The bus slowed down as the truck in front stopped to pick up half a dozen hollow-eyed, emaciated men in rags, standing in front of a closed gate bristling with barbed wire outside an open-cast mine. As the truck pulled away, the gate opened and a black Cadillac with tinted windows and a US number-plate drove out in front of the bus and sped away in the opposite direction towards Santiago.

Mawi knew the scenario, thanks to his *limpiabotas* friends, had heard about the poverty caused when mines were closed, because they were exhausted or less productive than expected. The owners left their luxury homes in Antofagasta on the coast west of the desert, with their underground reservoirs of fresh water shipped to the port in tankers, and headed back to the capital in their chauffeur-driven limousines. The miners, like the mines, were simply abandoned. They thumbed lifts to the towns, sitting among the ore on the backs of trucks, then scavenged through dustbins for scraps of food and in rubbish tips for junk they could sell. Those who had lost limbs in mining accidents simply sat on the pavements and begged.

The bus had left Santiago at seven o'clock on Saturday morning. Every few hours there was a stop of twenty minutes for passengers to stretch their legs, use the stinking toilets that didn't flush and had never been disinfected, and to buy sandwiches and bottled water. For the first twelve hours Mawi and Julieta had bought food at the stops. It was now ten o'clock on Sunday morning. They were too exhausted to feel hungry but their need for water had grown. The temperature inside the bus and out rose degree by degree as they crossed the Tropic of Capricorn and edged towards the equator.The air-conditioning didn't work and it was impossible to open the windows. They longed with growing desperation for the stops every three or four hours: for the cleansing draught when the front and rear doors opened, for another litre of water from a tumbledown kiosk.

Julieta was sitting in the window seat on Mawi's left. Since daybreak at half past five she had spent half the time dozing and the other half either peering anxiously down at the cars that overtook the coach or scanning the road ahead for road-blocks. When she dozed, her head slipped slowly sideways on to Mawi's shoulder. He felt protective, as he used to when his little sister fell asleep on his shoulder on the bus between Temuco and the stop five kilometres from his village. He didn't dare move when Julieta's hair brushed against his face and he smelt the now faint scent of orange-blossom, for fear of waking this new member of his family, this mermaid who had appeared in his lifeboat of survivors, this child, newborn but fully grown, his two-days-old wife. Mawi was mostly elated at the prospect of marriage but the occasional wave of panic bore down on him when he thought of the challenge and responsibility he had taken on.

Julieta was no child when it came to shrewd planning. They mustn't head south, she had told Mawi, because Araucanía was the first place the police and army would look for them. They would also be watching roads and flights into Argentina. They must head north, she said, cross the border into Peru and make their way to Cuzco, where her grandparents would welcome them and let them stay as long as they liked. While Father Lorencio went for their passports, Julieta had phoned Lan Chile to book herself on to a flight to Argentina she had no intention of taking. And while he prepared lunch, she had been at the bank cashing all her money, then at Thomas Cook's, with her passport in the name of María Inmaculada Morales, buying traveller's cheques.

Mawi tried to keep awake so as not to miss Julieta's head when it sank towards him but heat and exhaustion got the better of him. He woke from his doze to a view not of desert any more but of the town the bus was passing through: huts with crumbling adobe walls and mangy thatched roofs. Men in high-crowned felt hats stood talking in groups, and women in bowler hats led llamas and carried their babies and belongings on their backs wrapped in shawls wound round their shoulders. A gaggle of them were washing clothes in an all but empty reservoir, then spreading them out to dry on the cactuses growing out of the top of the adobe wall that separated them from the road. Mawi felt a glow inside him: these were indigenous South Americans like himself, even if they belonged to a different part of the continent. They must be Aymara Indians, who had prospered in the fertile lands to the north and east for more than three thousand years until the Spanish arrived with their frontiers, their names and their quarrels, desecrated the holy places and massacred, enslaved and impoverished the inhabitants. Their dispossessed descendants would have shrugged when this region was seized from Bolivia in the War of the Pacific a century ago and they were told they were now Chilean. Julieta's hair stroked Mawi's face. He rested his cheek on her head and went back to sleep.

The bus braked sharply. Mawi and Julieta sat up, wide awake. A mongrel finished crossing the road, tail erect, head held high, unaware that he had nearly been run over, and cocked his leg against a battered metal sign. The sign, damaged presumably after being struck full in the face by a heavy vehicle, informed travellers that they had arrived in Arica.

The air outside, as passengers disembarked stiffly at the bus station at five in the afternoon at the end of their thirty-four-hour journey, was a little cooler than it had been in the middle of the day but the smell was as nauseating as inside: not unwashed bodies and clothes worn too long any more but choking, black diesel fumes from engines that were serviced only when they broke down. The two tireless drivers fished and lifted the passengers' luggage from the depths of the compartment under the bus and handed Mawi and Julieta their haversack and canvas bag. The couple scanned the coach station for posses of soldiers or police, then walked unhurriedly and without glancing left or right into the fresher air of the terminal.

The man at the information desk had thinning blond hair, skin cooked lobster-red by the sun, a squint in one eye and a

German accent. He gave Mawi and Julieta a scrap of paper with the name of the nearest *hostal* photocopied in large print. As they made their way out of the terminal and into a street lined with Cadillacs, barrows and broken bicycles, Mawi saw him reflected in a glass door. He was watching them and, as he did so, he picked up a receiver, dialled a number and, without taking his eyes off his two enquirers, talked into the mouthpiece. Mawi told Julieta what he had just seen. They turned into the Avenida de la Victoria, paused to give some change to one of the beggars and, at a word from Julieta, walked straight past the *hostal* recommended by the German. Two hundred metres on they came to another simple hotel, dwarfed on either side by two newly-built concrete mansions fortified with electric fences, looked behind them to make sure they were not being watched, darted into the Hostal del Pacífico and asked for a *matrimonio*.

The management's idea of a double room was a large room with two small single beds placed as far apart as possible, one under the window, the other by the door. The bedsteads were made of iron. Between the beds stretched an expanse of linoleum designed to look like brown tiles. The window had an iron shutter on the outside, with slats that weren't quite closed, so that the far wall was lit with bands of reddening sunlight. There were no curtains. No lamps either: just the overhead strip light, with a switch beside each bed. The only furniture apart from the beds were the two plain bentwood chairs that also served as bedside tables. There was a built-in wardrobe for anyone wanting to unpack and put down roots. At least the bedroom had its own shower-room.

'Not much like home,' Mawi said apologetically, as if he had dragged his wife from a life of affluence into the gutter.

Julieta kissed him on the cheek. 'Who cares? I don't want to be reminded of home. Nice white sheets and covers, spotlessly clean. Not a speck of dust anywhere. You could eat off the floor.'

They took turns in the shower-room and put on fresh clothes.

'Are you hungry?' asked Julieta, when Mawi had washed and dressed. 'There's a restaurant just opposite.'

'Famished. But...'

'I've looked up and down the road. I can't see any men in parked cars or lurking in doorways.'

'It's not that. The problem is I'm running out of money.'

'I've got plenty.'

'Yes, but...'

'What?'

'I don't want you paying for everything... When we get to Cuzco, I'll find work. What I earn will be for you.'

They listened outside the bedroom door for a minute, then went downstairs, across the road and into the restaurant. Julieta was welcomed by a young waiter in black trousers and a maroon waistcoat, with unctuous black hair whose oil seemed to have found its way into his toothy smile, his bows and his gestures. For a moment Mawi thought he was going to embrace Julieta, but she paid no attention to him. He threw Mawi a dismissive glance as he led his prize across the glazed tiles and showed her to a table with a tablecloth as white as fresh snow. Mawi and Julieta sat down opposite each other and opened the leather-bound menus that were handed to them. The waiter lit the candle in the little glass bowl and glided to a spot a discreet distance from the table.

Mawi felt a growing panic as he looked at the lists in front of him. He could decipher the words with considerable effort but most of them meant nothing to him: fish, sauces and cuts of meat he had never heard of. He wished he had the courage to explain all this to Julieta and confess that he had never eaten in a restaurant before – not one with candles, tablecloths and menus. Instead he said: 'You're better at decisions than I am. Choose something for me.'

'Meat or fish?'

'Fish.'

Julieta ordered two *parilladas de mariscos* and a bottle of *rosado* and asked the way to the ladies' room.

Mawi was sitting alone when the waiter brought the *rosé* in a little silver bucket full of ice which he placed on a stand near the table.

'What's a Mapuche like you doing out with a good-looking girl like that?' the waiter said quietly.

It took Mawi a moment to get over his surprise. He wasn't a *limpiabotas* any more, he told himself: there was no reason now to take offensive remarks on the chin, to be spat on and take no notice.

'You're right,' he replied in a voice of authority he didn't know he possessed. 'I'm lucky to be married to the most beautiful girl in Chile. I'm lucky to come from a land of mountains and forests, a fertile land of wheat, fruit and wine. What about you? How does a young Chilean end up doing the job of a *roto* in the most god-forsaken town in South America?'

Mawi looked the waiter in the eye. If the creature had had fangs, he would have bitten him. Instead, he minced quickly across the dining-room and disappeared through a swing-door into the kitchen.

'Who were you talking to?' asked Julieta when she got back. 'I could hear your voice from the ladies' room.'

Mawi explained.

'Let's go,' she said, and led the way across the dining-room and out of the door.

'That's what happens if you go out with a Mapuche in Chile,' said Mawi as they headed along the Avenida de la Victoria towards the sea.

'Good reason for staying out of Chile. What bothers me is that he knew you were a Mapuche. How? You could have been Peruvian or Bolivian.' She lowered her voice and went on more urgently: 'If the man at the information desk really did recognize us, and if the waiter did too, it means the authorities are sending our profiles all over Chile, on television, in the papers, probably with a reward for whoever helps them find us. Arica's an obvious place to cross the border. We must travel inland to one of the smaller frontier posts and cross into Peru there, or into Bolivia. We'll get up while it's still dark, before the police start their raids and watches, and take the first bus heading east. And we must keep putting on different clothes and changing our appearance as much as possible.'

The rows of shops, hotels and restaurants stopped suddenly as the Avenida de la Victoria turned sharp right and became a sandy track between the dunes and shanties on its way to join the bypass to the port. A path rose from outside the angle formed by the turn and climbed to a flat summit a hundred metres from the road. On top of the dune was a kitchen on wheels with a brazier outside, two or three collapsible plastic tables and a dozen or so folding wooden chairs. Mawi and Julieta were drawn to the smell of fish and meat cooked over charcoal, and climbed up towards the van, one side of which folded in half to make a counter. The menu was scrawled in chalk on a board above the brazier.

Julieta laughed. 'Have you seen what their speciality is? *Parillada de mariscos*. They even have chilled *rosado*.'

They took a bottle and two hard plastic wine-glasses to one of the tables and sat sipping the cold *rosé* and eating dried seaweed while the Aymara chef cooked prawns, peppers and pieces of shark, marlin, swordfish and sea bass on a grill over the charcoal brazier.

'This is going to be ten times better than the restaurant at a tenth of the price,' said Julieta. 'And look! Between the dunes! We even have a view of the sea under the stars.' She sipped her wine, stared into the starlit night for a few moments, then went on: 'I've been a rich girl up till now. When we were hungry and away from home, we just walked into a restaurant and spent enough to feed an average family for a month.' She put a piece of seaweed in Mawi's mouth and another in her own. 'Think of the millions that could be saved every year if people like me – like my family – stopped eating in restaurants and came to places like this.'

'Enough to build proper homes for all the miners in Chile,' Mawi said softly, 'and schools for their children.'

He looked at Julieta sitting a little way round the table from him in her mimosa dress, smiling gently not just with her pale rose lips but with every tiny muscle around her mouth and in her cheeks, and with her oval black eyes, filling the air with the scent of orange-blossom, her hair springy after her shower, one side of her face lit by the brazier, the other by the stars.

'The gods are pleased with me,' he told her. 'They have given me the most beautiful woman in the world to be my wife.'

Julieta moved her chair closer to Mawi's and gave him a long kiss on the mouth.

The chef smiled proudly as he set two plates of charcoal-grilled fish, garnished with seaweed fried in a little oil, in front of his guests. So delicious was the *parillada* that for several minutes Mawi and Julieta were too engrossed in their meal to speak. At last they paused to sip their wine.

'I don't care what happens to me during my life,' Julieta told Mawi, taking his hand in both hers. 'So long as you're with me, I'll be happy. The bad things won't matter, because I'll still have you. The good things will be ten times better because you'll be there to share them with me. If you went and died on me, you wouldn't have long to wait: I would soon be with you again.'

Mawi no longer had the feeling of being alone in a jungle, a single voice demanding justice from the unjust, or swimming with no horizon in view, barely able to keep his head above water. Now he felt part of the world, with a companion to share its wonders and struggle with him against its outrages.

Mawi and Julieta ate their *parillada* and sat looking out to sea as they finished their wine. A soft light crept over the blackness of the ocean. They looked over their shoulders and saw a massive crescent edging up over the mountains to the west.

'The moon's come down for a closer look at us,' said Julieta.

The light brightened over the Pacific. A fishing-boat took shape between the two dunes, floating above the sea, so it seemed. Mawi felt a tingle of excitement as he gazed at the ocean and the boat. He was leaving Chile to be with his wife and to escape arrest, imprisonment and possible death, but for the first time he saw his flight as more than an escape from the Chilean authorities. It was also a challenge. Abroad he might be able to provide a happier life for Julieta than would have been possible in Chile even without her father's determination to break his daughter's spirit. And he might find a way of telling the world about the massacre and humiliation of his people.

They strolled back to the hotel, waited for ten minutes on the next floor up from theirs to make sure they hadn't been followed, then went down to their room. There they kissed as they hadn't been able to since their first kiss at the presbytery, with passion and abandon. Mawi's body ached for Julieta's but he sensed that she too didn't want to consummate their marriage in the discomfort of a single bed in a clinical hotel room, with the risk of a police raid and with a four o'clock start in the morning. They kissed more gently, went to opposite corners of the room, undressed with their backs to each other and climbed chastely into their separate beds.

19

Thirty-six hours after his arrest Father Lorencio was moved from a police to a prison cell, from a windowless space about three metres by two to one measuring four by three, with a barred opening high in the wall letting in daylight and fresh air and keeping the cell from getting stuffy and smelly. The iron bed had not only a mattress free of stains but also coarse linen sheets and a thin red blanket, though no pillow. A wooden chair and small wooden writing-table, without pen or paper, made up the furniture, all of which was bolted to the floor.

Father Lorencio sat on the chair, with his forearms resting on the table, lost in thought. There had been no trial. He hadn't been charged with any offence. He had been questioned for two hours in the police cell by two *carabineros*. They seemed satisfied with his answers. Why was he being kept behind bars?

Shrieks and raised voices from somewhere below made Father Lorencio's heart race and his hands, armpits and forehead clammy. A prisoner was being interrogated.

Mawi was right. Not much had changed since the heyday of the Inquisition. Then it was the rack: hooded men tying you to an extendible frame and turning a wheel until your arms and legs were pulled out of their sockets and your muscles and tendons torn. Or the lash: your head and hands were fastened in a pillory while your back became a pattern of red cuts, as if a razor or glass shard had been drawn across the skin. Or suffocation: your mouth was filled with wool, then with water, so that the wool expanded and stopped your breath. In Chile the police and army had taken over from the Church. Today it was all done with steel and electricity – with a perverse concentration on the genitalia: electrodes attached to the testicles; wire inserted into the urethra and litres of water poured down your throat which you were in too much agony to expel as urine, so that your bladder ruptured.

Father Lorencio had heard of an entertainment for police and army officers at the women's prison said to have been thought up by the President himself: the spectacle of mastiffs amok in the shower-room, having been trained to attack and rape the prisoners.

'Why have you endowed man with such a taste for cruelty, God?' Father Lorencio said aloud. 'For imposing such monstruous suffering on members of his own species? You have made man more savage than any wild beast. Why? And if I fall victim to that savagery, how will I have the strength to bear it?'

Father Lorencio heard no answer to his questions but saw a vivid image in his mind of Christ on the cross, with nails through his hands and feet and an expression of agony on his face, and he heard the gentle voice of a man asking weakly, 'Father, why have you forsaken me?'

Father Lorencio felt a surge of anger and banged his fist on the table. 'Is that your answer, God? That Christ also suffered the cruelty of man? It doesn't answer my question: why the cruelty in the first place? Are you some kind of divine Marquis de Sade who delights like a psychotic father in torturing his own children? Is Jesus Christ no more than your stepson? Are the real sons of God Tomás de Torquemada and Genghis Khan?'

Father Lorencio's anger brought him to his feet. With this simple movement came a moment of relief. Then some instinct told him to look for strength not in his faith but in himself – in physical activity to start with. He started to walk up and down his cell. It was a slow, relaxed walk, more like a Sunday constitutional than the anxious pacing of a caged animal. The sound of his own breath reassured him. He began to hum, then to sing quietly, and the sound of his voice was an assertion of his existence and identity. His body, breath, voice and mind belonged to him, not to the police or the State. Men in their cruelty could make him suffer in body and mind but they couldn't take them from him, as they could take his books, his job, his home. Even if they killed him, his body, mind and identity would still be his: he would simply have taken them with him into death.

Father Lorencio heard the sound of approaching footsteps.

'Are they going to take me away to be tortured?' he wondered, while he continued to walk and sing. 'You can barge into my cell and sink your claws into my flesh, but you'll never be able to get inside my breath, my voice, my mind.'

There was a jangle of keys and the door was unlocked. One of the warders came in with a tray, which he placed on the table with all the civility of a waiter in a restaurant. 'I've brought you an extra roll, Father,' he said. 'I noticed you only ate your bread last night.'

Father Lorencio stopped his walking and singing. He felt like hugging this warder who was capable of showing friendship to a prisoner. 'You're a good man,' he said. 'What's your name?'

'Francisco, Father.' He stepped towards Father Lorencio, glanced over his shoulder and added quietly, 'What's the country coming to when it starts putting priests behind bars?'

'No one should be behind bars without a charge or fair trial, priest or no priest.'

'If there's anything I can do for you, Father, to make things a bit easier...'

'My... clothes... I've been wearing the same shirt, socks and pants for days.'

'I'll wash them for you, Father. But you'll have to wear prison things while you wait for them to dry.'

Father Lorencio felt embarrassed: he had nothing to offer the young man except his thanks. 'I wish I could pay you but they took away my money with my keys and other things.'

'I wouldn't take your money, Father. There's just one thing I'll ask for. Will you give me your blessing?'

Father Lorencio could hardly refuse, in spite of his recent disagreement with God. The warder bowed his head. The priest made the sign of the cross and murmured a formula. The warder thanked the prisoner and went with his blessing, like a boy with a bag of sweets.

Father Lorencio sat down in front of his tray, with hunger but no appetite. The stew tasted not of the butcher's but of kennel or lair; the mashed potato was cold, and soggy from the juices secreted by the infected meat. He tore into the rolls and gulped his water. He longed for dishes he would normally never eat. Kentucky fried chicken: he had often driven past the kindly, smiling, bearded face but had never thought of stopping. With a double portion of French fried and a blessing from Colonel Sanders. Or a hamburger with melted cheese. Father Lorencio had always enjoyed his wine. Now he longed for it with the thirst of an addict. It didn't have to be the best. Communion wine would do: two bottles at least. He ate his bread and drank his water as slowly as he could. When both were gone, his hunger was the keener for being whetted. He wondered if the warder would bring him coca leaves to chew, to kill his craving.

Francisco: now there was a pure-hearted, unquestioning Christian. St Augustine had a point when he condemned the pursuit of knowledge as diabolical. Blessed are those who concentrate on the image of Christ, who never ask if the image is the real Jesus or a re-creation by the Gospelists, who never cloud their vision with doctrine, who identify with the pure being who is the focus of their thoughts and find peace in his company. The Calvinists and the Jansenists may have been right: either you were born touched by the hand of God, or you weren't. Christianity was for those who were already pure of heart. If you were not one of the elect, it would probably do you more harm than good. You were better off with another religion or with no religion at all.

Thomas Aquinas may have done his best to rescue Christianity from its veneration of ignorance and blind obedience, but in doing so he had started a process that would one day undermine the faith. As Mawi said, Christianity had poached on a reality where it had no business to be and explained myth in terms of science and science in terms of myth. Galileo may have recanted after explaining science in terms of science but the truth once told cannot be untold.

There were no more shrieks from below. Had the interrogators got the information they wanted or was the prisoner unconscious or dead? The answer to Father Lorencio's question lay in the sound of feet being dragged over concrete, the rattle of keys, the slumping of an agonized body and the crash of a cell door. The footsteps of officialdom receded. Father Lorencio was spared for the present.

Where was the Bishop? He must know that one of his priests was behind bars. The congregation of Santo Domingo would have told him that their rector hadn't been there to celebrate mass. The Bishop could get Father Lorencio out today if he wanted to.

20

Mawi and Julieta had left Arica soon after five. At eleven they had still not reached Putre. The distance was only a hundred and twenty kilometres and the first half of the road was paved. The next sixty kilometres slowed the bus down, sometimes to no more than a walking pace, as it climbed from only a few hundred metres above sea-level to nearly three and a half thousand on an ever steeper road round ever sharper hairpin bends, edging nearer and nearer to precipices of more than a thousand metres to avoid the deepening pot-holes. Twice the bus overheated and had to rest for twenty minutes to cool down. Once it stopped far from any signs of human habitation to let a tanned, wrinkled old *campesino* on board with his livestock: six chickens, two goats and a black pig. What was there for them to eat in this wilderness broken only by an occasional clump of oat-grass? Another time it stopped on the sharpest and steepest of all the bends to allow the driver a long chit-chat with his counterpart on the bus heading down towards Arica.

Mawi and Julieta were sitting at the back, out of view of the other passengers. Julieta was wearing Copihue's dress and shawl, with her hair pinned up and the scarf wrapped round it and knotted at the nape of the neck. Mawi was trying to look the part of a farmer or labourer in his jeans and white shirt, and a cloth cap bought for twice what it was worth from a surprised workman waiting for a bus at the Arica terminal. His black shoes were a give-away but he had covered them in chalky dust to make them look as much like boots as possible.

The higher they climbed and the further they travelled from mines, fast roads and urban life, the more Mawi was in his element. Julieta should have expected this but it came as a surprise from the man she was still discovering. She loved him totally and would cheerfully take the tiller every day of her life, but the fact that the rôles could be reversed, and that she would be able to place herself in his hands in some situations added a new dimension to their relationship and to her happiness.

When the bus at last docked at Putre Terminal in a miasma of diesel fumes, burning clutch and melting rubber, it was as if Mawi had known the market-town all his life. He led the way to the main square, an area of sand and dust where half a dozen planted palm-trees struggled to survive and a group of barefoot children in torn T-shirts were playing baseball with a brand-new bat and ball, paused to look around, then headed for a patio on the far side of the square which he had identified as a café.

He and Julieta sat down on two vintage wicker chairs at what had once been a card-table, under an awning of corrugated cardboard. Beyond the patio was a ramshackle plywood cabin. Julieta had never till now been surrounded by such poverty and had to make a special effort not to let Mawi see her unease. Would they be robbed? Or poisoned with salmonella or listeria?

A man in jeans and a smock emerged from the cabin and limped towards his two guests. He had a gentle manner and a face a little like Mawi's but about twenty years older. Mawi ordered coffee and whatever there was in the way of bread or bun. The café-owner limped back to his cabin and returned a few minutes later with coffee in two pristine mugs and slices of fresh bread straight from the oven, spread with home-made papaya jam and served on a spotless plate.

The current of recognition that had been flickering between Mawi and the *dueño* exploded into lively conversation in a language new to Julieta. Mawi listened for three or four minutes while the owner spoke, then he paraphrased what he had heard.

'Chol is a Mapuche,' he explained. 'He was born not far from my home. He travelled three and a half thousand kilometres to the north of Chile, because he had heard you could make good money in the mines. He found work in a mine that had been bought cheap by one of the big landowners when the

Government was privatizing mines after Allende. Crístobal Valdivia de la Cagalera spent most of his time in Santiago and put as little work into the mine as he could. He paid poor wages and spent nothing on maintenance. There were accidents. Chol's leg was crushed. He lost his job and was paid no compensation for the injury. A year later the miners went on strike. The army surrounded the mine and shot every one of them. Valdivia was afraid of retaliation by the miners' families, sold the mine to a US company and fled to Bolivia. When Chol was well enough to walk, he spent all his savings buying this café. He earns just enough to live.'

Chol smiled at Julieta. 'I'm sorry,' he said in Spanish. 'I would have spoken *castellano*.'

There was such frankness in Chol's face that Julieta was ashamed of her fastidiousness. She forgot the torn baize and chipped plate and started to feel at home in the humble surroundings.

'Where are you travelling?' asked Chol. The question was addressed to both his guests.

Mawi glanced at Julieta with a look that asked how much he was allowed to disclose, but Julieta answered for him.

'To Cuzco, in Peru, to see my grandparents.' Julieta was surprised at herself: after all the false trails she had been laying, here she was nonchalantly confiding in a stranger.

'Are there any buses from here to La Paz or Puno?' asked Mawi.

Chol shook his head. 'You could catch a bus into Peru from Arica and change at Arequipa for Puno and Cuzco.'

'We've just come from Arica,' Mawi said. 'We don't want to go back there. Is there any other way of travelling?'

Chol thought for a moment, then said, 'By donkey.'

There was a silence for a few seconds. Was Chol serious?

'And where do we find donkeys?'

'Here in Putre. I know someone. You buy the donkeys, follow

the Bolivian border north to Visviri, cross into Peru and take the road to Titicaca, where you sell the donkeys and take buses to Puno and Cuzco.'

Chol went out on to the plaza and disappeared from view, leaving Mawi and Julieta to have their breakfast. Ten minutes later he was back, followed by an old Indian in a grey smock, with a wrinkled face the colour of mahogany, leather trousers to match, and long grey hair tied at the nape of his neck. He stood at the edge of the plaza engulfed in sadness, with a donkey at each elbow. The animals, unlike their owner, seemed to be smiling at Julieta. There was such intelligence in their eyes, such alertness in their twitching ears, that she smiled back, said *'Hola'* and half-expected them to reply.

'This is Chumu,' said Chol, placing himself between his guests and the edge of the patio. 'He understands Spanish but speaks Aymara. Chumu is willing to sell his two donkeys.'

'How much is he asking?' asked Mawi.

Chumu replied in Aymara. Chol translated. 'A hundred thousand each.'

'How old are they?'

They were ten years old.

'That means they're already half-way through their useful lives.'

Julieta noticed Chumu press his head against the neck of one of the donkeys. The donkey responded by nuzzling the old man. 'What are their names?' she asked.

'The children call them Pablo and Pedro,' Chol answered for Chumu.

'How will he manage without them?' asked Julieta.

'He will miss them,' Chol replied. 'He lives alone. They're his family. But he needs the money.'

'We'll look after them,' Julieta said to Chumu.

'They'll be our brothers.'

Chumu hugged the other donkey and managed a smile.

'Gracias, señora,' he murmured.

'We have a journey of – what? – two hundred kilometres ahead of us,' said Mawi. 'Will they be able to carry us, as well as our belongings?'

The old man nodded.

'They may be experienced,' Mawi went on, 'but they only have ten years to go. Eighty thousand each would be a fairer price.'

The glimmer of sunshine that had appeared in Chumu's eyes disappeared and his face was once again enveloped in sadness. He hugged the donkeys. No price would ever compensate for the loss of his two friends.

'I have no idea what the donkeys are worth in terms of money,' Julieta said gently, 'but I'm prepared to pay a hundred thousand each for them. I'll need to cash traveller's cheques.'

There was a bank the other side of the plaza. By the time Julieta got back, the deal had been clinched and Mawi had bought a round of beers and paid for breakfast out of the little change he had left. Chol was sitting on a box between Mawi and Chumu, who was still standing below the patio with the donkeys. Julieta gave Chumu the two hundred thousand pesos and sat down beside Mawi.

Chumu started to speak in Aymara, quietly at first. Soon be became more animated. Chol tried to translate but Chumu didn't stop for breath, and he had to wait for the old man to wind down at last and pause to drink his beer.

'Chumu's family have lived in Putre for over a century,' Chol began. 'His grandfather was comfortably off, with a herd of more than a hundred donkeys. In those days this part of Chile belonged to Bolivia and there were no cars or lorries. Trade between La Paz and the port of Arica was done with horses or by donkey and cart. His grandfather would take twenty or thirty donkeys to Arica or the capital and come home when he had sold all but the one he was riding. War came. Chile seized Putre and

Arica. Trade stopped. Chumu's parents saw no future in donkeys and opened a bakery. The years went by. A North American firm built a supermarket in Putre and started selling sliced factory-made bread at half the price of his parents' home-made loaves. The shop was sold and his parents retired on the proceeds. But Chumu was out of a job. He revived his grandfather's business and made enough to live taking children for rides on his donkeys. The North American firm expanded and started selling mechanical toys. Now parents spend all they can afford on toy tanks and machine-guns, and there's nothing left for rides on donkeys. That's why Chumu has to sell Pablo and Pedro.'

Julieta and the three men finished their beers in silence. She got up and went over to the old man.

'If we pass this way again with the two donkeys,' she said, 'we'll give them back to you and you can keep the money.'

'Gracias, señora,' said Chumu.

Julieta scratched the donkeys between the ears, and they nuzzled her neck.

Chumu spoke to Julieta in Aymara and Chol translated. 'People say donkeys are stupid. They're not. They act stupid when they're badly treated.'

'We won't treat them badly,' Julieta promised him. 'They'll be like our children.'

Chol stepped off the patio, took the reins, which were no more than cords tied loosely to the donkeys' cheek straps, and led them along the side of the patio to a yard he had at the back. Mawi shook Chumu by the hand. Julieta embraced the old man. Together she and Mawi watched him walk slowly away across the plaza, with no donkey for company for the first time in his seventy or eighty years.

'You will have things to buy for the journey,' said Chol, who had tethered the donkeys and was back on the patio. 'The old market is the other side of the plaza, behind the church. Do your shopping, and I will have lunch ready for you when you get back.

Remember: you need warm clothes. The nights are cold at four or five thousand metres – sometimes minus ten or colder – and the wind is icy. Leave your bags. I will look after them.'

Julieta dictated her shopping list as they crossed the plaza and Mawi's memory served for pen and paper: carrots for the donkeys and food for themselves that wouldn't rot or melt or freeze or evaporate; bottled water; llama-wool or alpaca gloves; balaclavas with the bobble on top that tie under the chin; thermal underwear or, if they couldn't find any, old newspapers to stuff under their clothes. And pullovers. And a poncho for Julieta.

Mawi and Julieta found the market among homes with walls made of other people's discarded plywood and roofs of cardboard or brown paper held in place by pieces of rock from the mountains that surrounded the town. Lightweight roofing might be what you needed in a town with more earthquakes than millimetres of rain but what kind of shelter could plywood walls provide from the freezing winds at night that Chol was warning them against, Julieta wondered, even if you did stop all the holes and gaps with whatever you could find: newspaper, rags, plastic bags, pieces of old carpet. Arica, with its hotels, restaurants, port and airport could show the world an affluent face; Putre was uniformly poor. Every cabin had a patio pennoned with brightly coloured tatters pegged to a clothes-line, floored like Chol's with earth trodden till it was as hard as wood, protected from the sun with sheets of cardboard supported on a metal or wooden frame. The furniture under the flimsy awnings was a mismatch of plastic or wicker chairs, wooden or metal tables, boxes, planks on trestles. The market-town looked to Julieta like an endless junk-shop or scrapyard.

In the market tanned faces peered out from spaces no wider than cupboards crammed with towering piles of cheap clothes, pots and pans, bags of rice, fruit, vegetables. Mawi and Julieta found what they needed, bought two zip-up plastic shopping-bags to put it all in and headed back for the plaza.

Chol's café, which a few hours ago had made Julieta uneasy, now drew her like a beacon as she crossed the plaza laden with shopping. Hospitality was like sunlight, she thought. It could shine down on you in the middle of a pile of old junk and, because you were welcome and cared for, the junk felt more like home than roomfuls of antiques and chandeliers in a house that didn't smile.

It was the same with food. A meal had to be prepared with thought and care to be remembered. Chol cared. You could tell from his hands and thoughtful smile as he delicately added mint and coriander leaves to his *yaen-chupe* of cheese, potatoes and onions and poured the soup into bowls, set plates of paella in front of his guests, as if for old friends, and filled their glasses with a long cool drink flavoured with cherry-brandy.

Mawi and Julieta were contentedly sipping their lemon-grass tea at the end of the meal, when Mawi froze, like a puma at the sight of a gun, then slowly put down his cup. Julieta looked across the plaza and saw what Mawi had seen. Moments later Chol was at their side.

'Don't worry,' he said. 'They can't see you here: they're in the sunlight; you're in the shade. Do you want to finish your tea in the room at the back?'

Mawi and Julieta followed Chol into his kitchen: not a speck of grease on the cooker, Julieta noticed, not a crumb or drop of oil on the wooden table. A bead curtain led into the only other room in the cabin. In the semi-darkness she saw that it was entirely bare except for a mattress on the earth floor, and a blanket carefully folded at the foot of the bed.

Mawi and Julieta heard Chol hurriedly finish the washing-up, then saw him through a crack in the wall take a bottle of Cristal and a book, go out on to the patio, sit down at a table, put his feet on one of the boxes that served as stools, have a swig of beer and start to read.

The police car pulled up outside the café. One of the two

carabineros, a bull of a man, got out and sauntered on to the patio. Mawi and Julieta held their cups in one hand, their saucers in the other, to stop them clinking.

'Things quiet today?' the policeman called out to Chol.

Chol looked up, shut his book, took his feet off the box and got up. 'Too quiet. Can I get you a beer, *señor*?'

'No time… We're looking for a girl in her early twenties and a boy about the same age. Have you seen them?'

'How would I recognize them?'

'Pretty girl with dark, shoulder-length hair. One metre seventy-three. Good figure. Boy looks a bit like you, only twenty years younger.'

'What have they done? Robbed a bank?'

'They've gone missing. Sighted in Arica yesterday. Possible sighting here in Putre today.'

'If I find them, who do I return them to?'

'If they stop here for a drink or a meal, send someone straight over to the police station… Understood?'

'I understand.'

'Hasta luego.'

'Hasta luego, señor.'

Chol sat down again, put his feet back on the stool and opened his book. The *carabinero* got into the police car. The car slid away, like a predator that has stopped to sniff around, found nothing to gorge its appetite and is off to prey somewhere else.

Mawi and Julieta breathed again. Julieta put her head through the bead curtain.

'Is it safe to come out?'

Chol put down his book, got up and came into the kitchen. Mawi and Julieta put their cups and saucers on the kitchen table.

'I ran away from home,' Julieta explained. 'My father was trying to make me marry a man I didn't love. Mawi is my husband. We were married three days ago.'

Chol took Julieta's hand with one of his, Mawi's with the

other. 'Congratulations to you both!' he said. 'I will help you in any way I can. First, a warning: don't leave Chile at one of the border crossings.'

'We've borrowed passports,' said Julieta. 'The names are different.'

'That's an old trick. They won't fall for it.'

'So what do we do?' asked Mawi. 'Cross west of Visviri?'

'No!' Chol was emphatic. 'The whole of the border with Peru is still heavily mined after the last war. You'll have to leave Chile south of the frontier post at Visviri and cross into Bolivia. Head north-west for fifty or sixty kilometres, then cross from Bolivia into Peru – not at a border crossing, because you won't have visas. It shouldn't be too hard to get from Bolivia into Peru. The two countries have always been on good terms. They may not even bother with a fence.'

'The border between Chile and Bolivia,' said Mawi. 'Is it easy to cross? With donkeys?'

Chol replied that the Chilean army kept all borders well festooned with barbed wire but that the barbed wire stopped whenever it came to a ravine, and started again the other side. Not all the ravines were sheer. 'Trust the donkeys,' he said. 'They know if a path's safe or not.'

'We'll have to travel at night,' said Mawi. 'It's too risky by day. The police are on the look-out for us. Probably the army too. There's no cover. No bushes. Nothing. I haven't seen a tree for days. We'll travel by night and sleep during the day.'

'How will we see?' Julieta asked sheepishly. She felt a bit out of depth with these two sons of the outdoors.

'There's a full moon,' replied Mawi. 'Not a cloud for hundreds of kilometres.'

'The safest way,' said Chol, 'would be to avoid Chilean roads altogether and cut across the Parque Nacional Lauca…' He hesitated and glanced at Julieta.

'Yes?' she said.

'It's tough going even for a Mapuche, but…'

Julieta read the unspoken half of his thought: for a girl – one who wasn't even a Mapuche and had probably spent her life in Santiago – the Parque Nacional Lauca was out of the question.

'Come on!' said Chol. 'I'll help you load the donkeys.'

Chumu might be missing his donkeys but Pablo and Pedro seemed ready for a change from the quiet life. They brayed for joy at the sight of Chol and their two new companions and kept still while bags were loaded on to their backs. Their saddles were no more than pieces of carpet with long strips sewn on to them that were passed full circle round the donkeys' bodies and tied on top either end of each saddle. Chol padded the pieces of carpet with foam from his store, to make them more comfortable. He and Mawi then tied the straps and handles of the bags into the knots that kept the saddles in place, while Julieta fed Pablo and Pedro a carrot each as a reward for their patience.

By the time the donkeys were loaded, the sky was beginning to turn red and a chill had crept into the air. Julieta and Mawi took turns in the bedroom to put on warmer clothes.

They paid for lunch, which cost even less than the previous day's meal outside the caravan at Arica, knocked back the two glasses of *pisco* Chol poured for them, and felt the blood course through their veins and set the tips of their ears, fingers and toes atingle. They hugged their host and mounted the donkeys.

'How do we get to the Parque Nacional Lauca from here?' Julieta asked as Chol was about to lead the two travellers and their mounts to the plaza.

Chol looked at Mawi, hesitated again, then replied: 'Take the Visviri road. After two kilometres you come to a sign for the Parque Nacional. Turn right just after the sign. You can't always see the path but the donkeys will keep to it. After thirty kilometres you come to the road that follows the border south from Visviri. Bolivia lies a few hundred metres beyond the road.'

Mawi and Julieta put on their *chullos*, more to hide their heads than to protect themselves against the cold. The church clock was striking six as they waved to Chol and set off across the plaza towards the main road.

It took Julieta a few minutes to get accustomed to Pablo. She had ridden horseback in her early teens, but with stirrups, and reins attached to a bit. She quickly learnt to grip with her knees to keep herself upright and to tap with her hands for a right or left turn.

The main road took the two riders past the police station. They would have gone another way if they had known but it was too late now. They rode calmly past, glancing to their right just long enough to take in the poster on the notice-board outside: *MISSING... REWARD...* and underneath a photo of Julieta taken at the end of her last school term two years ago: not much of a likeness any more but just about recognizable to a stranger who had recently seen her in person. She and Mawi needed to get out of Chile as fast as they could.

By the time they reached the battered board with *P.N. LAUCA* scrawled on it, all that remained of the sun was an orange arc low in the western sky. In the east the moon was even more massive than last night in Arica: on a collision course with Earth by the look of it. The stars were the brightest Julieta had ever seen, Lupus, Centaurus and the Southern Cross shining through the dry, dust-free air like Christmas lights festooned along the snowy mountain peaks.

Mawi and Julieta pulled on their gloves and enveloped themselves in their ponchos as the donkeys left the desert road and started north-eastwards towards the stars up the mountain that towered many hundreds of metres above them like a white-crested tidal wave of rock which if it turned to water would engulf and crush them.

21

Adolfo Cortez was sitting at his utility desk at army HQ in Santiago. His office was small – Cortez was only a major – but as uncluttered as a town purged of its inhabitants. So free of clutter was his office, so bare his desk, that when he glided out with his briefcase, he left behind scarcely a trace of himself: no papers or pens on the desk or filing-cabinet, no photos or maps on the walls. The only clue to his occupancy was the fly-swatter that hung on a hook within reach of his swivel-chair. Twice during the past eighteen months Major Cortez had reported for duty and found his office occupied by a newly arrived junior officer, who had looked through the window in the top of the door and assumed the office was vacant.

Franco Reyes had wanted to meet at the Café O'Higgins but Cortez had made his excuses. He had had enough of watching that fat hog stuffing his chops with cream, beef, pudding. Reyes' daughter had absconded or been abducted but still his first priorities were his mouth and stomach. The media were turning the family drama into a national crisis but for Reyes it was no more than an excuse to sit on plush upholstery, surrounded by marble pillars and table-tops and rich old men, and make leisurely plans for his daughter's recovery and her kidnapper's arrest some time towards the end of the week. The recovery and arrest had become the object of an urgent military operation on the orders of no less a man than the President. Major Adolfo Cortez was involved professionally and was not prepared to turn an assignment into a gentleman's pastime over cream cakes in a lush coffee-house. He would rather deal with the girl's father on the telephone but Reyes was always in a meeting at the Ministry or afraid of being overheard by his wife or maid at home.

Franco Reyes needed to hear a few hard truths. First, if and when Adolfo Cortez married his daughter, authority would pass from father to husband. Father would not be controlling either daughter or son-in-law. If he threw his weight about at the major's, he would be banned from the premises. If he put pressure on either of them on his own territory, Cortez would stop going to the house and would prevent Reyes' daughter from going there. If he tried to manipulate the girl behind the scenes, by post or phone, she would be forbidden all contact with home. Reyes' money would be welcome, to pay for the extra expense of a wife, but if the worst came to the worst Cortez had money of his own. Plenty of it: his family was the richest in Chile.

Secondly, Franco Reyes was not going to make the marriage an excuse for regular blow-outs with his daughter and son-in-law. Among officers below the rank of lieutenant-colonel fitness was the unspoken rule, which meant a work-out at the gym twice a week and a sensible diet. There would be no more than one meal a month with Reyes to start with; this would in due course be reduced to a meal every two or three months.

Thirdly, there would be no marriage at all if any sexual contact had taken place between Reyes' daughter and her Indian, even if she was forced into it at gunpoint. A Cortez accept shop-soiled goods? Never! The honour of being admitted into the Cortez family and of being paraded round Santiago like a new filly would be denied Julieta Reyes if she came to him second-hand, especially from an Indian. The father's leisurely approach was not good enough. The Indian was unlikely to keep his hands off a good-looking girl like Reyes' daughter for long. Getting her back was a matter of urgency. Cortez would have the Indian mutilated when he was caught, for stealing his woman, but that wouldn't rescue the marriage if he had been playing ram to her ewe.

Fourthly— The phone rang. Fourthly was what Reyes was going to hear first.

'Cortez.'

'Señor Reyes to see you, sir.'

'Send him up.'

Twelve minutes late. The man was a self-indulgent, unpunctual slob. He was for ever boasting about his army days. If Cortez had him in his battalion, he would keep him on a diet of spinach and soda-water for six months and have him flogged every time he was a minute late.

A knock at the door.

'Come!'

The door opened and Franco Reyes stumbled in, panting and mopping the sweat from his forehead after climbing the one flight of stairs. He looked round the room in surprise. His own study was filled with pieces of furniture the size of galleons and as ornate as the reredos in Santiago Cathedral. His desk was always piled with papers. Books fell about the bookshelves. There was always a glass or cup of something on the go, and a plate with the sticky remains of a cake or two to make him the darling of flies and bluebottles. He had presumably been expecting the same confusion in Cortez' office because he stood looking disorientated, as if he had found the right person in the wrong room.

'So sorry I'm late, old chap,' he blustered. 'Been at the O'Higgins. Lost track of time.'

Cortez didn't get up. Why should he show that much respect to this mountain of jelly and indiscipline? 'Do sit down, sir.'

The desk and interviewee's chair were at right angles to the window and door. The room got the sun all day. At noon Cortez moved his desk, which was on wheels, from one end of the room to the other, so that he stayed in the shade while anyone he was interviewing was blinded by sunlight. Reyes sat down and at once started waving his right arm about between his face and the window, as if to ward off a swarm of wasps.

'No change to the passenger list? Julieta hasn't cancelled?'

'No changes, sir. Developments.'

'Developments?'

'We believe your daughter has no intention of taking that flight.'

'What?'

'She's been sighted, we think, sir, in a different part of Chile. With her Indian kidnapper. Assuming that he is her kidnapper.'

'Of course he's her kidnapper. Where?'

'Arica. Two locals recognized her from our poster.'

'The Communists are trying to smuggle her into Peru.'

'We're also investigating traveller's cheques cashed under a different name at a bank in Putre, a small town near the borders with Bolivia and Peru. There may be no connection but—'

'Send reinforcements to all the crossings!'

Cortez paused for a deep breath, to stop himself raising his voice to Reyes. 'We'd thought of that, sir,' he said, kicking at the final plosives as he would like to kick the bag of fat in front of him. 'We've also got troops patrolling the borders between the crossings. Half the Chilean army is looking for your daughter.'

'She's also your—'

'If she leaves Chile, there's nothing more we can do here at HQ. It's over to you then. Or your colleagues at the Foreign Ministry. You could try the old carrot with Bolivia: you find daughter and Indian; we give you a few square kilometres of land. The least they can do is put out your daughter's photo. You can always mislay the carrot when you've got what you want. Anything you can tempt Peru with?'

'No… There's Herman Gorringe, of course.'

'The CIA man?'

'He's in Peru on a mission, I think, doing the same sort of thing he does for us: tracking down dissidents; eliminating them. He might be able to help… Can't get over the rector of Santo Domingo being involved in all this… A priest…Clean as a whistle… So we thought…'

'It's hard to know how involved he is. Or how important he is to your daughter. We were hoping to use him as bait to get her back.'

Reyes was sitting with his mouth open, staring at the ground, punch-drunk. He didn't appear quite able to grasp the turn events had taken. Cortez sensed there was something he wanted to ask but the question seemed lost somewhere inside all the blubber. The sooner it found its way out, the sooner Cortez would get rid of the man, who seemed to have had as much truth as he could take for one day. The major didn't want a stroke or heart attack in his office.

'Anything else?' he asked.

'Er... This hasn't changed your feelings about Julieta, has it, Cortez? Your intentions?'

'Let's concentrate on getting her back, shall we, sir?' Cortez got up, went over to the door and opened it. 'We can think about other things later.'

Reyes realized the door was being held for him. His knees only just took his weight and the arms of his tubular steel chair nearly buckled as he hauled himself to his feet.

'We'll contact you as soon as we have any news, sir. By phone. Save you calling at HQ.'

Reyes stumbled out of the office. The major shut the door behind him.

'I wonder if Father Lorencio knows more than he's letting on,' thought Cortez. 'I can't very well question my own confessor. I'll get one of the interrogators to give him a grilling.'

22

Julieta woke and sat up. Was it a sound that had woken her, or a sound dreamed? Mawi slept deeply but woke at a whisper or a breath of wind, he had told her: he was stretched out like a puma in the sand, fast asleep. Perhaps it had been the sun catching her full in the eyes, transmuted by her unconscious mind into a sound.

Bed for the four companions was a sandy hollow on the eastern side of the Parque Nacional Lauca, within view of the frontier from the tops of the dunes either side of them. Two hundred metres away was the road that separated them from Bolivia and followed the frontier at a distance of half a kilometre. Mawi was one side of Julieta, within arm's reach, the two donkeys were on their flanks the other side, their eyes closed, their heads nodding. The sun was low in the sky and filling what had been the shady side of the hollow when Mawi and Julieta lay down in the shadow of the eastern dune. Julieta had been falling asleep on Pablo's back after more than ten hours' riding, in spite of her streaming eyes, the pain in her toes as the cold bit into them, and her face that stung with the arctic wind as if she had thrust it into a hive full of bees. If silence hadn't been the golden rule, she would have sung for joy when the sun rose over the frost-flecked rock and sand, dazzling her and Mawi, warning them it was time to get their heads down, promising to keep them warm while they slept. No bed had ever felt so comfortable or so welcome as this cupped hand between two dunes. She had fallen into a deep sleep as soon as her head touched the soft sand. Now the dazzle was from the west, a silent ringing warning them to wrap up warm and be on their way.

Julieta's feelings for Mawi had begun with a need to protect him, take him under her wing, as if he were her son or little brother. They had quickly grown into a girl's love for a boy, and into a young wife's for a young husband. Now it was Julieta who felt protected: not just held in Mawi's strong hands but carried on his wings as if he were some great bird of the mountains, defying vertigo, terrain and the savage cold. She had followed him spellbound through the moonlight as he led Pedro calmly, without stumbling or varying his pace, through this Andean desert among the stars up a path often so steep that even the donkeys had to stop for breath. Sometimes the path divided and Pablo and Pedro didn't know whether to turn left or right. Mawi would study the sky, as Europeans study the maps they are fond of making to support their claims to land they have seized the world over, find his bearings thanks to Libra, Sagittarius and the Southern Cross, and trace his way among the stars. Sometimes it was the ground he studied with his sharp eyes, when Pedro and Pablo lost the spoor for a few seconds and started to wander, searching metres ahead of him in the pale blue light for the prints of hooves not yet spotted by the donkeys, the droppings of pack-animals whose scent they hadn't yet caught, the remains of cigarette-ends barely recognizable after months in the baking sun, for the hairs of humans and animals. He moved as silently as an owl and never hesitated or took the wrong path. He never forgot Julieta and every few minutes turned to give her an encouraging smile or wave as she rode or led Pablo close on his heels. Not a word did he utter, having told her it was safer not to speak. During their ride through the night Julieta discovered in her husband the skill of a detective and the nerve and self-discipline of a tight-rope walker. And at the end, after eleven hours of concentration and physical exertion, he had been as fresh as when he had started. Even the donkeys were starting to flag, but not Mawi.

Julieta was famished. She wasn't going to eat before her husband but she would lay the provisions out, so that their frugal meal of hard-boiled eggs, fruit, biscuits and water would be ready when he woke. If he hadn't woken by the time the sun disappeared behind the dune, she would give him a shake.

Julieta sat up. She was getting to her feet when she heard the sound of an engine being started east of the hollow. Instinctively she crouched down, though her head was several metres below the top of the dune. She listened to the engine as it idled, and recognized the throbbing that had woken her. A lorry? It must have stopped on the border road south from Visviri. Did she dare look? The sun would be in the eyes of anyone facing this way. She put on her poncho, which she had taken off when she lay down to sleep, pulled it up over her head to form a hood and throw her face into shadow, scrambled to the top of the dune and peeped over.

The lorry was painted in khaki and brown camouflage whirls designed to look like foliage and visible for kilometres around in all this yellowy desert. Soldiers wearing the same pattern and colours were climbing into the lorry – sitting ducks if Julieta had a gun and a Neanderthal urge to end the lives of the young men. When all but two were aboard, the motor revved and the lorry trundled off north towards Visviri. The two soldiers, their rifles over their shoulders, set off on foot along the road in the same direction as the lorry.

A hand touched Julieta's arm, gently so as not to startle her. Mawi was beside her, his movements as silent as the motionless air, his head hooded under his poncho. He beckoned her down and she followed him to where the picnic was laid out. He went over to the donkeys, got them on to their feet, unfastened the two nosebags Pedro was carrying on his back and tied them over the muzzles.

'Best to start with the donkeys,' he whispered when he was back at Julieta's side. 'If they see us eating while they haven't got food themselves, they may start to bray.'

'What are the soldiers up to?' Julieta whispered back.

'Dropping off patrols at intervals along the road. We mustn't miss our pair when they get back. We need to know the distance each patrol covers, so as to pick the safest moment to cross the road. Let's eat. We'll be all right for a while.'

They hadn't eaten for twenty-four hours and tore into their food like wild animals. Never had food tasted so delicious as their ration of four plain biscuits each, a hard-boiled egg, an orange and an apple. They were too hungry to say a word until every mouthful had gone. Julieta poured water for them both, which they drank slowly, savouring every drop, then filled two plastic bowls for the donkeys, which they emptied in seconds. She packed away the food, water and plastic cups and bowls.

Mawi whispered his plan of action. One of them needed to keep watch on the brow of the dune while the other talked to the donkeys to stop them braying. They would take turns: fifteen minutes a shift. They were about to start when Mawi froze, listened for a few seconds, then said, 'Can you hear it?'

Julieta listened but heard nothing.

'Quick!' said Mawi. 'Get the donkeys into the shadows and lie down under your poncho!'

The sun was sinking behind the dune, so that the western side of the hollow was in deep shadow. Mawi and Julieta led the donkeys into the shade, where they tapped their rumps to make them lie down. Then they lay down themselves, pulled their ponchos over their heads and tucked their knees into their chests, so that they were completely covered by the ponchos.

Only now did Julieta hear what Mawi had heard: the chop-chop-chop of a helicopter's blades slicing through the air. The aircraft approached quickly. Twenty seconds after Julieta heard it, it roared a hundred metres over their heads. The noise quickly receded.

'Don't move!' Mawi whispered. 'It'll be back.'

They lay still for five or six minutes. Julieta was about to suggest checking on the foot patrols when she heard the throb again and stayed where she was. The helicopter didn't fly overhead this time but followed the road on the far side, scanning the ground along the frontier.

'They haven't seen us,' whispered Mawi when the sound of the blades had faded.

'Wouldn't it be better to go back to Putre and wait for the soldiers to give up and go away?'

Mawi shook his head. 'They'll be asking around the town and doing house-to-house searches. Lots of people must have seen us. It only takes one snake to give the fatal bite.'

'I'll take first watch and you feed the donkeys.'

Julieta was about to climb up the dune when she heard the distant neighing of a horse from the west, the direction she and Mawi had come from. She looked at Mawi. 'We're being followed,' she whispered.

'That was two kilometres away,' Mawi replied. 'Donkeys are quicker than horses going up steep, rocky paths. It'll take whoever it is at least an hour to get here.'

Julieta pulled her poncho over her head and scrambled to the top of the dune.

She had been watching for only two or three minutes when two soldiers appeared. They were coming from the south, not the north, so they couldn't be the first patrol returning. They reached a post with a little red pennant attached to it, like a flag at the corner of a football or hockey pitch, turned and set off back in the direction they had come from. If they weren't in military uniform and carrying guns, Julieta would guess they were fitness freaks doing laps in a walking contest. She half slid, half ran down the dune and reported what she had just seen to Mawi.

Mawi thought for a few seconds, then said: 'It's half an hour since the first lot set off north. If the patrols are synchronizing their walks, it means there are about three kilometres between each pair. Our best time to cross the road is when the two patrols are furthest from us. That's roughly a kilometre and a half each way. It takes about fifteen minutes to walk a kilometre and a half. We'll wait for the first pair to get back and turn round. That should be in half an hour. By then the sun will have set. Fifteen minutes after that we can get going. I'll watch till the first patrol are back.'

'Another three quarters of an hour?' In her alarm Julieta almost forgot to whisper. 'Whoever's behind us will be here by then.'

Mawi smiled. 'Not quite,' he said. 'We've got another hour.'

He climbed to the top of the dune, while Julieta went to talk to Pablo and Pedro. She stood between them and they nuzzled her. She pulled their heads close to her to keep her arms and ribs warm. Even with her poncho on she could feel the cold starting to bite. The sun had already set behind the western dune, so that the whole hollow was in shadow except for the very top of the eastern shoulder, where Mawi was lying scanning the road. In the space of half an hour the temperature had dropped about fifteen degrees from mild to not much more than freezing.

Julieta was surprised how exhilarated she felt, in spite of the danger she and Mawi were in. She felt alive. She loved and was loved. And she was with the man she loved, having chosen to be true to herself and to the love that filled her, instead of her father's prisoner, sacrificing her identity and her heart to his schemes. She had left the fettering safety of home for freedom, risk and danger, where one false move could end the life that was so vibrant in her. If she died, she would die happy, even though she wanted the life she had seized to shine like the sun and moon and stars for ever.

Julieta was woken from her reverie by a neighing that couldn't have been more than a few hundred metres away. The last orange rays of the sun had faded and the moon was casting its cold blue light over the sand.

Mawi appeared in front of her. 'The first two soldiers have turned and are heading north again,' he whispered. 'Let's start for the road. Best to lead the donkeys. It'll be quicker than riding them.'

Pablo and Pedro had been loaded and were ready to set off at a moment's notice. Mawi and Julieta took the donkeys by the reins and led them up the eastern dune and down the other side, where they were now in full view of the road. They broke into a run. The donkeys were fresh, and happy to be led at a fast trot. Mawi and Julieta slowed down as they reached the road. They looked both ways. There was no sign of vehicles or foot patrols. They crossed the road on to an area of stones and broken rock and started to run again, lifting their feet so as not to trip. They kept running for three hundred metres until they reached a dune running parallel with the road and were safely behind it. They stopped to recover their breath, then left the donkeys and crawled to the top of the sandy ridge, where they saw four figures on horseback appearing out of the hollow that had been refuge and bed for the past twelve hours. All four were carrying rifles. Two of them seemed familiar to Julieta. Could they have been the waiter and the man from the information desk in Arica?

'They're not police or army,' she whispered when she and Mawi were back with the donkeys. 'They're freebooters out for the reward.'

'They'll lose our tracks in the stones this side of the road,' Mawi whispered back. 'Look! You can see the frontier from here. All that barbed wire. The trouble is anyone on the road can see it too. We need to keep the dune between us and the road until we find a safe place to get over to the barbed wire.'

They set off again and headed north, still leading the donkeys. Walking kept their heads below the ridge, the rhythm was calming and reassuring, and the exercise kept their blood flowing now that the temperature had dropped to minus two or three.

The desert was transformed by the moonlight. The blinding reddish-yellow expanse had turned to an icy pale blue. By night the desert with its dunes was a cold ocean whose great rollers had been frozen into immobility. Like the moon itself, it was full of shadow and contrast. By day it was as though part of the sun had spilt from the sky to form a molten lake without shade or relief. Mawi and Julieta followed the dune northwards, and it was as if God were holding the sea back for them as he did for the Children of Israel fleeing from Egypt.

The sand had thinned out and sometimes they were walking on bare rock. The dune on their left had less and less sand to give it height and at last petered out. The border and the road to Visviri had separated, the road bearing left, the frontier right. The road was now two or three kilometres away and there was less risk of being spotted from vehicles or by foot patrols. There was no sign of the four horsemen: they had hopefully turned south instead of north.

Pedro, who was a little way ahead of Julieta, stopped dead, and Pablo followed suit. Mawi didn't pull his donkey to try and make him go on because he must have known something was wrong. He stepped slowly and carefully forward, then froze. He took one more slow step, knelt down, leant forwards and looked left and right. He studied whatever it was he saw for well over a minute, got to his feet and walked back past Pedro to Julieta.

'Ravine,' he whispered. 'Sheer drop. Runs east-west. West towards the road as far as you can see. If it goes beyond the road, there will be a bridge. That may be the only way over.'

'Back to the road?' Julieta heard the dismay in her own whisper. 'What about the other way – east?'

'It runs well past the frontier with Bolivia, then turns north. The barbed wire finishes at the edge of the ravine. There's a ledge half a metre wide below the edge. Chances are the army didn't put barbed wire there because they reckoned nobody would stomach the ravine.'

'How deep is it?'

'Impossible to say. Some ravines in the Andes are thousands of metres deep. It makes no difference. Twenty metres or three thousand metres: the risk is the same.'

'Let's use the ledge.'

'Are you sure?'

Julieta could hardly believe what she had just said. She had never been any good at heights. Even the three-metre drop from her bedroom window in Santiago made her head spin.

'Yes. I'm sure.'

They set off again, this time east along the top of the ravine towards the frontier.

Twenty metres from the barbed wire it was Mawi's turn to stop in his tracks. He led Pedro back to Julieta and whispered: 'The earth has been disturbed in one or two places. Follow me closely. If you see any other places where it's been dug, don't go near them.'

They circled to the right round the patch of disturbed earth. Ten metres from the barbed wire Mawi paused again and they made another detour.

They reached the barbed wire, huge loops of it arranged in two rows. Mawi removed a bag from each of the donkeys' backs.

'They stick out too much,' he whispered. 'The ledge isn't wide enough. Wait here while I see if we can get across.'

He took one of the bags, went to the edge of the precipice and disappeared.

There was a wind now, blowing from the east through the ravine – not much more than a breeze but cold enough to numb Julieta's face and make her eyes water.

'This isn't a dream,' she thought. 'Barbed wire, guns, a wind to freeze the blood, three-thousand-metre ravines. This is what I want, isn't it? Life? Even when it scares me half to death?'

The minutes went by, stretched almost to breaking-point.

'What if he doesn't come back?' thought Julieta. 'What if he's fallen over the edge? What do I do then? Will I still want to live? No, I'll throw myself after him.'

Another minute passed. Mawi's head reappeared over the edge of the precipice and seconds later he was back beside her.

'There's a sentry,' he whispered. 'You can't see him from here.

We'll be all right if we don't make a sound: the sentry's in the moonlight; the ledge is in the shade. I'll go first with Pedro. You follow Pedro, and let Pablo follow you. Take it slowly. Tread carefully. Keep your feet close to the wall and don't look down. Watch the back of my head.'

'What if the donkeys bray?'

'They won't. They understand.'

Just then a horse neighed two or three hundred metres behind them.

'That's good,' Mawi whispered. 'The sentry will be looking for the horses, not at the ledge. Come on! Let's go!'

'There's no going back now,' thought Julieta. 'Not with the gunmen behind us.'

Mawi took the second bag in his left hand, Pedro's reins in his right, and led the way to the brink of the ravine.

The ledge was half a metre wide, almost as wide as the average doorway. Mawi knew this and stepped on to it without hesitating. Julieta followed, glimpsed the mass of black on her left and stopped. She was afraid of seizing up, of not being able to move forward or back. The wind was stronger in the ravine, and blowing in her face, but not strong enough to make her lose her balance. She concentrated on the back of Mawi's head, kept repeating 'I love you' to herself and edged forward, not putting one foot in front of the other but stepping with the right foot and dragging her left foot after her. She was shaking all over, like someone with a high fever. She caught a glimpse of the sentry in the moonlight on her right but didn't look round. All she wanted to see was the back of Mawi's head.

The ravine was inside Julieta now: a vast empty space in the pit of her stomach through which she was falling. Nothing would make her do this on her own. She would rather have all the soldiers and gunmen in Chile close in around her and machine-gun her. The thought of Mawi and the sight of his head gave her strength. Would it be enough strength, she asked herself.

The moments and minutes were slowed down and drawn out, and with them her torment. Mawi was walking at not much more than a snail's pace, so as not to leave Julieta behind. He stopped. Why had he stopped? Julieta drew close to Pedro's tail and waited.

Then she heard it too: the throb of the helicopter. Its searchlight appeared above the opposite wall of the ravine like the headlamp of a motor cycle on full beam but ten times brighter. Night almost turned to day as the helicopter flew directly towards the two fugitives and their donkeys on the ledge above the ravine.

Julieta was on the verge of panic and of screaming to a crew who would never hear her: 'Here we are stuck on the edge of this precipice! For God's sake help us! Lower a rope and get us out!' Julieta felt Pablo's muzzle on her hand, and her moment of panic passed.

There was a roar and an explosion of light as the helicopter swept by not ten metres overhead. All was black for a few seconds, then Mawi's head took shape again. The helicopter was still there, hovering just beyond the top of the cliff. Julieta heard the sound of men's voices shouting.

Mawi and Pedro started to move again. Julieta followed. The ledge climbed. After a minute or two it broadened. Mawi and Pedro disappeared from view for a few seconds. A hand caught Julieta's and helped her up the last two metres of the ledge on to the plateau.

'We're just out of view of the soldiers,' Mawi said quietly. 'We need to find a hollow with shade and wait there out of the moonlight till the helicopter's flown off.'

'We're in Bolivia, aren't we?' Julieta replied, her voice shaking. 'We're safe.'

'Not so long as Chilean soldiers can see us.'

'The helicopter: what's it up to?'

'They're changing sentries. They haven't spotted us yet.'

Mawi and Julieta led the donkeys quickly away from the ravine and back into the sand. Three minutes later they reached the shade of a dune and took shelter from the freezing wind.

'Not even a Mapuche woman would dare do what you have just done,' said Mawi, keeping his voice down in spite of the roar of the helicopter.

Julieta kissed Mawi on the mouth – a long, watery kiss of relief and love in equal measures. Her knees gave way and he lowered her on to the sand.

'The donkeys,' she said. 'What would we do without them? They never bray. They walked along that ledge as quietly and calmly as you did.'

'They understand,' replied Mawi. 'They trust us. If they like you and trust you, they'll do anything for you.'

'Why was the earth disturbed the other side of the barbed wire?'

'Mines. That's why there was no barbed wire across the ledge. They laid mines instead.'

The noise of the helicopter crescendoed. The aircraft rose twenty metres from the ground and hovered like some huge insect. Mawi and Julieta tapped the rumps of the donkeys, lay down themselves and covered their heads and bodies with their ponchos. The helicopter flew off in the direction of Visviri. The roar of its engine faded to a hum, the hum to a murmur, and the murmur to silence.

It was the silence that disturbed Julieta at first more than any mechanical noise she had ever heard. She had never known a silence like it: no voices, no engines, no bird-calls or animal cries, not even a rush of air, as there were no obstacles in the wind's path to create sound-waves. She listened to the sound of her own breathing to escape the utter stillness. Then she thought: the world was created to be a place of peace and only occasional sounds – birdsong, the roar of lions, the lap of waves, now and again a clap of thunder. Why are men and women afraid of the world's silence? Why do they destroy it with their towns and engines, their bombs and guns, with their screaming and shouting and deafening music? Is it because they are out of tune with the world they live in, too proud to accept the laws of Nature, terrified at the thought of death?

Mawi and Julieta strapped the two bags on to the donkeys, climbed back into their saddles and, soundlessly as the silence all around them, set off on the next leg of their journey. The setting was the same: the same moon, the same dunes, the same freezing wind. The difference was that they no longer felt hunted. The further they travelled from Chile, the safer they seemed to be.

Julieta was still shaking but felt neither the cold nor her exhaustion. She was wallowing in a warm bath of relief. And when after an hour or two the warm water started to cool, it wasn't the landscape round her she saw in the moonlight but the blackness of the ravine, the barbed wire, the helicopter's search-light, and the patches of fresh earth that could have exploded into inferno and killed them all. The same footage played over and over in her head, as her nerves and brain came to terms with her experience. Mawi and Julieta rode for eight or nine hours. When Julieta wasn't asleep on Pablo's back dreaming of barbed wire, ravines and helicopters, she was awake remembering them.

'Trees!' Mawi called out, waking Julieta from a doze. There was no need to whisper any more.

The black sky was turning to navy blue, and the pale lemon light of dawn was lining the eastern horizon and already eclipsing the paler light of the moon. Trees, yes: the first they had seen for nearly four days. Pine-trees, she thought: their resinous smell made Julieta think of Christmas, or of a freshly run bath. The sound of the wind in the pine-needles was like the distant rushing of an express train. There was another sound: the babbling of water.

'Stream,' said Mawi. 'It must flow into Lake Titicaca.'

They dismounted in a copse a little way from the stream, took two blankets from their baggage to cover the ground, and without even bothering to tether the donkeys lay down side by side in the shade of the trees and fell into a deep sleep.

23

Father Lorencio was walking briskly up and down his prison cell, breathing deeply, releasing endorphins and serotonin, oxygenating his blood, in an effort to dispel the agitation the Bishop's visit had caused him. The not yet quite doubting Thomas had allowed himself to find fault with the makers, the managers and the fabric of his faith but at the back of his mind there had always been the comfortable thought that he was simply satisfying a human need to complain about the slightest restraint imposed on individuals by whatever authority they had submitted to, or had forced on them. Until now Father Lorencio had been carping about the brickwork and the builders; now he felt the first shudderings of an earthquake that threatened to bring the whole house down on top of him.

A short phone call from the Bishop to one of his many contacts in the Government would release his fellow-priest in less than an hour. Why didn't he pick up the phone and make the call? Because he was afraid. Afraid of the men in power. Afraid of breaking with tradition, the tradition of Church serving State, however monstruous the actions of the governments it supported. Were there any grounds for fear? Even the President would think twice before trying to unseat a bishop, and it would take more than a phone call to make him consider it.

The thought of his own sermons at Santo Domingo continued to haunt Father Lorencio. For every hundred lives saved by his trips to the mountains, a hundred or more could have been lost through the incitement he had given the colonels and generals in his congregation to pluck the serpent, heresy, from its nest and crush it under their heels – under the steel-rimmed heels of their jack-boots if only he had dared. What excuse was it that he didn't believe a word he was saying when pewfuls of uniforms and worsted suits were hanging on every syllable he uttered? The thought that when he was looking into the shifty, flabby, weak-mouthed face of the Bishop he was in fact seeing a reflection of himself did nothing to calm his agitation.

The only book prisoners were allowed was the Bible. Once Father Lorencio would have found comfort reading the New Testament. Now it seemed full of structural cracks. St Paul and the four Gospelists were writing decades after Jesus' death. None of them had ever met the great teacher. Their knowledge of him was anecdotal. He was useful to them as a point of reference for their own visions and agendas, thought Father Lorencio.

St Paul, who was closest to Jesus in time, could have interviewed dozens of eyewitnesses but had shown no interest in Jesus the man and teacher. The new religion St Paul brought to the Greek-speaking world centred on the death and resurrection of its central figure, not on his life and teachings. And St Paul's new religion set out to reject, not fulfil Jewish Law, which appeared to Father Lorencio to be the exact opposite of what Jesus had intended. Christianity, as the new religion came to be called, was coloured not by the serene figure who seemed to emerge hazily at moments out of one or two of the Gospels but by St Paul, with his anxiety, his psychotic hatred of sexuality, his torment.

Father Lorencio had re-read the Gospels from cover to cover. Jesus didn't spring from their writings as an authentic, living personality. For Mark Jesus was engaged in a struggle with Satan that could be won only through the agony of crucifixion. More eccentric – 'Crackpot, even,' the prisoner said aloud as he paced his cell – was Mark's idea that Jesus spoke in parables so as *not* to be understood. For John Jesus was a spiritual more than a human figure, God's revelation of himself to mankind.

What was lacking, it seemed to Father Lorencio, who was voicing his thoughts now, was a written eyewitness account of Jesus' life and teaching to cut through the undergrowth of literary devices – virgin birth, miraculous cures, resurrection and so on – and superimposed theology. 'If only one of the disciples had been a Jewish Pliny or Herodotus. He would have left an authoritative record of a man who must have possessed exceptional charisma and compassion. Hundreds of interpretations and distortions of the great but shadowy figure could have been prevented and Christians would be able to find their inspiration in the man of genius portrayed as he really was.'

Gabriela was right: the greatest damage to the new movement was done by its acceptance as a state religion by Rome in the early fourth century. Until then it had been a secret society of recusants who were looking either for a deeper spiritual experience than paganism could provide or for an identity and mode of self-expression outside the imperial framework. The many thousands of martyrdoms only fuelled the movement and increased the determination and sense of identity of its followers. Then in 313 the Emperor Constantine snatched Christianity from the ever more subversive opposition and made it one of the established religions of the Roman Empire.

The outsiders of the past two centuries were now on the inside, and they lost no time taking advantage of their new position of strength. Constantine found himself dealing with 'a group of bad-tempered malcontents' – Gabriela's words, endorsed now by her brother. Imperial Christians bore no resemblance to the gentle, tolerant teacher who had unwittingly given his name to the new faith. They were fiercely intolerant both of one another and of all other religions. The doctrinal differences within the movement, instead of enriching it as Hinduism is enriched by its diversity, led to violent quarrels between bishops, who didn't hesitate to send hit-men to kill or maim their brothers in Christ.

Things were not going quite as smoothly as planned, so Constantine decreed that doctrinal uniformity would be imposed by the Emperor himself. 'Saints like Ambrose and Augustine collaborated with the State and by their authoritarianism and intolerance turned the Church into a fascist organization that would have made it the darling of Benito Mussolini had he lived fifteen centuries earlier and been Emperor.' Gabriela's words again, now her apostate brother's. Metaphor was imposed as if it were scientific truth. The imaginative retelling of the Christian story, to keep it fresh and alive in the absence of a historical account of events, was regarded as heresy and punished with crucifixion and later by disembowelment, garrotting, burning at the stake and other tortures dreamt up in hell. Monks were encouraged by bishops who would later be canonized to tear limb from limb men and women who dared to take a rational approach to Christian doctrine.

Father Lorencio became conscious of his voice and surroundings, found himself standing now, no longer pacing, directing his words to an imaginary congregation beyond one of the walls of his cell. He smiled when he remembered his arguments with Gabriela and realized he had become her convert. And he laughed out loud at the imagined outrage on the faces of his rigid, unthinking congregation at Santo Domingo and their shouts of indignation as they rose spluttering from their pews and headed for the door. 'Traitor!' 'Heretic!' 'Satan!' 'Beelzebub!' He laughed with relief too at having freed himself from the lies he had been feeding his colonels and admirals and ministers and civil servants Sunday after Sunday, month after month. This was the first time for eight years he had preached what he believed.

'From now on Christianity was the religion of the aggressor, not of the oppressed, and a convenient rubber stamp for centuries of atrocities against those who stood in the way of greed and power,' Father Lorencio went on with feeling, aware now of his voice and imagined listeners. 'Jesus was no longer represented as the victim of Rome but of his own people, the Jews – impossible, since crucifixion was a uniquely Roman punishment. For centuries he was portrayed not on the Cross but in Roman armour, waving a banner. The Jews were punished not just by the Romans but for two millennia by every nation in Europe for killing a man who was in fact killed by the Romans. The contradiction between Jesus' message of peace and the forging from the fourth century on of St Paul's fraught religion into an instrument of violence first by the Romans, then by the rest of Europe, has never ceased.'

Nor had the Church's involvement in the material and political affairs of the world, sometimes as a body wielding even more power than monarchs, today as the cringing servants of the State, thought Father Lorencio as his audience faded from his mind and he sat down on the edge of his bed. No servant could be more obsequious than the Bishop who had called at the prison and sheepishly declined to lift a finger to help his brother priest but promised to raise his hands in prayer. Prayer! God must be fed up with listening to the prayers of frightened men. Action and courage were what Father Lorencio would want to see if he were God.

The concrete hangar echoed with the noise of the iron gate at the end of the row of twenty cells opening and clanging shut. The prisoner recognized Francisco's light step and got to his feet again. He almost shouted for joy when the steps came to a halt outside his cell. The friendly warder's visits were the highlights of his day.

'I've brought you your clothes, Father, all washed and ironed,' Francisco said, unlocking the cell door.

Father Lorencio loved Francisco as if he were his own son. He was almost in tears as he thanked him. He had never imagined what joy one could feel at the sight of a clean shirt and clean socks and pants. Half an hour in a hot bath and he would be in heaven, even if a two-minute cold shower every two days was better than not washing at all.

'It's not much, Father,' said Francisco. 'I'd unlock all the doors and let you out, if I dared. Any luck with the Bishop?'

Father Lorencio shook his head.

'If I was the Bishop, I'd be straight on the phone to the President. Locking up an innocent man. A man of God, what's more. It's not right.'

Father Lorencio gave Francisco his blessing, which was all the young warder asked in return for his kindnesses.

When he met someone like Francisco or Mawi, Father Lorencio couldn't stop himself thinking he was meeting Jesus. Even when he received a moment of kindness from a soldier or policeman, for as long as the moment lasted he saw Jesus Christ. He saw him as a local preacher in Galilee, a simple man with an exceptional commitment to God and to his fellow-men and a unique gift for communication, who for a few days had become a national figure and who would be astonished if he returned and saw how much of world history over the past two thousand years he had helped to shape. Even if the Jesus Christ of Father Lorencio's imagination were not the real man, would this make his image of the charismatic teacher and healer of the soul a less valuable response to goodness and kindness?

Francisco paused in the doorway on his way out. 'I'm not supposed to tell you this,' he said quietly. 'They like to spring it on prisoners. You've got an interview with the major tomorrow evening – Major Santos, the one who does all the questioning. I thought I'd warn you. It'll give you time to prepare yourself… I'll leave you to change back into your own clothes.'

24

Julieta lay somewhere between dream and day-dream, her head comfortably pillowed, having risen from the blackness of sleep and insensibility but not yet surfaced into sunlight and full consciousness. Her brain was busily processing and filing away the stack of memories from the past few days, and exorcising her fears and phobias. She was half-conscious of the plash of water: a stream, perhaps, dividing as it met a rock.

In her memory the moonlight danced on the tumbling, sluicing torrent they were following, and the sky to their left faded from red to lavender, pink and duck-egg blue, as they rode gently downhill on easy terrain, their fear of a gun-barrel over the crest of every hammock diminishing with each kilometre they travelled.

They had bathed and had their meal between sunset and twilight. Julieta remembered the smell of pine and the sound of the breeze soughing through cones and needles. There was another smell: the smell of earth. They had left behind sand and aridity and were now in a region of moisture and growth. She had undressed, put one foot in the water and gasped at a temperature not much above freezing. Grabbing her soap she had marched into the middle of the stream, sat down and all but screamed out in shock.

As she laid out the hard-boiled eggs, fruit and biscuits, her body tingling and warm now that she was dry and dressed, Julieta watched her husband stroll nonchalantly to the edge of the stream, take off his clothes, wade without hesitation into the water and sit down without a gasp or convulsion. How she longed to seize him and hold his brown, strong body against hers! No: she didn't know him well enough yet, this husband she had kissed for the first time only a week ago.

They were on their donkeys once more, side by side, following the stream. The eastern sky was turning from navy blue to gun-metal grey. They said little as they rode, both of them at ease in their separate worlds of thought. The chasm, barbed wire, helicopter and land-mines of the night before no longer throbbed in Julieta's head like a fresh wound; instead she found herself framing letters to her mother, Copihue and Father Lorencio. Would they believe a word of what she told them?

'Achacachi! Achacachi!' a voice half-croaked, half-sang in answer to a question from Mawi. The face Julieta saw in front of her was an old woman's, grinning toothlessly under a black bowler hat, wrinkles crowding into every part of her leathery skin, the black and cinnamon looking the darker for a poncho that had more colours than a parakeet. The old woman was behind a hatch cut out of the wall of her shanty, ladling a drink into two glasses from a steaming cauldron, filling the cold dawn air with the smell of fruit and herbs and spices.

A shaft of light fell on a sail out in the little harbour, turning it from white to orange. Mawi and Julieta looked round and saw the sun peeping over the horizon. The jetties were abuzz with activity as the fishermen arrived back with their night's catch. Women in black and brown bowler hats, and ponchos and long skirts as colourful as a flower market, chattered and laughed while they waited with big wicker baskets for their husbands or sons or brothers to moor at the jetties and unload their fish, to be sold at the market, as likely as not, before the sun was high.

'Achacachi! Achacachi!' The old woman was pointing along the lakeside now.

The fishermen's huts stood two or three metres out from the shore on stilts. They were made from flotsam and jetsam: the roofs were thatched with reeds and the walls cobbled out of old pieces of sail nailed to wooden posts. There were no windows: maybe the gaps in the walls let in enough light. What the huts lacked in substance they made up for in colour: bright pinks, reds, greens, blues.

Señor Achacachi led the way up a plank bridge to a boat-house, which was no more than a thatched and gabled roof sloping down on both sides to the water and supported at its four corners on posts driven into the bed of the lake. Under the roof Mawi and Julieta saw a boat six metres long and nearly two metres wide made entirely of reeds, interwoven and tied so that they formed a structure as solid as wood. The hull curved upwards at each end. The prow was shaped like a fish's mouth, the stern like its tail. Between the mast and bow was a space about two metres by three for cargo or passengers, and behind the mast a covered area, providing shelter from the burning sun.

Señor Achacachi was standing with Mawi now, on the ledge surrounding his hut, which was the same colour as the lake and sky and in a different class from the others with its properly built slatted wooden walls and glazed, wooden-framed windows. Señor Achacachi was perfectly groomed and obviously not a fisherman – model haircut, carefully pressed green linen trousers, short-sleeved white shirt. He was broad-shouldered and square, with the brown skin, flat nose and wide nostrils that gave indigenous Bolivians their Manchurian look. He had pearly, even teeth, and features to eclipse every cardboard cut-out face in Hollywood. Julieta saw him laugh gently. 'Cash only,' he was saying to Mawi. 'You can sell your donkeys at the market five minutes away.'

The walk to the market with Pablo and Pedro played like a lament in Julieta's dreams, her steps slowed almost to a standstill to add minutes to the little time they had left together, the donkeys' heads close to hers as she followed the women in their bowlers and colourful ponchos, some with baskets to fill, others with basketfuls of fish or vegetables to sell.

'Your animals for sale?' a man's voice called out from among barrows and stalls piled with corn-cobs and potatoes.

Pablo half turned his head to give Julieta a look full of sadness and reproach, and in her dream she heard him say in Chumu his previous owner's voice, 'You couldn't have done without us. We're more than useful. We're your friends. One doesn't sell one's friends.'

She felt tears in her eyes and on her cheeks as she lay with her head almost in water in her dreamland between sleep and waking, remembering the market where donkeys were bought and sold.

Then she was back following the stream, riding side by side with Mawi, and the eastern sky, having turned pale grey to mark the end of night, was now decked in pink for dawn, with a line of orange along the horizon like the flames of a forest fire but without the smoke, burning brightest at its centre where the rising sun was about to erupt. From the crest of a hill they saw Lake Titicaca stretching away from them like a vast sheet of azure ice, or an ocean without waves, broken only by islands – huge black rocks, some jagged, some smooth – and bordered in the north by a chain of snowy peaks.

Julieta heard a rush of air overhead, looked up and quickly raised her arms to protect herself as the two witches on broomsticks swooped down out of the sky, filling it with their black skirts.

'Condors,' Mawi said calmly. 'There must be a troop of animals on the move.'

The two immense birds swept over their heads, their wingtips juddering like the spinnaker of a yacht as it turns into the wind, then soared away from them, beating their wings languidly three or four times before allowing warm air currents to carry them skywards.

Julieta heard pan-pipes, looked down and saw a shepherd striding down the middle of an unpaved road. His face was lit by the dawn sky and he wore a floppy brown felt hat and a multicoloured poncho. His flock of a hundred or more sheep hurried after him. A mongrel jogged along behind, ready to nip the heels of stragglers.

'Listen!' said Mawi.

After a while Julieta heard it too: the sound of engines. They led the donkeys out of view of the road, ran back to the top of the hill and lay down in the grass. A convoy of lorries painted in khaki and brown whirls appeared from round a bend in the road, heading west. The shepherd stopped playing, turned and started to herd the sheep on to the grass verges. Julieta caught a glimpse of Hispanic faces through one of the windscreens as the lorries roared along a long stretch of dirt highway straight as a railway line, ploughed through the dozen or so sheep still on the road and rattled away in a cloud of dust. The shepherd shouted after them in Quechua or Aymara but the lorries charged on without slowing down.

Mawi and Julieta went back for Pablo and Pedro and hurried over to the shepherd, who was bent over the victims of the soldiers' act of capricious brutality. He straightened up when the two travellers approached. He was a sturdy young man about Mawi's age with a face that seemed to hail from somewhere north of China. After months living in the open, taking his flock from pasture to pasture, his clothes were in tatters: the poncho, which had looked so colourful from a distance, was full of holes, his trousers were torn and his toes showed through his home-made leather shoes. The shepherd's eyes and cheeks were wet with tears. He pointed down at the sheep at his feet and said something in his own language. His soft voice and gentle manner were out of keeping with his rough appearance and the villainous look the gaps in his mouth gave him.

Mawi crouched down to examine the damage. One sheep had been killed outright. Another had a broken leg but could hobble on three. A third was badly injured. The rest of the flock were bleating and close to panic but unhurt. Mawi took a shirt from one of his saddle-bags, tore it into strips, clicked the two halves of the broken femur into place and bandaged the leg tightly. Then he helped lift the badly injured sheep on to his fellow-Andean's shoulders and drape it carefully round his neck. These two men were brothers, Julieta thought, true South Americans whose ancestry in these mountains dated back thousands of years, united by their oneness with the land and by the pain of having had it seized from them by invaders from across the ocean. The shepherd held Julieta's hand respectfully in his for a moment, then took hold of Mawi's and shook it in both his own, and set off along the road, undefeated, robust in his poverty, followed by his mongrel and the bleating sheep.

'Let's not stop to sleep this morning,' said Julieta as she and Mawi mounted the donkeys. 'There may be a price on our heads, even in Bolivia. The faster we go, the more likely people will be looking for us in the wrong places.'

'This must be the road to Peru,' Mawi replied. 'The less we have to do with roads the better. We can follow the stream to the lake and find a village where they sell boats. Half of Titicaca is in Bolivia and half in Peru. There are no frontier posts in the middle of the lake. We just sail from one country into the other.'

Julieta now saw Mawi tug at the ropes of a boat until the sail swung slowly round and started to billow, the bow turn from the shore out towards the lake and the sail fill with air. The bales of reeds under her feet were caught up and propelled towards the open water.

The pillow under Julieta's head heaved. She woke. The images inside her half-sleeping mind faded quickly. 'The swash of water can't be a stream,' she thought, opening her eyes. 'We left the stream behind early this morning. And what's this thing over my head?' She tore at the material covering her head and shoulders.

'I put my poncho over you. The sun burns at four thousand metres.'

Julieta heard Mawi's voice and waited a second or two for her conscious mind to focus and the words to make sense. She felt the flank of one of the donkeys heave again under her head and saw the ghosts lingering in her subconscious vanish like mist. She lay still for several seconds, basking in the relief of knowing Pablo and Pedro were on board. Her memories were snapshots now, no longer film sequences: the boy who had held the donkeys for a few *bolivianos* while she went to the bank for money to buy the boat; the bank clerk who had stared and seemed to recognize her; the boy trotting along with her to Señor Achacachi's hut; the armed man in uniform who had trailed them; the disappearance of the donkeys; their reappearance in the reed boat under the thatched roof, lying contentedly on their flanks in the area in front of the mast, Pedro with his head raised in interest at the unexpected turn events had taken, Pablo with his eyes closed, like a churchgoer who has nodded off during his devotions, while the boy who had won their trust stroked their heads and talked to them as if he had known them all his life.

Julieta removed the poncho from her head, and her head from Pablo's flank, and saw that the sun was in front of the boat now, instead of behind, and already sinking towards the horizon. The lake had narrowed, so that it formed a strait between two mountain masses rising more than a thousand metres on either side. These were so drenched in blue light from the sky, and its reflection in the lake, that they had been transformed from the colour of earth or rock into the same azure as the air and water. The white sail above Julieta's head was flapping like a seagull over a shoal of fish. Her skin tingled from the sun and wind. Mawi was still standing in his place forward of the shelter, the ropes in his hands, the square sail protecting him from the sun.

'How long have I been asleep?' Julieta asked.

'Five or six hours.'

'Aren't you tired?'

'You can take the ropes for a while, if you like.'

As Julieta stood beside Mawi, holding the ropes, it was less like steering a boat than clinging to the feet of a great white bird that needed no guiding, and allowing it to lead the way.

The straits broadened, the water became choppy for ten or fifteen minutes, and then they were on the main body of Titicaca, a sheet of deep blue glass, more ocean than lake, stretching before them until it merged with the sky. The snow-covered peaks Julieta had glimpsed at dawn now reappeared from behind the blue mountains on the eastern shore of the lake. Julieta knew they were more than six thousand metres high and among the giants of the Andes but because Lake Titicaca itself lay high above the clouds, at four thousand metres, in air free of vapour, the mountain-tops were in sharp focus and looked only a few minutes' flight away with the wings of a condor. Julieta could feel their icy breath on her hot skin and saw it puffing in wisps from the summits. They formed a semi-circle round the lake like a chain of gigantic icebergs.

Julieta closed her eyes, to rest them from the dazzling sun. In her mind she saw the boy who had helped with the donkeys on the shore they had left behind waving, waving for all he was worth. Señor Achacachi stood next to him, watching, not waving – watching the boat that was his father's life fly away across the lake like a departing soul. Behind them was a third figure. Julieta's heart beat faster. Why was he there? He hadn't been at the boat-house when she had waved to Señor Achacachi and the boy. Why could she see him now, the armed man in uniform who had followed her from the market? She opened her eyes, to wipe him from her view.

The boat had altered course a few degrees, so that the sun was no longer directly in Julieta's eyes. She could see the islands now: dark blue shapes, some long and low, others sudden eruptions of land climbing sharply to pointed peaks, then falling steeply to the water.

Señor Achacachi had told Mawi and Julieta about the islands. He had spoken almost with awe about the nearest two, the Isla de la Luna and the Isla del Sol.

He had told them also about his father's boat, bought with

borrowed money in a struggle to escape the poverty of a fisherman's life. The risk had paid off: his passengers spoke of the peace and silence of their journey on a traditional reed boat between Guaqui and the Islas del Sol and de la Luna, of the spirituality of a part of the world that had been home to the gods for many thousands of years. The venture paid for secondary school and university for the ferryman's son and daughter. Then a firm from Philadelphia set themselves up with fast boats, a smart new jetty and half-page advertisements in all the papers. Old Señor Achacachi went out of business and returned to fishing and poverty.

Meanwhile his son prospered: worked for a travel agency in La Paz, married a Swiss girl, borrowed from the bank, built a lakeside hotel at Copacabana, rescued locals from unemployment and poverty, trained them, paid them a fair wage. Two years later a company from New York built their own hotel a few hundred metres from his, brought their own staff, spent millions on publicity, drew guests by the busload. Achacachi was trying to sell his business, but who wants a hotel a stone's throw from one that gets all the visitors? He had already sold his flat in La Paz to pay the interest on his loan. His wife and two children no longer had a home of their own and were staying with Achacachi's sister. The reed boat had been a family treasure. Now that was gone too.

The Isla del Sol was only a few hundred metres ahead now, a long rocky altar on which Julieta watched the sun rest for a minute, turning the island from dark blue to burning red and orange, until it seemed to melt the rocks, sink through them and leave behind it a molten afterglow mirrored in the face of the rising moon.

Mawi took the ropes as they rounded the north-east corner of the island and turned south-west, looking for a place to moor, or a beach between two rocks where they could pull the flat-bottomed boat out of the water.

Julieta sat down on the reed deck, closed her eyes and rested her head on Pablo's flank. Was it her imagination or could she hear singing? Had Mawi heard it too? At first men's and women's voices, then children's. The singing grew louder. They rounded a small promontory. Tucked deep into a little bay bordered by orange rocks was a sandy beach, also orange in the setting sun. The twenty or more people on the beach were not tourists. Julieta wondered if they were even islanders. Some were collecting shellfish from the rocks on both sides of the bay; others were fishing with nets thrown out into the lake and passing what they caught to a group of women for them to cook over braziers on the beach. Their clothes were Bolivian: scarlet, orange, magenta, sky-blue, sunflower yellow, emerald green.

'They're waving to us,' said Julieta.

The singing died down.

'Who are you?' one of the women called out.

Julieta seemed to recognize her, without knowing who she was. 'We're looking for a place to moor,' she called back.

The singing swelled. The boat was a good hundred metres from the shore and at least twenty voices were singing together in harmony and counterpoint but Julieta could hear the words as clearly as if they were the brightest stars in the sky, though she didn't catch their meaning at once.

For centuries we've waited:
Viracocha, rise again!
Free our children from the beast
That holds them gasping in its coils.
We implored the warriors from the north;
They promised but they never came.
Viracocha, break your silence!
Did you send these two young travellers?
The Sun has touched their hearts and eyes;
Viracocha, give them wings!

The singing faded, the woman conferred with her companions, then a man called out: 'The harbour's crowded. Why not try the steps?'

'What steps?' called Julieta.

'The steps Manco Capac and Mama Ocllo climbed,' the woman chimed in. 'You will have no trouble finding them.'

'A few hundred metres along the coast,' the man called to them.

The singing swelled again.

Viracocha, give them wings
To lift our children from despair,
From hunger, cold and sickness,
And the conquerors' injustice;
Wings to soar with in triumph
Over a continent restored.
And bring them to us at the end
To sing with us and share our joy.

Julieta had never heard singing like it. She had been to concerts in Santiago given by world-famous choirs but none of them came anywhere near this group of fisher-folk. This was like a blessing from a choir of angels.

Mawi and Julieta rounded the next promontory. The singers disappeared from view. Their singing became fainter and soon faded.

How did they get to their bay, Julieta wondered, the singers with their fishing-nets and braziers and godlike artistry. The place seemed inaccessible from above and they had no boat. Were there caves and tunnels behind the rocks, invisible from the lake? Did a boat drop them off and pick them up? Or were they as immaterial as their singing, appearing to have substance only as long as the sun made them visible, spirited here by their own thoughts or the thoughts of those who evoked them? Would they be gone from the bay once the sun had sunk into the lake and the sky had turned from orange to black?

Julieta opened her eyes and gazed at the huge slice of orange heat and light almost touching the water, glowing now instead of blazing, so that she could look at it without being dazzled and contemplate its perfect roundness. How simple and sensible, she thought, to worship something so perfect in form and so indispensable, since without it there would be no heat, no light, no life.

Three or four hundred metres along the coast a flight of steps appeared as promised, carved out of the wall of rock, climbing more than a hundred metres to the tableland above. The steps were worn and looked as old as the rock itself. Julieta started to count them but soon gave up. She had never seen such a long flight of steps. They made her think of the picture in her children's Bible of the climb to St Peter's Gate.

Two rocks had been carved so ingeniously that each had a stone ring not added on but forming part of it. Mawi and Julieta moored their boat to the two rings designed for the purpose, got their two companions to their feet, made sure the loads were fast and nudged the donkeys towards the steps. Pablo and Pedro knew what was expected of them and started to climb. Julieta went next, Mawi last. There was no railing and the bottom steps were wet and covered in moss. They would be less slippery covered in banana skins, thought Julieta as she scaled the first five or six steps in slow motion, treading as carefully as she would over land-mines.

She was surprised how easy the rest of the climb seemed. During the past few days she had learnt to overcome fears that would once have paralysed her. Instead of imagining the dangers, as she would have done only forty-eight hours ago, she narrowed her thoughts down and concentrated them on spreading her weight and breathing evenly. She climbed as Pablo and Pedro climbed, on all fours, using her hands to steady herself and take some of the weight off her legs. After a few minutes she was conscious only of the scrape of footsteps and the clip of donkeys' hooves, sometimes sounding together, sometimes creating complex cross-rhythms.

Julieta had no idea how long it took them to get to the top. She emerged almost from a trance as she stepped from stone on to soil, found herself among trees and breathed in a smell of pine and resin. A stony path led two or three hundred metres from the pine-grove through a landscape of occasional bushes, trees and clumps of grass to a more fertile area of olive-trees and oleanders, where roof-tops could be seen among the foliage and flowers. Mawi and Julieta led the donkeys along the path and found themselves in the upper part of a terraced village of thatched adobe houses covered in clematis and bougainvillea. A path wound steeply down to a cove, where fishing-boats were moored to a wooden jetty or pulled up on the beach. Fishermen the size of ants, seen from this height, were helping one another drag their boats into the water. Others were lighting their oil-lamps. Women leading heavily laden llamas and alpacas or carrying heavy loads wrapped in colourful shawls on their own backs made their way up and down the zigzagging path.

'This is paradise,' said Julieta. 'I wonder if there's somewhere to stay. Here's someone who may know.'

Clogs clacked on the stony ground. A woman in a wide-brimmed straw hat, multi-coloured shawl, red skirt and red woollen stockings appeared round a bend in the path, the last on her long climb from the harbour, leading a chestnut-coloured llama. Mawi and Julieta wished her *buenas tardes* and asked if there was a hotel or guest-house on the island.

'You can stay with me,' the woman replied.

Her bright smile revealed teeth that dazzled against her dark brown face. She was petite, with delicate hands, two black plaits that hung down her front and a face pretty as a columbine, with only thin lines around the mouth and eyes to season its youthfulness.

'I often have guests to stay,' she said. 'Visitors from all over the world. I've just been down to the harbour for fresh fish: *paiche*.' She pointed to the open box on the llama's back. 'My garden is full of potatoes and mint. My name is Yucuma Choquechinchay. This is Caramelita.' She indicated the llama, who looked superciliously down her nose at the four travellers.

Mawi and Julieta introduced themselves and the two donkeys, then followed Yucuma and Caramelita off the main path on to a smaller one past olive-trees and under canopies of oleander and bougainvillea, whose pinks, reds and purples were deepening with the fading light, through cool air thick with the scent of honeysuckle and ripe apples to a single-storey thatched house hidden among trees and built of flowers, it seemed. In front was an open verandah, and below that a meadow. At the end of the meadow, facing them, nestled a smaller thatched adobe house, with no verandah but with the same mantle of flowers and foliage, and with a well in front of it.

Yucuma opened a rickety wooden gate and drove the indignant llama into the meadow. 'You can put your donkeys with Caramelita. She gets on with other animals. She likes people too but she prefers children to adults, because they don't make her work.'

Yucuma led the way across the meadow to the garden-house, where Mawi and Julieta unloaded the donkeys.

'This is the guest-room,' she said, opening the French windows. 'My husband made the furniture. My mother wove the tapestries: they're a blessing of the gods, the people and the animals of the island on those who sleep here.'

The room took up most of the garden-house; a wooden-framed double bed filled half the room. Two oil-lamps stood on a table, the earth floor was strewn with reeds and the unplastered adobe walls were decorated with brightly coloured tapestries covered in llamas, fish, condors and cabbalistic geometric figures.

'Have you always lived on the island?' asked Julieta.

'My family came from Cuzco when the Spanish invaders destroyed the town.'

'That was five hundred years ago.'

Yucuma nodded. 'Are you hungry? Supper in half an hour?' She smiled cheerfully and disappeared into the garden with her box of fish.

Mawi drew two bucketfuls of water from the well in front of the summer-house, took them through a door at the back of the bedroom to the shower-room, and filled the cistern.

'It's the same all over South America,' he called, unpacking a clean white shirt and a pair of clean black trousers while Julieta had first shower. 'They remember the distant past as if it were yesterday. When a temple collapses in an earthquake or gets destroyed by invaders, they build an identical one on top of the ruins, so that the past is always present. They remember the days when their lands belonged to them, and they still hope for them back. The spirits of their ancestors live in the forests and the mountains. Their gods are in the earth and in the air.'

Julieta put on the lemon dress she hadn't had a chance to wear since Arica, took Mawi's arm and strolled with him first over to Pablo and Pedro, who had found their own paradise of clover and friendship in Yucuma's garden, then up to the house.

'Who is Viracocha?' Julieta asked Yucuma as she and Mawi sat down in their ponchos at a table on the verandah and watched the western sky turn a deeper shade of lavender and the now familiar face of the moon rise above the trees. A smell of fresh fish grilled in butter, of mint and thyme, wafted from the house.

'Viracocha?' Yucuma was about to set plates of *paiche* and new potatoes in front of her guests but stopped in mild surprise. 'He's our god of creation.'

'And Manco Capac and Mama Ocllo?'

'His two children, the first of the Incas, the founders of Cuzco.

He created them out of the waters of Lake Titicaca.'

'And the long flight of steps to the right of the cove down there?'

'They're the steps Manco Capac and Mama Ocllo climbed when they rose out of the lake. They were built by Viracocha himself when he and Inti, the sun-god, and Pacha Mama, the goddess of the earth, made the Isla del Sol their home. It was Viracocha who taught the Incas the art of stone-cutting.'

'And who are the warriors of the north?'

'They came in their curved ships a thousand years ago from the other end of the earth. The Spanish call them *vikingos*. In those days our land covered most of the continent of South America. When the Spaniards killed many of our ancestors and made those who survived slaves, we prayed Viracocha to send the warriors of the north to free us. We are still praying today.'

Yucuma set down the plates and lit the oil-lamp in the middle of the table.

'What about the singers on the little beach a few hundred metres past the steps?' asked Julieta. 'Who are they?'

Yucuma's black eyes opened wide in surprise. She stared at her guests for so long that Julieta started to feel uncomfortable. 'How did you find out?' she murmured at last. 'You're the first visitors I've met who know about them.' A question hovered between her parted lips, afraid to take flight. 'Have you seen them?'

Julieta nodded.

Yucuma put a hand on the table to steady herself. She pulled up a chair and sat down between Mawi and Julieta. She spoke quietly and with urgency, afraid perhaps of waking spirits in the surrounding bushes and trees and bringing calamity on herself for betraying a secret.

'People here close to our gods and ancestors say this holy island is inhabited by the souls of past generations who have been purified of all the passions and vices of humanity and now appear only to privileged mortals somewhere near the steps, in bright colours to make them visible, singing, offering kindness, welcoming travellers and showing them the way. I've never seen them myself.' She paused. 'Perhaps I don't believe strongly enough… I've never even met anyone who's seen them till today.'

Yucuma waited a few moments, then got up and filled her guests' glasses with the wine she had made from lemon-grass and herbs. Her eyes were still full of surprise and wonder as she smiled at Mawi and Julieta, wished them *¡Que aprovechen!* and went into the house.

Mawi and Julieta tore into their *paiche* and new potatoes. When Julieta had taken the edge off her hunger, she put down her knife and fork for a few moments to sip her wine and look at the very last of the daylight, a band of dark blue just above the horizon soon to be painted over in black, and at the full moon smiling down on them.

'Let's forget about Peru and stay here for ever,' she said softly. 'In a house like this one. You could collect sightseers from Copacabana in our Viking ship, and I could give them a guided tour of the island in Spanish, English or French. Their children could go for rides on Pedro and Pablo.'

There was still time to change her mind, Julieta thought. A marriage wasn't irrevocable in the eyes of God until it was consummated. She was about to consecrate her life to a boy who might soar like a great bird when he was in the wildest mountains and deserts, or behind a mast intuitively harnessing air currents to drive a boat across an expanse of water, but who would be ridiculed by Adolfo Cortez at a Santiago cocktail party.

Santiago, fashionable parties: Julieta felt no regret for a world she had left behind. Cortez had paled into a featureless memory. She felt nothing for him: neither anger nor contempt, not even pity. The wealth she had chanced on would never be found among the crystal chandeliers, silver candelabra and cold hearts of Hispanic Chileans. Julieta had discovered her eldorado among the simple-hearted Indians of the Andes, who laughed and smiled with candour and welcomed strangers as if they were old friends. She had found it in a world of plywood walls, cardboard roofs and threadbare clothes, far from Cadillacs and motorways, riding her beloved Pablo, sailing a boat designed long before Spaniards arrived on the continent, with a view not of treasuries and banks but of an azure sky, and azure water and islands, and the snowy peaks of the high Andes. Would Cortez ever discover the treasures Julieta had learnt to value? She said good night to Yucuma and walked arm-in-arm with Mawi back across the meadow to the garden-house and their bed hidden among the flowers and blessed by the gods, the people and the animals of the island.

25

A smooth-faced man of about thirty-five, with a Roman nose and black swept-back hair smelling of lacquer, sat in a metal chair at a metal desk in a windowless room in the bowels of Santiago. His short-sleeved shirt and trousers were khaki and he wore brown lace-up shoes. On his right was a panel of dials and switches. The only light came from the Anglepoise over the desk, positioned so that the interviewer was almost invisible and the interviewee half blinded. A bruiser, also in khaki, with a shaven head and stubbly chin, stood in front of the only door.

'In case I make a dash for it,' thought Father Lorencio. 'Where would I dash to? Into the iron grille at the end of the corridor?'

Around the room, neatly placed on metal trolleys, were transformers, amplifiers and junction-boxes, and the earphones, probes and manacles that plugged into them. Father Lorencio noticed what looked like the jump-leads from his car and a metal armchair with shackles for the hands and feet and a cable connecting it to an adaptor. All this equipment was presumably controlled from the switchboard on the interviewer's right.

Father Lorencio was sweating and shaking, not for fear of the two men and their gadgetry but because of what he had just been shown in another room through a spy-hole in the door. And been made to listen to: the screams of pain and terror. There were three men: an interrogator and a bruiser, and in a regulation jump suit a handcuffed prisoner old enough to be their father. The bruiser had jerked his knee and the prisoner had doubled up. The bruiser then tore away part of the jump suit, seized a metal rod connected to a cable and, as far as Father Lorencio could see, thrust it into the old man's rectum. The interrogator switched on the current. The prisoner lurched about like a man with St Vitus's dance. 'The names!' shouted the interrogator. 'Tell us the names!' The prisoner was in too much pain to tell anyone anything. The bruiser replaced the metal rod in its free-standing rubber sheath, passed two arms as big as tree-trunks under the prisoner's shoulders, folded two hands like loins of pork behind his head and, with a quick movement and a crack like the sound of a branch snapping, broke his neck.

Father Lorencio wasn't handcuffed. This gave him a grain of hope: perhaps he would be treated like a priest, not a convict. Then he noticed a pair of handcuffs on a hook on the wall above his metal chair.

He breathed deeply and concentrated his mind on the course of instruction he had received twenty years ago at theological college. It had been given by a visiting Dominican, a hawk among Franciscan doves. He had even had the face of a hawk: Father Lorencio could see it now, with its curved beak and hard little eyes. His tongue was like a sword, stabbing and slicing at the soft shells of the ordinands. His teaching was not so much by catechism as through drilling in a kind of spiritual ju-jitsu, in parrying verbal onslaught against the true faith. The principle wasn't counter-attack but deflection, never yielding, gradually deflating and at last disarming your attacker. Father Lorencio would have tried the technique in his discussion with Mawi, if Mawi's arguments hadn't always taken him by surprise.

The attacker lunges: your god can't be both good and omnipotent; if he were, his world wouldn't be awash with evil. The defender parries: God allows evil, so that man can choose good; a man without the possibility of moral choice is no different from animals. Lunge: man has no moral awareness; if he had, he wouldn't choose evil more often than good. Parry: he is still learning; in the end he will discover that good is more to his advantage than evil. Lunge: man evolved from his simian forbears a million years ago; he still hasn't learnt to choose good over evil. Parry: a million years are a moment in eternity; God is prepared to wait. Lunge: a god who is good wouldn't allow humans to lose their loved ones in wars and massacres. Parry: it is through suffering that men and women become strong and learn to make the right moral choice. Lunge: what lessons in moral choice will ever be learnt by the children your god allows to be crushed in earthquakes and to die of painful diseases? Parry: they suffer for a moment in this world only to find eternal joy in the next. And so on, like a radio quiz where you must never say yes or no, repeat or hesitate. Father Lorencio had been able to keep it up for hours, having learnt the hard way, being screamed at by Father Domingo if he lost his concentration for a moment.

This was an interview with an army officer, not the Inquisition, but the technique was the same. It was the technique, not the theological substance, that Father Lorencio would use when the questioning began. Thanks to Francisco, the warder, he had had a day to pace his cell, exercise his brain and get his eye back in.

The smooth-faced man unctuously invited Father Lorencio to take a seat.

Father Lorencio sat down and took the initiative. 'I haven't been charged with any offence, Major,' he said. 'I have done nothing wrong. May I ask why I'm being detained?'

'Believe me, Father,' replied the major in a voice as smooth as oil, 'I would release you here and now if the matter were in my hands. I have the greatest respect for your work at Santo Domingo. I'm not one of your parishioners but I have had the good fortune to hear one of your sermons: stirring, stirring. Can I offer you a brandy?'

'No thank you, Major. You haven't told me why I'm being detained.'

The major poured two glasses of brandy and pushed one across the desk. The smell made Father Lorencio think of the rectory, and his study after supper when he sat down in his armchair with a book and a glass of wine or brandy and started to feel sleepy. He was about to succumb when the smell of the major's after-shave, sharp, clean and expensive, cut through the comforting, crushed-grape fumes of the brandy and put him on his guard.

The major's face looked badly over-exposed behind the bright light from the Anglepoise but his hands were clear enough. The left hand, steady as a marksman's, held a cigar, while his trigger finger closed round a silver cigar-cutter and snipped a triangle out of the sealed end – with a stillness and precision learnt from snipping the ends off fingers and toes, thought Father Lorencio. The major lit a match, puffed on his cigar and disappeared completely behind a bonfire of smoke and flames.

'Small matter of Julieta Reyes' trail being picked up in the patio of your presbytery,' he said at last from behind his smoke-screen. 'Dogs followed it up to one of the bedrooms, then down and across the patio to your quarters. How do you explain that?'

'I have a cleaner who comes once a week,' Father Lorencio replied. 'The dogs probably mistook the maid's scent for Julieta Reyes'.'

'Do you give the maid a cup of coffee after work?'

'No. Tea.'

'She prefers tea?'

'Yes.'

'Which does Julieta prefer?'

Father Lorencio just stopped himself tripping over the wire and saying 'Coffee'. 'I have no idea, Major. I have never offered Julieta Reyes anything to drink. Except wine at Communion.'

Father Lorencio longed for a sip of brandy but fought the craving. He needed to keep his mind in razor-sharp focus.

The major eyed Father Lorencio for a few moments, then said, 'We've contacted the maid. The scent isn't hers.'

'No other woman comes into the presbytery.'

The major sipped his brandy and puffed on his cigar. 'You are Julieta Reyes' confessor, I believe. When was the last time she confessed?'

'The Sunday before last.'

The major gave Father Lorencio a conspiratorial smile. 'And she confessed that she was in love?'

'I can't repeat what I hear in the confessional. You know that, Major. I can promise you that nothing Julieta Reyes tells me would interest you.'

'How do you know what would interest me?'

'The imagined wrongdoings of an innocent girl?'

'Julieta confesses wrongdoings?'

'People don't usually confess their good deeds.'

'Julieta came to confession a few days ago. Did she have her own key or did you open the gate for her?'

Another trip-wire, thought Father Lorencio. 'Confessants don't come to the gate, Major. They go to the church, which is open from seven o'clock.'

The major swigged and puffed again. 'And her boy-friend? How long had he been staying at the presbytery?'

'What boy-friend? Where are all these questions leading, Major? What has happened to Julieta Reyes?'

The major gave Father Lorencio an impatient look. 'You're here to answer questions, not ask them, Father. There was a young man staying in one of the guest-rooms at the presbytery. How long had he been there?'

'Pedro Moreno? He's a trainee priest from Puerto Montt. I was giving him a week's instruction in the teachings of St Augustine and St Thomas Aquinas.'

'Indian?'

'Pedro Moreno? I don't think so. I'm not interested in my students' racial origins. If they want to learn, I'm happy to teach them.'

'How did Julieta meet him?'

'She's never met him, so far as I know.'

The major scrutinized Father Lorencio's face for a few seconds, then made a small gesture of irritation with the hand holding the cigar. 'We'll speak again later, Father,' he said tersely.

Father Lorencio was led up the flight of metal steps and to his cell by the bruiser, who must be the chief warder, Father Lorencio guessed, and probably the chief torturer and executioner. The lights had been turned down and there were groans and snores from the other cells. It could only have been about eight o'clock but the prisoners settled down early: sleep was the best way of filling the long hours and days of waiting. It felt to Father Lorencio as midnight used to feel. He sat down on the bed. He was too exhausted to undress. He stretched out to doze and fell sound asleep.

He couldn't have been sleeping more than twenty minutes when he was woken by the rattle of keys. The executioner was back, with an extra half-hour's stubble on his chin. Father Lorencio was led down to the interview room again, stumbling with fatigue.

The smell of after-shave, hair lacquer and cigar was almost overpowering. There was a milder smell of black pudding and cabbage. The major had obviously been keeping his energy up on *prieta*. The mere thought of blood sausage and tepid cabbage would normally have made Father Lorencio retch. Now the smell made his mouth water. It was the cigar, after-shave and lacquer that nearly made him vomit.

The major was at his desk, fiddling with the switches on the panel to his right. He found the one he wanted and flicked it. A machine behind Father Lorencio crackled like summer lightning. Father Lorencio felt drops of cold sweat running from his armpits down his ribs.

The major made a show of having only just noticed the prisoner and switched off the machine. '*Buenas tardes* once again, Father. I hope you feel refreshed after your break.' He relit his cigar and poured more brandy for himself. 'Another glass, Father? No, you haven't finished the first one. Where were we? Oh yes! Julieta Reyes contacted you to ask if you would mind having her Indian boy-friend to stay because she couldn't invite him home: her father is trying to get her married to someone else and wouldn't in any case allow a racially and socially inferior guest under his roof. Am I right?'

Father Lorencio was so tired that he almost blurted out angrily that he had been offering sanctuary to an innocent boy Reyes had threatened to have arrested for something he hadn't done, not providing a love-nest for a girl he knew only as a confessant. He controlled himself and said nothing.

The major waited a few seconds for an answer, then went on: 'Julieta spends the night in your guest-room with her Indian. The two of them cross the patio to your kitchen, where you give Julieta toast and peach jam for breakfast. And coffee. Or was it tea?'

Father Lorencio nearly tripped over the same trip-wire. He was exhausted and no longer alert enough for word games. His best plan was to say as little as possible. He waited for a good ten seconds, then replied quietly and slowly: 'Your story is a complete invention, Major. Julieta Reyes never contacted me or asked for a bed for a friend.'

The major puffed on his cigar. 'And the coffee and peach jam?' He gave Father Lorencio a mischievous smile, as if to say: 'I'll give way on the bed and the boy-friend if you let me have the coffee and peach jam.'

'Part of the same invention.'

The major sipped his brandy. 'How is it then that Julieta's fingerprints were found on your jam-jar?'

Father Lorencio felt a blush behind his ears and drops of cold sweat in his armpits. After another pause he said quietly: 'If Julieta Reyes' fingerprints are really on the jam-jar, she must have called at the presbytery while I was out, to see me about goodness knows what. Pedro Moreno must have heard the bell, let her in and offered her something to eat and drink while she was waiting for me.'

The smile remained on the major's face. 'Shall we see if you're telling the truth?' He flicked the switch again and the machine behind Father Lorencio crackled and sparked like a firework.

Father Lorencio felt sick and almost retched. 'They're going to plug me into that thing,' he thought. 'I won't be able to keep this game up with all those volts tearing through me.'

'No, we'll wait,' said the major. 'Confessions can take time to ripen, can't they, Father? We'll meet again in a day or two.' He bowed his head in mock respect and gestured towards the corridor and stairs.

The chief warder held the door for Father Lorencio, with an ironic smile that mirrored the officer's, and accompanied him as far as the hinged grille leading up to the cells, where they stood and waited.

The warder had positioned himself between Father Lorencio and a door with a little wire-reinforced window at the top. He raised his head to scratch his chin and in that moment Father Lorencio caught a glimpse through the window of the elderly prisoner, now in khaki, and his two torturers sitting chatting with wine-glasses in their hands and a bottle on the table in front of them. So the scene Father Lorencio had been forced to watch was a fabrication to scare the daylights out of him. He felt an urge to break into peals of laughter but suppressed it and remained deadpan. His relief quickly cooled when he remembered the major's last words. Today's charade could be replayed for real in a day or two, with one obvious change of cast. The only comfort was that the suave major seemed to be keeping torture as a last resort for his reverend prisoner. Father Lorencio needed to come up with a perfectly crafted story before their next meeting.

There was the sound of footsteps on the stairs. The chief warder unlocked the gate and handed the prisoner over to Francisco, who escorted him up the metal steps and back to the cell.

'This is for you,' Francisco whispered when the cell door was shut. He gave Father Lorencio something in a paper bag. 'I bought two, so that we could each have one.' He whispered even more quietly: 'I overheard the major talking to my boss. Don't breathe a word or I'll end up inside too. They're keeping you here for two reasons. They're hoping Julieta will write to you at your church, which will tell them where she is and make it easier to frame you. If that doesn't work, they'll send news reports of your arrest and imprisonment all over South America, hoping she will see or hear one of them and come running back to try and get you out. It's wicked keeping an innocent man locked up to use as bait. And a man of God at that.' He squeezed Father Lorencio's hand in both his and left the cell, locking the door behind him.

Father Lorencio opened the paper bag. Inside was a cheese sandwich. 'Bless the boy,' he said aloud.

'Don't write to me, Julieta,' Father Lorencio thought as he scoffed the sandwich. 'If you find out I'm in jail, don't come and try to rescue me. Stay quiet, keep away from Chile, and you and Mawi should be safe. Sooner or later they'll get tired of keeping me here and they'll let me go. Write to me and there'll be no more cat-and-mouse games: the chances are they'll torture me to death.'

He emptied the crumbs from the bag into his hand, threw them into his mouth and put the wrapping in his pocket. He stumbled to the bed, collapsed on to it and fell into a deep sleep.

26

Mawi and Julieta were at the apex of the Isla del Sol, sitting on a flat rock that might have been placed there for Manco Capac and Mama Ocllo so that they could rest and watch the course of their brother the Sun. Mawi's arm was round Julieta; her head was resting on his shoulder. They were sharing a silence broken only by the lapping of water, the bleating of goats, and far away a mother calling to her child. In front of them the inland ocean was being transformed minute by minute into shimmering light by the rising sun.

They had left Yucuma's soon after their breakfast of fresh orange juice, papaya and home-made bread and passion-fruit jam to look for the sacrificial altar she had told them about and the pointed rock on which, soon after dawn every day, Inti paused for a moment in his endless journey, to make sure his island hadn't been shaken to pieces in a fit of anger by the God of Thunder, before soaring over the lake, wrapping islands and water in his folds of light as he climbed to his zenith. The rock and altar were only a few metres from where Mawi and Julieta were sitting.

'Yucuma is forty-one,' Julieta had told Mawi as they followed the path south-west along the ridge of the island. 'Her husband, Huanuni, was a coca-grower until the US sent the Marines into Bolivia to wipe out coca production and put hundreds of thousands out of work. An ex-mine-owner persuaded him to go and work in the mines at Potosí in the south of the country for two or three years. While he was away, the mine-owner tried to get Yucuma to sell her house to him at a knock-down price. When she refused, he told her Huanuni had been killed in a mining accident. Two weeks later he proposed to her.'

Mawi had been first up this morning for a change. He had walked down to the overcrowded harbour to see if there was anywhere to moor their boat, to save Julieta and the donkeys climbing down the three or four hundred stone steps in case they all had to leave the island in a hurry. When he got back to the house, Julieta was on the verandah, deep in conversation with Yucuma.

Huanuni had been at Potosí for only two years, Julieta had told Mawi, but it was long enough for him to develop silicosis. He gave notice. Two weeks before his contract was due to end he was badly injured in a cave-in. There was no compensation but he had managed to put some money by, which he and Yucuma used to restore the house. He died three months later. Julieta saw two little sun-hats on pegs behind the verandah door and asked how old her children were. Her ten-year-old son had died a year after her husband of yellow fever, her seven-year-old daughter two years later of typhus. Now she was alone with Caramelita. 'It's all so unnecessary,' Julieta had said. 'This is the twentieth century, not the sixteenth. You can inoculate people against typhus and yellow fever. You can enforce safety regulations, so that mines don't cave in. You can give miners masks to wear to stop them getting silicosis.'

They had walked in silence for a minute or two, then Mawi had said quietly: 'You would cure the diseases and end the suffering of every human and animal in the world if you could.'

'Not cure, because I'm not a doctor,' Julieta had replied, 'but prevent. Most suffering and diseases are unnecessary. They could so easily be prevented.'

The path along the top of the island was also its thoroughfare. Mawi and Julieta had followed women in their bowlers and colours leading llamas laden with wool or cheeses to sell, and met others driving goats or jet-black sows, each with its litter of piglets, sometimes as many as a dozen, in search of tufts of grass for pasture among the rocks. Mawi and Julieta had greeted everyone they met and received smiles and greetings in return. The piglets Julieta picked up wriggled and squeaked in her arms, while the mothers grunted in consternation.

'In the fourteenth and fifteenth centuries this was all part of the Inca Empire,' Mawi had told Julieta as they walked, with a gesture that took in the islands, the lake and the surrounding mountains. The Incas had mined quantities of gold and silver but no one had damaged his health or lost his life underground. They had doctors – brain surgeons, even – who used coca to prevent thrombosis and altitude sickness, and as a tonic and an anaesthetic. There were no drug-dealers then to buy the coca for a few *centavos* a kilo and send it to basement laboratories in the US to be converted into cocaine and peddled at a thousand times the price on the streets of Chicago and Los Angeles. If the Spaniards hadn't conquered the Incas and destroyed their civilization, there would be Inca doctors on the island today and children wouldn't be dying of typhus, yellow fever and other diseases brought to South America by the invaders. 'The Mapuche never lost their respect for the Incas,' Mawi had said, 'even though they were our enemies and tried to conquer us. The Incas built houses and palaces that didn't fall down in earthquakes. They understood the stars and used them to navigate. They knew how and where and when to plant crops, fruit and vegetables. Everybody had enough to eat. They never ran short, even in a bad year, because they knew how to store their food. The Inca Empire stretched six thousand kilometres from north to south, yet everyone lived near a paved road straight as the path we're walking along. The rulers at Cuzco knew what was going on in every corner of the Empire thanks to the relays of runners who carried news along the roads. If your father was Pachacutec or Atahualpa or one of the other sun-kings, he'd know where we were by now. We would be under arrest and on our way to his royal palace.'

'If my father were Sun-King,' Julieta had replied, 'he would be wise enough to give us his blessing and leave us in peace.'

The path had climbed and, as it did so, the sunlight, coming from behind the summit in front of them, had grown brighter. Another few minutes and they had reached the crest, the highest point of the island. The light was so dazzling that they stumbled and had to stop. It was as if the Sun had changed his course so that he could brush his cheek against the island named in his honour, and they had stepped inside his orb without being incinerated or even scorched. They had groped their way blindly to the stone bench where they were sitting now in silence, listening to the distant sounds and waiting for contour and colour to return as the sun rose almost visibly to its zenith.

'If the Incas had searched the whole world,' Julieta murmured at last, 'they could never have found a more perfect place to honour their god: these huge black rocks, this vast lake as deep and still and blue as the sky, the white heads of the gigantic mountains all around. Nothing green any more. Nothing apricot, peach or orange. Just black, white and blue. It's primeval. Elemental.'

Before Mawi and Julieta had started their journey with the two donkeys, he thought he had married a town girl who would miss the comfort and ease of her parents' palace and never grow used to the rigours of outdoor life. Never once during their arduous three-day journey had Julieta complained or shown any sign of stress, fatigue or cold. And she was always the first to wake. What if she had broken under the strain? He would be racked with guilt for the rest of his life. Or if she had lost her nerve or footing crossing the frontier and fallen into the ravine? He would have thrown himself after her. Had there been an easier way to get her out of Chile? He couldn't think of one. Mawi was more than in love with Julieta now. He admired her, and was proud of her.

'I'm not an Inca and I don't worship the sun,' Julieta said gently, 'but I've never felt so close to my own god as I do up here, with you beside me, the altar and lake and mountains in front of us and the sun overhead. Closer than I've ever felt in a church.

Why couldn't he have made the rest of the world like this, and filled it with people like you, and Copihue and Yucuma and Chol and Father Lorencio?'

'If everywhere looked like this, nowhere would be special.'

'I could look at this view every day for the rest of my life – for all eternity – and never grow tired of it. Just as I'll never grow tired of you.'

She lifted her head and looked up into Mawi's eyes. He leant and gave her a long, gentle kiss. Her mouth tasted of salt and the peppermint leaves she had picked on their walk.

In his thoughts Mawi was with Julieta in the garden-house at Yucuma's, when they had strolled back there after supper last night. Their huge bed was waiting for them and Mawi knew that Julieta was as ready as he was to end the ache of waiting and consummate their marriage. They lay on the bed, Mawi in his white shirt and black trousers, Julieta in her lemon dress. Julieta told him more about the singing she had heard as they were sailing past the cove where the fisher-folk were casting their nets, and Mawi had the strong sensation that they were being watched as they lay there – by divine, not human, eyes. He was certain then that Julieta was a gift to him from the gods. What he couldn't tell was whether she had been sent to him by her own gods or by his. If she was a gift from Pacha Mama, it would be sacrilege to refuse the blessing of his wife's body. If her own gods had sent her, he couldn't be sure. Father Lorencio had never explained how a woman could be a mother and a virgin at the same time. The last thing Mawi wanted was to steal Julieta from her gods, as the Spanish had stolen so many of his own people from theirs, or encourage her to do something that would displease them. Julieta needed her gods as much as he needed his, Mawi guessed, and the Spanish gods certainly needed someone gentle and loving like Julieta after all the outrages committed in their name. He was ready to spend the night fully dressed on the bed, as separate from her and unshakeable as the rock he saw in front of him now, planted on the bed of the lake.

'I've been thinking,' Julieta mused. 'There are more important things to do than ferry tourists to and fro and give their children rides on donkeys. That would be fine in a country with a health service and a helicopter to fly the people here to hospital in La Paz. They haven't even got a nurse on the island. Yucuma wanted to be a nurse but she can't read or write and couldn't afford to train. If we lived here, we could make part of our house into a surgery. I could do a course in nursing and dietetics and we could stop children getting ill and dying unnecessarily.'

Mawi would happily spend his life as a boatman, he told Julieta, if that was what she wanted, ferrying the sick to the mainland and bringing them back healed. He would do whatever she asked, so long as she was happy and he could be with her. He would even ruin his lungs down a mine for her, he thought, though it would take a cataclysmic change in Julieta to make her want to live among arid piles of dirt, with not a tree or flower in sight.

The sound of a horn from out on the lake behind them made them look round.

'There's another harbour down there,' said Julieta. 'Bigger than the one the other end of the island.'

'That must be where the larger boats dock, the ones from the mainland. Look! There's one coming in now. The women are waiting to load their llama wool and goat's cheese on to it.'

'I wonder if anyone sells postcards. I want to send one to Father Lorencio.'

The path that wound from the altar and temple ruins down to the port was paved with stones that fitted so that the joins were barely visible.

'Built in the days of the Inca Empire,' said Mawi.

'And as firm and even today as they were seven centuries ago. We would have been in togas then, instead of jeans and T-shirts, here for Midsummer's Day, with pilgrims from all over the continent.'

The port was modern, and a stark contrast with the harbour the other end of the island. Concrete jetties and a concrete quay were punctuated with iron bollards. There were no flowers. A single valiant pine-tree provided the only shade. A crowd of women waited on the quay with their llamas and wares as the boat approached the dock.

Mawi and Julieta were overtaken by an old woman with a bundle on her back almost as big as she was. They asked her if anyone sold postcards.

'*¡El chileno! ¡El chileno!*' she called, pointing at a group of kiosks at the far end of the jetty.

'Chilean?' Julieta said, with a hint of wariness in her voice.

El chileno was seated in his jeans and red checked shirt in an upright deckchair outside his kiosk surrounded by a knot of women flourishing pieces of paper. Julieta looked through the rack of postcards hanging on the side of the stall while Mawi watched *el chileno,* his hand adorned with a gold signet-ring, writing what each woman dictated and putting her piece of paper in an envelope, which he addressed and sealed. He took one *boliviano* for a stamp and another for his skills, then handed the stamp and envelope to his client. Julieta chose a card and went to the stall-owner to pay.

In the cluster of faces watching Julieta, *el chileno*'s was the only one that didn't smile. His mouth was small and tight and he looked impatiently up at Julieta, who had interrupted his work, and fixed his hard little eyes on her. When she spoke, in her Chilean accent, a look of unease blew like a cold wind across his face, and his eyes became restless and suspicious and looked everywhere except at Julieta. He made Mawi think of a middle-aged weasel, with his pointed face, so different from the Manchurian faces around him, his wiry body and his reddish-brown hair touched with grey at the temples.

Mawi and Julieta sat on two rocks under the solitary pine,

which had lost most of its needles and provided little shade.

'The ex-miner who sent Yucuma's husband off to Potosí,' said Mawi. 'Do you know if he lives on the island?'

'Yes, He's squandered his fortune and now runs a small business here.'

'Selling magazines and postcards and writing letters for the islanders. Did you see the initials on *el chileno*'s signet-ring? CVC: Cristóbal Valdivia de la Cagalera, the mine-owner who crushed Chol's leg for him.'

Julieta paused to take in what Mawi had just told her. 'This wouldn't be Eden without a snake,' she said quietly.

Julieta wrote her card to Father Lorencio, while Mawi watched the boat, half tug and half barge, moor alongside one of the jetties. The women with their llamas moved from the quay to the end of the jetty, out of the way of two square-bodied, square-headed Manchurian stevedores who were starting to unload boxes, bundles and bales with the strength of cranes and fork-lift trucks and carry them to the shore. *El chileno*'s customers waited in a group on the quay in a flutter of packets and letters. One of the men dumped a bundle of newspapers and magazines outside the Chilean's kiosk and whisked some of the packages and envelopes from the women on his way back to the boat.

'This is the mail-boat,' said Mawi. 'Do you need a stamp?'

Julieta gave him some change and he went back to the kiosk. The bale of newspapers was where the stevedore had left it, bound with metal bands. Mawi glanced at the photo and headline on the front page of the paper at the top of the pile, looked again and felt his heart pound and the pulse in his neck throb. The headline consisted of one word: *MISSING!* The photo was unmistakeably of Julieta. *El chileno* was sitting in his deckchair smoking a cheroot and hadn't looked at his papers yet. Mawi worked a copy free of its bands. He paid for a stamp and the paper, went back to the pine-tree, stamped Julieta's postcard and showed her the photo and headline.

'You take the card to the boat,' she said. 'I'll see what the paper says.'

Mawi hurried to the jetty, where one of the crew was plucking letters in his oil-stained hand like leaves from the forest of outstretched arms and throwing them into an open basket on the boat-deck.

Mawi became conscious of Julieta's voice calling to him. 'Mawi! Stop! Don't post it!'

Mawi withdrew the postcard just as the oily hand was about to snatch it and made his way through the crush back to Julieta. One or two of the women on the jetty had heard Julieta calling and were looking over their shoulders at her with curiosity. *El chileno* threw his cigar-butt on the ground, got up and went to deal with the bale of papers.

'They've arrested Father Lorencio,' Julieta said with quiet urgency as Mawi sat down on his rock. 'Listen to this!' She read from the article on the front page, skipping through the details of her education and father's career and slowing down for the parts that involved Mawi. *'A seat had been reserved in Señorita Reyes' name for a flight to Mendoza in Argentina but this was almost certainly a diversion forced on her by her kidnapper, who is thought to have entered Bolivia with her from the far north of Chile. In spite of tight security, there have been no reports of anyone of Señorita Reyes' name or description leaving Chile from any airport or frontier crossing. The border between Chile and Bolivia is fortified with barbed wire and regularly patrolled by soldiers, who report no sightings and no damage to the barbed wire. Señorita Reyes' alleged appearance at Guaqui on the shores of Lake Titicaca today is a mystery. However, there is no doubt that the false passport and the traveller's cheques believed to have been used by Señorita Reyes at Putre in Chile several days ago were used again at Guaqui today. The rector of the Church of Santo Domingo de Guzmán in Santiago, which Señor Reyes and his family attend regularly, is under arrest on suspicion of being party to Señorita Reyes' disappearance. He claims to have had no contact or involvement with her except as her confessor. Señor Reyes has offered a reward of ten thousand bolivianos to anyone providing information leading to Señorita Reyes' recovery and return to her family.'*

'It's a bluff,' said Mawi. 'They can't prove it was you who cashed traveller's cheques at Putre and Guaqui.'

'That's not going to stop anyone who sees the picture and recognizes me from going to the police. The islanders are poor. Ten thousand *bolivianos* would make a poor family rich.'

'The people here can't read or write. They only buy a paper to see if they've won the lottery. They send letters but they have to pay someone to write them.'

Julieta said nothing. When her silence had lasted a good ten seconds, Mawi glanced at her and saw her eyes riveted on the lake. He looked at the boat and jetty and at the women handing their cheeses and bundles of wool to two of the crew. Then he noticed a man in a khaki uniform with a holster attached to his belt stepping on to the gangway down to the jetty.

'That's the man who followed me in Guaqui,' said Julieta, half to herself.

They watched the policeman or soldier – whichever he was – walk down the gangway and make his way unhurriedly along the jetty to the quay. He stopped, looked about him, then sauntered in the direction of the kiosks at the far end of the quay.

'He hasn't seen us,' said Mawi in a voice not much more than a whisper. 'There's enough shade here so that we don't stand out. But look at *el chileno*! He's got one of his papers in his hand and he's staring at us. He must have recognized you. It'll only take the *guardia* a minute or two to get to him and the only way out of here is up the steps, which are half-way back to the kiosks.'

The crowd of women had finished handing their wares to the crew and were preparing to leave the jetty with their llamas. A minute later they were crossing the quay on their way to the steps, so that the man in khaki and *el chileno* were lost from view.

'Come on!' said Mawi. 'This is our only chance.'

They crossed as nonchalantly as they could to a woman in the middle of the throng who was leading the largest of the llamas, engaged her in conversation and walked with her across the quay and up the steps, making sure to keep themselves well hidden behind the llama.

At the top of the steps the women stopped to rest. Mawi and Julieta looked down at the port. There was no sign of *el chileno* and the uniformed man.

'They haven't seen us,' said Mawi. 'It's too exposed here. We must keep going.'

They smiled and waved to the women and set off briskly back along the path towards the north-east end of the island.

'The *guardia* may not be here because of us,' Julieta said a little breathlessly. '*El chileno* may not have recognized me, or may not shop us if he has.'

'It's not worth the risk,' replied Mawi. '*El chileno* has spent all his money and has to earn his living as a stall-keeper. There's nothing he'd like better than a cheque for ten thousand *bolivianos*. He's afraid of hit men from Chile finding his hide-out. Strangers with a Chilean accent are not going to make him jump for joy. If he shops us, he'll win his money and get rid of us in one go.'

'We'll be safe with Yucuma.'

'Not for long. Other people have seen us. Nowhere on the island is safe for us any more.'

'What are we going to do for Father Lorencio?'

'Nothing. If we say and do nothing, there's a chance they'll let him go.'

Their return to the north-east end of the island was nothing like the carefree walk earlier in the day, full of light and peace. Instead of exchanging smiles and greetings with goatherds and swineherds, they now saw them as potential enemies and betrayers and left the path to avoid meeting them. The views either side across Lake Titicaca were the same but the magnificence was only seen now, no longer felt.

Mawi and Julieta came to the path that led down to the little harbour and left it for the smaller path through the trees and bushes to Yucuma's. As they approached the house, they heard voices and slowed down. They caught a glimpse through the foliage of several heads at the gate into the meadow and advanced even more slowly and cautiously. After a minute or two the voices became clear of the foliage that had muffled them, and the heads fully visible. Mawi and Julieta looked at each other in relief: three little girls and one little boy, aged seven or eight, were standing at the gate talking to Pablo, Pedro and Caramelita. They walked over to the children, who were dressed in the same brilliant colours as the women of the island. Their eyes and hair were polished jet and their skin was like shining mahogany.

'What are they?' asked one of the girls.

'What are what?' said Julieta. 'Pablo and Pedro? They're donkeys. Have you never seen a donkey?'

The children shook their heads.

'They don't look like llamas but they carry loads like llamas.'

The children looked at the donkeys, sizing them up.

'Do they spit?' asked one of the other two girls.

'Can you eat them?' asked the boy.

'Do they grow wool?' asked the third girl.

'No, they don't spit or grow wool, and you can't eat them, but you can ride on them.'

'Can we ride on Pablo and Pedro?' the four children chimed out in chorus.

'Shouldn't you be at school?' Julieta asked.

'At what?' said one of the girls.

Julieta explained. The children listened spellbound. All the boys and girls on the island in one big room, learning to read, write and count: it sounded almost as good as *chirimoya* ice-cream.

'My mummy can read and write,' said the boy. 'She's going to teach me.'

'Did you go to school?' the oldest girl asked Julieta.

'Yes, for twelve years.'

'Did you, *señor*?' asked the same girl.

'For three years,' replied Mawi. 'My family taught me most of what I know.'

'Are you going to live on this island?'

'We want to,' replied Julieta.

'If you live on this island, will you make a school, so that all the children can learn to read and write and count?'

Julieta thought for a moment, then replied: 'We'd like to, more than anything else in the world. Now, do you want to ride on the donkeys or don't you?'

'Y-e-e-e-s!' The chorus was so loud and shrill that Caramelita retreated several steps in alarm.

Mawi's instincts told him not to be distracted by the children and to keep watch while Julieta entertained them. He made his way back along the path, then took a short cut through the bushes and trees, clambered for two or three metres up a steep, rocky bank and found himself standing next to the path that followed the ridge of the island to the temple ruins and the port. His sharp eyes made out a pair of men not much more than a kilometre away advancing along the path towards him: one was *el chileno*, the other the *guardia*.

Mawi climbed back down the bank, sliding part of the way, hared through the bushes and trees and along the path to the meadow, where he slowed down so as not to alarm the children, who were taking it in turns to ride on the donkeys. He spoke quietly to Julieta.

'We've got to leave straight away,' he told her. '*El chileno*'s on his way with the *guardia*. Yucuma might throw them off our scent but the children will tell them everything. I'll take the bags to the boat. Can you pay Yucuma and get the donkeys down to the harbour and on to the pier? We'll never get them down the steps in time. I'll find a way through the fishing-boats. You'll have to jump aboard with them as the boat sails along the jetty. There won't be time to moor. The men are only a kilometre away. They'll be here in ten minutes.'

Mawi and Julieta left the children to go on playing with the donkeys and dashed across the meadow for their luggage.

'Look!' said Julieta. 'Yucuma's filled our room with flowers.'

She threw her things into her bag and ran up to the house, while Mawi tore back across the meadow with the bag and haversack, through the gate and on to the little path. He charged between the bushes like a wild boar, tearing off twigs and leaves, scratching his arms, catching whiffs of laurel and verbena. Two minutes later he was on the broader path that climbed up from the port past the adobe houses smothered in oleander and bougainvillea. He reached the top of the path and turned north-east towards the steps that led down to the boat. When he was fifty metres short of the steps, he stopped, put down Julieta's bag and took off his haversack. The sun was on his back and he was perspiring and out of breath.

'We'll never do it,' he thought. 'They're only five minutes away. She's got to get the donkeys down to the harbour. I'll never get the boat to her in time. What am I going to do? Will Yucuma hide her? What if she doesn't? I can't leave Julieta to face those men alone. I'll have to go back.'

He was about to start back when he heard footsteps behind him: someone running this way along the path. He turned and saw Julieta, who was clutching a bundle. Where were the donkeys? What had gone wrong? Mawi scanned the path and trees behind her but saw no one in pursuit.

Julieta caught up with him and paused for breath. 'I sent the children home, then told Yucuma everything,' she said. 'As much as I could in half a minute. She says the men will call at her house first. She's going to keep them talking as long as she can, then send them down to the harbour.'

'What about the donkeys?'

'Yucuma's going to look after them. They couldn't be in better hands. They love it here. They're in heaven. I've brought the rugs we used as saddles. I thought we might need them.'

They walked the last fifty metres to the steps and began their descent.

'Take it slowly,' Mawi called to Julieta as he started down in front of her. 'Even if the men think of looking for us here, they won't be able to hurry down the steps.'

'Shall I take my bag?'

'I can manage.'

'Thank God we didn't moor the boat at the harbour!'

'We have your fisher-folk to thank for that.'

Fifteen minutes later Julieta was helping Mawi hoist the sail. They cast off. Mawi turned the boat slowly until the bow was facing north-west. A south-easterly breeze was blowing: just what they needed. A gust caught the sail, which started to billow. The boat was propelled away from the cliff and out on to the lake.

'There's someone at the top of the cliff,' Mawi called to Julieta, who was laying the rugs in the shelter behind him.

Julieta came out to look. 'It's Yucuma,' she said. 'She's waving. That's a good sign. She must have got rid of them.'

Julieta waved back, and went on waving for fifteen minutes or more, till Yucuma was a tiny speck on top of a rock a few centimetres high. Even then Julieta went on waving, until she could no longer see the speck.

'Let me know when you want me to take over,' Julieta called to Mawi as she settled down on the rugs to watch the sun sink into the water, turning it from deep blue to orange.

The moon rose and the blue-black sky filled with brightly twinkling stars. Mawi looked up at the chart that would guide him to the port of Moho in Peru.

27

Franco Reyes sat at his presidential desk in his dark grey, three-piece serge suit, lost in thought. It was after ten in the morning, and sunny outside, but the window was closed and he had forgotten to draw the maroon velvet curtains. The room was dark, except for the light from the wrought-iron table lamp with its faded parchment shade. Reyes stared down at his folded hands in the puddle of light on his desktop, at the gold signet-ring on his little finger, the large glass ashtray, the silver lighter, at the untouched glass of cherry brandy and the plate where a bluebottle was feasting on a half-eaten chocolate cream, but his eyes were blind to it all. A Havana cigar protruded from his mouth but had long since gone out.

Reyes was thinking knights, bishops and kings, going over every possible move in his head and racking his brains for one that wouldn't checkmate him. And like a chess-player he sat and sat, looking for a way out of his impasse. He had been sitting hunched over his desk since before nine o'clock.

Where were Julieta and her Indian? In Bolivia by the sound of it. Were they planning to stay there, in hiding with the gun-runners and drug smugglers somewhere in the northern jungle, or make for Brazil or Peru? Peru… Cuzco… Julieta's grand-parents. Is that where she was heading? No point phoning: Reyes wasn't on speaking terms with Nicole's parents.

And he couldn't very well bother Cortez again. If Julieta and her native were abroad, they were outside his sphere of influence. In any case, the major would lose interest in the marriage if Reyes kept pestering him.

The Bolivians had been helpful: their Foreign Ministry had traced the bank where Julieta had apparently cashed a cheque under an assumed name, and their newspaper editors had published photos and articles.

Peru was a different story. Reyes' opposite number at the Ministry of Internal Affairs in Lima had refused all help: no monitoring of cheques cashed at their banks, nothing in their papers, no *WANTED* signs at their airports and police stations. 'Scumbags, the Peruvians,' thought Reyes. 'Wait till they have their next earthquake! I'll make sure not a peso's worth of aid gets to them from Chile.'

If only there were some way of contacting Gorringe. He was on a mission in Peru at the moment. If Julieta and the Indian were on Peruvian soil, Gorringe would find them: he had a sixth sense, that man.

The President? He had shown an interest, expressed his concern. Maybe, but he wasn't going to phone the President of Peru on the off-chance that the daughter of his deputy, deputy Minister of Internal Affairs might turn up with her ethnic lover.

Would Thomas Cook's help? They were a British firm. The British were making friendly noises in Chile at the moment, in the hope of winning support for their crass adventure in the Malvinas. Cook's had shown willing so far, releasing details of traveller's cheques cashed by María Inmaculada Morales. The problem was this told Reyes and his associates where Julieta had most likely been two or three days ago, not where she was today. He didn't know anyone at Cook's, but there was no harm in inviting one of the directors out for a meal.

What about the police? Sometimes they had good relations with their counterparts in other Latin American countries when diplomats were closing their embassies and political leaders were on the point of declaring war. What was the name of the superintendent who had trailed Julieta to Santo Domingo? Garrote. It might be worth meeting him at the O'Higgins.

How would Julieta and her Indian be travelling, Franco Reyes wondered. Garrote was bound to ask. Not on foot, presumably. By car, bus, train, aeroplane?

Reyes was damn sure Nicole knew more than she was letting

on. Not that she was letting on anything at the moment, because he had stopped speaking to her. Maybe she had masterminded the whole operation, planned the escape, booked air tickets and hotels. Could he scare her into confessing all she knew? Hose her with boiling water? Whip her round the garden with a ringmaster's two-metre lash from one of the circuses? Break all her grandmother's precious plates over her head? No: the maid or the neighbours might call the police and he would find himself without a job, a future or a wife.

Then Reyes thought of the cellar, with its thick oak door that was as good as soundproof. Yes, that's what he would do: he would give the maid a week's holiday, starting on Monday, and as soon as she was out of the house lock Nicole in the cellar and starve her until she confessed.

Reyes' mind was made up: he would work on Nicole. And contact Garrote. He had found a way out of the maze. Not the logical way perhaps, in Nicole's case – more a matter of lateral thinking – but better than sitting bogged down at his desk all day. He rose to his feet, rescued the chocolate cream from the fly and put it in his mouth, knocked back his cherry brandy, relit his cigar, and belched. Then he walked over to the door, removed the cellar key from the rack and put it in his trouser pocket. He would speak to the maid, then wait for Monday to ambush Nicole.

28

There was a rumble like distant thunder from behind Mawi and Julieta as the engine of the articulated lorry sprang into life. They shook hands with Warmi Imambari, the well-educated Andean who had bought their boat, and clambered with their luggage into the cab. Tikamaki, the driver, gently let the clutch in and the lorry pulled away smoothly and quietly from its waterside lay-by, gliding without a tremor over the holes in the dirt road. The only sensation of movement was the cab pulsing as the lorry tugged at the resisting trailer. Mawi and Julieta threw a last glance at the delicate reed bird, her wings folded now like a swan's, that had carried them across the water from danger to their new hope of refuge.

Tikamaki in his boots, jeans and green-check woollen jacket that zipped up at the front was as massive and tongue-tied as Warmi had been small, lean, elegant and articulate. The seat was wide enough for four or five, in spite of Tikamaki's size, and there was enough space between the driver and his two passengers for them to sit in silence without feeling awkward.

Warmi had been waiting for Mawi and Julieta on the quay when they sailed their boat into the harbour at Moho, as if the meeting and sale had been prearranged.

'Do you want to sell your boat?' the young man had asked them without introducing himself. 'I need one exactly like it.'

He had led them briskly in his smart navy-blue trousers and polished black shoes to a ramshackle quayside bar, where they sat down on three boxes at a white plastic table under a Coca-Cola sunshade. Mawi was all set to ask ten per cent more than Julieta had paid for the boat, to recover some of the money she had spent on them both, when Warmi produced a wad of notes from his black leather handbag and made an offer: a thousand *soles*. As this was nearly twenty-five per cent higher than Señor

Achacachi's price, they accepted without a murmur.

'There's just one condition,' said Julieta. 'When you've finished with the boat, we'll buy it back from you.'

'Why do we want it back?' Mawi asked Julieta when Warmi was in the bar buying a round of beers. 'To ferry sick people from the Isla del Sol to the mainland?'

'No, we'll need a fast boat for that. To return it to its rightful owner. The money we paid Señor Achacachi we'll consider as a hire charge.'

Warmi returned with the drinks. 'Where are you heading?' he asked as he sat down on his box.

'Cuzco,' said Julieta. 'My family are there. I've been travelling with my husband. I'm on my way home.'

'How will you get there?' asked Warmi.

'We're going to hitch to the main road, then pick up a coach.'

Warmi pondered this for a moment, then said, 'It could take you two days. And it's not safe: there are bands of armed robbers between here and Cuzco. They hold up buses and pick up hitch-hikers in their cars and rob them. Why not travel by lorry? It will only take you six hours. I have a friend and... fellow-traveller who will take you.' He leant back on his box and called: 'Tikamaki!'

Within minutes Mawi and Julieta had their day arranged for them, and less than an hour after reaching Moho they found themselves on board a lorry bound for Cuzco, with their boat sold and a thousand *soles* in their kitty. Why Warmi should want a reed boat or how this dapper, quick-witted young man came to be a friend and fellow-traveller of a taciturn lorry-driver twenty years older than himself they couldn't imagine.

Julieta nudged Mawi, who was sitting in the middle of the seat. He followed her glance to the three posters fastened to the back of the cab.

'They can't be real,' he thought. 'Even a cow would blush.' The peroxide blondes looked out from behind their false hair, teeth and smiles at a cab that was as clean and simple as Father Lorencio's church, with a smell of lemon and a crucifix hanging above the windscreen.

'What are you carrying?' Julieta asked Tikamaki, to break the silence.

The driver paused before replying, as if the words had to be mined from deep inside him. 'Fruit and vegetables,' he said at last, his voice rumbling like his lorry. After another pause he added: 'Potatoes and maize from the mountains; apples and pears from the lower slopes; papaya, passion-fruit and pineapples from the jungle; oranges, lemons, grapefruit, aubergines and avocados from the coast.'

'All of it for export?' said Julieta.

A pause while Tikamaki dug for more words. 'Most of it for markets in the towns and cities,' he said. 'Some of it for what they call fair trade buyers from abroad.' Another pause for thought. 'I work for a *cooperativa*: growers and sellers part of the same organization. It's good work but there's no money in it. I could earn more driving for a foreign *empresario*.'

'Why don't you?'

'Because foreigners don't pay our growers a fair price, *señora*. They keep them in poverty. Our country is blessed with sunshine and fertile soil but the blessing has been stolen from us to feed the rich countries of the north.'

Now that Tikamaki's convictions had loosened his tongue, Mawi was changing his opinion of him: if he said little, it wasn't because he had nothing to say. Tikamaki's friendship with Warmi started to make sense: the older man obviously hadn't had the same schooling, but he might have a deeper mind than his more polished, more fluent friend.

'You don't like foreign *empresarios*,' said Julieta. 'Nor do we. But you seem to like their women.' She indicated the posters with a glance and a sly smile.

Tikamaki blushed. Mawi had never seen a blush like it: the

whole of Tikamaki's brown face and tree-trunk of a neck turned purple as an aubergine. So deep was his blush that it made Julieta blush too.

'The man's shy,' thought Mawi. 'That's why he finds it hard to start talking. Inside that mountain of a body there's a shy little boy who imagines the little people around him are much bigger than him, and an uneducated man who thinks everyone else is cleverer than he is.'

'I've a wife and four children,' said Tikamaki. He pointed at the curtained bunk above the posters to show where he put the pictures of his family. 'This stuff is wallpaper for the authorities.'

'Authorities?' said Julieta, who seemed determined to tease all the shyness out of the driver. 'Are the authorities crazy for blond wigs and plastic bosoms?'

Tikamaki glanced at his two passengers as if to be sure he could trust them. He seemed trapped between the shame of his posters and the secret they concealed. 'The authorities prefer North American dreams to South American reality,' he said at last. 'You can take a look behind the sham, if you like.'

Julieta hesitated, then unbuckled her seat-belt, knelt and carefully peeled away the synthetic faces and ballooning bosoms from the back of the cab, to which they were stuck with Blu-Tack. Behind the marshmallow mountains of blond hair and pink flesh were smaller black-and-white portraits of faces Mawi had seen before, though he couldn't put a name to them: a middle-aged man with a bushy black and grey beard, wearing a military uniform; a young man, clean-shaven, with black, shoulder-length hair; and a small, emaciated man, with a bald head like a brown egg, peering out wide-eyed from behind a pair of wire-rimmed spectacles.

Julieta recognized them at once and saved Mawi from his ignorance. 'Fidel Castro, Che Guevara and Mahatma Gandhi.'

The people's leaders went back into hiding behind the teeth, breasts and peroxide hair. Mawi buckled Julieta back into her seat-belt.

'The day will come when I don't need to hide their faces,' said Tikamaki. 'When Peru belongs to the Peruvians and people can hang whatever pictures they like in their own homes and in their lorries.'

Tikamaki slowed down for two vicuñas, delicate as fawns, that had strayed on to the road. They realized their danger and leapt back into the scrub like two lithe ballerinas.

'Peru could be an economic and social success story,' Tikamaki went on, 'if our leaders put their trust in Peruvians instead of in foreign banks and businesses.' There was no stopping him now, thought Mawi: the rock had finally been given a big enough push and had started to roll. 'The *cooperativa* I belong to is one of half a dozen that have started up in the Andes. They're working so well that the Government's beginning to get worried.'

'Worried?' said Julieta. 'They should be dancing for joy.'

'They're afraid. They're afraid because the US and others are afraid. They're afraid of Peru standing on its own two feet. Economic success means higher wages. Higher wages means less cheap exports to the rich countries. And they're afraid of what they call the left: of Peru turning into a society that helps the poor, instead of the rich.'

Tikamaki took his foot off the accelerator. The lorry was approaching a road junction, where the dirt road from Moho met the paved highway between Puno and Cuzco. From now on they could expect to be waylaid by gangs of armed robbers at every turn, if Warmi was to be believed.

The plateau they had been crossing since leaving Moho was no more than a wasteland: the backyard into which the gods had thrown their rubble when they worked the miracle of Titicaca and the surrounding peaks. The landscape was becoming more fertile as the road followed a river through a valley between two ranges of high hills. Fields of potatoes, maize, alfalfa, barley and quinoa swept up the hillsides until they met the rocky summits. Settlements of adobe huts with straw roofs were set in the middle of pastureland and were surrounded with adobe walls to keep out the grazing sheep and cattle. These were the crops and herds that fed the rich countries of the world, thought Mawi, while those who owned and cultivated them lived in poverty.

'Hello, there's a police car ahead!' said Tikamaki. 'Two! They've stopped the Puno-to-Cuzco bus. Checking brakes and tyres, very likely.' He slowed down, then pulled out to overtake. 'They're searching inside the bus. I wonder what they're after.'

'Or who they're after,' thought Mawi, as he exchanged a glance with Julieta.

'Warmi and I belong to a movement that has its headquarters in Cuzco,' Tikamaki told his two passengers, while the lorry picked up speed again. 'Not a political movement: we don't want trouble with Lima. Dialogue is what we want, not confrontation. The long-term aim is independence for the Andes but we're not in a hurry: we can wait. We're a peaceful movement. We believe in evolution, not revolution. We've had a couple of marches, without a shout heard or a fist raised. We don't want bombs and guns. We don't cause unrest and strikes. We just want the Andes to be a place where people have enough to eat, learn to read and write, and can see a doctor when they're ill.'

'Do you take recruits?' asked Julieta. 'Can women join?'

Mawi would like to have given Tikamaki's vision the same positive response Julieta gave it. He shared Tikamaki's belief in peaceful change, in the right of the Andeans to a fair wage for their work and to food, education and health care. What he didn't believe was that the authorities would quietly enter into a dialogue with Tikamaki and his fellow-idealists. Mawi was less than half Tikamaki's age but just now he felt years older than him. He remembered the peaceful marches of his own people, who were murdered in their dozens for daring to speak out. Soldiers and police must be much the same in Peru as in Chile.

Tikamaki had never seen what men were capable of when they were given guns and uniforms.

It was Julieta's brainchild that rang true with Mawi, her plan of action, the fruit of her ideals. What was there to excite the barbarity of the soldiers and police in a young woman opening her door to the children of the Isla del Sol, teaching them to read, write and count, and teaching their mothers how to look after their children's health?

Julieta's plan answered a fundamental need in Mawi. For five years his only thought had been of justice after the outrage to his people. Deep in his heart he knew there was little hope of this. He had found himself at a dead-end, struggling against despair. Julieta had taught him that the way forward lay in giving yourself to others and peacefully, patiently helping them to a better life.

Where had she learnt this basic principle of finding happiness for yourself by giving it to others? Not from that monster of a father of hers. From her mother? From nature perhaps: from the bees, who collect nectar to make honey, and in turn carry pollen from anther to stigma, so that the flowers multiply and spread. From her gods? From the Spanish gods of love and gentleness in whose name hundreds of thousands had been tortured and killed? From gods you couldn't see or hear and who never spoke to you? It seemed to Mawi that the Spanish gods were whatever you wanted them to be, created in the image of their worshippers, fashioned by Spaniards with their own cruel or gentle hands, having the true nature of gods only when they were imagined by a Julieta or a Father Lorencio.

Julieta was born with her knowledge, Mawi guessed, just as she was born with the gentleness and beauty he fell in love with – beauty of character, beauty of looks. Her gift was her own but it was inseparable from her womanhood: from an impulse to create, not destroy. Men – Chilean, Spanish, North American men – had been bred for violence, as Spanish bulls are bred for the ring. They had something to learn from Mapuche men, who worked peacefully alongside the women, rethatching the roofs of their *rukas*, making furniture, taking the animals to pasture, while the women looked after the small children, wove, milked the goats and cooked. They cherished their own land and respected other people's; never in their long history had they even trespassed on their neighbours' land. Only when they were threatened with invasion themselves did they take up arms, hoping not to have to use them. When they did fight, they fought fearlessly, outwitting the enemy wherever possible to avoid loss of life.

Tikamaki braked. 'Road-block ahead,' he said. 'The police are out in force today. Break-out, maybe: prisoners on the run.' The lorry slowed to a crawl.

Mawi edged down the seat until his head was below the bottom edge of the windscreen and he was completely hidden from the driver's window by Tikamaki's bulk. Julieta took the cue and did the same. The lorry stopped. They waited.

'They're waving us through,' Tikamaki said at last. The lorry eased forward and slowly started to gather speed.

'How will Warmi help the movement with the boat he's bought from us?' asked Julieta with a catch in her voice. She was obviously trying hard to sound unmoved by road-blocks and police searches.

'Warmi's a special case. He's not a farmer or weaver or fruit-grower. Warmi's a doctor. He's Bolivian, not Peruvian. It makes no difference: we're all Andeans; we were Andeans thousands of years before the Spaniards carved up our land and gave it their own names. When he was a boy, Warmi saw his brothers and sisters, and then his parents, die of diseases that could have been prevented or cured with drugs. Why weren't they? Because his family couldn't afford them. They were sold at prices that made the North American pharmaceutical companies rich but did nothing for ninety-nine per cent of Bolivians. Warmi's a clever operator – was so even as a boy. When he was sixteen, he got a job with one of the foreign companies delivering drugs on his scooter all over the province of La Paz. He made a careful note of the ingredients on the packets of drugs he delivered. After four years he'd saved enough to pay for his training as a doctor at Lima University. Now he travels to Lima once a month to buy the chemicals from his friends at the university labs. He takes them to Bolivia, makes the medicines himself and sells them at a quarter of the price the foreign companies charge. He's been getting the ingredients across the border at one of the frontier crossings in compost and fertilizer bags, but the customs officials are starting to get suspicious… Those houses and church towers five kilometres ahead: that's Cuzco.'

They had almost made it, thought Mawi. He and Julieta had left Santiago a week ago. They had been on the move ever since, giving police and soldiers the slip, travelling by bus, donkey, boat and lorry to reach Julieta's relatives, whose home town now lay within view. Their luck would surely hold for the last thirty or forty minutes of their journey.

'That's why Warmi needs the boat,' Tikamaki went on. 'He'll sail it into Bolivia once or twice a week with a group of sightseers on board and the chemicals hidden in the fish's head at the bow of the boat and the tail at the stern. He only makes a two per cent profit on what he sells but, because he'll soon have half the population of Bolivia buying their medicines from him, the chances are he'll end up richer than the pharmaceutical companies. He's promised to start a hospital, or even a chain of hospitals, with some of the profits. Warmi's a drug dealer with a difference. The world needs more drug dealers like Warmi.'

On the outskirts of Cuzco Tikamaki slowed down. A dozen or more lorries, a few battered vans and a couple of jalopies were parked on a lot fifty metres ahead. He pulled off the road and docked alongside one of the other lorries.

'This is a drivers' halt,' he said, switching off the ignition. 'It's also where our movement holds its meetings.' He opened his door and swung his huge frame effortlessly out of the cab.

The parking area was bordered on the south-east side behind them by a hill covered in pine-trees. On the far side of the lot from the road was a refuelling centre for lorries and their drivers: filling-station, bar and restaurant in one. Most of the paint had peeled from the row of antique pumps in front of the building, leaving more rust than metal, but their lighted dials showed that they were still in service. A big shed made of breeze-blocks and corrugated metal stood immediately behind the bar and restaurant and had the look of a repair hangar for lorries.

Mawi could feel that Julieta longed to get to her grandparents'. He didn't want to delay but Tikamaki had given them a six-hour lift in his comfortable cab and the least they could do was buy him a drink.

Julieta opened the passenger door. The air was abuzz with conversation from the bar. Mawi started down the metal steps after her with the bags but froze when he glanced into the wing-mirror.

'What is it?' asked Julieta.

'Don't look round but there's someone lying in the wood behind us pointing what looks like a gun in our direction.'

'A hunter?'

'What do you hunt in a car park?'

'Jaguars?' Julieta said, biting her lip. '...Perhaps it's just a fallen branch.'

'Painted khaki and brown to match the other branches?' thought Mawi. 'Maybe I only imagined it.' He followed Julieta and Tikamaki across the car park towards the reassuring crush, and the image quickly faded, like a dream at the moment of waking.

Forty pairs of men's eyes turned to stare at Julieta when she opened the glass door and walked into the brick and linoleum bar. The icon of these long-distance drivers' imaginations as they journeyed through the night on lonely passes and hairpin bends high in the Andes had apparently stepped out of their heads and made their fantasies a reality. Mawi put his arm round his wife's shoulders.

More lorries were berthing in the parking area. Jalopies and battered vans were arriving. There would soon be a gridlock at the bar, so Mawi and Julieta bought drinks for Tikamaki and themselves and headed for a corner away from the hubbub.

Many of the newcomers were women, all of them wrapped in shawls and ponchos to protect them against the cool evening air. Some had babies cocooned in a second shawl on their backs, looking solemnly at the world out of large, curious eyes. Mawi guessed these were the fruit- and vegetable-growers and weavers Tikamaki had been telling them about.

There was a movement towards the door next to the bar, with the usual jam when fifty people try to get through a narrow space at the same time.

'I'm off,' said Tikamaki. 'I have to pick up produce from over twenty points in the Cuzco area. You don't need to go. There's a guest speaker at tonight's meeting. Why not stay?'

Julieta gave their friend a hug. Mawi shook his hand warmly. The big, friendly bear stepped his way gingerly through the crowd to the glass door and disappeared into the dusk.

Mawi and Julieta were less impatient to get to her relatives now and were curious to learn a bit more about the cause Tikamaki believed in. They joined the throng at the bar and waited their turn for the door.

The lorry hospital had been stripped of metal body parts and scrubbed clean of all but the most resistant oil stains. It had more the look of a schoolroom than a garage. Rows of benches without backs faced a dais where two chairs and a table with a lectern were set out for tonight's speakers. A bottle of spring-water and two glasses had been placed on the table. The lecture-hall was lit with strip-lighting. Butane heaters sent out waves of warm air.

A woman of about thirty wearing jeans and a white smock was standing at the bottom of the steps leading up to the dais, talking to an elderly nun wearing a grey habit and carrying a book. The benches were filling with the broad, dark brown faces and round, black eyes of Quechuan men and women, all of them cleanly turned out, the women in their long skirts and shawls or ponchos, their hair tied in a single plait worn either in front or behind, the men, including the lorry-drivers, in jeans and polished black shoes, and spotless shirts under their ponchos.

Mawi and Julieta sat on a bench at the back of the hall, to be able to slip out, if necessary, before the end of the meeting.

The nun and the younger woman climbed on to the dais, the audience applauded and the nun sat down. The younger woman introduced her guest in a strong, warm voice, speaking Castilian so as to be understood by the nun and Quechua out of respect for her audience. She had the face of a *mestiza*: half Spanish and half Quechuan.

'Sister Thérèse has lived for the past sixty years in the poorest areas of Lima,' she told her audience, 'in El Alto and El Salvador, where she and a small group of Franciscan helpers cook and provide medical care for some of the two million poor who live there in shanties made of cardboard – food, medicine, but also friendship and hope. Sister Thérèse has travelled all the way from Lima specially to talk to us on a subject that has troubled some of you. She has called her talk *Communism and Christ*.'

She turned to Sister Thérèse, who got stiffly to her feet. The audience rose with her spontaneously and broke into applause. The nun walked with the stiffness of age to the table, put her book on the lectern and smiled down broadly and kindly at her audience. She was tall and stooping, probably in her early eighties, with at least one wrinkle for each of her years. She started by blessing everyone in the room, speaking Spanish with a slight foreign accent. Her voice was weak with age but there was a brightness in her eyes, and conviction and authority in her words. The audience listened without a rustle or murmur. When she had finished her blessing, they followed the younger woman's example and sat down quietly.

Communism had a sinister ring, Sister Thérèse told her listeners, not because of the social and ethical ideal the word represented but because of the reality those in power in most Communist countries had made of the ideal: enslavement of the mind instead of freedom of expression and worship, fear instead of confidence, oppression instead of brotherhood. In the Soviet Union millions of innocent people had been sent to their deaths by Stalin, for no better reason than his paranoid fear of personal disloyalty or of opposition to the régime. China and Albania were as far from the Communist ideal as the Soviet Union.

Sister Thérèse had studied the minutes of past meetings of the Andean movement and found nothing to suggest a tendency towards the totalitarianism of the Soviet Union, China, North Korea and Albania. She was reassured by the independent-mindedness of the areas surrounding Cuzco: clusters of villages organizing themselves into co-operatives willing to collaborate with one another but opposed to the centralization of many Communist régimes.

'It's a social structure that leads to fellowship, peace and a respect for man and nature. If you doubt me, take a look at the way the Mapuche, an indigenous people of what is now Chile, organize themselves. The Mapuche are a federation of independent communities. They hold elections every year to choose their leaders and representatives. Their land is fertile and their animals are well looked after. The Mapuche offer us a model of egalitarian practice, social harmony, and harmony with the seasons and the soil.'

Mawi felt himself blush. He was so used to being treated as a pariah in Chile that praise for his people produced a shock of pleasure. He glanced left and right. Only Julieta seemed aware that he was one of Sister Thérèse's chosen people. She smiled and slipped her hand into Mawi's. The thought that had first occurred to him in Arica appeared again in sharper relief: the place to look for recognition and justice for the Mapuche people was not behind the mountains and barbed wire and media silence that guarded fortress Chile but abroad, in other Latin American countries and on other continents.

Warmth from the heater two metres away spread through Mawi's body, and with it a feeling of contentment. For the first time for years he felt secure, part of a group, an equal among equals. And at his side, her hand resting in his, was the girl whose love for him was as infinite as his for her. Mawi's eyelids began to feel heavy. He had been on the go for thirty-six hours, walking the length of the Isla del Sol twice, racing to escape capture by a *guardia,* sailing a boat across Lake Titicaca and riding on a lorry for six hours. He straightened his back and willed himself to follow the thread of the lecture, which had led back over two thousand years to a desert region of Ancient Palestine.

'Hidden among the dunes was a monastery where a community of Jews called the Essenes lived,' Sister Thérèse was saying. 'The Essenes were weary of the endless occupation of their homeland by Assyrians, Romans and others and retired to the desert away from the fanaticism of some of their fellow-Jews to live a life of peace and brotherhood. The teachings of the Essenes are close to those of our Lord. He almost certainly spent part of his life among them.'

Sister Thérèse paused to put on the pair of wire-rimmed spectacles she wore on a chain round her neck and opened the book she had placed on the lectern. During the silence Mawi's sharp ears caught a man's voice outside the hangar, quiet as a breath of wind. Normally the noise would have woken him from his drowsiness in an instant and put him on his guard, but he felt too secure in this crowd of good-hearted Andeans to give it more than a few moments' thought. Probably a lorry-driver talking to himself as he checked his oil level or topped up with water.

'The book I have here describes the life of the Essenes,' Sister Thérèse went on. 'The author is the philosopher Philo, a Greek Jew who was born twenty years before Our Lord and died twenty years after his crucifixion and resurrection.' She read from the book:

' *"The Essenes share their possessions and pool everything they earn. The sick are cared for and, if they can't work, are fed and clothed at the expense of the community. The old are looked after and, even if they are childless, feel as if they were surrounded by their children and grandchildren. The Essenes farm, keep bees and work as shepherds, cowherds, artisans and craftsmen. They make no weapons. There are no masters and no slaves. The Essenes practise fraternity and equality. They believe that brotherhood is the natural relationship among human beings and that this relationship is destroyed by commercial competitiveness and greed."* '

Sister Thérèse closed her book, took off her glasses and let them hang from their chain. She looked down at her audience and smiled.

'Theologians argue that Christ's teaching owes much to the Essenes,' she said. 'What is the Essene way of life but Communism in its purest form? Some of you are troubled because you have heard that a Communist can't at the same time be a Christian. I tell you you can't be a true Christian if you are not also a Communist.'

This was as much of the talk as Mawi heard. As he fell asleep, he felt Sister Thérèse's love for humanity and not for the first time found himself baffled by a religion that could produce followers as barbaric as the conquerors of South America and as gentle as Sister Thérèse and Julieta.

There it was again! Lying in the shadows of the pines. The khaki and brown branch with eyes and a blackened face and the barrel of a gun pointing at Julieta and himself. When Mawi had seen it earlier, he had suppressed his instincts and feelings. Now, seeing it in his dream, he was gripped by fear.

He was woken by an insistent patting on his arm.

'She's giving her blessing and then she's finished,' Julieta whispered. 'The other one's going to drive her to the airport for her flight back to Lima. My grandparents live the other side of the airport. She might give us a lift home. If we stay here, we'll be stuck in the crowd. Let's go outside and wait by the cars.'

Mawi and Julieta got up and tiptoed to the back of the hall and into the bar. Opening the glass door was like stepping under a cold shower. They took their ponchos from their bags and put them on. The sky was a sheet of navy-blue ice, fringed at the horizon with orange.

'Perhaps it's too soon to go back to the Isla del Sol,' said Julieta as they walked towards the cars.

Mawi looked at her questioningly.

'Wouldn't you like to be part of this movement? Helping build a fairer society for the people of the Andes? A society where they're not marginalized and exploited?'

Mawi was doubtful. 'My people wanted a fairer society for themselves. They marched peacefully through the streets of Temuco and were massacred.'

'What are you saying? That the poor should sit and let the rich exploit them? Should accept their poverty without complaint and hope for a miracle? If the poor wait for a change of heart in the rich, they'll be waiting for all eternity.'

'And if they do too much too soon, they'll be destroyed. The people here are sitting on a time-bomb. The Government's against them. So is the Church. Your idea of a school and medical centre on the Isla del Sol stands a better chance of success: of growing quietly, invisibly from a seed into a tree.'

Mawi and Julieta came to a row of parked cars. A series of explosions caused them to spin round, then instinctively duck down beside an old Chevrolet. They had a glimpse of three or four jets of flame from the wood behind them. Guns: several of them. Not sporting rifles, these, not with bangs as big as that. Grenade- or rocket-launchers.

Another explosion, so loud this time that Mawi and Julieta clapped their hands to their ears and threw themselves to the ground. When they looked up, the lecture-hall was ablaze, there was a large hole in the wall and part of the roof had collapsed. Shouts and screams lashed at their ear-drums. A baby was howling. The flames spread. The screams turned from alarm to agony and there were yells of 'No!' and 'God!'

Julieta got up. Tears were pouring down her face. 'We've got to help them,' she shouted.

Mawi scrambled to his feet. As he did so, the near wall of the lecture-hall collapsed. The heat from the flames inside, even at thirty metres, was so intense that Mawi and Julieta tore across the parking area away from the fire to avoid being burnt. They crouched down in the shelter of a van, only a few metres from the fuel pumps. The screams from the burning building had grown more desperate and a smell of burning flesh filled the air.

Mawi and Julieta heard a click behind them and looked round. A man in combats was standing with his face in shadow, a revolver in his hand.

'Get up!' he said, quietly in Spanish. He had a North American accent.

Mawi and Julieta stood up. The man took several steps towards them. His face was now lit by the flames.

Julieta gave a gasp.

'Here's a couple of birds I didn't expect to bag this afternoon,' the North American said with a grin.

'Herman Gorringe,' murmured Julieta.

'We'd better shift,' the man said. 'We're standing on five thousand litres of motor fuel.'

29

A tall, blond lieutenant in his early twenties sat in Major Adolfo Cortez' shoebox office, blinded by sunlight, trying not to blink, receiving a dressing-down from the senior officer, who sat in the shade watching his prey trapped in the threads of his web.

Lieutenant Manuel Görisch was Chilean by birth but Hispanic only on his mother's side. His father had emigrated from Germany in 1945, to avoid the embarrassment and inconvenience of answering questions from British and other investigators into the activities of the Third Reich. Lieutenant Görisch thought of himself as Chilean, when he thought at all, had never been to Germany but had inherited his father's looks and height and been drilled to speak German and yell and raise his right arm in salute twice a day, at sun-up and sundown, to the fylfot draped above the altar in the family chapel.

Major Cortez' complaint was entirely fabricated. Lieutenant Görisch was beyond reproach as an officer. Cortez had had to rack his brains to think of something, and had come up with some nonsense about arrangements for the inter-regimental football tournament being behind schedule. How credulous and guilt-ridden the young officer was! He wouldn't dream of denying the spurious charge. The Germans were born to obey.

Major Cortez had a craving for Lieutenant Görisch. He couldn't get him out of his head. He imagined him sitting opposite him at table whenever he dined alone at the luxurious villa he had inherited from his Chilean grandfather, on the terrace overlooking the ocean; he even lit the candles and opened a bottle of vintage wine in his honour. At night, Lieutenant Görisch lay chastely to attention in Major Cortez' thoughts, stark naked on the opposite side of the bed. The major decided the only way to stop himself going mad was to meet the lieutenant face to face at an interview, no matter on what pretext.

The only fantasies Cortez reproached himself for were the ones following his decision to interview Görisch. They would have to be whispered in God's ear at the next of his increasingly rare visits to the confessional. The interview had been planned in his imagination down to the smallest detail. In the top right-hand drawer of his desk, next to the Bible, would be secreted a sturdy wooden chair-leg. The major would reduce the blond lieutenant to a state of abject guilt and remorse, then invite him to kneel with him and recite the Nunc Dimittis. Major Cortez would take the Bible from his desk, being sure to leave the drawer open. The lieutenant would kneel and close his eyes. Reading from his Bible, the major would rise to his feet, remove the chair-leg from the drawer, walk over to the lieutenant and club him over the back of the head with it, concussing him for a good fifteen minutes. No mess, no noise. Major Cortez would go quickly to the door, lock it and close the shutter over the spy-hole. He would return, unfasten and lower the lieutenant's khaki trousers and unzip his own. Having done his business, he would adjust his own and the unconscious lieutenant's dress, sit him on his chair, open the shutter, unlock the door and wait for the junior officer to regain consciousness. When he did so, the major would express concern. 'Dear me, Görisch, are you not feeling well? You seem to have had a black-out. Would you like me to call a doctor?' 'No, no, sir. I'm perfectly all right. I do apologize. It must be the pickled herring I had for supper last night. Seems to have inflamed my lower intestine.'

Fantasy had remained fantasy. There was no chair-leg in the right-hand drawer of the desk. All the chair-frames were made of steel or aluminium. The only object in the room suitable for whacking was the fly-swatter. If Cortez hit Görisch over the head with this, the lieutenant would be surprised but not concussed.

It wasn't the major's moral scruples that stopped him turning fantasy into reality: these were threadbare after nearly a decade in the services. He was paralysed by a memory: of his German grandfather the day the *Kommandant* had caught him alone in his bedroom at the age of fifteen experimenting with his new-found sexuality; of being flogged with a leather strop, then dragged across the landing to the bathroom, where the old man had thrust his grandson's head into the unflushed lavatory and pulled the chain; of being sent to the Augustinians for two months to be purged of his bodily needs, then on a cadet course to have his testosterone converted into nitroglycerine and gunpowder. At the end of it all Adolfo Cortez still had a body, and therefore bodily needs. He had simply learnt to feel disgust: disgust at most of what went into the human body; disgust at the sewage that came out, even if it was sweat, spit, blood or semen. The mess of the sexual act he found repellent. He might still enjoy copulation if it could be dehydrated – sex through a pea-shooter – but scientists had apparently not yet managed to do for the sexual act what they had done for sweet and sour pork with noodles. Until they did, Major Cortez would go on getting his thrills in another way: from pain, the infliction of it, sometimes on himself, more often on others. The trouble was, pain was often messy too. And noisy. Why couldn't thumbs be cut off without all the blood and screaming? Why couldn't people suffer in silence – communicate their suffering only through their eyes? It was not so much physical as psychological pain that excited Major Cortez. He was working on ways of inflicting pain cleanly and quietly.

The major's experiments with Lieutenant Görisch were showing promising results. The lieutenant was sitting bolt upright on the edge of his chair, racked at the thought of having been remiss in the discharge of his duties, blinking like an owl in a cage, unable to see his tormentor. The major was enjoying the experience as much as grosser men might enjoy pot-holing their way through Lieutenant Görisch's alimentary canal.

Desire was getting the better of the major's usual caution. If he ordered Görisch to strip naked, he wondered, would the younger officer be fool enough to obey. Of course he would. He was programmed to obey. A Spanish American lieutenant would storm out of the room in disgust. But not this blond Adonis. He would undress by numbers with the same precision that he performed his drill, lay his clothes neatly on the chair, then stand to attention while Major Cortez ran his fingers over the young man's torso and down his thighs.

What if the other officers got to hear about it? Major Cortez would be lynched or court-marshalled by guilt-ridden homophobes making their imprudent fellow-officer the scapegoat for their own secret cravings. What acceptable reason could he give them for ordering the lieutenant to remove his clothes during an interview? Could a doctor be bribed to say the major had medical qualifications? Then it dawned on Major Cortez: there were no witnesses. If the lieutenant blabbed, Cortez' word was as good as Görisch's – better, thanks to his age and rank. 'You're telling me I ordered Görisch to undress? The young man's fantasizing. Hallucinating. He must be disciplined.'

Major Cortez was on the point of getting up, locking the door and ordering the lieutenant out of his clothes when there was a shuffling outside the office, a fumbling for the handle and the sound of panting. The door swung open and in stumbled Franco Reyes, perspiring.

'They've found them!' he blurted out.

'Get— !' For a moment the major's steely self-control nearly snapped. He recovered quick as a viper, and hid his fangs. He paused for his blood to run cold again, then fixed a gaze full of venom on Reyes' face and hissed: 'I'm in the middle of an interview, Señor Reyes. Would you mind waiting outside till I've finished?'

'What? Oh, right.'

'Bumbling idiot,' thought Cortez when the intruder had stumbled back out. 'Picked up some rumour about that slut of a daughter of his and comes shambling round to me, so that he's got an excuse for coffee and cream cakes at the O'Higgins.'

'I think I've made my point about the tournament,' Cortez told Görisch. 'The interview is terminated.'

'Thank you, sir.' The lieutenant jumped up, half-raised his arm in front of him in the salute he had learnt from his father, quickly corrected it to the one he had been trained to give, and left the room, closing the door smartly behind him.

Cortez kept Reyes waiting two or three minutes, then got up and opened the door.

'Sorry to barge in like that, old chap,' Reyes brayed as he came back into the room. 'Couldn't wait to tell you the news.'

'Do sit down!' Cortez said curtly. He shut the door and returned to his desk.

Reyes sat and was at once blinded by the sun. He shifted his chair five or six centimetres but was still blinded. He resigned himself to being baked in his suit like a jacket potato, and blinded with it.

'They've found them,' Reyes repeated.

'I suppose you mean your daughter and her companion.' He sat down.

'Her kidnapper. Of course.'

'Who found them?'

'Herman Gorringe. Pure chance. He was with a contingent of US Marines helping the Peruvian army contain a Communist uprising in Cuzco. Damn nearly contained my daughter while they were about it. Her kidnapper turns out to be not only an Indian but a Communist with it.'

'I thought we knew that already.'

'Forced her to go to some kind of meeting. They left moments before the troops went in. Gorringe nabbed them just as they were about to drive off in the Indian's car.'

'Where are they now?'

'Gorringe is putting them on a flight to Santiago.'

'I'll make sure my men are at the airport to meet them.'

The Indian was going to pay for this, thought Cortez. He had made a fool of the major and his plans for a wife who would have added glamour to his image and ensured his speedy promotion. And he had cost the army an arm and a leg in their search for him.

'I say, this hasn't changed your intentions so far as Julieta's concerned, has it, Cortez?'

The same old question. Marry an Indian's whore and be the laughing-stock of his regiment and the whole of Santiago? If she weren't Reyes' daughter, he would arrest her too. There was nothing he would enjoy more than watching her being gang-banged by the regiment, or satisfying the sexual needs of the guard-dogs at the women's jail.

'Has it occurred to you, Señor Reyes, that your daughter may have left Santiago of her own free will?' the major asked brusquely.

Reyes took umbrage. 'Leave home with an Indian? And a Communist with it? Julieta? I'd strangle her with my own hands.'

Cortez smiled to himself. No need for guard-dogs or the regiment. Leave it to Father.

'She was kidnapped, I tell you. Abducted.' Reyes lashed out with his right arm: he had identified his daughter's kidnapper with the sun in his eyes. 'By an Indian!' He swung his fist at the sunlight, nearly smashing the window-pane. 'And a Communist!' Another punch. 'If I lay my hands on him, I'll— I'll— I'll—' Reyes was gnashing his teeth and clawing with his hands. 'I'll cut off his balls.'

'Why don't you leave that to my men?' Cortez said calmly and quietly. 'They've had plenty of experience. They'll do it without any fuss.' And they would hold the parts in question in a candle flame for five minutes before cutting them off, while Cortez watched the Indian's face from a soundproof room and relished the agony in his eyes. 'Government ministers gelding Indians attracts public attention. You don't want any more publicity for your daughter, do you?'

Reyes got up, which at once solved the problem of the blinding sunlight. 'You're a good man, Cortez,' he said, advancing towards the desk. 'Thinking of my feelings, and Julieta's, when you've so many other things on your mind.'

Cortez stayed sitting and looked up at Reyes as if he were asking the waiter for the bill. 'If you give me the flight number and arrival time, my men will roll out the red carpet for her at the airport.'

When Cortez had noted down the information Reyes gave him, he got up, went over to the door and held it open for Reyes to leave.

'All this worry must have given you an appetite,' said Major Cortez. 'Why don't you walk over to the Café O'Higgins and order a meringue or two and a coffee topped with whipped cream?'

Reyes stumbled out. Cortez closed the door, returned to his desk and removed the fly-swatter from its hook on the wall.

Marry Reyes' daughter? If it were proved beyond all doubt, broadcast on every channel and published in every newspaper that she had left Santiago against her will and that the Indian had kept his hands off her? Who would believe a story like that?

He swatted the fly that had been irritating him, took the stunned insect to the window, pulled off its wings and allowed the body to fall to the pavement below.

30

Mawi and Julieta were squeezed into a seven-seater, four-wheel-drive Chrysler station-wagon as it steered a course between pot-holes and precipices and negotiated hundred-and-eighty-degree hairpin bends on an unmade road that climbed two thousand metres, dropped two thousand metres, then climbed them again while it improvised its way, or seemed to, coastwards across the mountains from Cuzco. The technicolour sky as the sun was setting – bright orange modulating to apricot, then to lemon, pale blue, lavender and mauve – had given way to monochrome and moonlight. There was always a precipice on one side or the other – a wall of rock dropping anything from a few hundred to two or three thousand metres: a nightmare by day for anyone with no head for heights; bearable by moonlight, when night filled the chasms with solid darkness.

Vertigo and iridescent skies were far from Julieta's thoughts as she sat in the back seat of the Chrysler shoulder to shoulder with the US Marine on her right. Mawi was in the middle seat, sandwiched between two more Marines. Herman Gorringe was sitting in front, on the passenger side. A fourth Marine was driving. The car was unmarked but the Marines were still in camouflage gear, having got out of Cuzco fast: blackened faces, khaki and brown whirls on their peaked caps and jackets and on the trousers tucked into their boots. There was no question of escape: there were no doors behind the middle seat, three of the four Marines carried machine-guns and, even if they all fell asleep, Herman Gorringe had a revolver which he had been cleaning and reloading.

Julieta's thoughts were not for her own safety. They were not even for Mawi's. They were with the men, women and children at the meeting in Cuzco, all of them burnt to death by the killers with whom she was forced to share a car: with Sister Thérèse, who had dedicated her life to helping the poor of Lima; with the younger woman, who held the audience with her strong voice and her ideals, her defiant smile and her mixture of indigenous and Spanish American good looks, and who perhaps had a husband and young children; with the lorry-drivers, farmers, fruit-growers and weavers, who had very probably worked fourteen hours a day seven days a week to earn just enough to stop themselves and their families from starving, and from freezing to death during the Andean nights for want of clothing and fuel. These people had died in agony for wanting a society free of injustice and inequality. Who had carried out the killing? Lackeys of the White House and Pentagon, self-styled champions of justice and democracy, gangsters posing as keepers of the peace. Once Rome, the Middle Ages, Genghis Khan, the massacre of the Cathars in France, the conquest of the Americas and the Thirty Years' War had been the extremes by which barbarity was measured. Today it was the twentieth century.

From where she was sitting at the back of the car Julieta had a clear view until nightfall of Herman Gorringe's head two rows in front. There was a time when his copper hair, broken nose, strong jaw and powerful build had suggested avuncular good humour. Then Jekyll turned Hyde, and teddy bear became crocodile. Now, when Gorringe turned to the driver or looked over his shoulder and grinned, Julieta wished the crocodile back. Crocodiles were more ethical: they killed only to eat. Instead she saw a human male – a man who earned his living by killing fellow-humans in cold blood. Julieta would like to be able to look at the copper hair and thick neck and pray for a repeat of Paul's experience on the road to Damascus. But pray to what or whom? To a god who allowed a roomful of good-hearted, innocent people to be burnt alive? If she prayed for anything, it would be for Gorringe to be struck dead by a heart attack; unfortunately his heart seemed to beat as confidently at four thousand metres as it did at sea level in Santiago.

The ad hoc rule Julieta had made for herself when she was pushed into the car at Cuzco was to keep her mouth shut. To speak to her captors was to grant them some kind of legitimacy. The best they deserved was for the driver to misjudge a bend and take the car over the edge of a precipice. She and Mawi would die with them, of course, but they were probably going to die anyway – machine-gunned by their North American guards at some remote spot between Cuzco and wherever the car was heading.

But to keep quiet was to give the Marines the idea that she understood no English and allow herself to be the butt of their salacious remarks. Gorringe could have spared her the unpleasantness by letting them know she understood every word they spoke, but he said nothing.

'When are we going to pull over for a break, chief?' asked the Marine on Julieta's right. 'Me and the guys are waiting to shag this good-looking Hispanic bird.'

'Sorry, buddy, no go,' replied Gorringe. 'I got to get her back to her dad unspoiled.'

'Unspoiled? You reckon she hasn't already been spoiled by the Red Indian jerk?'

Julieta clenched her fists and bit her lip to stop the rush of invective with which she longed to purge this cesspit on wheels. How the Marines' feet smelt! Even through their thick boots. She didn't know which she found more disgusting: their language or their feet.

After a silence of an hour or more Gorringe took it into his head to launch an attack on Mawi, who had been as silent as Julieta since their capture at Cuzco. Whether he thought Mawi spoke English or knew he didn't understand a word of the language was uncertain.

'What's a Commie Indian bastard like you doing with a respectable white girl?' he asked. When Mawi didn't reply, Gorringe went on: 'Your tribe short of squaws, sonny, or do you make a habit of abducting girls racially and socially superior to yourself?'

Julieta could contain herself no longer. Putting muscle into her voice, so that she could be heard from the back above the noise of the engine, she said to Herman Gorringe in impeccable English: 'Commie bastard? My husband is a hundred times more of a democrat than you are. He didn't abduct me. I left Santiago of my own free will. If he's a bastard, what does that make a mass murderer like you?'

There was a silence of several seconds. Julieta had the small gratification of sensing the discomfiture of the Marine sitting with his shoulder pressed against hers, who now knew the Hispanic bird on his left spoke English as well as he did, and was a married woman, like his own mother perhaps.

There was an explosion of laughter from Gorringe. 'Democrat? What's a democrat doing with his broad at a meeting of Commie subversives?'

'An elderly nun telling a group of local farmers, weavers and fruit-growers about the influence of a religious community two thousand years ago on the teachings of Jesus Christ? Do you call that subversive?'

'That's how it starts. You get the blessing of God and the Church, then you go blowing up trains, bridges, factories, ships, aeroplanes.'

'Which means less caviar and champagne for US businessmen and shareholders. I can't think of a better way of encouraging terrorism than murdering a hundred innocent people at a community meeting. That's when the poor say goodbye to non-violence and start planting bombs. If I had a brother, sister, husband, father at that meeting, I'd be out there myself blowing up trains, ships and aeroplanes.'

There was another silence, this time lasting ten or fifteen minutes. The Marines might still be queuing to shag Julieta but they were queuing in silence. She even sensed their respect for her. Julieta was indifferent to it. The respect of killers was something she could do without. Their obscenities of earlier on no longer stung. These men were outside God and nature. They inhabited a hell that would always set them apart from the rest of creation.

Julieta wanted to ask Herman Gorringe where she and Mawi were being taken but to do so would be to sanction Gorringe's right to be taking them anywhere. Instead, she said: 'We've been on the road for more than two hours. If you're planning to shoot us, why not do it now? You won't find a remoter spot than this.'

Gorringe exploded into laughter again. 'Shoot you? What kind of a dumb-bell do you take me for? You want me to trigger an international crisis? Every US citizen would be kicked out of Chile. The mines would be nationalized. Wall Street would collapse. The President of the United States would geld me with his own hands. I'd wind up driving a cab or hanging around street corners picking up fags. No, lady, I got to get you back to your daddy free of bullet-holes. What happens to Túpac Amaru here doesn't bother me. I guess Chilean Intelligence are drooling to give him the high voltage treatment, so I'll just put him and you on the same flight from Lima.'

A flight from Lima to Santiago. The wheels of Julieta's ingenuity started to turn. A bomb scare in mid-air, forcing them to turn back to Lima? If she and Mawi had weapons, they could disconnect the radio, hijack the plane to some remote jungle airstrip and disappear among the rubber plants and raffia palms.

The road had given up its daredevil, cliff-hanging character for the time being and was making its way across the flattened crown of a mountain between moonlit verges of snow that probably never melted. They rounded a bend and saw a dilapidated filling-station in the moonlight five hundred metres ahead. The pump lights were on. So was a light in the stone cabin next to the pump, and smoke was rising from the chimney. The headlamps revealed a sign a hundred metres ahead: on it was scrawled the word *queso*.

'Food and fuel stop!' Gorringe shouted from the front seat.

The Marine on Julieta's right, who had been snoring quietly with his head slumped away from her against the window, woke up with a jolt and blurted out: 'McDonalds?'

Herman Gorringe guffawed. 'That's right, buddy,' he said. 'You just jump out, if you can find a door, and buy us each a Big Mac with mustard and relish.'

'Reckon they have Coke, chief?' asked the driver.

The road dipped and the stone hut disappeared from view. The station-wagon pulled up. Two Marines stayed to guard Mawi and Julieta while the other two each grabbed a bundle of clothes from their kit, leapt out and stripped down to their underpants. Julieta glanced at the thermometer on the dashboard: twelve degrees Fahrenheit. Minus eleven Celsius she reckoned after a few seconds' mental arithmetic. The first two Marines returned to the car in civvies, and the other two leapt out with their bundles. Gorringe stepped into the snow and unhurriedly removed his camouflage jacket and trousers: underneath he was wearing his copper-coloured suit. In less than three minutes the station-wagon was on its way again. Gorringe's fellow-killers sat with their crew cuts in their crumpled blue suits and patent leather black shoes, their faces scoured red with snow, shivering as they waited for the shock of the cold air to wear off. They had the lean, muscular physique of plain-clothes bodyguards and the off-the-peg look of insurance salesmen. The smell of feet was stronger than ever.

The car stopped at the filling-station. A Quechua wearing a poncho, gloves, and a *chullo* to keep his head and ears warm, opened the door of the hut and peered at the car. A goat looked out after him but decided to stay in the warm. The Indian stepped outside and closed the door.

'You got eats?' asked Gorringe when the Quechua had filled the tank. 'Chow? Nosh?'

The Indian looked blank.

Gorringe pointed at his own mouth.

'¿Comida? Sí, señor.'

The guards formed pairs again and took it in turns to go to the cabin. Mawi and Julieta were offered food and drink but shook their heads. Gorringe and the Marines returned with slices of goat's cheese on chunks of home-made bread.

The guard on Mawi's left took over the driving and they got under way again, bumping over stones and lurching in and out of pot-holes.

'What in hell is this? A soap sandwich?' asked Gorringe after he had taken several bites of bread and cheese. 'It's a soap sandwich. Did you get your Coke?'

'No, chief,' replied the first driver, who was now sitting next to Mawi. 'Goat's milk.'

'Soapy water,' said Gorringe. 'Soap sandwich washed down with soapy water. What can you expect for twenty cents?'

The temperature dropped as the night advanced. Snow still lined the road, left over from a snowfall perhaps weeks or months ago. The heater was on full but the warm air didn't reach the back of the car. Julieta rearranged her poncho but remained cold. She longed to be beside Mawi and burrow into him for warmth.

The back of Mawi's head was only fifty centimetres from Julieta's hands. She could tell from the breathing next to her that her guard was asleep. She reached out with one hand and stroked Mawi's hair. He half-turned his head. This little gesture sent a thrill through Julieta that warmed and reassured her, and she fell asleep.

In her dream she was the prisoner of her father, under house arrest at home in Santiago. Copihue had been sacked. Mawi was in prison. Julieta begged to be allowed to visit him but her father refused. She was to be married to Adolfo Cortez. The wedding-day was approaching. She went to her mother's bedroom and took a bottle of sleeping-pills from the drawer. The doorbell rang. She knew it was Cortez, come to claim his bride. She reached for the pills – and woke.

The ringing in Julieta's dream was not the chimes at home but the church bells of Puquio calling the faithful to early mass. The little town the killers and their captives were driving through was almost empty. The faithful were few and old. The rest obviously preferred to stay warm in bed. No hope of rescue in Puquio.

The sky in front of them as they left the town was black but Julieta could see the pale orange and yellowy green of dawn reflected in one of the wing mirrors. There were no silhouettes of high mountains ahead and the road was dropping steadily, so she reckoned they must be getting near the coast. It was no comfort to Julieta to be leaving the mountains and the night behind: daylight and the coast brought her and Mawi inexorably nearer to Lima, the airport and the flight back to Santiago.

Suddenly the lurching stopped. For hundreds of kilometres they had been bumping along a dirt road full of pot-holes; now they were on tarmac. After the unconscious strain of being buffeted hour after hour, the relief was better than a feather-bed, and Julieta fell into a deep sleep.

She was woken by heat and bright light. The heater was off, the windows were open, the tropical sun was beating down on the roof. Julieta was suffocating in her poncho. She tried to take it off but her neck was so stiff from leaning as far away from the guard as possible that she had to wait for it to unjam. She got the poncho off at last, rolled it up and put it behind her head as a cushion.

Mawi was in his shirtsleeves, holding his poncho. Julieta longed to reach out and stroke his hair again but her guard was awake and she thought better of it, not for fear of what he might do to her, but of what she might say to him if he tried to stop her. His machine-gun had disappeared, presumably inside his salesman's briefcase.

Julieta ached for a pee but would rather wet herself than beg these gangsters to stop and let her relieve herself.

Nasca: a sign beside the road told them they were at one of the most famous towns in the Americas for historians and archaeologists. Julieta had learnt at school about the geometric figures and giant monkeys, birds and spiders carved into the rocky desert for the gods to see when they looked down from the heavens. If the gods were looking now, perhaps they would see her plight and Mawi's, reach down, rescue them both and transport them to live for ever enfolded in their protection on the Isla del Sol.

The distance from Nasca to Lima was the same as from Cuzco to Nasca but the coastal road was fast and they reached the outskirts of Lima by early afternoon.

Julieta was unprepared for the poverty that spread in every direction as far as the eye could see: hillside after hillside covered in the cardboard shelters that served as home for the millions of emigrants from the mountains who had come with their illusions of a better life in the capital. The pavements were lined with starving beggarwomen sitting with their backs against the wall, hardly strong enough to hold up an imploring hand. Some had collapsed and lay motionless, while flies buzzed about their heads and emaciated dogs sniffed at them. The most agonized dogs had also collapsed and died and lay rotting in the gutter. Only the rats were well fed: they waddled from one towering pile of rubbish to the next, not even waiting for nightfall to scavenge. A water lorry sold clean water to those who could afford it, queuing with their plastic bottles and cans. Those who couldn't spare the two or three *soles* washed their clothes and faces in the cess-water that trickled through the gutter. The buildings that lined the streets were half collapsed after the last earthquake but no one had the money to rebuild them.

'It makes you sick to look at it,' was Herman Gorringe's

comment. 'Needs a flood to wash it all away.'

It was in surroundings like these that Sister Thérèse had spent her life, also with her illusions perhaps. Did she believe that God would one day change all this? Did she ever ask herself where all the wealth was going that should have been used to provide food, medicine, education and jobs for this multitude of paupers? Did she sometimes wonder who the men in suits were, with briefcases and North American, European or Australian accents, who stayed in the heavily policed four- and five-star hotels, dined behind electric security fences in the most expensive restaurants and went back to their own countries even richer than when they had arrived? Julieta felt a growing hunger to challenge the bankers, industrialists and politicians who destroyed the lives of so many millions of Andeans, even if it cost her her own life.

At Jorge Chávez Airport the Marines formed a wide semicircle round the sales counters in the departures precinct, revolvers in pockets, machine-guns in their briefcases, while a young woman in a blue and red uniform and a mask of foundation, mascara and eye-liner copied Mawi's and Julieta's assumed names on to their tickets.

'You're paying in *soles* or dollars?' she asked.

'We're not paying in anything,' Julieta replied. 'We haven't enough money.'

Herman Gorringe, who was standing within earshot, switched on his avuncular grin, took a wad of dollars from his pocket and counted out ten hundred-dollar bills.

Mawi and Julieta checked in but kept their bags as hand luggage. Gorringe and his men accompanied them to the barrier.

'In case you have second thoughts about flying and head for the street,' he said, switching on his grin again, 'Uncle Herman and his friends will be at the door waiting for you.'

Mawi and Julieta showed their tickets and passports and rid themselves of their captors. Julieta paid the airport tax and they moved on to passport control.

'We've got no entry cards and our passports aren't stamped,' Mawi murmured.

'Could be our salvation,' Julieta murmured back.

'We'd both end up in a Peruvian gaol. Then they'd send us back to Chile under armed guard. At least this way we stand a chance.'

Julieta trusted to her instincts and singled out a young man who had perhaps once had more of the poet than the official in his soul, and they joined his queue.

'We're students,' she explained, playing the innocent. 'We hitch-hiked up from Chile a week ago. We were on our way to Cuzco to stay with my grandfather. The immigration officer was sound asleep. We didn't want to wake him.'

The official scrutinized the two passports. 'Where did you cross the border?' he asked.

'At Visviri.'

The young man looked at Mawi's and Julieta's faces and at the photos in their passports.

Julieta held her breath. The seconds went by.

The official put on his sternest expression. 'You should have woken him,' he said.

'I know.' Julieta smiled sweetly. 'We didn't have the heart.'

'There'll be a fine to pay. Go to desk fourteen.'

He handed back the passports. Julieta paid the fine, the bags were cursorily searched for guns and bombs, and she and Mawi arrived safely in the departure lounge.

'I'm bursting for a pee,' said Julieta. 'Then we must eat. We haven't had anything since breakfast yesterday.'

Mawi and Julieta cast a wry glance at the *M* over the only restaurant in sight. They bought a meal of imported meat, bread, potatoes, fruit and flour and took it to a plastic top with two stools. They tore into their double-decker chickenburgers so ravenously that the feathers all but flew. The piping hot turnovers smelt deliciously of cloves and tasted of apple-flavoured cardboard.

'Better?' asked Mawi, when they had finished.

'Strong enough to hijack an aeroplane.'

Julieta's bravado hid the anxiety she felt: not for herself – she could handle her father – but for Mawi. It was the danger Mawi was in that had brought them together in the first place. Now Mawi was her husband, dearer to her than anyone else in the world, and his danger was also hers. Prison and torture had changed from possible to almost inevitable. If he disappeared – a euphemism that turned her blood to ice – her heart would shatter into a thousand pieces.

They made their way to the departure gate. On the way they passed a large crowd of English-speaking men, women and children, waiting for their flight: refugees from Argentina unable to get a direct flight to London, to judge by the snippets of conversation Julieta overheard. They seemed to have clubbed together to charter a jumbo jet. They were lucky, she thought: they were going home to safety. Mawi was going home to possible execution.

They mustn't give up hope, Julieta told herself as they waited to board their flight. But the longer they sat, the more down-hearted they became. They ran out of things to say: nothing seemed worth talking about any more. They sat hand in hand at the end of a row of seats, waiting.

There was a sound of stirring clothes and scraping shoes, like a congregation rising at a funeral service. The passengers were on their feet, queuing to show their boarding-passes and walk down the covered gangway to the tarmac.

Mawi and Julieta inched their way forward, still hand in hand. At last it was their turn to show their papers. Once through, it was like being clear of a roadworks. They followed the ramp, turned sharp left, then sharp right. At the bottom they came to a service road. The passengers ahead had already crossed the road and almost reached the Lan Airbus parked near the terminal.

They were about to cross the road themselves when a bus came into view – a shuttle bus, used for ferrying passengers whose aircraft weren't within walking distance. As it approached, Julieta saw that it was empty and that the doors were open. She heard no footsteps behind them.

'Jump in the back and crouch down!' she said to Mawi, without time to plan, reflect or explain.

Mawi understood at once. Moments later they were on the bus, crouching behind a partition that hid them from the driver's rear-view mirror. The bus drove on fifty metres and pulled up outside another gangway. A small crowd of passengers were waiting on the kerb to board. This seemed to be a relief bus for one already full pulling away ahead. As the crowd started to move towards the door of the bus, Mawi and Julieta eased themselves on to their feet. One or two passengers looked at them in mild surprise but Mawi and Julieta remained calm and looked bored, as if they made a habit of crouching in empty airport shuttle buses. More passengers came hurrying down the ramp and soon the bus was full.

'We've got the wrong boarding-passes,' Mawi whispered to Julieta as the bus pulled away.

'We're past the gate: that's what matters,' Julieta whispered back. 'It's our only chance. We have to take it.'

The bus stopped outside a two-storey aircraft the size of an ocean liner and disgorged its passengers, who made a dash for the steps up to the cabin, seeing in every fellow-passenger an enemy intent on stealing the seats they had reserved. Mawi and Julieta followed. The later the better: it was the empty seats that might save them from being found out.

'Whatever you do, don't show your boarding-pass stub,' Julieta murmured as they climbed the steps.

At the top she made a show of fumbling in her bag for the stubs.

'I've got them here somewhere,' she told the fair-haired

stewardess who was waiting at the door with a glued-on smile. 'I remember the numbers: W one and two.'

'Far side at the back,' said the stewardess.

Mawi and Julieta made their way down the starboard aisle in a cabin the size of a cinema, hardly daring to breathe. Each row had twelve seats: three each side with a block of six in the middle. A few single seats were unoccupied but there seemed to be no pairs of free seats. P,Q,R,S,T. At last they came to W and were able to breathe again: an elderly lady was struggling to sit down in W one by the window, but W two and three were free. The three seats in front of W were unnumbered, as they were next to the emergency door, and they were empty.

'Oh dear, I don't think I'll ever be able to sit here, with my bad leg,' said the elderly lady.

A very young stewardess, still wet behind the ears, appeared from the service area at the back of the aircraft. Julieta explained that her grandmother was having trouble sitting down and asked if they could all move forward a row. As soon as they were seated in the emergency row, Julieta in the middle seat, her new-found grandmother by the window and Mawi next to the aisle, a couple approached, scanning the seat numbers, and laid claim to W two and three, in the row behind. Mawi and Julieta exchanged a look of relief. Julieta took hold of Mawi's hand. Hers was clammy; his was quite dry.

'Where are you travelling to?' Julieta asked the elderly lady.

'Paris. London first, of course. Then I change planes. What about you?'

Julieta hesitated. Only now did she realize that the people about her were speaking English and that she and Mawi must be with the crowd of Britons who had had to leave Argentina. 'We're travelling to London,' she said.

There was a hum as the first of the engines started up. The loudspeakers in the airport would be putting out calls for the two missing passengers for Lan Flight 437 to Santiago. Did Herman

Gorringe realize she and Mawi were travelling under assumed names? What if all flights were grounded while a search took place? Julieta would only be able to relax when the Boeing 747 was airborne.

31

Nicole Reyes sat in her burgundy bathrobe tying her hair into a loose bun in front of the eighteenth-century Spanish dressing-table her husband had bought for her at great expense as a first wedding anniversary present. It looked awkward beside her graceful bedside table, desk and chairs, the ceiling-to-floor cotton curtains and Monet reproductions, like an ox in a field of fallow deer. She had made a show of liking it at first but over the years its lack of delicacy and charm, its clumsiness, the size of its legs, its grandiosity had become associated in her mind with a husband she found more and more insufferable.

Nicole wondered why she took so much trouble with her appearance. Not for Franco. He wouldn't notice now if she let herself run to fat, allowed her hair to hang like a mop, her skin to dry out, her teeth to rot, dirt to collect under her fingernails. Wouldn't notice whether she used Eau de Rochas or *eau de javelle*. Was it a subconscious need to attract the attention of men who might be sensitive to her elegance, gentleness and subtlety of mind and value her for them? The only men Nicole met were Spanish Chileans, men very much like her husband. No, she did it for herself. It was a way of surviving, keeping her identity, not allowing her personality and values to be crushed by the boorishness, insensitivity and philistinism of her husband and his colleagues and cronies.

Julieta driven from her home by her father: it was the final straw. She had been the only reason left for the marriage, the only thing Nicole and her husband still had in common. Not that they shared the same feelings for Julieta. Nicole had watched in wonder as her daughter grew from a baby into a little girl and then into an adolescent for whom everything in the world was possible. Now she was a young adult with a sharp mind and strong will, but above all with a loving heart. She was the best friend Nicole had. For her father Julieta was a possession, someone to dominate and manipulate, to marry to a man who would raise his social standing and speed his promotion. Thank goodness Julieta hadn't inherited her father's Chilean coarseness, his need to crush and control. Thank goodness she did have her father's will. It might get her the life she wanted, instead of the life her father wanted for her.

Franco hadn't been speaking to Nicole for the past ten days, ever since Julieta left home. He must imagine she was behind Julieta's disappearance, or knew it was going to happen. Let him imagine what he liked: it didn't interest her. But she would like to know how and where her daughter was. She and Copihue took it in turns to eavesdrop when Franco was on the phone but so far hadn't found out much. His conversations were conducted in shorthand or code: Nicole guessed he was meeting army officers or the police regularly and just using the phone for newsflashes and urgent messages. Most of what he said was incomprehensible but Nicole and Copihue could tell from the tone of voice that he wasn't in control, which must mean Julieta and Mawi were free.

Most mothers would be frantic with worry if their daughter had absconded. Not Nicole Reyes. Copihue had told her about Mawi. Nicole trusted Copihue's judgement and her own instincts. He sounded a sweet boy. Julieta had too much insight to fall for someone who would ill-treat or take advantage of her. And she was sensible. She was unlikely to be starving or catching pneumonia or running out of money. The girl had been more of a worry at home under her father's control.

Nicole nearly always changed in the early evening, as if her husband had been a polished, well-educated French government minister instead of a brainwashed apparatchik in a military dictatorship. She finished her hair in front of the full-length wall-mirror, took off the bathrobe and slipped into the three-quarter length dress she had laid out on the magnolia bedspread. She buttoned it in front of the mirror and felt summery and light-hearted at the sight of the purple and white orchids on their pale green background. She crossed to the top drawer of the rosewood bureau, where she kept her costume jewellery, and took out a necklace of large white beads, gold bangles for her wrists and rings for her fingers. She put them on and went over to Julieta's flowers in the white vase on the mahogany side-table. The mimosa had lost its scent and the fluffy globes had dried into little yellow pellets, but the freesias still smelt as fresh and sweet as innocence, and the red roses still reminded her of summer holidays at her grandmother's house at Les Andelys.

Nicole was happy that Julieta had broken free and escaped a living death married to that cold-eyed, cold-blooded major, but she did miss her company, especially in the evening after dinner, when they used to sit out on the terrace, sometimes chatting, sometimes in silence, enjoying the mild air and garden scents, watching the moon rise, listening to the bees drawing pollen from flowers, and the nightingale in the locust-tree. Nicole had always meant to do a portrait of Julieta sitting on the terrace, to capture her in the flower of youth. She wondered if the opportunity was gone for ever.

She went downstairs to the kitchen, put on an overall and helped Copihue prepare the evening meal. Chicken this evening: *à la provençale*. As a change from steak. Nicole and Copihue liked it, even if Franco considered it lightweight. *Muscat* grapes to follow. He would have to fill up with biscuits in his study afterwards.

Nicole took a bag with two large bunches of grapes covered in bloom to the dining-room and laid them on the stack of Limoges fruit plates. These had belonged to her grandmother. Whenever she touched them, she was transported to the terrace outside the French windows at Les Andelys, with wistaria covering the wall behind her and filling the air with its delicate, springlike scent, and a view along the path made of crazy paving and bordered with roses, irises and columbine, under the willows to the River Seine.

Nicole heard the clang of the metal security gate in front of the house. She felt the tension return to her shoulders and neck and the iron band tighten across her brow. A day of peace and friendship with Copihue was at an end and a conjugal evening with Franco was about to begin.

The front-door opened and banged shut and the Bally shoes clattered across the tiles to the study. The telephone receiver was picked up and a number dialled. A phone call with the door open? Was security-conscious Franco Reyes becoming careless? 'Hello?' he boomed. 'I'd like to speak to the President's secretary.'

The President's secretary, no less. This must be important. An important call with the door wide open? He obviously didn't care who heard. Or perhaps he wanted his wife and Copihue to hear. Nicole caught the barely audible pad of Copihue's shoes as she tiptoed to the kitchen door to listen.

'Good evening, *señora*. Franco Reyes here: Ministry of Internal Affairs. I wonder if it would be possible to speak to the President for a couple of minutes. I have good news.'

Good news for the President? Sounding cock-a-hoop? Nicole's heart sank.

'Good evening, Mr President. Forgive me for disturbing you. You were kind enough to enquire after my daughter two days ago. The good news is that she's been found and her kidnapper seized… In Peru, sir… They were escorted to Jorge Chávez Airport in Lima and put on a flight to Santiago. They should be arriving any moment now. Major Adolfo Cortez, the officer I told you about, is meeting them with a detachment at Arturo Merino Benítez Airport… Herman Gorringe, sir, our US security contact. He happened to be in Peru on an anti-terrorist mission… Thank you, sir. I thought you'd be pleased, sir. Thank you, Mr President. Thank you, sir.'

Nicole's husband replaced the receiver and started to hum

tunelessly. He went to the oak dresser, took a bottle and glass, removed the cork and poured.

Nicole pulled a chair out from under the dining-table and sat heavily. This was the worst news she had had since the death of Bonne-Maman eight years ago. She wanted more than anything in the world *not* to be reunited with the daughter she loved. Not here in Santiago. Franco wouldn't just put pressure on Julieta. He would force her to marry Cortez. Nicole wanted her child to be free, to live. She would rather Julieta moved to the other side of the world, to India or Australia, than came home to her father. She would travel anywhere in the world to visit her daughter. And Mawi: what would become of him? He had been labelled a kidnapper. They would torture him. Kill him, perhaps.

What could Nicole do? She felt helpless. What could one powerless woman do against the united forces of the barbaric and depraved Establishment? Kill Franco? She would commit murder for the sake of her daughter's happiness. Poison his beef and blame it on the Argentinians? This might save Julieta from marrying Cortez but it wouldn't get Mawi out of prison. Julieta would never be happy so long as Mawi was behind bars.

The phone rang. Franco broke wind, then answered it.

'Cortez, dear boy! How are you, old chap? Where are you? Just been on the phone to the President. Told him you—… What? Not—? I don't believe it. Not on the—?'

Hope, like the first snowdrop, raised a tiny head in Nicole's mind.

'Of course I gave you the right time and flight number. Phoned Lima myself to double-check… I don't know what to say… Herman Gorringe? No, he's a cracker. Never gets anything wrong. Have they looked in the lavatories?… I said, have they looked in the lavatories on board the aeroplane? And the kitchens?… Already thought of that… Yes, yes, of course I'll keep you informed. I— I'm sorry, I—'

There was a pause. Franco banged down the receiver.

Nicole got up. She pushed the chair under the table and went out on the terrace. The tension had gone from her shoulders and neck, the iron band from her head. Julieta and Mawi were still free. They had somehow managed to elude the forces of oppression. Nicole couldn't imagine how they had done it. She wished there were some way of communicating with them, by Morse or telepathy, to tell them she shared in their triumph.

She heard shouting from the study. Her husband was in a rage. Nicole couldn't hear the words. She wasn't interested. The autocrat had been thwarted. Let him storm.

Franco came into the hall. Nicole could hear what he was saying now. 'I know who's behind this,' he was shouting. 'Where is she? Where is the bitch?'

Where was who? He couldn't mean Copihue. 'He must be looking for me,' thought Nicole. Her husband might be an autocrat but he had never called her a bitch or inspired uneasiness in her before. For the first time in their marriage she felt apprehensive. Reyes sounded beside himself with fury. He wouldn't attack her, would he?

He was stamping his way upstairs now, still shouting. Was there somewhere Nicole could disappear to until the storm blew over? The bottom of the garden? Too late: he was on his way downstairs again, like an elephant on the rampage.

Reyes puffed and snorted his way into the dining-room. Nicole took her courage in both hands and went inside.

'You're behind this, aren't you?' her husband trumpeted.

'Behind what?' Nicole replied, meeting *passion* with *raison*, as her French education had taught her to do, and forcing herself to sound calm.

'Behind what? Behind what? Peru! Peru! My daughter jumps ship in Peru and you tell me you're not behind it, you Peruvian bitch?'

'I don't know what you're talking about. I'm going to my room. I'm not prepared to stand here and be insulted. Please let me past.'

'Not prepared to—'

Reyes lunged at the table, grabbed the grapes from the topmost fruit plate and hurled them at the wall. Most of the grapes fell to the floor. Some burst when they hit the wall, stuck to it and stained the designer wallpaper.

'The grapes were for dinner,' Nicole said quietly, holding on to reason and calm like a shipwrecked sailor clinging to a timber in a stormy sea. 'Now we have no dessert.'

'Dessert? Dessert?' Reyes bellowed. His hand landed like a jellyfish on the empty Limoges plate. It stuck to his hand. He raised his arm and like a discus-thrower sent the plate spinning into a top corner of the room, where it smashed into fragments. His hand descended on the next plate.

Nicole let out a cry of pain. 'No! No! Not Bonne-Maman's plates! Please!'

One by one the plates were thrown spinning against the ceiling and walls. The sixth plate flew towards the portrait of Franco Reyes' strong-jawed mother and landed fair and square in her mouth. Not a blink, not a tooth broken, but the plate was reduced almost to the humble clay from which it began its ascent to porcelain and prestige.

Except for one shard. Nicole saw it coming and shielded her eyes. The splinter drove like a knife into her cheek. She felt no pain. Only warmth flowing down her face and shoulder. She touched her face. Her hand was covered in blood. She grabbed a napkin from the table and pressed it against her cheek. In less than a minute the napkin was saturated. She seized another and held it to her face. Her head was spinning: she pulled out a chair, sat down and closed her eyes. When she opened them, Copihue was standing over her, tearing off sheets from a kitchen roll, trying to staunch the flow of blood. Reyes had left the room.

'The napkins are ruined,' Nicole said weakly. 'So is my dress.'

'It doesn't matter, *señora,*' Copihue said soothingly. 'They can be cleaned.' She was almost in tears.

'Give me the roll. You'd better phone for a doctor. I'll need stitches. And…'

Copihue pressed the kitchen roll into Nicole's hands, went to the door, paused.

'Look in the Yellow Pages. Find an antique dealer and get a price for my dressing-table.'

'Yes, *señora*.' Copihue left the room.

The table should pay for two rooms for Copihue and herself at the Hotel Santa Lucia for a fortnight, thought Nicole, while she waited for her money to arrive from France.

She reached for the silver bowl in the middle of the table, emptied the pomegranates from it and held it up as a mirror. Her face was distorted out of recognition. She turned the bowl until the hand holding the paper towels was seen as if through a magnifying glass. She removed the towels to examine the wound for two seconds before the blood started to pour again. The gash was deep. For a moment she thought she could see her tongue behind it. No, she would be tasting and swallowing blood if the splinter had pierced her cheek.

'I'm scarred for life,' Nicole murmured. She tore off another few sheets from the kitchen roll and pressed them to her face.

32

As the Boeing 747 climbed out of the smog hanging over Lima and headed north-east for the mountains, Mawi's and Julieta's apprehension subsided and they started to relax. No one had asked to see their tickets or boarding-passes or realized they were sitting in the emergency seats because they had no seats of their own. Julieta dropped her guard a little and turned her attention past their fellow-passenger to the view of the Andes.

At first there wasn't much to see: foothills far below. But the hills quickly grew into mountains that reached higher and higher and became whiter and whiter, until the highest and whitest almost touched the aeroplane: mass after mass of brute weight and size, with only the occasional trace of vegetation, like the beginnings of moss on a garden wall. In themselves they were not beautiful, not in the way that a flower or bird is beautiful, but they were a foundation on which beauty could be built. Veil the snow-covered summits in mist, backlight them as if through a gauze with the lemon light of dawn, and mass and size would be alchemized into weightlessness and translucence. Soak them in the deepening orange of sunset, and earth and rock would be transformed into light and colour.

'Look!' The elderly lady on Julieta's right was pointing out of the window and down at something.

Julieta got up and leant across to look. Half a dozen condors were circling like gliders round one of the snow-capped peaks not far below.

Julieta had already said a few words to her neighbour. This was expediency on her part, in case one of the stewardesses happened to glance in their direction: Julieta would hardly sit and ignore her own grandmother. She now felt more and more drawn to her fellow-passenger, and they were soon engrossed in conversation. The elderly lady was French, on her way back to

Europe after fifty years with a Catholic mission in Lima. She would have preferred to end her days in Peru, serving the mission, but her sister was widowed, ill and alone, and God had told her half a century helping the poor among the rubble and rubbish of Pamplona Alta and El Salvador was all he asked of her and that she must devote her remaining years to her only surviving relative, soothed by the grassy slopes of the Western Pyrenees and rung to prayers not by the angelus but by the sound of cowbells. She would live out her life not among brown faces and colourful ponchos in the shanty-towns of a land seized from the Andeans and ravaged by Spanish adventurers but among the red berets of the Basques, who settled in those mountains ten thousand years ago and had for centuries been trying to reclaim them from the occupying French and Spanish.

'It's the poor people of Peru I shall miss,' said Julieta's neighbour. 'We go there to help them but it's they who help us, with their warmth and neighbourliness and their acceptance of life's difficulties without stress or complaint. The Basques make good friends once they get to know you. I prefer to live among the colonized, not the colonizers.'

Julieta's thoughts were in Cuzco, with the outrage perpetrated by a modern Pizarro and his killers, agents not of the Spanish Crown but of a back-door empire preaching democracy but practising commercial exploitation, claiming the world for God and his favoured people, priggishly policing land that wasn't theirs and burning to death the gentle visionaries of a truly democratic society that would have received the blessing of the Essenes and of Christ. She could feel the heat of the flames, see them greedily devouring the walls and roof of the lecture-hall, hear the screams, smell the burning flesh as vividly as if she were still crouching in front of the blazing building. Julieta would take upon herself, if she could, the entire debt owing to the good people of the Andes – to the millions who had been burnt, shot, stabbed or sliced to death, or had died from hunger or disease – and the guilt most European South Americans were too thick-skinned to feel.

Julieta's attention had wandered for a moment from the conversation with her neighbour. She gave a start at the mention of a name that touched a wound in her memory.

'Sister Thérèse is the best of them,' the missionary was saying, 'the friend I'll miss most. And the most dedicated of the Franciscan sisters. Tireless, in spite of her years. Nothing she wouldn't—'

'Did you say Sister Thérèse?'

'Yes. Do you know her?'

'A tall nun in her eighties? A bit shaky on her feet? Wrinkled face?'

'That's it. How do you know her?'

Julieta couldn't reply at once. She saw Sister Thérèse enveloped in flames, heard her call out, trying to make herself heard by God, saw the flames licking and pawing at her nun's habits, the terror in her face, heard her husky screams of agony. Julieta's head began to spin and she reached out for Mawi as she would for the gunwale of a boat in rough waters. Mawi had heard the conversation and was ready with his hand for her to clutch. 'Dear Mawi! May I always be as thoughtful to you as you are to me,' she thought.

'I've heard her speak,' Julieta replied at last. 'At a meeting. Not in Lima.'

'Oh, she goes everywhere in Peru, giving hope to the poor, inspiring and encouraging. She's quite radical in her views. Tells everyone our Lord was a Communist.' The missionary chuckled.

Should Julieta tell her? Cause her distress at the start of a long and tiring journey? Spoil the homecoming? No, let her settle into her new life with her sister in the Pyrenees. Let time and distance throw Lima into softer focus. She would hear about the terrible end of Sister Thérèse sooner or later.

Julieta longed to stretch out her other hand and take hold of her adopted grandmother's. How like her great-grandmother she was! The same youthful joy and curiosity. The same willingness to talk to her fellow human beings, especially those fifty or more years younger than herself. Julieta would love to have spent more time with Bonne-Maman. If only they hadn't lived so many thousands of kilometres apart.

Julieta found herself thinking of the fisher-folk on the Isla del Sol, and wondered why. She saw the face of the woman who had called to them from the shore, and then she understood: it could have been Bonne-Maman's face – not Bonne-Maman as Julieta had known her but as she remembered her from a photograph taken about forty years earlier. The resemblance was striking. Instead of being surprised or unsettled by it, Julieta was filled with a feeling of peace.

She looked out of the window. The mountains and condors had gone. They were over jungle now, following the River Amazon to the Brazilian border on its three-thousand-five-hundred-kilometre course to the Atlantic Ocean. Instead of the stark, elemental grandeur of the Andes, where nothing grew, Julieta saw its antithesis: luxuriant vegetation growing so fast and thick that only insects and reptiles could penetrate it. She knew emerald humming-birds drew nectar from the exotic flowers, blood-red, orange, canary-yellow, sky-blue and indigo, that dotted those billions of acres of green, unbroken except for countless rivers that snaked through the jungle, tributaries of tributaries of the Amazon; knew that riotous parrots flapped from branch to branch and jewelled butterflies the size of dinner-plates fluttered among the palms. But she also knew the air was thick with malarial mosquitoes, that vipers lay coiled under orchids, anacondas seven or more metres long lay in wait, still as tree-trunks, ready to crush their animal or human prey, and that the rivers were full of caymans and alligators. The jungle disappeared from view for a few seconds behind one of the many columns of vapour, generated when icy mountain blasts meet the equatorial heat, spiralling upwards six or seven kilometres before spreading and breaking into puffs of cloud. Rows of columns joined to form arches. At the end of the massive cathedral was a vast screen of haze reflecting and dyed orange by the setting sun. The vision of heaven disappeared as the jet flew through another pillar of gas. When it emerged, they were among thunder-clouds, outlined by the sun in red, burning like huge lumps of coal and darting out forked tongues of lightning. This was South America, thought Julieta, where heaven and hell meet, where peaceable Andeans eke out an existence, eating the potatoes and maize they grow, weaving clothes from the wool of their llamas and alpacas to protect themselves against the bitter nights, and where profiteers from abroad dynamite whole mountainsides and help themselves to the vast wealth of copper and gold walled behind them, cut down millions of hectares of rubber- and mahogany-trees and turn medicinal coca into ruinous cocaine.

Julieta was still holding Mawi's hand. It had lost its grip, because he had fallen asleep. Her new grandmother was asleep too. Julieta wished she could pull a curtain round Mawi and herself, gently unbutton his shirt and burrow into his brown chest. She felt like taking a rug from the overhead locker, undressing underneath it and, when Mawi woke, wrapping herself and the rug around him.

The clatter of a trolley from behind woke Julieta from her reverie. A minute later the stewardess with the fair hair and glued-on smile was shaking Julieta's two sleeping neighbours. She had a hospital nurse's taste for apple-pie order: this was the time for eating, not sleeping; you would be told when you could sleep. Tray-holders swung out from the arm-rests, and indented trays ingeniously designed so that a four-course meal could fit into a space no bigger than a sheet of A4 paper were placed on them.

Mawi and Julieta were still digesting their chickenburgers and turnovers and had no appetite, but to refuse the meal would have been to draw attention to themselves. They struggled with their egg mayonnaise, chicken with sweetcorn, cheese and biscuits and lemon mousse, all tasting of the carcinogenic plastic lids that made it sweat, and sipped their quarter-bottles of Rioja a thimbleful at a time to make it last. They could have done without the food but with another litre of wine. They said little to each other as they supped; the only thing they wanted to talk about was the one thing they mustn't mention: their unscheduled change of flight and fortune.

A monitor swung down in front of them and a picture appeared on the screen. Dinner was over; the passengers were now to be entertained.

Skyscrapers. Cars eight metres long. A police station. Policemen at their desks, most of them white, the two black ones kosher thanks to their immaculate uniforms and good looks. Outside, somewhere: a shooting. The police station again: alarms sounding. A police car squealing round a corner. A chase. Brakes screeching. An accident. Villains running. Policemen running. More shooting. One villain limping. An arrest. Back at the police station: black police officer with respectable haircut and white man's speech and gestures interrogates Rastafarian drug-smuggling villain with dreadlocks and not a clean word in his vocabulary.

Julieta yawned. Why were the passengers being shown North American pulp on a British aeroplane flying from Peru to London, she asked herself. South America was full of talented film-makers. So was Britain perhaps. Factory food and cliché-ridden movies hardly constituted a culture. Yet countries the world over with thousands of years of history and culture eagerly traded what was real for what was false.

'How are you enjoying the film?' she asked Mawi.

'The buildings: they're as tall as mountains. How do people get to the top floor? Do they have wings?'

Julieta lifted the arm-rest, laid her head on Mawi's shoulder and closed her eyes.

It was all a matter of business, she decided: of buying your way into other people's minds and markets. The aim of business was profit, so *profitable* had taken the place of *good, moral, ethical.* God's most favoured people had reinterpreted his word and given the world a new commandment: poison stomachs, numb minds, kill with cancer, provided thy balance-sheet sheweth a profit at the end of the year; starve the poor, steal their land, finance corrupt régimes, destroy families and communities, to feed and fatten thy shareholders' portfolios. Was it worth trying to resist this mighty life-denying force with her little project on the Isla del Sol? Wouldn't it be like trying to hold back an oil-slick with a teaspoon? For several minutes she felt overwhelmed, discouraged, depressed. Then she heard a faint voice inside her head. The more she strained to listen, the more it sounded like a voice from ten years ago: Bonne-Maman's. If the project worked, her beloved ancestor told her, it would touch the hearts of those who thought like her but hadn't yet turned thought into action; it would inspire other projects, until at last there would be a life-asserting force to match and sap the strength of the monster that starved millions of children in its greed for gold and thirst for oil.

Julieta's thoughts turned to those she loved but couldn't be with, as they always did when she grew drowsy: her mother, Bonne-Maman, Copihue, Father Lorencio. She snuggled into Mawi's neck and fell asleep.

The hours felt more like minutes when Julieta woke dazzled by the rising sun on her face. They had been flying east through a series of time-zones, adding their own speed to the speed of the spinning Earth, thus shortening the night by nearly half.

The monitor had disappeared from above her head. The only picture was on the cabin monitor, a large screen twenty rows away that showed a map of the North Atlantic, with France in prominence and a dot representing the aeroplane inching like an insect over Brittany.

Mawi was sound asleep. No need to wake him. Julieta lifted

her head from his shoulder and leant across Grand'mère, who was also asleep, to look out of the window. She had glimpses of forests, rivers and fields between mountains of cloud. The cloud broadened and thickened as they flew northwards. By the time they reached the English Channel there wasn't a single break in the greyish-white expanse.

The fair-haired stewardess wheeled a trolley along the aisle, serving breakfast with her glued-on smile. Next on the timetable came the filling in of immigration forms.

Mawi was awake now and watchful. His anxiety passed like a current to Julieta and made her stomach ache. Gorringe was in cahoots with Cortez and her father. The Chilean Government could have sent out a request to the countries concerned for all flights out of Lima yesterday afternoon to be searched on arrival for two stowaways.

The figures on the monitor started to tumble. A minute later the bright sun and black sky were gone and they were in twilight.

'Swallow!' Julieta told Mawi, who was poking at his ears, trying to unblock them.

2500, 2200, 1900, 1700. Still they were in cloud. Julieta leant across Grand'mère, straining to see through the murk. Droplets of moisture scudded across the outside of the window. At last an image appeared, faintly: an impression of roads and houses, not much more than five hundred metres below. Long lines of houses, like rows of boxes. Long lines of rain on the window. Was it day or night? What season was it? It was autumn in Chile, so it should be spring in England. Nothing but roads and houses: an endless built-up area. Where were the mountains and countryside?

Then Julieta remembered: poems at school by a poet called William Wordsworth, and the English teacher telling them Wordsworth and his friend, Samuel Taylor Coleridge, another poet, used to go for long walks in the Lake District. It was somewhere in the north. She remembered thinking what a coincidence it was that William Wordsworth and Samuel Taylor Coleridge should belong to the English Lake District, and Gabriela Mistral and Pablo Neruda to the Chilean Lake District. Then there were the pictures in her first English school-book of little thatched houses covered in climbing roses, with gardens in front of them overflowing with flowers of all colours. Green – everywhere was green. Even the hills: not rock but soft earth, covered in lush green grass.

Was this where Mawi and Julieta were going to spend their lives, if they were not arrested as soon as they arrived and put on the next flight back to Chile? In England, in one of those little houses buried in flowers? Her mother and Copihue could come over. They could get away from the Chilean winters and spend summers with them in the English Lake District. Summer in England must surely be sunnier than the spring. They would all go for long walks even in the rain, along the lakes and through the landscapes of Wordsworth's poems. Mawi and Julieta would carry their two children, a boy and a girl, on their backs. What would they be like, their children?

A little girl appeared before Julieta's eyes, as clearly as if she were on the aeroplane with her. She had a brown face, long jet-black hair and ebony eyes. Her frayed dress and poncho were made of all the colours of the rainbow and she wore a floppy white sun-hat.

'You promised,' said the little girl.

'Promised what?' whispered Julieta.

'You said you were going to live on this island and make a school, so that all the children could learn to read and write and count.'

Before Julieta could reply, there was a whirring as the undercarriage was lowered, and the little girl disappeared. Muzak started to play and the airliner began its approach to Gatwick Airport.

33

A well-fleshed gentleman in his early forties, carrying a frayed leather bag, closed the front-door of his stuccoed, late Regency terrace house, turned the key in the mortise lock and strode off in his dark grey, tailor-made Austin Reed suit for Baker Street Station and the tube to Westminster.

The gentleman hated rush hour on the underground, but traffic jams were even more stressful: sitting in a taxi for over an hour for a distance he could walk in an hour and a half, and occasionally did on his way back from work on a fine evening in spring or summer. Parks almost all the way: Green Park, Hyde Park, a gap for Gloucester Place, then Regent's Park and home. It was the only exercise he took. He arrived home exhausted, wallowed in a hot bath for half an hour, downed half a bottle of whisky after supper, replacing the weight lost from the walk, and slept like a log.

The gentleman was against tube journeys for the same reason as everyone else: he didn't like the bodies of people he didn't know pressed against his. Perhaps that was why nobody talked to anyone else on the underground: silence created a barrier that space didn't allow. The alternative would be to make it a brotherhood-of-man experience: everybody embracing everyone else, laughing and talking and shedding tears. A congregation of born-again charismatics on wheels. It might be possible in Africa, if Africa had tube trains, but while English people still outnumbered Africans on the London underground, such effusiveness was unthinkable. Until the Great Revolution of Kisses and Tears arrived, the gentleman would ride the tube like everybody else, in a bubble of silence, isolated as far as possible from the malodorous lepers and potential pickpockets with whom he was forced to travel.

Stick it up your Junta! was today's headline on the newspaper stand outside Baker Street Station. And one of the papers was advertising a competition, with prizes for the most abusive jokes about Argentinians.

How could one love one's fellow-men when they went to war with such obscene relish? Boys of eighteen and nineteen would perhaps be blown to pieces by shells, burnt alive and maimed for life. For the tabloid press it was a game and a way to make money. A game for sick minds. But if the newspapermen were depraved, so were the millions who read what the papers printed. If only it were a just and unavoidable war, instead of an excuse for the PM and her rabid right-wingers to indulge themselves and their fellow-countrymen with fantasies of a glorious past reborn, of John Bull with his cudgel clubbing the dagos who were threatening to overrun those dismal islands, then with his torn old atlas and crumbling crayons recolouring that forgotten corner of the South Atlantic pink. The gentleman found this warmongering and sentimental journey into a colonial past offensive, as did many of his fellow civil servants. Theirs not to reason why, however, but to serve the inferior minds of the government of the day.

Her Majesty's not yet quite senior civil servant was among the ticket-machines now, easy to mistake for pale blue refrigerators, heading for the Bakerloo Line. He slowed his pace for a moment to listen to the busker sitting on a box playing some kind of flute. The boy played well. He looked East Asian: a Uighur or Kazakh perhaps.

The civil servant had once played well himself – the violin – but his fingers seized up years ago for lack of practice, when the world of dream had to give way to the world of grind: when his family and milieu expected him to give up everything he enjoyed doing, that is, and embrace futility, frustration and regret. He could have rebelled. Could still rebel. Dig his violin out of the attic, don jeans and a smock, grow his hair long and start busking in the London underground. More enjoyable than his mind-numbing job at the Home Office but harder to take the plunge when you were older: the civil servant was forty-two, with a steady and well-above-average income and his pension secure.

The East Asian boy might not be counting on a pension but his own income looked steady enough: coins fairly pouring into that hat of his. A sombrero: that was it. He wasn't Asian; he was Latin American. The civil servant would have liked a word with the boy, to ask where he was from and what instrument he was playing, but he hadn't time. There had been an instrument like that in a television film about the Andes. He must be Peruvian or Bolivian or something. The gentleman hoped he wasn't Argentinian. Some of these people would lynch him if they found out: those who read and were swayed by the tabloid press.

Although he had to get to work, the gentleman found he had stopped with several other passers-by to listen to the boy. He had never stopped for a busker before, not just because the playing usually wasn't worth stopping for but because his social class and education set him apart from the rabble. Middle- and high-ranking civil servants were not οι πολλοι (hoi polloi: the gentleman's Greek was in better shape than his violin-playing). They didn't stand with the crowd gawping at pavement artists.

This boy was exceptional. For the first time in his life the civil servant felt at ease rubbing shoulders with a crowd of random strangers: they might not be wearing ties, their jeans might need laundering and their gym shoes whitening but their response to the music was the same as his. The others gave their small change without counting it, whether they could spare it or not. The gentleman carefully took two pound coins from his black leather purse, bent down and dropped them into the sombrero at the feet of the musician, who managed to smile his thanks without pausing in his playing.

The civil servant put away his purse and strode towards the ticket barrier. On his way he passed another busker, sitting on a newspaper on the ground, his back against a wall, grimly plucking a guitar. His T-shirt, jeans and plimsolls were falling apart. Both his arms were tattooed with what the gentleman mistook for the staff of Aesculapius. Then he saw that the snakes were coiled round each other, not round a staff: not medicine but poison. The tin at the busker's feet was empty except for a 5p coin and a few pennies.

'I bet that little chap wishes he could play as well as the Latin American,' thought the civil servant as he showed his ticket at the gate. 'He might be able to afford a new pair of shoes.'

34

Mawi's lips ached. It wasn't just that he hadn't played for over a fortnight. This was the first time in his life he had kept playing for six hours at a stretch, with only the odd break of a minute or two for a sip of water from his plastic bottle. In spite of his aching lips, Mawi had found his second wind and would happily have kept going for another two or three hours.

He had been afraid of performing in public at the start but for the first two hours most people were in too much of a hurry to notice him, and the hubbub cushioned him from those who did pause. His confidence had grown: he was pleased now when passers-by stopped and listened. As they had started to, once the rush to get to work was over. Little groups of them. Not just English speakers with white faces. All the world seemed to pass through Baker Street Station: Africans, Indians, people from the Far East. Were they all English? Had England become the colony of the once colonized? Was this the new London? Anglo-Saxon men with shoulder-length hair, black men with dreadlocks, white women with green hair and Indians wearing turbans stopped, listened and applauded.

Mawi felt more at home in London after only two days than he had after five years in Santiago. London was like an open hand, it seemed to him, Santiago like an iron fist, militarist, intolerant, modelled on Fascist Spain. The thought of transporting Baker Street Station to Santiago made him smile at first, then shudder. Chilean *machismo* would be outraged by the men with long hair. They would soon be beaten up by soldiers with crew-cuts, the green-haired women would have their heads shaved, and anyone – let alone a Mapuche – daring to busk in a metro station would quickly be arrested by the police as a leftist subversive, thrown in prison without trial and more than likely tortured to death. London seemed to Mawi a city where a

Mapuche could be accepted and feel safe.

The passers-by not only stopped, listened and applauded but they also paid. Mawi wished he could spend the rest of the afternoon playing for them. The problem was they had given him so much money he didn't know where to put it all. The hat he had bought at a fancy dress shop in Camden Town to give the right exotic look was brimming over with coins, most of them silver- or gold-plated: twenty pences, fifty pences and pounds.

Mawi put his flute in its case, surrounded it with as many coins as would fit and stuffed the rest in his jeans pockets. He wished the endlessly swirling crowds would vanish for just five minutes, so that he could count his hoard. He placed the hat on his head, tucked the case under his arm, picked up the wooden box he had been sitting on, bought for a pound from a builder working on a site in the Marylebone Road, and was about to head in the direction of the Post Office Tower when he saw the little guitarist with tattooed arms again, standing not two metres away, clutching a guitar case almost as tall as himself in both arms and watching his fellow-busker with a mixture of curiosity and hostility.

Mawi felt embarrassed. He knew he must have taken the guitarist's usual spot. Mawi had been the first to arrive, at half past seven. The guitarist had arrived an hour later. He had stood at a distance glaring at Mawi for a minute or two, then found himself another spot, just out of earshot.

The guitarist said something to Mawi in English.

'No entiendo,' Mawi replied with a bright smile. *'No hablo inglés. Lo siento.'*

'Per-mit?' asked the guitarist, almost spitting the question at Mawi.

'¿Permiso? No. ¿Es necesario?'

The guitarist shrugged. He let go of his case with one arm and used his free hand to mime smoking a cigarette.

Mawi shook his head apologetically. 'Poor fellow!' he thought.

'He hasn't even made enough for a packet of cigarettes.' He looked at the young man's shoulder-length hair, unwashed and uncombed, and the shoes that belonged more to the streets of Lima than London, and remembering the Mapuche principle of helping out anyone down on his luck took a handful of coins from his pocket, counted out five of the gold-plated ones and offered them to the guitarist.

The five one-pound coins disappeared into a pocket of the guitarist's disintegrating jeans and an old tobacco tin appeared in his hand. He lifted the lid off with his thumb and revealed three cigarettes he had rolled himself and a cluster of sweet-papers twisted at each end. A moment later the tin was in his pocket and he was giving one of the sweet-papers to Mawi, and a square of cardboard with writing on it.

Mawi looked at the card. It was a beer-mat with the name of a bar or club: the Trafalgar. The name had a Spanish ring.

The guitarist pointed at the card and mimed Mawi playing his flute. Next he clenched his fist, threw back his head and drank in gulps from an imaginary mug. Last he indicated Mawi's sweet-paper, raised his thumb and forefinger to his nose and sniffed.

Mawi unwrapped the sweet-paper. Instead of a fruit drop or toffee, he found half a teaspoonful of what looked like salt or powdered sugar. Was this a joke? He looked up, hoping to learn something from another mime or from the expression on the guitarist's face.

Mawi gave a start. The guitarist had vanished. In his place stood a man so emaciated that his skull and facial bones showed through the tissue-thin white skin that covered them, and his knuckles through the thin bluish skin of his hands, which were shaking. He was wearing a threadbare royal blue suit without a tie, the collar and cuffs of his white shirt were frayed and his bare toes showed through the ends of his worn-out black shoes. His hair was falling out in tufts, he had purple bags under his eyes, two of his teeth were missing, the rest were black and broken and he had a drip at the end of his nose. It was hard to tell the man's age: twenty-five, perhaps, going on sixty. He seemed to have risen from the dead, a skeleton in clothes that were almost rags.

The cadaverous man was looking at Mawi in dismay out of dilated pupils that made his eyes black: Mawi was clearly not the person he was looking for. He stammered something and stumbled off. A moment later the guitarist reappeared. The skeleton lurched towards him and thrust a wad of bank-notes at him. The guitarist counted the money, then took his tobacco tin from his pocket and emptied the sweet-papers into the skeleton's hands.

Mawi kicked himself for being so blind. He rolled up his sweet-paper and dropped it into the litter-bin two metres from where he had been playing. Now he had seen for himself what happened to the life-giving coca leaves of the Andes when they were no longer treated as sacred: seen how they had been scorched and bleached and blended with several dozen chemicals and reduced to a fine white snow that turned life and vitality into a living death.

No sooner had Mawi got rid of his twist of cocaine than he heard shouts and footsteps from the nearest entrance to the metro station. Before he could turn round, four men in navy uniforms, two of them with tracker dogs, were tearing across the concourse. Seconds later two of them headed back for the exit, dragging the skeletal man between them like a sheep's carcass half eaten by vultures. There was no sign of the guitarist. Maybe he had a powder that made him disappear.

Mawi put the beer-mat in his shirt pocket and walked casually to the exit. He looked behind him at the sound of the panting dogs. They had led the other two uniformed men to the litter-bin and were sniffing at it excitedly. Outside the station he turned left along the Marylebone Road towards King's Cross.

After a minute Mawi glanced over his shoulder: there was no

sign of dogs or uniforms; he had not been linked with the sweet-paper in the bin. He began to breathe again.

To be arrested on suspicion of possessing or dealing in narcotics, and separated from the girl whose life had joined to flow with his, would be painful for them both but disastrous for Julieta. For the past fortnight she had been providing for the two of them. Now Mawi had to support his wife. Yesterday Julieta had tried to take out sterling at one of the banks, only to find her traveller's cheques had been stopped, presumably by her father or one of his cronies in the Government or the army or police. The second shock for them both was when the *soles* Warmi Imambari had paid them for the boat were refused by the bank, then by a *bureau de change*: nobody would change a currency for which there was so little demand, they were told. For Mawi the shock quickly wore off and became a challenge. He located a busy metro station in a well-heeled part of London half an hour's walk from their own less affluent area, bought his sombrero and box and started work at once. Today Mawi was taking home his first pile of coins. Julieta would know she had a man who could provide for her. The title of husband was starting to feel comfortable, like new shoes that had stopped pinching.

Walking along this stretch of the thoroughfare no longer made Mawi apprehensive. Among the grander houses of Santiago the Mapuche had been as welcome as stray dogs would have been in the city's Christian temples. Armoured buses were for ever disgorging police in riot gear in the smartest areas, so that members of the public who didn't look respectable or Hispanic enough could be rounded up and jailed as potential troublemakers. In London the police weren't even armed, most of them. They wore helmets that looked like bowler hats, or peaked caps that made them look like chauffeurs, and were glimpsed about as often as some rare species of wild duck. The houses and offices, which Mawi at first took for temples, with their white columns and façades, had no security fences.

Businessmen came and went self-confidently with their brief-cases, housewives arrived home with their shopping without looking nervously over their shoulders for muggers. This was obviously a wealthy area but the well-to-do white men in tailor-made suits, and their manicured, coiffured wives wearing designer clothes, were happy to share the pavement with Blacks, Asians, tattooed misfits with tattered jeans and holes in their shoes, and green-haired women with rings in their noses, fish-net stockings and shorts as short as underpants.

Mawi stopped to cross a street, looked to his left and saw a clump of cherry-trees in flower. He changed his mind and walked towards the mass of pink blossom. A garden extended as far as he could see left, right and in front of him. On this side was an endless terrace of white palaces. 'You can walk through Regent's Park,' Julieta had said to him, showing him the way in her A-to-Z. This must be Regent's Park. Was it for the public or only for the people living in the palaces, Mawi wondered. He saw an open gate and crossed the road. There they were again: the tailored suits and dresses, the torn jeans, the green hair and salon sets, the white, black and brown faces, the polished Italian shoes and the trainers that were falling apart, hurrying or strolling through the pink confetti, some with dogs trotting behind them on leads. He walked through the gate and caught glimpses through the cherry-blossom of a lake covered in ducks, swans and geese, and children standing at the edge throwing bread to them. For a vivid instant Mawi was in Chile, not in Santiago but near Temuco, a thousand kilometres further south, where he had grown up among forests and lakes teeming with wild life, and orchards full of blossom in the spring and fruit in the summer. Not that this park in the middle of a city was really much like Araucanía but the cherry-trees, the water and birds, the sunshine and mild air had conjured up his homeland for a moment. Mawi was a creature of the mountains and forests, not of cities. Santiago had been hell, Lima had promised worse, but London with all its trees was bearable. It seemed to be a city built by people whose roots were in the countryside. If Mawi had to live in a city, he would choose London. He hummed the tune of a Mapuche song, then started to sing to himself, as he walked through the park in the direction of King's Cross.

Mawi longed to be with Julieta. He hadn't been separated from her since their marriage nearly two weeks ago. He felt as he used to feel as a boy when he led the animals back from pasture at dusk, having left the village with them at daybreak. He remembered how hungry he used to be and how he hurried to be with his parents and sister, and his uncle and grandparents, and eat with them at the long table in the warmth of the *ruka* on chilly evenings in the spring and autumn, or in the shade of the jacaranda at the end of a hot summer's day. Now he was a young man, and family and physical pleasure had taken on a new dimension and intensity. Julieta was more than a table-companion: she was the very meal itself. Danger and discomfort had made their journey together a time of self-denial and restraint. Famine had become plenty and they could give themselves to each other now, body as well as soul. As they had done once during their journey, in the safety and comfort of Yucuma's guest-room. From now on, whenever they made love, even in London a few hundred metres from a busy railway station, in their thoughts they would be on the Isla del Sol, in the garden-house at the bottom of the meadow where they had left Pablo and Pedro grazing.

The park and road came to an end. Mawi rejoined the main road, where his song was lost in the din of passing cars and lorries, red double-decker buses and black taxis that looked like hearses for short corpses. If the road had been built to match the life-styles of those who lived along it, it would be going steeply downhill. The company directors and their wives had disappeared from the pavements, even if their shiny Mercs and BMWs could still be glimpsed speeding along the Marylebone Road past second-hand Minis and rickety Fords. By the time he reached King's Cross, Mawi seemed to have walked for years, rather than minutes, from the white palaces of Regent's Park, with brass plaques that were polished every day and three-metre-high windows that sparkled like diamonds, to the little brick houses near the station, whose coating of soot must have been deposited in the days of steam-trains.

Mawi was struck how the national flag became more important the further he walked down the social hill from Regent's Park, and how much like a prohibition it looked: two crosses on a blue background, like a sky seen through a heavily barred window. Many of the passers-by were holding little flags on sticks and most of the little terrace-houses had a flag in one or more of their windows, whose panes like the brickwork dated from an age of soot and steam-engines. Were the disadvantaged more patriotic in England, or simply less afraid to nail their tribalism to the mast? Their young began their lessons in belligerence at an early age, it seemed, as they toddled behind their mothers dressed in camouflage fatigues and wielding toy machine-guns.

Less than a hundred metres ahead Mawi saw the bar he had passed this morning on his way to Baker Street Station. It had a sign hanging high on the wall with a picture of a mounted army officer dressed in red, white and blue waving his sword and leading a mass of foot-soldiers in pursuit of a fleeing enemy. Mawi recognized one of the words under the picture. It was the same as the word on the cigarette-machines in Santiago: Marlborough. This morning the bar had been closed. Now the wooden tables with the benches attached to them on the pavement outside were full, large glasses of beer covered the table-tops and there seemed to be some sort of celebration going on: a group of about ten young men with shoulder-length hair were standing unsteadily with their arms round one another's necks, singing loudly and tunelessly. Forty or more empty beer-glasses were on the table next to them.

As Mawi got closer, he saw that the area outside the bar bristled with flags. All the drinkers were holding them. Flags festooned the walls and windows. The young men yelling out their song were wearing T-shirts made of flag. There must be an international football match, thought Mawi. He could hear the words of the song now but only two of them meant anything to him.

Ru Britannia, Britannia rus de vais,
Britain neva, neva, neva chalbi slais.

The singers kept repeating the same two lines. Perhaps these were the only two they knew. Gradually they formed a ring and, after a few more repetitions, they started to move, stamping, bending their knees and slowly circling.

Mawi had stopped twenty metres short of the gathering to watch the spectacle. It looked to him more like a war-dance than a celebration.

As if in response to his thought, the singing stopped and the chanting began.

Kil! Kil! Kil! Kil! Argentina!

The meaning of the display dawned on Mawi: the war with Argentina. He had completely forgotten about it. There were so many coups and revolutions in Latin America that he lost track of all the violence. Argentina was fighting Britain instead of Chile for a change, and this crowd of patriots were drinking vast quantities of beer, waving their flags, singing out of tune and performing a tribal dance to mark the event.

One of the warriors caught sight of Mawi. The chanting petered out and one by one the heads turned towards him. Some of the drinkers at the tables had looked round to stare at him too.

'They're looking for a victim to sacrifice to their god of war,' thought Mawi. Chilean? Argentinian? It didn't matter: anyone foreign-looking would do.

He stepped unhurriedly to the kerb and jay-walked to the other side of the road, safe in the knowledge that if the warriors tried to do the same with the amount of alcohol they had inside them, they would be bowled over like ninepins by a passing bus or lorry.

Mawi continued eastwards for two hundred metres until he came to the small street off the main road where he and Julieta had rented rooms. As he walked, he glanced over his shoulder. The beer-drinkers were no longer interested in him. Their attention had turned to one of their tribe – one of the warriors – who was kneeling on the kerb, vomiting into the gutter.

The only thing these rows of little brick terrace houses had in common with the palatial white ones in Regent's Park was that they all looked alike, the little houses like the other little ones, the big like the big. It was a mystery to Mawi how the residents, rich or down at heel, remembered where they lived, especially since hardly anyone bothered to put a number on the door. He would have found his way more easily in the forests of Araucanía. Luckily he had had the foresight to count the number of houses to the nearest lamp-post, and the number of lamp-posts to the main road.

Some instinct made Mawi glance behind him again. A fraction of a second later and he would have missed it: the brisk movements of someone about his own age, the shoulder-length hair, the tip of a black case disappearing into the newsagent's a hundred metres down the street on the opposite side. He waited two minutes. No one left the shop, so he turned and walked the last two lamp-posts to the little house where he and Julieta were staying. London must be full of young men with black cases: why should Mawi imagine he had seen the guitarist from Baker Street Station again?

There were three doorbells, each with its security microphone. Mawi and Julieta hadn't yet written their names on the strip of card that slipped under the piece of plastic beside their bell. They hadn't met or even seen the other tenants. The door of the ground-floor room opened a crack whenever they came in or went out but not enough to see who was peeping at them. Once they had heard the sound of a man shouting and a woman crying for a minute or two that seemed to come from downstairs, and a different man yelling and a small dog yelping that came from the first floor. Otherwise the house was as silent as a waiting predator, and the only sound was the distant rumble of traffic from the main road.

Mawi let himself in and closed the front-door quietly behind him. At once the door of the downstairs room was jerked open wide enough for Mawi to see a pair of bloodshot eyes and two bramble-bushes, one growing on a man's head, the other on his chest. The man growled something and banged his door shut. One of the neighbours was starting to make friends, it seemed.

He climbed the stairs past the two smouldering men. Mawi's and Julieta's rooms were on the top floor: *debajo del alero,* as Julieta put it. Under the eaves. Mawi had never heard the expression before. He liked the idea of being under the protective wing of the house. He found it exhilarating to be near the roof. Until his stay with Father Lorencio at Santo Domingo he had never slept above ground-floor level.

Mawi and Julieta had a big room *debajo del alero* with a window looking out on to the backs of the houses in the next terrace, like rows of drawers, each with its little rectangle of garden divided from the garden either side by a fence of vertical wooden slats. Some of the gardens were as tidy as chess-boards; others were overgrown. The window itself was in two parts, which slid up and down instead of opening like doors. The two halves stuck when you tried to slide them and couldn't be closed properly. It didn't matter in the spring or summer, Mawi thought, but the room would be draughty when the weather turned cold.

He reached the top of the stairs, opened the door and was welcomed by a smell of cooking.

'Salmon and new potatoes with mint,' Julieta called to him from the kitchen. 'Spanish strawberries the size of apples. They have lovely things in the shops. A bottle of French wine: Anjou *rosé* to go with the fish. I bought it chilled. And look! Real coffee! It's the same price as instant in England.'

'How did you pay?'

'Last of the dollars. I changed them this morning. Don't worry. I've got a job. Three pupils: two Japanese and one Iranian. First lesson tomorrow: they're paying sixteen pounds each when they start. Cash.'

'What makes two Japanese and an Iranian come to London to learn Spanish?'

'They're learning English. They say their English teachers can't speak or explain their own language, so they want me to teach them. I met them at the language school where I was trying to get work teaching Spanish.'

'Are you sure it's your English they're interested in, not your good looks?'

'I hope so,' Julieta laughed. 'They're all women. How did you get on? Did you find somewhere to play?'

'Baker Street Station. There was another busker. A guitarist. I think he wants me to play at a bar or club.'

'Are you going to? It can't do any harm, can it?'

'I'm happy playing in the metro station.'

Julieta came through from the kitchen in her jeans and a white blouse, with a white apron round her waist, put her arms round Mawi's neck and gave him a long, soft kiss. Her hair smelt of orange-blossom, as it had at Santo Domingo, the night of their first kiss.

'How much did you make?' she asked at last.

Mawi opened his flute case and poured the coins on to the bed.

Julieta's eyes opened wide in wonder. 'There must be twenty or thirty pounds,' she said.

Mawi emptied the contents of his pockets.

Julieta gave a cry of astonishment. 'Baker Street Station must be an Aladdin's cave. You sort it out while I dish up.'

Julieta went to the kitchen for the plates and Mawi arranged the coins in piles on the floor. She set the plates of salmon and new potatoes either side of a white vase full of apple-blossom, then counted the money while Mawi went to the table and opened the bottle of wine.

Contentment spread through Mawi's body, as if he had already taken his first sip of wine. He felt at ease in their room, which they had found with only one phone call, having bought a paper at the airport and scanned the property-to-let page. The doors into the little kitchen and little bathroom were open and it was full of sunshine at the moment, even if the sea-green curtains absorbed some of the light. Mawi was mystified by the decorations: by the primroses, brown with age, that covered the walls, painted on a pale blue background that had turned yellow in places, and printed on paper that was scratched and peeling at the corners; by the mainly dark red carpet, threadbare in places, with its ornate design fading, that hid most of the varnished wooden floor. In spite of the embellishments, this was home of a kind for Mawi and Julieta – not quite their own home, but a place on which someone had bestowed time and care years ago. They were pleased with their find, even if the rent would have paid for a suite in the presidential palace in Santiago.

The flatlet was furnished and crockery, glasses, cutlery, cooking utensils and bed linen had been provided by the landlord. The furniture was old and solid, made of dark wood: a dining-table, a bedside table, two chairs, a wardrobe, a standard lamp in the corner and a table lamp beside the bed. Only the bed was new: Mawi and Julieta were the first to use it. Mawi was relieved: he would rather sleep on the floor than on a smelly, stained old mattress but he could hardly ask Julieta to do the same.

'Ninety-six pounds forty-five pence,' Julieta called out as Mawi poured the *rosé*.

Julieta put the coins, one fistful after the next, into a plastic bag, took her wine from Mawi and clinked glasses with him. They drank to Father Lorencio, to Copihue and Julieta's mother, to the friends they had made on their journey, Chol, Yucuma, Tikamaki, to themselves and a future without fear.

35

When Mawi and Julieta walked out of the spring sunlight through double swing-doors into the miasma of beer dregs and ashtray at the Trafalgar in Camden on an evening in early May, they were greeted with a cheer as loud as an overhead thunderclap. They paused for a moment, touched with panic, then realized the cheer wasn't for them but for the picture on the giant television screen at the end of the large bar-room, where thirty to forty long-haired male beer-drinkers, mostly in their twenties and thirties, stood clutching mugs the size of chamber-pots.

'The home team must have scored a goal,' said Julieta.

She and Mawi edged across the dark brown lino for a clear view of the screen, past mainly solitary drinkers seated on green leatherette-upholstered chairs and stools at round black high-gloss wooden tables in front of beer-mats, square glass ashtrays and partly drunk mugs of beer. Occasional exchanges of monosyllables between tables, without a glance exchanged, were like ships' sirens calling to one another through the fog.

'They 'ad it comin' to 'em,' spluttered a red-nosed woman in her fifties or sixties from under her black straw hat crowned with cherries, fag in mouth, her chihuahua yapping at her feet.

'Teach 'em a lesson,' croaked an octogenarian with a collapsed face framed by a shiny black nylon Sofia Loren wig.

'Argy-bargy,' a man with swept-back greying hair honked sourly as he slouched on his stool in his stained beige mack.

The pictures that covered the walls of the Trafalgar reminded Julieta that the British were a seafaring people: reproductions of three-masted men-of-war firing their cannons, portraits of Admiral Horatio Nelson, one-armed, one-eyed but triumphant at the helm of his flagship, *HMS Victory*, Spanish galleons on fire, victorious British naval vessels being proudly refitted for their peacetime activities of slave-trafficking and piracy. She scanned the room in vain for paintings of merchant ships engaged in friendly trade with their European neighbours, or for peaceful yachting and trawling scenes like those she remembered from her book of Mediterranean artists.

When Mawi and Julieta found a gap between the heads of the beer-drinkers, it wasn't a football field they saw but the grainy picture of a massive warship. Black smoke was pouring from it – not from the funnel but from the body of the vessel. Every few seconds another mass of black smoke billowed up, as ammunition or fuel exploded in the spreading flames. Streaks of light like slow-moving sparks kept falling from the deck into the sea. Julieta asked Mawi, who had sharp eyes, what they were.

Mawi looked at the fountain of little lights for a moment, then murmured: 'They're men on fire, jumping into the water.'

Julieta clung to Mawi as they stood and watched a ship the size of a fortified mountain collapse into the sea, sucking down with it burnt men who were struggling not to drown. After two or three minutes only the bow was left above water. When this also disappeared from view, an even more thunderous cheer went up from the beer-drinkers.

Chile and Argentina had been fighting each other sporadically for centuries. Even during her own life Julieta had seen outbreaks of violence, though none of them had escalated into a full-scale war. She didn't remember any feelings of hatred in Chile towards Argentina. Disagreement between the two Hispanic neighbours over a strip of land in the far south of the continent was seen as inevitable. From time to time the leaders of the two countries felt compelled to send their armed forces to play out the old ritual for honour's sake. It was never accompanied by the blood-lust Mawi and Julieta had just witnessed.

'Let's go!' she said. 'This is horrible.'

This was the moment Mawi had been hoping for, to judge by his look of relief. It had been Julieta's idea to come to the

Trafalgar. He was happy busking, he had told her. Mawi had been busking eight hours a day and coming home rich but exhausted, Julieta replied; a gig would bring the same money in an hour that busking did in a day. They turned to leave and were greeted by a small man about their own age who had emerged from the crowd like a mole from the ground. Mawi's face fell.

'You – buy – drinks,' said the young man in a voice squeezed out through the long nose that drooped over his embryo moustache. 'Drink – with – us. Me and me mates is sittin' in corner.' The words were accompanied by a mime show to make their meaning clear to Mawi and Julieta.

'Is that the guitarist?' whispered Julieta when the young man was back with his mates.

Mawi nodded.

Julieta had had a vision of a dashing, dark-haired virtuoso, like the flamenco guitarists she had seen on television. When was the last time this little fellow had washed his mouse-brown hair or had it cut? He would have to be a genius of a musician to make up for his appearance. Julieta was now even less keen to stay. She waited for Mawi to give the signal to go and Mawi waited for Julieta to do the same. They were carried like a boat with a jammed rudder to the bar, where they stood hoping not to be noticed by the massive, middle-aged Anglo-Saxons in their shirt-sleeves, perched in pairs, top-heavy on their stools, conversing in undertones as if the rule of silence in churches and libraries also applied in pubs, except to those drinking for the glory of their country.

A good-looking black man in his late thirties, with the physique of a heavyweight boxer, appeared behind the bar, dressed in a white linen smock, and gave Mawi and Julieta a big smile as he turned on a tap and filled two bucket-sized mugs with frothing beer for a pair of giants spread over their stools like mushrooms on their stems.

'Welcome to the Trafalgar!' he said. 'Where you from?'

Julieta gulped. She didn't want to broadcast the news that she and Mawi were South American: some of these people might not realize that Chile wasn't Argentina. She could say France but what if the barman was from Senegal or Guinea and started speaking to Mawi in French? Spain? He might spend his holidays in Spain and know every corner of the country. 'Chile,' she replied at last, as quietly as possible.

'Chile?' boomed the friendly barman, pulling more beer as he spoke. 'That's South America, isn't it? Anywhere near Argentina?'

'The other side of the continent,' Julieta replied, quickly this time. Then, to be on the safe side, raising her voice slightly, she added: 'Chile's been at war with Argentina for centuries.'

'I wouldn't care if you was Argentinian,' said the publican with a hostile look at the crowd in front of the television. 'Everybody's welcome at my public house: Chilean, Argentinian, black, brown, white.'

The publican interrupted his welcoming speech to take an order. Julieta translated what had been said into Spanish.

'I come to England from Jamaica,' he went on, filling six more flagons with beer. 'The white boys at school called me a black bastard. I went to the gym every day for eight years and built up my muscles, made a few hundred grand wrestling, bought myself a public house. Everybody, I told myself, everybody will be welcome at my inn. Anyone calls me or one of the customers a bastard, black, brown or white, they'll be picked up like a sack of rubbish and pitched out of that door.'

The publican's speech didn't win him a glance from the large men on their stools. Julieta guessed they had reached an age when their testosterone was no longer at boiling-point and they preferred a quiet drink to a brawl and the risk of being swept up like refuse and tossed into the street. The only reaction was from the publican's assistant behind the bar, a small, thin Anglo-Saxon in his thirties with the chinless face and unblinking eyes of a lizard. He listened to what his boss was saying and darted him a poisonous glance.

'There's going to be changes here,' the publican went on, when he was back at his tap after working the till. 'All these paintings: I don't want to be looking at slave-ships and men-of-war all day.' He seemed to have taken to his two young South American customers. 'The television's going too. I'd switch it off now if I didn't know those savages would start smashing my windows. Music is what this public house is going to be about. Music brings people from all over the world together.'

Mawi paid for two glasses of wine – at the price of a crateful of bottles in Chile – and he and Julieta joined the guitarist and his mates at a table beyond the television screen, where they sat down on stools. Comment and discussion had followed live coverage on the speakers and screen behind them, and the nationalists' thirst had turned from blood to beer.

Julieta shuddered at the sight of the snakes tattooed on the guitarist's bare arms. His two companions could have been soap opera hit men in their studded black leather jackets and hobnail boots. Their hair was as short as his was long. Their fingers were stained with nicotine and they were wearing Rolex watches. They gripped their beer-mugs like vices in their tattooed hands. Their jaws were clenched as tight as their fists. The smell at the table was of beer, cigarette smoke, fried food and cheap after-shave.

'Don't – mind – me – mates,' said the guitarist, enunciating his words as if he were on a bad line to Bombay. 'They – bin – guests – of – Her – Majesty – for – past – six – months. It's – made – them – a – bit – tense – like.' He raised his voice for the introductions that followed. 'My name Johnny. They calls me Snake. Meet Dave.' He jabbed with his forefinger for the benefit of the two foreign half-wits. 'That's Dave. This is Jake – Jake.'

'Is that 'is bird?' said Jake. 'Reckon she's a good screw?' He raised his glass to his lips and seemed about to take a bite out of it. Julieta noticed the scar on his cheek and his filthy fingernails.

Moments later a bucketful of beer was gurgling down his throat like dirty water into a drain.

Julieta remembered the gentleness of men like Señor Achacachi and Warmi – of all the Peruvian and Bolivian Indians she had met. She thought of her own husband and his tenderness and friendship. Then she looked at the young Anglo-Saxons in the bar quenching their thirst without enjoyment, swilling down beer with a look of disgust, as if they were being forced to drink their own urine. Was this also how they ate and had sex? Grabbing, gulping, hogging? Julieta thought of her mother and Copihue. How she longed to see them! How they would love Mawi!

'Where you from then?' asked Snake.

Julieta pretended not to understand the question at first. She wanted to make communication as heavy-going as possible, in the hope Snake and his mates would lose interest and go. 'Chile,' she said, when she had feigned incomprehension for as long as she could.

Snake looked blank. 'Where's that? Iceland?'

Julieta drew an imaginary triangle on the table and ran her finger down one side of it. 'Peru. Bolivia. Chile.'

'South America,' said Snake.

Julieta nodded.

'Argentina,' said Jake, and belched.

Julieta shook her head. 'Chile.'

'Got your work permit, have you?' Jake asked Mawi.

He exchanged glances with his mates, then looked across the room at someone behind Julieta. She followed his glance to the bar and saw not the publican but the lizard glancing back at him from behind the row of beer taps. Alarm-bells jingled for a moment inside her head.

Julieta didn't translate the question. Mawi's affairs were no business of these people. She wished she hadn't persuaded Mawi to come to the Trafalgar against his instincts. She now wanted to get him out of the place as fast as she could.

'Through that door – big space for gigs,' Snake was shouting, having decided Mawi was deaf, as well as half-witted. 'Black publican – music freak. Different group every night.'

Mawi looked at Julieta. She translated. He nodded.

'You play couple of numbers for Tobias,' Snake went on. 'That's the publican. Show Toby what you can do. If he likes you, you got a guaranteed audience. A 'undred minimum. Maybe two or three 'undred. Five quid a punter. That's five 'undred quid. A grand or fifteen 'undred if you pulls the crowds. Twenty per cent goes to the 'ouse. We splits the rest fifty-fifty: 'alf for you, 'alf for me and me mates. You'll be gettin' two 'undred quid minimum, six 'undred if you're lucky. What do you say?'

Julieta translated.

'I don't want to work with these people,' said Mawi. 'I'm happy busking in Baker Street Station.'

Julieta decided to give up playing the soft-headed foreigner and bring the discussion to an end. 'My husband's very grateful for your offer, and your interest in his work,' she said curtly, 'but he can earn the sort of money you're suggesting playing on the street for a few hours. He wonders if you could double the ticket price and guarantee an audience of three hundred.'

Snake and his cronies stared open-mouthed at Julieta. Jake's beer hung ten centimetres from his mouth like dish-water in a blocked sink. The foreign bird talked English almost as good as they did. And she had the nerve to ask twelve hundred quid for an evening's piping by a total unknown.

'Er – right,' said Snake when he found his voice. 'The problem is, you see, I can't give them sort of guarantees. Sure you could make a couple of 'undred quid buskin' on a good day but you wouldn't get no kudos. A pub like the Traffy 'as kudos, you see. It may not be the Albert 'All, and the money may not be what Marlon Brando pulls for a lead part in a 'Ollywood blockbuster, but for up-and-comin' jazz musicians and the like the Traffy 'as kudos. What's your name by the way? I didn't ask.'

'I'll tell him my name but that doesn't mean I'll work with him,' said Mawi when Julieta had finished translating.

Mawi borrowed Julieta's biro and wrote his name in capitals on the back of a beer-mat.

'Crumbs!' said Snake, trying to pronounce the polysyllabic words. He pocketed the beer-mat.

As if to celebrate a contract that had just been signed, a band struck up from somewhere behind Mawi and Julieta, in the bar area. They left their drinks to go and investigate.

They brushed aside the curtain covering a doorway just next to the counter and found themselves on the threshold of a room three times the size of the bar-room behind them. A group of four black musicians with dreadlocks were in full swing in a warm-up jam session on the stage at the far end of the room: trumpet, sax, percussion and bass. They played with easy professionalism. There were about fifteen rows of chairs, with an aisle in the middle leading from the platform to the door. The decorations were a world away from those of the bar: autographed photos in clip-on frames of Louis Armstrong, Ella Fitzgerald, Thelonius Monk and a dozen others, even if the autographs had a printed look about them. The electrician was experimenting with his filters, bathing the musicians first in violet light, then working his way through the spectrum: indigo, green, yellow, orange, red.

'You can't work with those three,' Julieta said quietly to Mawi. 'It would be a pact with the devil. Two of them are just out of prison: that's why their hair's so short.'

'I like the owner,' Mawi replied. 'Tobias. I trust him. He cares about music. Musicians as good as these four wouldn't play for him if he didn't.'

Mawi and Julieta went back into the bar, finished their drinks and took their leave of Snake and his two ex-convict mates.

'We got a deal then?' asked Snake.

'We'll think about it,' replied Julieta.

They were about to go out through the swing-doors when Mawi stopped, turned and walked over to the bar. 'Good-bye,' he called in English to Tobias.

'Come again!' Tobias called back. 'Do you like music? I saw you listening to the quartet.'

'My husband's a musician,' said Julieta, who had followed Mawi to the bar.

'What do you play?'

'He plays the Mapuche flute.'

'Why don't you come and play a couple of pieces for us? We might be able to fit you into one of our evenings.'

Mawi and Julieta walked out into the mild spring air and set off in the twilight back towards King's Cross.

Gotcha! was the headline on the newspaper-stands. News of the sinking of the Argentinian warship was already in print. If Englishmen could raise their glasses and cheer at the sight of hundreds of young men enveloped in flames throwing themselves into the sea, thought Julieta, what hope was there for the millions of children dying quietly of dysentery, thirst and starvation in those parts of the world that were printed pink in the old atlas she used to leaf through as a child?

36

Mawi stood on the platform of the music-room at the Trafalgar, calm, self-assured, floating above his listeners, playing for them as if they were family or friends.

The five musicians grew younger as they played. The music was working its transforming magic. Time had gone into reverse. Job and Paul, the sax and double-bass players, were twenty-five at the most now, having started the gig in their middle or late thirties. Ricky and Lou, the trumpeter and percussionist, were even younger – early twenties instead of early thirties. Their everyday cares vanished visibly as the music filled them: the tension disappeared from their faces, a childlike sparkle returned to their eyes. Their energy grew with every note they played. Their bodies became as supple and relaxed as the bodies of teenagers, and their music almost made them dance.

Snake, Jake and Dave, who couldn't have been much older than Mawi in years, had changed ages with the four black musicians and left whatever youth they had behind. Snake's small, closely set eyes glittered with a miser's avarice as he sat hunched threadbare over his growing pile of sovereigns and fivers. Dave and Jake, in black leather, stood over him like two security guards, their faces as lined as old crab-apples with tension and hostility.

Job, Paul, Ricky and Lou might be a joy to watch and listen to, with their bright, clean clothes, youthful energy and musical talent, but to Julieta's mind they were little more than a background for Mawi. Mawi was the youngest of the band by nearly a decade and with them he had shed his years since the gig began. He was the best-looking and best-dressed member of the band – of everyone in the room. This wasn't partiality on Julieta's part. She had heard it confirmed by people in the audience, both black and white. She didn't mind taking a little of the credit for his appearance: she had trimmed his thick black hair so that it now fell just over his ears but didn't hide them, and covered his neck without touching the collar; and she had washed and ironed his pale brown cotton trousers and long-sleeved white Mapuche shirt, taking care not to damage the bird and butterfly wings embroidered down the front. Credit also had to go to Emmanuel, the black electrician, who had lit the platform and wall behind so that Mawi was playing in what looked like soft sunlight against a cloudless azure sky.

Julieta had tried to do a head-count but the concert had only just got under way and people kept arriving or changing places to be with friends. There must have been nearly two hundred already. Ages ranged from five or six to about eighty but most of the audience were between twenty and forty. Clothes were loose and informal, with a few flamboyant touches: a jacket covered in gold and silver buttons, a young black woman whose head was a mass of silk flowers and butterflies pinned into her hair, a man with one green and one yellow shoe. Julieta looked colourful herself in Copihue's Mapuche skirt and shawl. She didn't recognize any of last week's beer-drinkers. There didn't seem to be many drinkers at all. A few of the crowd were holding glasses but most had come to listen, not to drink. And not to bay for blood. This audience was as relaxed and peaceable as last week's television audience had been tense and bloodthirsty. The drinkers in the bar that day had almost all been men. Julieta could see as many women as men in the music-room tonight. At least half the faces were black.

Julieta looked around her for Tobias but there was still no sign of him. Where could he be? He had been in the bar earlier and had promised to come through as soon as the music started. Without Tobias there would be no concert. He had been in raptures when Mawi played for him. It was Tobias who had brought together Mawi and the quartet. It was thanks to his enthusiasm and hard work that there were so many here tonight.

Where was he?

Mawi's playing was sometimes joyful and celebratory, sometimes sad and thoughtful, sublime in its simplicity, breath-taking in its virtuosity. Julieta was among the peaks of the Andes as she listened, riding on Pablo under a sky filled with bright pinpoints of light while Mawi led the way as masterfully as he played the flute, or lying on the deck of their reed boat, suspended between the gentian sky and its reflection in the waters of Lake Titicaca, watching Mawi work the ropes and steer his course, using his sharp eyes by day and the stars by night.

Mawi was beautiful to listen to and to watch, with his brown, outdoor skin and strong, supple body, his long, thin fingers that seemed to fly like birds up and down his flute, and his facial bones as fine as those of his hands. But if the beauty of his music and appearance touched the senses, thought Julieta, it did so to carry his audience's thoughts and feelings beyond the experience of pleasure, just as the statues crafted by the Ancient Greeks aimed to concentrate the minds of those who contemplated them on virtue, beauty of thought and perfection of form. Mawi had told Julieta that his music brought him close to his ancestors, to the surviving members of his community, to the forests and lakes of Araucanía and the birds that called from the branches and shallows. For Mawi music was the language of his gods. His flute was the voice with which he spoke to them and which they listened to. Art and morality were one when he played, it seemed to Julieta; there was goodness in his music, and this communicated itself to his listeners.

Julieta was roused from her thoughts for a moment by the stillness in the room: not a cough, not a breath or rustle, not a shuffle of shoes or a brushing of clothes. Mawi was playing quietly. Julieta had heard the piece before, this lament without despair. All the suffering of the Mapuche people seemed to be there for those who were attuned to it – in the breathing and rise and fall of the music. Where did the suffering of Mawi's people end and his own begin? Julieta had no idea. His own wife hadn't asked him about his past, and hadn't been told. Their intimacy was a continent on which they had only just set foot together.

A voice spoke to Julieta through the playing. It took her only a few seconds to recognize it. It was the voice of the missionary on the flight from Lima to London and it was as clear as if Julieta's borrowed *grand'maman* were sitting next to her in the music-room. 'Flowery cottages and country walks are for poets and dreamers, my dear,' said the voice, 'and for old people like me who have been put out to grass. Your place is not with the Romantic poets, who rhapsodized over the grassiness of English hills and the tranquillity of English lakes while English slave-raiders prowled the African coast and traded in human misery, but among the poor of your own continent, rebuilding their lives after nearly five centuries of exploitation, helping the hungry to feed themselves, the sick to recover their health and the illiterate to read and write.'

Mawi and Julieta had found a home in London and could earn enough from their teaching and playing to live comfortably. Mawi could make a reputation as a musician. Yet Julieta longed to get back to the Andes and Lake Titicaca, to help the *cooperativa* at Cuzco and start her project on the Isla del Sol. She knew London was only a temporary home for Mawi too, that he would lose touch with his gods if he stayed and that his music would lose its sublimity. Julieta would like her children to say of their parents, as she said of her sixteen-hour *grand'maman*: 'This was life well spent, blessed by God, a model to follow.'

Julieta remembered now where she had heard the piece Mawi was playing. It was at Santo Domingo, the night she left home to get away from Adolfo Cortez, Herman Gorringe and her father, and to be with Mawi. It was the piece he was practising in his room with the window open, while Julieta stood in the shadows below, touched by the sorrow and joy in the music. Now she was as spellbound as her fellow-listeners.

Julieta heard shouts from the bar: not of disorder and havoc, as far as she could tell, but of command and control. Where was Tobias? Why didn't he stop the disturbance? She was about to leave her seat near the exit to slip out and ask for quiet when the connecting door was thrown open and a group of men barged in and marched along the aisle towards the platform. Julieta jumped up and went after the four men.

The sight of their machine-guns and uniforms did nothing to stop her. She had spent the past ten years under a régime where it was usual for men in uniform to march into a room full of people, massacre them all and return home after the day's work to gurgle at their babies and dandle them on their knees. If these men were going to riddle Mawi with bullets, they would have to riddle Julieta first. Policemen, were they? They looked more like park-keepers in their navy-blue uniforms with their peaked caps and black-and-white check cap-bands. Two were thick-set and obviously spent their spare time straining in the gym. The other two looked too puny for anything more strenuous than ping-pong.

The four policemen fanned out at the foot of the platform. Mawi brought his playing to a close, not stopping dead but finishing on a cadence. The other musicians followed suit.

'Is your name— ?' The voice of one of the two thick-set policemen sounded through the last notes of the music like a car-horn. He stopped in mid-sentence either because he couldn't read his own writing or because he couldn't pronounce the name.

Julieta's feet hardly touched the steps as she flew from the floor of the room on to the platform. She turned and looked down at the policeman holding his notebook.

'My husband's name is Mawi,' she said in a voice loud enough for everyone in the room to hear, feeling and sounding calm in spite of the situation. 'He doesn't speak English, so I'll have to translate whatever it is you want to say to him.'

The officer took a moment to try and remember whether the

rule-book allowed him to use a suspect's wife as an interpreter. Realizing he had no alternative, he continued with his police-speak.

'We have received information, Madam, providing reasonable grounds for us to believe that your husband, if this gentleman is in fact your husband and if his name is—' The policeman stopped once more to try and decipher or pronounce the name written in his notebook.

'Mawi,' said Julieta, coming to his assistance again.

'...That he's a foreign national engaged in gainful employment in this country without the permit required by law.'

'My husband was invited to play here tonight,' Julieta replied. 'If he's not allowed to be paid, he'll play for nothing. He's a musician. He plays for the love of it.'

'Yes!' a voice called out from behind Julieta – Ricky's, she thought.

The audience had been sitting in silence listening to the exchange between Julieta and the police officer, as if it were part of the performance they had paid to attend. Now they were on their feet, applauding – not riotously but warmly: the gifted flautist and his feisty wife had won their hearts and their support.

The policeman was nothing like the ones Julieta had come across in Chile, who shouted and pointed their guns and, as often as not, fired them. This English policeman was more like a postman who had delivered bad news. He was more apologetic than officious and wore his machine-gun like an embarrassing stain on his uniform.

'The information we have received,' said the officer, struggling on, 'is that the foreign national believed to be gainfully employed without the legally required permit agreed to accept eight per cent of the revenue from the public performance currently taking place on these premises.'

Julieta noticed Snake and the two ex-convicts standing at the back of the room observing their victim caught in the trap they had set for him. Who else could have told the police? Why did they do it? What did they have against Mawi?

'I've already told you,' Julieta said to the policeman. 'If my husband can't be paid, he'll play for nothing.'

'We need to hear that from the suspect himself. If he'll be good enough to accompany us to the police station, one of Her Majesty's interpreters will translate what he says for us.'

Julieta explained to Mawi what she and the policeman had been saying. Mawi quietly put his flute in its case and unhurriedly climbed down the steps from the platform.

'Why do you need four men with machine-guns to arrest an unarmed musician who hasn't done anything wrong?' Julieta asked as she followed Mawi down the steps. 'It's because his skin's a few shades too dark, isn't it? Because he's South American, like me, and your leaders like to believe that all dark-skinned people bristle with bombs and guns? We're not Argentinian. We don't believe in war. We believe countries should relate to one another through music, not with weapons.'

Another 'Yes!' from behind Julieta and more applause from the audience. The clapping continued as Julieta followed Mawi and the four officers along the aisle to the door. Murmurs of 'Pigs!' and 'Bluebottles!' from each row of seats as the policemen passed were mixed with words of encouragement for Mawi and Julieta.

'Are you arresting me too?' asked Julieta when they reached the bar.

'No, madam,' replied the officer who had done the talking.

'I want to come with you. I want to be with my husband.'

'I'm afraid that won't be possible, madam.'

'At least tell me where you're taking him.'

'Marylebone Police Station. Just down the road from here.'

'When can I visit him?'

'If we can find an interpreter quickly, he may be home before you, madam. If not, your best plan is to phone or call at the station tomorrow morning.'

The four policemen swept through the swing-doors with Mawi, and Julieta was left standing alone in the bar. She looked at the counter in the hope Tobias would be back in his place. Instead, she saw the lizard smirking at her as he filled a mug with beer from a tap.

'Where's Tobias?' Julieta asked him.

'I'm afraid they took him in for questioning too… madam,' he replied glibly, his voice unctuous, his face puckered into a sneer. 'Something about hiring foreign musicians without work permits.'

Julieta just stopped herself picking up the partly drunk mug from the table next to her and throwing the beer in the barman's face.

The audience were starting to come into the bar from the music-room. Julieta would rather meet a crowd of lepers than the three rats who had shopped Mawi. Nor did she want to be the centre of everyone's curiosity. She went out into the twilight and waited in the shadows under the spread of a plane-tree. She needed to talk to Job, Paul, Ricky and Lou.

Snake and the two ex-cons were among the first out, Snake with his hunched, busy walk, the other two taking ostrich strides, their gorilla arms hanging beside them, knuckles facing forward, their hobnail boots grating on the pavement. Snake was carrying a knotted plastic bag that presumably contained the evening's takings. They hurried away into the growing darkness. A minute later Julieta heard two motor cycles start up.

The rest of the audience were in no hurry to go. Some must have stayed for a drink or to talk to the musicians. Others were standing just outside the doors, chatting.

With every minute that passed, Julieta's patience was stretched a little further. At last, when it was near breaking-point, the four musicians came out of the Trafalgar, carrying their instrument-cases. Julieta hurried over to them.

'All this is Snake's doing,' she said. 'What's he got against Mawi? And Tobias? They've arrested Tobias too.'

'Not just Snake,' said Job the sax player, the oldest of the four. 'Ken, too.'

'Ken?'

'The barman. He's got friends in one of the big breweries. Wants Tobias to lose his licence so his friends can buy the pub and sell him the concession at a knock-down price.'

'And Snake? What's in it for him?'

'We'll tell you in the car if you want a lift. Where d'you live? First thing tomorrow morning we'll call for you and drive you to the pig farm. They're arresting South Americans all over London. It's called national security. They'll let him go as soon as he can prove he's not an Argentinian spy.'

Julieta couldn't help thinking of her father, and smiling, as she climbed into a rattletrap of an old blue Ford with four young black musicians she had met at a far from smart pub in not the most elegant part of London. How he would rant, if he could see her, at the folly of a daughter who strayed so far from the affluent, respectable areas he remembered, Knightsbridge, Belgravia and Westminster, and associated with men of the wrong social class and race. Julieta felt safer with Job, Paul, Ricky and Lou than she would ever have felt with the sons of her father's colleagues in high office.

37

Mawi was astonished at the friendliness and courtesy of the police officers at the Comisaría de Marialabuena, as he called his new home, especially of the two policewomen and two young men not much older than himself, one of them with a face browner than his own and the other with the blackest skin he had ever seen. After yesterday's armed raid on the Trafalgar Mawi had steeled himself for shouting, beatings and torture. Instead, he was treated almost with gentleness by his keepers, who offered him cigarettes, which he declined, having tried one and not liked it, and endless cups of tea with milk and sugar, some of which he accepted, mainly out of politeness. At first Mawi thought he was being softened up for a brutal interrogation but, when the two young policemen brought him his flute, having first made sure it wasn't a blowpipe filled with poisoned arrows, and indicated that he could play whenever and for as long as he liked, he decided he was being treated more like a guest than a prisoner. Instead of being the victim of an exclusively Anglo-Saxon organization of thugs, he felt almost welcome among these racially mixed guardians of civil peace. Would the day ever come, he wondered, when the Mapuche were admitted into Chile's Hispanic *policía*.

Through the barred opening in his cell door Mawi had a good view of the open-plan office area of the police station. There the two brawny members of the Trafalgar raiding party, unarmed now, spent their time between call-outs tapping slowly on electric typewriters, making and receiving phone calls and drinking one cup of tea after the next. They bantered with each other and their younger colleagues and were more like favourite uncles than members of an anti-terrorist squad. The two shrimpish, pale-faced policemen who had made up the quartet seemed in their element doing clerical work and were obviously rattled when some crisis forced them to leave their desks and sent them hurrying to a car waiting for them in the yard, its blue light flashing.

A woman in a white overall brought Mawi lunch the day after his arrest and seemed devastated, and racked by maternal worry, when he didn't eat it. It wasn't that Mawi had lost his appetite – just that swallowing the food she brought was more of a punishment than being locked in a cell. The cell was no worse than the hotel room at Arica, and a lot safer: clean, whitewashed, dry, not too hot or cold, with a single bed that was the height of comfort by Mawi's standards, and a little barred window with a view of the police car park. The surprising thing was that Mawi's jailers in the office he could see through the bars of his cell door were given exactly the same food as their prisoner and seemed to enjoy it. English palates and appetites – those of the police, anyway – were obviously titillated and satisfied by stringy meat and mushy boiled potato in cold gravy. Mawi wished he could share their tastes as he watched them at their desks gorging their stew. The woman in white made a discovery: the young South American liked eggs. During his first few hours in custody she brought him more eggs than he normally ate in a year: hard-boiled, soft-boiled, fried, poached, scrambled.

When Julieta called for the first time, soon after Mawi's breakfast of egg, toast and tea, she was given VIP treatment. The young black officer brought her an upholstered chair to sit on while she talked to her husband, closed the cell door but didn't lock it, to allow her some privacy without making her feel a prisoner herself, and went back to his desk. Mawi guessed his own friendly welcome at the police station was almost certainly thanks to Julieta and her defiant stand on the platform at the Trafalgar.

It was only when Julieta seized him and hugged him that Mawi realized how much he had missed her since last night and how painful it was to be parted from her for more than a few hours now that his life drew all its energy and purpose from her love and companionship.

'They want me to bring your passport for them to see,' Julieta said when she had let Mawi go and found her breath and voice. 'Then they reckon they should be able to release you without waiting any longer for their translator.'

'The police came looking for me at the Trafalgar,' Mawi said quietly. 'Something about a permit. How would they have known? Somebody must have given them my name.' Mawi had lain awake in his cell till after he heard a church clock strike two, trying to guess who had been behind the raid. Chilean agents working for Julieta's father? British agents tailing all recent arrivals from South America?

'Snake gave them your name. Who else? Snake and his two cronies and the reptile behind the bar. It wasn't forty per cent of the box office takings they were after. They were blackmailing Tobias: a thousand pounds each or they would go to the police and torpedo the concert. Tobias called their bluff.'

'Where is he now?'

'In a police or prison cell somewhere. Paul, Ricky and the other two told me. They said it was all done by letter and phone. Tobias didn't realize who was behind it. He put Snake and his friends in charge of box office. I saw them walk off with all the money before the audience came out.'

Julieta went back to the flat for Mawi's passport and called again as he was finishing his lunch of eggs – scrambled topped with fried. She was greeted in the office like an old friend. Soon after she arrived the mood inside the police station changed. The young black policeman opened the door and spoke to Julieta. He was obviously embarrassed. He returned to the office area, leaving the door open.

'It's your passport,' Julieta explained, keeping her voice down. 'The name on it is nothing like the one we gave the three rats at the Trafalgar.'

'Easy,' replied Mawi. 'One name for the Spanish, the other for the Mapuche: my Mapuche name for music; the Spanish one for passports.'

'They can't keep you any longer without charging you. They don't want to let you go without questioning you, but their Spanish translator's in hospital having his gall-bladder removed. They regret very much, madam, but feel compelled to charge my husband.'

'What with?'

'They'll think of something. Having two names? Playing the flute in public without the Queen's permission?'

The black officer reappeared in the doorway and announced that the time allowed for Julieta's visit had run out. She got up. Her upholstered chair was removed. She told Mawi she would come and see him as soon as they let her. She seemed shaken and close to tears.

'Be careful!' Mawi whispered when the policeman was out of sight for a few moments. 'Your own passport. Your two names.'

Julieta gave Mawi a quick kiss and went out through the door being held for her, which was at once closed and locked.

Visits from the two young officers stopped, as did the flow of tea. The only cups now came with the eggs, which were brought with unchanging maternal concern by the woman in white. The black policeman came in again and, with an apologetic look in his eyes, confiscated Mawi's flute.

Mawi watched the sun set over the roofs the other side of the car park, then went to bed. He had no fear for himself. The police were as gentle as lambs. He almost wished they had more of the wolf about them: he would be able to worry about himself instead of about Julieta. If they put one and one together to make a couple, they would guess that Julieta's identity was as ambiguous as his own. If she wasn't arrested herself, and if Mawi was kept locked up for more than a week or two, she would run out of money. Three pupils were not going to bring in enough to pay the rent and buy food. What then? She would be forced to phone her father and try and persuade him to have her traveller's cheques reinstated.

Mawi fell asleep and dreamt he was in a cage hanging from a beam near the ceiling of an immensely high room. The door of the cage was open, but without wings he had no way of escaping. As soon as he started to play the flute, wings appeared from his shoulders but the door of the cage slammed shut. He woke and heard the church clock striking. With the clarity of thought and purpose the brain has at four o'clock in the morning, Mawi knew he must stop Julieta from seeing him again while he was in custody, however painful this might be for them both. Running out of money was a lesser evil than losing one's freedom. Julieta was intelligent and resourceful. She would find work to pay the rent and feed herself.

At half past nine, after his tea, egg and toast, the two young policemen arrived and indicated in a friendly but formal way that Mawi had to accompany them somewhere. He was escorted out of his cell, through the office, down a flight of steps and out into the car park he had been looking at through the bars of the cell window, along a walkway thoughtfully covered because of the daily threat of rain, to the building next door, up another flight of steps into a corridor full of people, some in jeans, others in dark suits, through double doors into what Mawi at first took for a modern place of worship but then realized was a courtroom. The officers gestured him to a row of padded blue chairs and sat down either side of him.

Mawi saw that what he thought was an altar for sacrifices – turning wine into blood, beer into some other body fluid: however the English communicated with their gods – was in fact a large desk on a dais, with three chairs like his own waiting to be occupied. Behind the desk were two massive curtains the colour of the sun at noon and, hanging in front of them, a sheet of heavy dark blue cloth with a design woven into it in gold, red, white and paler blue thread: a lion and a unicorn, animals presumably indigenous to England, a crown, a shield and a motto. Mawi wondered whether the curtains would open in the course of the morning to reveal the Queen of the English in all her majesty, dazzling in her pearls and gilded diadem and sequins, seated as Julieta had described her on a heap of diamonds and rubies pillaged by her piratical ancestors from the continents they had helped to impoverish.

There were two other people in the courtroom, both poring over files: a man in a suit and tie at a desk below the dais and a woman with pudding-basin grey hair at a table just behind Mawi and his escorts. The woman finished her reading, got up and came round the table to speak to Mawi. She was dressed in a pleated black skirt and a white blouse. For a moment Mawi thought she was a waitress come to offer him yet another cup of tea.

'Soy traductora empleada del gobierno de Su Majestad.' The words were right but the accent was so English that Mawi needed a moment or two to make sense of them: the woman was an interpreter working for Her Majesty's Government.

Mawi was mesmerized by her moustache. He had seen down on women's upper lips before but this woman had bristles, and hairs that curled. She had them on the backs of her hands too. Like an Argentinian gaucho, he thought: she just needed the stetson, black cigar, black leather trousers and horse. He couldn't resist a glance at her legs: even through the thick stockings he could see clusters of long black hairs like crushed spiders. She was flat-chested and had a contralto voice. Mawi's translator was either an unconvincing female impersonator, he reckoned, or a woman who had overdosed on hormone treatment when she was entering a professional world dominated by men.

The translator suddenly scuttled to her place behind the table, the suited man was on his feet at his desk and the two policemen stood up, gesturing to Mawi to do the same. Two more double doors the other side of the courtroom opened and a short, middle-aged woman, dressed in black and white like the translator, marched in, head held high, followed by two tall men in suits, older than she was, who kept their eyes on the floor half a metre in front of them and struggled to keep up with their leader as she strode towards the dais. In their wake hurried more women in black and white and men in suits who Mawi guessed were ushers and secretaries. Last into the court, scrutinized by two policewomen standing guard at the entrance, were a handful of people in more casual clothes – journalists, perhaps – who moved without the urgency and self-importance of most of the court officials.

An usher was about to close the double doors when a young woman in jeans and a white blouse stepped through them: Julieta. Mawi just stopped himself waving to her, then waving her away. His heart longed for her but his head told him it wasn't safe for her to be here. She saw him, raised the fingers of one hand to him for a moment and gave him an encouraging smile. Mawi felt a surge of self-confidence and courage – of joy, almost. All this gravity and formality, which could have oppressed him, now seemed absurd. What did it matter when he had Julieta's love and she his?

The woman on the dais and the two men flanking her paused behind their chairs, then all sat down together under the twinkling eyes of the lion and unicorn. This was the signal for the rest of the court to sit. The coat of arms perched just above the chairwoman's head like an enormous crown. She barked at her two colleagues, who nodded meekly, then at the translator, who barked back, then at Mawi, who looked blank. The two policemen led him a metre or so towards the dais, then stepped back, and the translator appeared at his side, handed him a laminated card and told him to read aloud the words written on it.

Mawi had learnt to read and write Spanish during his three

years at school but had received his more advanced education without books or writing from the elders of his community. As a result, he had long ago formed the habit of listening, rather than reading, and memorizing, instead of writing. His reading and writing were rusty, for want of practice.

The woman on the dais barked at the translator, who asked Mawi if he could read. Mawi nodded.

At last he deciphered the Spanish words on the card and swore by the gods of the English to tell the truth, the whole truth and nothing but the truth. What would their gods do to him, he wondered, if he told only part of the truth. Set him on fire, perhaps, and throw him into the sea to drown or be eaten by sharks.

'What is your name?'

The chairwoman was barking at him again from under her carnival crown. He had been about to retreat to his chair but one of the policemen was signalling to him to stay where he was. The translator translated.

'José Luis Gutiérrez, *señora.*'

'I have another name here: Ñan— Ñanko— Ñankomawi—' The woman on the dais was experiencing the same difficulty as the policeman at the Trafalgar.

'That's my Mapuche name, *señora.*'

'Your what?'

'I am a Mapuche.'

'You have a Chilean passport?'

'Yes, *señora.*'

'Are you Chilean?'

'The Mapuche live partly within the borders of Chile. They have been living there since long before Chile existed. For hundreds – no, thousands – of years. The Spanish arrived four hundred and fifty years ago and for three and a half centuries tried to drive us off our land. They defeated us a hundred years ago, and killed many of our people, but we still regard the land as ours.'

Mawi was proud to tell the court a little about a nation perhaps none of them had heard of. It didn't occur to him he might be setting a trap for himself.

'Where is this land of yours?' The chairwoman took a map of South America from among her papers.

'In the Lake District, *señora*. A thousand kilometres south of Santiago.'

The *señora* studied the map for half a minute, then exclaimed: 'Just across the border from Argentina!'

'Everyone in Chile lives just across the border from Argentina, *señora*,' Mawi replied, when he had waited for the translation. 'Except those in the far north, who live just across the border from Peru and Bolivia.'

'Have you ever been to Argentina?'

'Yes, *señora*. I have relatives living there. The Mapuche live both sides of the border. The border was placed there by the Spanish invaders thousands of years after the Mapuche made the region their home.'

'Do you regard yourself as more Chilean or Argentinian?'

'I regard myself as Mapuche, *señora*.'

'So you don't regard yourself as Chilean?'

'I have a Chilean passport. I am a citizen of Chile.'

'What is your native language?'

'Mapudungun: the language of the Mapuche.'

'But you speak fluent Spanish?'

'Everyone in Chile has to learn Spanish, *señora*.'

'Spanish is the main language of the Argentinians, is it not?'

'Yes, *señora*.'

'You have no special loyalty to Chile, you have relatives in Argentina and you speak the language of the Argentinians fluently. Am I right?'

Mawi realized what the woman was driving at and was too astonished to reply. What paranoid fantasies was the quarrel

Britain had fuelled with the tin-pot leaders of Argentina's dilapidated régime creating in the mind of this dragon of the English Establishment? Was she a true reflection of a country that a few years ago had ruled an empire many times larger than that of the Incas? She belonged in the law-courts of one of the smaller South American countries, Paraguay or French Guiana, hearing conspiracy in the buzz of every fly and suspecting the rest of the world of plotting her country's extermination. Or in the same games arcade as the louts at the Trafalgar, obsessively feeding in coins as she twiddled the knobs of her war game. This woman also had a moustache, Mawi noticed: not curling and bristling vegetation like the translator's but a definite bloom of black mould above her upper lip.

'Why are you in England? What are you doing in this country?' Having had no answer to her previous question, the dragon was firing another.

'I'm here on my honeymoon,' Mawi replied, after a pause for the translation.

'Honey— ?' Obviously nothing so simple as the love of a young man for his bride was thinkable in this psychotic's fantasy world of intrigue and espionage. 'Where are you living? In London? In a hotel?'

'London. Kincross.'

'King's Cross. Not very romantic, is it? What address?'

'Two streets after Kincross Railway Station. Turn left. Four houses after the fourth lamp-post on the right-hand side.'

A guffaw from the back of the courtroom – from a journalist perhaps – was silenced by a look of fury from the dais.

The man at the desk below the throne turned and whispered to the dragon queen.

'Oh yes,' she said. 'We're forgetting something. Read the charge, will you please?'

A clerical-looking man in black, thin, bald and bespectacled, rose from a table the other side of the courtroom and addressed

Mawi. After wrestling with the twelve syllables of the two Mapuche names, he said:

'You are charged with travelling to this country under a false name and with false documents. Do you plead guilty or not guilty?'

Mawi waited for the translation, then replied calmly: 'Not guilty.'

The man below the dais turned to the dragon again and half-rose from his chair. They whispered for at least a minute. The dragon turned to the colleague on her right and had to shake him to wake him up. She whispered to him. He nodded. She whispered to the old fellow on her left, who also nodded. She spoke aloud to Mawi.

'This court is not competent to make a judgement involving the technicalities of national security. The case is referred to a higher court. You will be remanded in custody pending trial or extradition.'

'You mean they're keeping me locked up till they've finished their war with Argentina?' Mawi said to the interpreter with cheerful contempt when she had translated the dragon's decision. 'Just in case I turn into a butterfly, fly through your Prime Minister's window, overhear her talking to herself in the bath, then phone the generals in Buenos Aires to report what she's said?'

The moustache quivered in outrage at this savage who scoffed at the solemnity of one of her great country's courts of law, whose judgement and integrity were beyond all doubt, and who showed disrespect for the chief of Her Majesty's ministers.

Mawi looked about him for Julieta as the two policemen escorted him towards the door. She was already at his side.

'I'll come and see you as soon as they let me,' she told him.

'Safer not to,' he said, hoping she would understand. 'You'll need money. Try phoning Father Lorencio. They could have let him go. He may be able to help.'

Mawi's escorts were not allowed to let their prisoner linger. They bustled him out of the courtroom, down the stairs and into the car park.

Mawi was baffled by a country where groups of white thugs yelled war-cries, stamped the pavement with their war-dances and yearned for a warrior past in which they had been cannon-fodder for prodigal kings and aristocrats, field-marshals and ministers for war; where effete men were dominated by belligerent women with moustaches who aped the crudest male instincts for confrontation, domination and tribal exclusion; where the police arrested you, then treated you like a son or younger brother; where being black was less of a crime than not being British. One moment the country seemed to be opening its windows to the world and looking out towards a future of tolerance and peace, the next pulling up the drawbridge and retreating into a past of nations, flags and wars.

Mawi was led back into the police station and to his cell. The black officer brought him a cup of tea.

If the country's female translators and small-time judges had moustaches and the character of bull-terriers, Mawi thought as he sipped his tea, the Queen of England and her Prime Minister must be as fearsome and hairy as gorillas.

38

Father Lorencio lay on his bed waiting for the crash of the iron door at the end of the block, the rattle of keys and the sound of the first cell door in the row being unlocked. The warder could carry only one tray at a time and it took him ten minutes to reach Father Lorencio's cell: enough time to get up, wash his face in cold water in the chipped white metal bowl on the table, and put on his clothes.

Father Lorencio slept twelve hours out of every twenty-four. Not from despair or indiscipline. Just the reverse: sleep was an intelligent use of time and was part of his programme to keep his mind either occupied or switched off.

After breakfast he spent an hour every day, usually at his table, looking to the future and making plans, or refining plans, for when he left prison. It was a way of keeping his spirits up and not losing hope of an early release.

He would return to Santo Domingo for only as long as it took to pack up his books and other belongings. He would hire a van from the garage near his sister's and move most of his things to the house, where there was plenty of storage space. The last thing he would do before leaving Santo Domingo was to write a letter of resignation to the Bishop, with no forwarding address.

In the northern mountains of the Lake District, Chile's Arcadia a day's journey south of Santiago, was a village officially classified as abandoned. What had in fact happened was that the inhabitants – subsistence goatherds and weavers – were driven from the village during the last war between Chile and Argentina and their homes commandeered by the Chilean army. The chapel had a little presbytery attached to it, where Father Lorencio had spent two summers more than twenty years ago studying before being ordained. He would make the presbytery his base and write a minimum of ten letters a day, to the UN, to the media in countries all over the world, to religious leaders, humanitarian organizations, government ministers in North America, Eastern and Western Europe and the USSR, reminding them of the tens of thousands of former supporters of Allende who had been sent, and continued to be sent, to their deaths. The village was accessible only on foot or by donkey. He would walk the five kilometres to the nearest village once a week to buy provisions and give his letters to the Continental bus-driver to take across the border and post in Argentina.

Father Lorencio would leave the established Church to rediscover the Jesus not of the Christianity he had never intended but of all religions whose followers bowed before superior forces and celebrated the fellowship of men. Father Lorencio was filled with excitement at the prospect of immersing himself in his thoughts and books as he had done during his stays in the village as a young man.

The next four hours until lunch were for physical exercise. Not pacing up and down his cell: he had grown tired of that after two days. Now he went for country walks, a different one every day, through forests, across rivers, up mountains, along precipitous ledges. He clambered over the table and bed and under them. He breathed in the smell of pine-woods and orange-groves; sometimes he stopped to pick an orange from an overhanging branch, peel it and eat it; he heard the sound of running water, of wind through the pine-needles, the raucous cry of herons and the song of orioles.

After his lunch of bread and water Father Lorencio exercised his mind for six hours. He recited prayers and hymns to himself over and over again till he remembered all the words. He played word games: said the first word that came into his head, then the first word he could think of beginning with the last letter of the word he had just said, and so on, word after word, as fast as he could, till his head throbbed with the effort: selfish heron nabs swordfish, heart throbbing, greedily, yellow water, river running, gratify yet tired. And number games: think of a number – any number; add six; add sixteen; take away two; add five; add seven; take away twelve; add three; take away the number you first thought of and you're left with twenty-three.

'Good morning, Father.'

Father Lorencio zipped up his trousers, pulled the buttonhole across and attached it to one of the buttons meant for braces: with his belt confiscated, and the amount of weight he had lost, his trousers would fall down otherwise.

'Good morning, Francisco.'

Thank goodness it was Francisco! Usually it was Francisco but every now and again it was the surly one who kicked the door open, banged the tray down without a word and slammed the door shut after him. When Francisco was on duty, breakfast was the high point of the day, with a double ration of bread, and a cup of hot coffee instead of a glass of cold water. There was nothing to go with the bread but it was always fresh when Francisco brought it. Father Lorencio suspected he bought the bread and made the coffee himself. Sometimes he knew it was Francisco because he could smell the coffee before it reached the door. Even powdered coffee had an aroma – one he didn't even like three weeks ago but which now smelt like nectar. He hoped the other prisoners couldn't smell it.

Bread, water and, on most days, coffee: this was his daily fare. An apple once a week: the State's concession to its prisoners' health. Father Lorencio's stomach had shrunk, so he wasn't famished any more. It was a good way of losing weight. Not that he had ever been overweight. He must have lost ten kilos in less than three weeks. He had a beard now. He would like to see himself with his beard but there were no mirrors or reflections.

Francisco put the tray on the table and hung what looked like a prison suit over the back of the chair. Father Lorencio's heart sank. His world had become so small and his life so predictable that even a minor change of routine caused anxiety.

'It's not wash-day,' he said in dismay. 'You washed my clothes only two days ago, bless you.'

'Oh yes it is, Father!' Francisco replied. 'Today's wash-day because tomorrow's a special day.'

'In what way special?'

'Can't you guess?'

The suppressed smile of joy on Francisco's face said it all. Father Lorencio had often felt like hugging this good-hearted young man for all his kindness but had always thought it wouldn't do for a prisoner to throw his arms round his warder. Now he couldn't contain himself.

'I've given you the good news, Father,' Francisco said, disengaging himself. 'Here comes the not-so-good news. They've found your Julieta and her husband. In England. He's been arrested.'

'And Julieta?'

'She's free.'

'In England?' Father Lorencio was silent for a good few seconds while he took in what Francisco had told him, then he said quietly: 'If staying behind bars could help those two, I'd ask you to take the suit away and wash my clothes on wash-day as usual. But I'm probably more use to them outside than in.'

He changed into the prison suit. Francisco took away the metal bowl and the clothes Father Lorencio had been wearing.

He sat down, sipped his coffee, ate his bread and felt calmer and able to think again. He decided today would be no different from any other day. There was no reason to change his routine. The hour after breakfast was when he made his plans. New events meant new plans. There was no time to lose. Father Lorencio finished his coffee, got up and started to pace the cell.

As he paced, the seed of an idea dropped into his mind. One of the Allende supporters he had helped – the one who swore he would assassinate the usurping President: what was his name? It was thanks to Father Lorencio that he had escaped to Peru. Now he was a director of Chile's most important airline. The seed grew into a seedling: the man – whatever his name was – had a daughter called Mercedes who worked for her father's airline as a stewardess on long-haul flights. There should be no problem contacting Mercedes and her father but how would Father Lorencio locate and contact Mawi and Julieta?

Father Lorencio had been pacing for only fifteen minutes. Forty-five to go: long enough for the seedling to grow and put out twigs, develop into a sapling, stretch out its branches and break into leaf.

39

If it hadn't been for Julieta, Mawi would have resigned himself without too much difficulty to a stay of four or five days, or even a week or two, at the Comisaría de Marialabuena. His cell was clean, with a firm, comfortable bed, sunshine through the window in the afternoon and early evening, a motherly cook who brought him tea and eggs, policemen who would have liked to be friendlier but whose duty compelled them to keep their distance and, across the corridor, a spotless lavatory and a wash-basin and shower with soap and hot water. As Mawi couldn't read English newspapers, they had brought his flute back to give him something to do – perhaps also for their own sake to relieve the monotony of filling in forms, filing statements and taking what sounded like calls from cranks, to judge by the police officers' tone of voice when they spoke on the phone. It would have been no worse than being locked in a hotel room if he had had no fears for Julieta – if she were staying in the safety of one of the palaces in Regent's Park, for example, with a passport in her own name and a wallet full of traveller's cheques she could cash. What if the war between Britain and Argentina dragged on for months, or even years, or if they deported him to Chile? What would happen to her?

The morning after Mawi's appearance in court, the woman in white brought him a poached egg on toast for breakfast, then a policeman he hadn't seen before told him to put away his flute, which he was about to play, pointed out of the window and mimed a steering-wheel. Ten minutes later Mawi was escorted down the steps into the car park. There he had to climb into the back of a black police-van. He wanted to ask the two new officers where he was being taken, and if Julieta would be able to phone him, but without a translator there was no way of communicating with them. In a rare moment of desperation he only just stopped himself shouting and banging the side of the van with his fists. It wouldn't change anything. A few English lessons from Julieta would have helped but there hadn't been time and now it was too late. The doors were slammed shut and locked. Mawi was the only prisoner in a van designed to seat twelve or more, on benches one either side. There was no view: the barred windows were narrow and near the roof. The van pulled away. Mawi sat down and awaited whatever the day had in store for him.

For the first half-hour there was a lot of stopping and starting – for traffic-lights, Mawi imagined. All he could see through the long, thin windows were tiles and chimneys. He knew Julieta mustn't come and see him, yet his unease grew closer to panic with every kilometre that took him further from King's Cross. It was when the stopping and starting ended that Mawi nearly lost control again. They must be on a dual carriageway, leaving London. There were no more tiles and chimneys. Only the passing sky. Where were the two men taking him? More than once he was about to bang on the partition and ask. What would be the point? If they understood the question and told him, the name wouldn't mean anything to him.

The van seemed to leave the dual carriageway and, to judge by the sound of cars passing in the opposite direction, follow a normal road. There was no stopping or starting, which meant there were no traffic-lights. The van slowed right down and turned. Mawi heard the sound of gravel. A minute later they stopped. The driver called to someone. There was the sound of iron gates opening. The van trundled forward and stopped again. The gates crashed shut. The rear doors of the van opened. Mawi was told to get out.

He found himself in an area the size of a small *plaza* surrounded by the towering brick façades of four dark, gloomy five-storey buildings. The windows were small and mean and functional. Many were no more than openings in the walls, thirty centimetres square and barred. He was escorted to a pair of large steel doors, which opened as he and the two policemen approached. He paused for a moment and gasped at the smell of farmyard that engulfed him. At the doors he was handed over to two men in navy-blue uniforms like those of his police escorts but without the check cap-bands. They had enormous bunches of keys jangling at their hips. The steel doors crashed shut at the touch of a button. The smell, undiluted now with fresh air, was almost overpowering. In a moment of confusion Mawi thought he had been brought to work on a pig-farm.

Or a steel-works? He was in a hall the size of a gymnasium. Everything was made of steel. Rows of steel doors with little steel-grilled openings lined the two longest walls of the hall on three floors. Steel columns supported perforated steel gangways giving access to the upstairs doors. The gangways were connected on each upper floor by a bridge built on steel girders. A spiral staircase made of steel met the centre of each bridge. The gangways, bridges and staircase had steel railings and were enclosed in steel mesh.

The warders barked at Mawi and escorted him through one of the ground-floor steel doors into a shower-room, where the smell of farmyard was less pungent. Between fifteen and twenty nozzles lined each side of the room, with no partitions or curtains between them. The floor sloped away from the door and the water ran away down two conduits and through grilles into the drains. One of the warders barked at Mawi again. He understood that he had to undress and take a shower. He handed his flute, then his clothes, to the warders, who put them in a transparent plastic bag, which one of them labelled. Mawi expected the water to be cold but it was tepid. There was no soap. One of the warders handed him a towel. When he had dried, a pair of torn blue jeans was thrust into his hands, followed by a frayed white shirt with faded blue stripes, a pair of grey socks with holes, a denim jacket and a pair of black imitation-leather shoes. The jeans and shoes were too small, the shirt and denim jacket too big. The socks smelt of the previous wearer's feet.

The warders opened the steel door and led Mawi from the shower-room back into the miasma, through another steel door into a little office smelling of fried bacon and manned by a small but powerful-looking warder with a scar all the way down one side of his face, perhaps from a knife wound. The warder took the plastic bag with the flute and clothes from his colleagues and put it in a locker, then glared at Mawi and barked at him to press his thumb on to a piece of coated paper on the desktop. Mawi did as he was told. When he looked up, he was dazzled by a flash-bulb as the scarred warder took his picture.

From the office Mawi was led along a row of steel doors with grilled openings. The doors were unmarked and identical but the warders seemed to know them as if they were painted in contrasting colours. They stopped outside one they perhaps saw as bright yellow. The more assertive of the two warders looked through the bars, barked, took a large key from the bunch jangling at his side, unlocked the door and opened it.

Mawi's heart sank as he looked inside. Instead of a clean, uncramped space with a view of the sky and of people and cars coming and going, he saw a windowless area smaller than the cell at the police station, with two beds end to end either side and a narrow passage between them. The only light was from the doorway, or through the barred opening when the door was closed. There were already three occupants, two well-built, one small and wiry. They were sitting on their beds, as there was nothing else for them to do. All three were wearing blue jeans, white shirts with blue stripes and shiny black plastic shoes, like Mawi. All had close-cut hair. Mawi guessed his own hair would be cropped soon.

The three men looked up when the door was opened. Mawi saw in the half-light that they had pale faces and bags under their eyes. The two larger men must have been in their late thirties. The small, wiry one was older. The older man was looking at Mawi with sneering contempt, the other two with murderous hostility.

The smell of excreta had been bad enough in the hall. Stepping into the cell was like opening the door of a lavatory that had never been cleaned and just been used. Mawi stopped in his tracks and wondered if he was going to be sick. He realized now that the stink that filled the whole building was like a quagmire fed by flushes of stench through the grilles in the cell doors. Like apples, he thought: the intoxicating fragrance of an orchard was the sum of all the apples growing there. The thought helped him hold back his nausea.

'Good afternoon,' he said, as cheerfully as he could. These were two of the dozen or so English words he had learnt.

The small, wiry man sneered up at him. One of the other two spat on the floor.

The assertive warder threw Mawi a grey blanket, piled on two sheets, a pillow-case, a towel and a toothbrush, gave him a push, banged the door shut and locked it.

For a few moments Mawi saw nothing and didn't move. When his eyes had adjusted to the gloom, he took two steps to the available bed, hesitated when he saw the state of the mattress, then lowered himself gingerly on to a landing-area between stains. The wiry prisoner was directly opposite him; the other two were sitting on their beds at the end of the cell.

The prisoner who had spat turned to Mawi. Words tumbled from his mouth like rubbish into a dustcart: the release of pent-up frustration, perhaps, at having to share a small, unhygienic dungeon with two, and now three, strangers. Mawi recognized the word *fuck*, which was repeated so often that he felt he was starting to understand English pretty well. But when the convict glared at him in fury, expecting an answer, Mawi was lost for words. He was afraid if he stayed silent much longer he would be assaulted, so he replied in Spanish, quietly and as calmly as he could:

'I'm afraid I don't understand what you're saying but you sound angry. I don't wish you any harm. I don't want to be here any more than you do. The best way of coping, in my opinion, is if we try to get on together.'

The three convicts stared at Mawi open-mouthed.

The wiry one was the first to recover from his astonishment. He leered across at Mawi, who saw that most of his teeth were missing. 'Ispaniola?' he asked.

'No soy español. Soy chileno.' Mawi decided that trying to explain Mapuche to his cell-mates was impossible at this level of communication. As it was, their faces were blank. *'Chile,'* he said.

The angry convict rounded on Mawi again. 'Chile?' he said. 'Argentina?'

'No Argentina,' Mawi replied quietly. *'Chile.'*

But Chile and Argentina were one and the same to Mawi's storming neighbour, who was ready with another dustbin-load of abuse to throw at him. Mawi wished he had said yes to 'ispaniola' and accepted the change of nationality and gender.

The wiry man interrupted the torrent of violent language, which at once stopped. Mawi sensed that the older prisoner had kudos, perhaps for the number of sentences he had served, robberies committed or throats cut.

He leered at Mawi again. 'You – like – ash?' he asked.

'Ash?'

'Hashish?'

'¿Hachís?' Mawi shook his head.

'Coke?'

'Coca-Cola?'

There was as much anger as mirth in the laughter that burst from Mawi's cell-mates, as if their bile and spleen had long ago flooded and stained all their other emotions.

The wiry man lifted his mattress and removed a small paper packet.

Not Coca-Cola but coca leaves? Was it possible? Mawi had a

sudden craving for coca tea, or for two or three leaves to chew, to soften the edges of a hard day.

The convict was leaning towards Mawi and leering at him. 'Me – give – you – pot,' he said. 'What – you – give – me?'

The laughter from the other two prisoners wasn't angry this time – more like the sniggers you hear from a group of men when one of them tells a dirty joke.

Mawi shrugged. He thought he had understood the convict but he had nothing to offer him. His pockets were empty. If he had a watch, it would have been taken from him by the warders.

The convict unwrapped the packet. It contained what looked to Mawi like tea: pieces of dried leaf with tiny dried white flowers. Whatever it was, it wasn't coca. The prisoner took a packet of cigarette-papers from the pocket of his jeans, skilfully removed one, filled it with tea, rolled it and with the delicacy of a cat ran the tip of his tongue along the edge of the paper.

He saw Mawi watching him, leered, leant towards him and raised a hand. Mawi flinched, expecting to be hit. Instead, the convict patted his cheek and chuckled. Then he sat back, pulled a throw-away lighter from his jeans pocket and lit his cigarette.

The older man's hostility seemed to be wearing off, thought Mawi. Perhaps it was only a matter of time before the abusive convict in the corner relaxed and became less unfriendly.

There was a heaving at the end of the cell as the third prisoner rose from his inertia. He had the physique of a heavyweight boxer. He threw his arms round the neck of his irascible cell-mate, who didn't seem surprised and offered no resistance. The assault was accompanied by a running commentary and appeared to be a demonstration of some kind. The attacker pointed to different parts of his victim's head, neck and shoulders and mimed blows to them. How to kill or injure a man from behind without weapons or mess appeared to be the prisoner's theme. He seemed to have difficulty articulating. Mawi guessed from his speech and the dull look in his eyes that he was brain-damaged. The wiry man was too preoccupied with keeping his cigarette alight to spare so much as a glance at his two fellow-convicts. The demonstration ended and the prisoner sank back on to his bed and into his torpor.

The older man passed his smoke to the two at the end of the cell, who each drew on it for a few seconds, then handed it back. He offered it to Mawi.

'*No, gracias*. No, thank you.'

'Go on!' He made a jabbing movement in Mawi's direction with his cigarette.

Mawi smiled and made a declining gesture. The wiry man kept on jabbing. Mawi kept on smiling and declining.

Mawi quickly realized he had offended his cell-mate by refusing his offer. The convict put the cigarette in his mouth, jumped up angrily, kicked a chamber-pot out from under his bed, spilling some of the urine in it, and unzipped his jeans.

Mawi was turning discreetly towards the door when he stopped, mesmerized like an ant thrush by a tree snake. The snake that had appeared through a gap in the unzipped jeans was out of all proportion to the rest of the little man's body.

The convict stood at a comfortable distance from his pot and started his flow, which was like the gush from a bath tap. Some of the urine went into the pot; most splashed on to the floor.

Mawi glanced at the other two convicts. They were watching the older man impassively, without a glimmer of interest or surprise, or a murmur of complaint at the mess on the floor.

Mawi felt a surge of revulsion at this display by a man old enough to be his father. Till today he had never seen another man's genitalia – not even his own father's or his uncle's. He had never undressed in front of anyone except Julieta. Even when he used to swim in the lake with his childhood friend – the boy who drowned himself when his parents were slaughtered – they always wore briefs. As for urinating all over the floor, even the animals Mawi looked after as a child never fouled their own or other animals' sleeping areas. He looked away, not out of discretion now but so as not to show his disgust and risk being lynched.

The flow of urine stopped at last. The pot was kicked back under the bed, with a splashing noise as the contents spilt over the edge. Why could he hear the sound of muffled laughter? What new obscenity were the convicts planning? Mawi turned from the door to find the little man's monstrosity centimetres from his face. It seemed to be studying him, like a fer-de-lance sizing up its prey before striking. Mawi threw himself back on to his bed and against the wall with a shout, dislodging one of the sound-proof tiles, which fell to the floor.

The three convicts exploded into laughter. The two men at the end of the cell doubled up and rolled about on their beds. The little man collapsed on to his, and in his glee didn't even bother to zip his growth back inside his jeans. Mawi reckoned laughter must be in short supply in prison and that this was the biggest laugh his three cell-mates had had behind bars. There were shouts from prisoners in other cells, who had probably forgotten what laughter sounded like and wanted to share the joke.

Having grown up in Latin America, Mawi had been ready for violence and torture at the hands of the police, warders and his fellow-prisoners, ready for fear and physical pain. What he hadn't been prepared for was schoolboy vulgarity.

Mawi heard shouts of a different kind from the other cells, the sort of shouts you hear from celebrating football fans when the team they support has won a match. Where had Mawi heard that kind of shouting recently? He remembered: at the Trafalgar, where the losing team numbered hundreds. They weren't on their way to the shower-room, smarting from a defeat. They were covered in fuel, burning like torches, throwing themselves into the heavily rolling South Atlantic. Had another Argentinian ship been sunk? Had the prisoners heard about it somehow, from the warders or from transistors smuggled into their cells?

'Kil! Kil! Kil! Kil! Argentina!'

The chant from the Marylebone Road pub. If the prisoners had been allowed flags, they would be poking them out through the bars of their cells.

Mawi got up and looked through the grille in the door, expecting to see warders rush into the hall with hoses and canisters of tear-gas to silence the prisoners, but no one came.

As he stood with his back to his cell-mates, he was seized from behind and forced on to his knees. The two heavily built convicts had him by the arms, one on either side. The wiry one pulled Mawi's legs from under him, so that he was lying face down on the floor. Mawi heard himself shouting, but he also heard his shouts lost in the hubbub from the other cells.

40

The day after the magistrates' judgement Julieta had two cups of strong Brazilian coffee and an orange for breakfast and set off for Camden to find a call-box and phone Marylebone Police Station. There were telephone-boxes all over King's Cross – there was even a pay-phone just inside the front-door – but after what Mawi had whispered to her in the cell she didn't want the police to find out where she was staying and call to look at her passport.

A policewoman told Julieta that Mawi had been moved to a prison fifty miles away because all the ones in or near London were full.

Fifty miles: that was eighty kilometres. Julieta knew it was safer not to try and see Mawi but she needed to know how to get to him in an emergency. She phoned British Rail and was told she would have to change twice and that with the waiting between trains the journey would take two and a half hours each way. She asked the price of a return ticket. The reply left her speechless: it was more than she and Mawi had paid for their two-and-a-half-thousand-kilometre haul through Chile – more even than her unused air ticket from Santiago to Mendoza.

Julieta's English lessons would pay for food, rent and other expenses for only two days a week but, thanks to Mawi, she still had several hundred pounds from his busking. She should be able to survive for two or three weeks – a month if she ate only one meal a day. She would try and contact her mother to ask for help. That meant waiting till mid-afternoon, because of the time difference.

She walked back to King's Cross, went first to the post office to change a five-pound note into silver, then to the Indian grocer's for a packet of spaghetti, a bottle of tomato sauce, a pair of chicken legs, a tin of peas and a bottle of cheap red wine – her supper ration for the week – and coffee and biscuits to keep her going during the day.

At three Julieta went downstairs to the pay-phone by the front-door and piled her coins on the window-ledge. She reckoned it was a good time to phone home: it would be ten in the morning, her father would have gone to work and Copihue would be at home doing the housework. She dialled the number. The phone rang and rang until the ringing-tone changed to a continuous hum. Julieta waited five minutes and tried again. Ring – ring – ring – hum. She collected her coins and went upstairs. Her stomach had tightened. She didn't feel like the cup of coffee and the chocolate biscuit she had promised herself.

An hour later Julieta tried again. Perhaps Copihue had had to go out or been in the loo. There was still no reply. Trying not to feel discouraged, she found Father Lorencio's number, which she had taken the precaution of writing in her address-book when she was booking the flight to Mendoza. She braced herself for disappointment: Father Lorencio hadn't yet served his purpose as bait to catch Mawi and her; why should they release him? Even if he was free, he might not be at Santo Domingo. Didn't Copihue say he had a sister who lived in the mountains?

The phone rang on and on, just as the phone at home had done. Julieta was about to hang up when the ringing stopped. This time there was no hum. Someone had picked up the receiver. There was a silence.

'Father Lorencio?'

'Who is this?' said a man's voice. He sounded suspicious. Was it Father Lorencio?

'Julieta.'

'Julieta who?'

Julieta's stomach tightened again. This couldn't be Father Lorencio. Another priest must have taken over at Santo Domingo. She put a second coin in the slot.

'Julieta Reyes.'

Suspicion turned to *bonhomie*. 'Julieta Reyes? Franco Reyes' daughter? Good morning to you! How are you? How is your father?'

Father Lorencio was the only priest Julieta and her family knew. If this wasn't Father Lorencio, who could it be?

'Who is that?'

'Speaking to you? Father Lorencio, of course.'

'I'm calling from—'

'From home, I expect. Not that it matters. It's a pleasure to hear you, wherever you are.'

'I'm not in Santiago. I'm…' Julieta hesitated. This could be a police agent trying to win her confidence. And yet the voice sounded more and more like Father Lorencio's.

Whoever it was didn't let her finish her sentence. 'You're on your way back to Santiago. That's good news. I remember now: your father told me you would be away for a few weeks.'

There was a beeping. Julieta fed in two more coins.

'I've been trying to phone home,' she said. 'My father must be at work.' She must be careful not to sound as if she were avoiding her father. 'Have you any idea where my mother and Copihue are?'

'None, I'm afraid. I haven't seen any of your family for the past three weeks. I've been— I've been away myself. I've only just got back. I'll try and find out where they are for you. Ring me again later. No, don't: I'm going out. I tell you what: I'll leave a message with another of my parishioners. Be sure to phone her: she'll help you. Her number in… in the capital is 286-0053. Her name is… Ana. To be sure you're speaking to the right person, ask her to tell you what you were wearing when you last called at Santo Domingo. She will ask you a question: same sort of thing. Then you can arrange to meet. She lives in the capital, not far from you. Much closer than you think. Have you got all that?'

A door behind Julieta – the door of the ground-floor flat – was yanked open. She turned and saw a hulk of a man looking angrily out at her. He had tousled greying hair, bloodshot eyes and a tangle of what looked like barbed wire bursting through his unbuttoned shirt. 'Got bleeding foreigners in the house, have we?' he growled loudly in an accent that didn't sound English to Julieta – could it be Australian or South African? – and banged the door shut.

Did the neighbour imagine Julieta could have a conversation on the phone without saying anything? She hadn't been speaking loud enough to disturb anyone. Churlish man!

'Julieta?'

Julieta put in two more coins.

'286-0053. Ana. What I was wearing. Answer her question. Will she then tell me how I can contact my family?'

'That among other things. Phone her in exactly one hour's time. From a different telephone: there seems to be some interference on your line. *Hasta pronto, Julieta.*'

Before Julieta could reply, the man had hung up. One of the coins was returned to her with a rattle. She took what was left of the others from the sill and climbed slowly upstairs.

Julieta felt as if her insides had been slashed with a knife. Mawi was in prison a long way from London. If they kept him there more than three weeks, she would run out of money. Her traveller's cheques were useless. When she tried to phone home, no one answered. The voice at Santo Domingo might not be Father Lorencio's. Her neighbour in London was a cantankerous xenophobe. If she had a shoulder to cry on, she would shed floods of tears. Mawi's was the only shoulder; if he were here, there would be no reason to cry. Julieta was alone: she had never felt so alone in her life. She let herself into the flat, closed the door, went to the bed, sank on to it and hugged her knees to her chest.

The telephone conversation kept replaying in her head. She was sure now it was Father Lorencio's voice. Unless it was a first-class impersonation. If it was Father Lorencio, why did he hardly remember who she was? 'Julieta Reyes? Franco Reyes' daughter?' Her father had told him she would be away for a few weeks? Father Lorencio had seen her on to the coach to Arica and helped Mawi load the bags. Perhaps three weeks in prison had affected his mind. They said poor diet caused loss of memory. They could have tortured him, poor man, and upset his judgement. What was all the business about phoning someone called Ana and exchanging security questions, just to find out where her mother and Copihue were?

Then it clicked. Julieta let go of her knees and sat on the edge of the bed.

Interference on the line? Calling from a different telephone? Of course there wasn't any interference on the line: Julieta would have heard it. Father Lorencio's own phone was being tapped, or he suspected it was. Someone called Ana was going to act as an intermediary between them. But now that he had given Julieta the number, Ana's phone could be tapped too.

A second dawning. With it Julieta got up, noticed the spring sunshine and walked to the window. Her insides had healed and she felt hungry. She went into the kitchen and took two chocolate biscuits from the packet.

Maybe the number Father Lorencio had given her wasn't in Santiago at all. Julieta had been careful not to give her whereabouts and yet he said that Ana lived not far away. He had kept on about the capital, instead of saying Santiago. Was this a clue for Julieta and a way of throwing anyone monitoring the conversation off the scent? Could the number be in London? Did Father Lorencio simply leave out the prefix: 0171- or 0181-? How on earth could he know she and Mawi were in London? Julieta's instincts defied her reason: she would try the number. In an hour's time, Father Lorencio had said. She looked at her watch: a quarter past five. She would phone at six.

The doorbell made Julieta jump: this was the first time anyone had rung the bell. She went over to the door to lift the receiver but hesitated. She was not a nervous person but the conversation with Father Lorencio had made her security-conscious. What would she do if it was the police come to examine her passport? Pretend to be out? What if they had a pass-key or broke down the door?

The bathroom window gave on to the street. She went into the bathroom, where the casement-window was open. She took her little mirror from above the basin and held it up so that she could see the front-door without being seen herself. What she saw, not six metres below, made her pulse race so that she could hear it beating in her ears: not men in raincoats, Homburgs and sunglasses but the three from the Trafalgar: Snake, Dave and Jake. How did the reptiles know where she lived? What did they want? To ask her forgiveness for putting Mawi behind bars? Never.

'She's not in.' Julieta thought she recognized Snake's voice.

'Pity! She must be frantic for it, seeing as her Red Indian bloke's in the nick.' No mistaking Jake's voice. 'We could have taken it in turns.' Salacious laughter from Snake and Dave. 'Not to worry! We'll call tomorrow or the day after.'

With that they pushed off down the street towards King's Cross.

Twenty minutes ago Julieta had been overwhelmed and depressed. Now she felt frightened.

41

The three convicts were on their beds, asleep. Two of them were snoring. Mawi was still lying face down on the floor. He was not badly hurt, as far as he could tell. Not if the absence of pain was anything to go by. He felt a bit bruised: the human body was bound to bruise when it was pounded on a concrete floor.

It wasn't defeat or despair that made him stay exactly as his cell-mates had left him. He had been schooled from childhood to suffer outrage and abuse. First it was the Spanish Americans, now the Anglo-Saxons: Europeans spread and burnt like poison-ivy. To suffer outrage but not accept it. Despair was acceptance. Acceptance was defeat.

Mawi had thought of killing the convicts while they slept. One of them had taught him how to do it. Mawi had seen and remembered the points on the head, neck and shoulders that could be pressed or stabbed with the fingers or rapped with the knuckles. He would start with the wiry man, who didn't snore and wouldn't wake his mates by his sudden silence, then take out the other two in quick succession. And then what? A lifetime in a cell like this one, with others like these for company. He would be doing the convicts a favour by ending their hell, and sentencing himself to decades of a worse hell. He would never have a life with Julieta, who would be condemned to widowhood with her husband still alive, or forced to marry a man she didn't love. Mawi was being kept behind bars while Britain fought its little war with Argentina. The war would be over in days or weeks. Mawi had only to hold on for as long as it lasted and then he would be free: free anyway from the company of these three nightmarish creatures, who even when they left this cell would be imprisoned in the hell they had made for themselves, the hell of their own depravity.

There was nowhere for Mawi to go. There weren't even any

warders doing the rounds of the cells. He longed for the shower-room, with its rows of nozzles and its tepid water. That would be a reason to move, even if he had to drag himself there. If there were still no soap, he would ask a warder for a bottle of disinfectant to pour over himself. As it was, there was only the bed to move to: better to keep the mess on the floor than spread it all over his blanket.

A convict in one of the cells opposite had decided the rest of the prison would share his insomnia and was giving full voice to his fury. It seemed to be aimed at the black inmates of the gaol. Mawi understood *fucking* and *niggers,* which were repeated over and over again. What was their crime against this paragon of the master race, he wondered. To have looked him in the eye through the bars of their cells? What was the crime against society that had landed them in prison? To have lost their families in an ethnic purge in Africa and to be looking for a safer life in one of the European countries that had ravaged and destabilized their continent? Was the convict only voicing what many of his politer, better-educated fellow-Whites felt behind their pious show of liberalism and tolerance?

Julieta had told Mawi about the lakes and green hills of northern England, where two famous poets once found friendship and inspiration. He would like to have travelled there with Julieta. Now he longed for the lakes and mountains of his own country, for the araucaria forests and the giant red campanulas, the copihues, for warm sunshine after cleansing rain. He wanted to take Julieta there to meet the few relatives of his who had survived the army massacre, to stand with her and listen to the gentle voices of all those who had been killed carried to them on the wind, blessing their marriage. He would take her even if he had to play fox and hounds with the police and army and risk being arrested and tortured for kidnap.

While Mawi lay quite still, the mess on the floor and on his body was bearable. To disturb it by pulling up his trousers and getting to his feet was to feel it and smell it – possibly to add to it by being sick. The wiry man's overturned chamber-pot was only inches from his face. A little further away was the metal bucket for excreta that had been kicked over in the struggle and had spilt most of its contents on the floor. Mawi's legs and buttocks were awash with blood and semen.

The two well-built convicts had held him face down while the wiry one lay on top of him and pounded. Mawi's shouts wouldn't have been heard even in the next cell, with the yelling and the banging of beds from all the prisoners. The two convicts holding Mawi down had chanted 'Argy-bargy! Argy-bargy! Argy-bargy!' while the wiry man hammered away, then gasped and dribbled all over Mawi's neck when he reached his climax. The abusive convict was next in turn and didn't even bother to wipe away the older man's slime. Mawi had been keeping his buttocks tightly shut but was now given a blow on the head or neck that made him relax all his muscles. He felt the convict inside him, like a prospector frantically grubbing for gold on another man's land. 'Argy-bargy! Argy-bargy! Argy-bargy!' Gasp. Dribble. After the third convict had had his turn, Mawi heard them snigger and smelt smoke as they sat on their beds and passed around another of the little man's roll-ups. Twenty minutes later one of them was snoring. Then the older prisoner's breathing became audible: slow and regular, like marsh gas rising to the surface of a pond. Soon the third man had been snoring.

Mawi's eye was caught by a beam of light dancing somewhere outside the cell. A convict shining a torch through the bars of his door? The beam moved through the hall. It couldn't be a prisoner; it must be a warder.

'Shut the fuck up!' Mawi recognized the warder's voice.

The insomniac stopped his yelling and there was a quiet cheer from some of the cells: from the black prisoners, probably. Mawi wondered if the publican from the Trafalgar was among them. He wanted to call out: 'Tobias, are you there?'

Instead, he groaned. Not from pain or distress but so as to be heard by the warder. He pitched his groaning so that it would be heard across the hall without waking his fellow-prisoners.

Footsteps approached the cell door. A torch was shone between two of the bars. There was a pause.

'Gugod!' said a voice.

Mawi felt like singing for joy but gave another groan for good measure. The two well-built convicts snored. The wiry one slept deeply, like an anaconda digesting its prey.

42

'Colombian or Brazilian?' asked Julieta. 'The Brazilian's stronger.'

'What heaven! Real coffee. That's one of the things I like best about working long haul: getting out of Latin America and being able to drink the coffee we grow.'

'That, and Scottish fruit-cake,' said Julieta, unwrapping the little cake she had bought for her guest and herself and putting it on a plate.

'How did you find such a beautiful flat?' asked the daughter of the founder and director of Chile's most successful airline, an exile from his own country living in Peru, in the wealthy district of Lima.

'We like it. But it's only one room, with a kitchen and bathroom the size of cupboards. You must have seen many more beautiful flats than this one.'

'It's full of light. Quiet. You've got a view of trees and flowers. You're free, independent: free to come and go without fear of the secret police; independent of your family.'

Julieta paused to take this in. 'That's not quite how things have worked out,' she replied. 'My husband's in prison and I've had my traveller's cheques stopped by my father, so that I'll soon run out of money.'

Ana was not what Julieta had expected. For one thing her name wasn't Ana; it was Mercedes: another of Father Lorencio's ploys to throw eavesdroppers off the scent. For another she wasn't a glamour queen, caked in make-up, with a smile of contempt for everyone not fortunate enough to be a dashing pilot or a passenger travelling first class. Attractive she certainly was, with her healthy skin, the natural buoyancy and lustre of her chestnut hair, her snow-white teeth, her warm smile, and her self-confidence and optimism. She didn't give herself airs, in spite of her father's fortune. She had just spent her leave walking alone in the Andes and looking out for condors through her binoculars and telephoto lenses. Julieta was at once at ease with Mercedes and felt they could be friends.

Julieta brought in cups and saucers, plates and the cafetière. There were two armchairs but they sat at the table, as Julieta's mother and French grandmother and great-grandmother had taught her to do with guests, and felt the warm spring sunshine on their arms and faces, filtered through the half-open leaves of a lime-tree.

'You seem to know Father Lorencio well,' said Julieta, broaching the matter that had brought them together.

'Father Lorencio is our family deity,' Mercedes replied with feeling. 'Without him we would have no family. Or no father. A tree without a trunk. He saved Papa's life. There's nothing we wouldn't do in return to help Father Lorencio or his friends.'

'He said you would tell me how to contact my mother. She doesn't seem to be at home.'

Mercedes looked at Julieta thoughtfully. 'She's not at home,' she said at last. 'I suppose you don't know: your parents split up. Your mother left. The maid went with her – Copihue: is that her name? No one knows where they are for the present. Your father's still living at your house.'

It was Julieta's turn to be thoughtful. The shock of Mercedes' news wore off and left her feeling both happy and sad: happy that her mother had at last escaped from a domestic tyranny that had allowed her no freedom, no opinions, hardly even a personality; sad because separation was an admission of failure, an acceptance that things couldn't get better, the breaking up of a family. Perhaps her mother would spread her wings at last. And perhaps her father would come to value the wife and daughter he had lost.

Julieta poured the coffee, cut the cake in four and put a piece on each of the two little plates. She told Mercedes everything: how her father had tried to force her to marry a cold-blooded army officer; about her elopement with the Mapuche boy she loved and who was now her husband; their escape into Bolivia; about Pablo and Pedro; about the Viking boat; the Isla del Sol; sailing by moonlight into Peru; Cuzco and the massacre by US Marines; their capture; jumping a jumbo jet to London; the concert at the Trafalgar; their betrayal by the three reptiles; the police raid; Mawi's custody on suspicion of being an Argentinian spy; his transfer to a prison outside London; the reptiles tracking Julieta to the flat.

'My jet-propelled life suddenly feels very dull,' said Mercedes in between sips of coffee.

Julieta laughed. 'Three weeks ago I longed for a life of adventure. Now I long for peace and quiet. We want to live on the Isla del Sol in the middle of Lake Titicaca. The people there are poor. The State does nothing for them. Tourists visit the island but all the profit goes to the mainland tour operators, many of them foreign. We want to start a school and medical centre for the islanders.'

'I've had enough of jetting round the world. I want to do something worthwhile with my life. Do you need anyone to help you?... Papa has been talking about sponsoring a project. Who knows? Yours may be the one that touches his heart. And his pocket.'

Julieta felt a tingle of excitement, a surge of confidence, as her idea for the Isla del Sol stirred inside her, became a hazy reality, took on the first traits of an identity. Could it really grow from a seed into a sapling, then a tree, and would the tree seed itself and spread, until South America was covered in forest?

'You'd give up your life as an international air hostess to live on an island with no cars or roads, three hours from the mainland on the fastest boat?'

'I never wanted to be an air hostess. Papa was so keen for me to join the company that I didn't have the heart to refuse. The job was handed to me on a plate. I wanted to be a flying nurse – one of the angels – instead of a waitress pushing a trolley up and down an aisle in the sky, serving drinks and snacks to the well-to-do. I would rather be serving the poor: saving them from starvation.'

Julieta poured a second cup of coffee for them both and put the remaining pieces of cake on the plates. 'That's the last of the cake,' she said. 'There are some chocolate biscuits. And there's lots of coffee.'

'You're running out of money,' said Mercedes, getting down to business.

'That's why I need to contact my mother. We lived on what we earned when Mawi was free: he was doing well busking at Baker Street Station. I've made a good start with my teaching but it doesn't even bring in enough to pay the rent.'

'How much do you need?'

Julieta felt herself blush with embarrassment. 'I wasn't expecting… I… I'd pay you back. As soon as they refund my traveller's cheques. Sooner if they let Mawi go.'

'Relax! I'm not a money-lender. My family are the ones in debt, remember. To Father Lorencio. Helping his friends is a way of repaying some of the debt… You need a good lawyer. Now. Today. Justice is for those who can afford it. Gaoling your husband on suspicion of being an Argentinian spy? It's outrageous. If we treated English visitors to Chile like that, their country would declare war on us. Papa will find you a lawyer specializing in this sort of thing. We must get your husband out on bail. By the time the case comes up, the war over that wasteland in the South Atlantic will be over and charges will be dropped. Or he could jump bail and leave the country with you.'

'We couldn't do that. Not if your father's paying. He'd lose his money.'

'He'd get it back charging foreign businessmen more for their first-class seats.'

'Where would we go? South America will only be safe for

Mawi when my father accepts our marriage. We were starting to enjoy our life in London.'

'Our airline's running flights between London and Santiago while most of the Aerolíneas Argentinas services to Europe are suspended. We refuel at Tenerife. We could give you a lift as far as the Canaries and get you off the aircraft and through the airport without the usual formalities. The Canaries are a beautiful place to live. Best climate in the world. Your husband could play his flute for the tourists and you could teach Spanish to the ex-pats and sun-seekers. Until it's safe to return to the Isla del Sol.'

The sun appeared between two branches of the lime-tree, filled the room with unfiltered light and poured its warmth on Julieta's shoulders. Mercedes' warmth filled her heart. She felt her face light up with a smile.

'You may not be a flying nurse, Mercedes,' she said, 'but you're certainly an angel. More coffee?'

'There's nothing I'd like better than to spend the rest of the afternoon drinking coffee with you by the open window, watching the sunlight dance through the leaves and listening to the birds in full throat, but I must get back to the office and on to the phone to Papa.' Mercedes got up, went to the bed for her brown leather shoulder-bag, took out an envelope and gave it to Julieta. 'Ring me at nine in the morning. We should have a solicitor for you by then.'

Julieta saw her guardian angel and new friend to the front-door, hugged her and kissed her on both cheeks.

'Are you sure you feel safe here?' Mercedes asked Julieta as she left. 'Nothing easier than arranging a hotel room for you.'

The safety of a hotel, without unfriendly neighbours and unwanted callers and with a private telephone that wouldn't be tapped. What a temptation! No: she mustn't ask any more of Mercedes.

'Quite safe. *Gracias, amiga. ¡Hasta mañana!*'

Julieta felt light-hearted with relief as she closed the door. She wasn't alone any more. She had found not just a rescuer but a friend. No: it wasn't Julieta who had found her. It was Father Lorencio, that rescuer of so many men and women in trouble or danger, that man of unfailing courage, that saint, who from twelve thousand kilometres away had sent Mercedes to be her saviour.

Julieta floated up the stairs to her flat. If a neighbour put his head out of a door and barked at her, she would smile and greet him and tell him the sun was shining, the birds were singing, the buds were unfurling from fists into little green hands and, if he opened his window, he would notice that the air was filled with the scent of lilac.

When Julieta had closed the door of the flat, she tore open the envelope Mercedes gave her and found five hundred pounds. Five hundred! She was going to ask for fifty. Five hundred would keep her going for a month. For two months if she gave regular English lessons. For ever if Mawi got out soon and started busking again. She would phone the prison and try to get the good news through to him; last time she phoned, the governor's office had refused to take a message and would only confirm that Mawi had arrived.

The doorbell rang. Mercedes must have forgotten to tell Julieta something. She was about to press the square of white plastic that sounded the buzzer and opened the front-door, without bothering to pick up the receiver, when she heard a distant laugh. It could have been a neighbour or passer-by but it was enough to stop her hand a fraction of a second before it touched the button. A man's laugh: had she heard it before?

'I'm becoming paranoid,' she said aloud to herself. 'But I'd better just lift the receiver and check that it's Mercedes.'

The laugh again. Julieta's hand left the receiver. She went into the bathroom, picked up her mirror and held it so that she could see the front-door through the open window.

It wasn't Mercedes at the door. It was Snake, Dave and Jake.

43

Paradise was relative, Mawi decided as he lay with his eyes closed between clean sheets under a clean blanket in a pleasantly warm room. For someone who had everything, nothing was paradise. For a walker lost in the mountains at night, a light in a window, a glass of *api* straight from the stove and a hot bath were paradise. For a beggar sleeping rough, the first ray of sun on his back, the smell of baking bread and enough coins for a couple of rolls were paradise. For a man rescued from the filth and violence of a prison cell, a bed in a ward of thirty in a prison hospital was paradise.

The yelling and abuse had stopped. Some of the patients were too ill to yell, but even those well enough lay quietly. There was no reason to yell and curse when you were being cared for. Perhaps it was lack of care that had driven some of these men to crime, in protest against an uncaring world.

Mawi had slept well. After the rescue he had been carried by two warders and a male nurse across the yard to the hospital, where there were private showers with hot water and soap. He had then been put on a trolley, so as not to make the bleeding worse, and wheeled face down into the ward, where the male nurse was joined by a colleague, a huge black woman who helped him push the trolley against a spare bed, pulled the curtains, examined Mawi's behind and applied ointment and a dressing. The two nurses got him into a pair of pyjamas and slid him on to the bed. He was given a sleeping-pill and soon slipped from the trauma of the day into a dreamless sleep.

Felicidad! The relief of being able to communicate again! The joy of waking not to the barking of prison warders or hospital dragons but to the softness, gentleness and sensuousness of a young woman whose sun rose over the same ocean into which the sun of the Mapuche and of Julieta set. Felicidad might not be pretty but at least she hadn't been reared in some northern citadel of imperialist rule. She was a Filipino, with looks that could have been South American and, like Julieta, a way of speaking Spanish Mawi found easier to understand than the gabble he had heard all his life in Chile.

Mawi was famished, having arrived at the prison after the last meal of the day, which he reckoned must be brought to the cells in the middle of the afternoon.

'The others get tea and bread and margarine for breakfast,' Felicidad explained to Mawi. 'It's a bit better than the food in the cells. I'm afraid we can't give you anything solid for two or three days. You'll have to survive on tea, milk, orange juice and broth. You can have as much sugar as you like in your tea.'

After a breakfast that only took the edge off Mawi's hunger, a doctor with brown skin and black hair started his round of the beds. Mawi was at the end of one of the two rows and was seen after about an hour.

'Where are you from?' he asked, when his turn came. Felicidad interpreted.

'Hackney,' replied the doctor.

Hackney? Mawi had heard of Delhi, Bombay and Calcutta but never of Hackney.

'And you?'

'Araucanía.'

The doctor looked blank.

Felicidad pulled the curtains round the bed. The doctor looked with cheerful detachment inside and outside Mawi's backside and dictated a string of medical terms. Felicidad, clipboard in hand, stood tactfully with her back to Mawi, half outside the curtains, taking notes.

Mawi was greatly relieved that the doctor and nurse weren't European or of European origin. Especially not Anglo-Saxon. After what had happened in the cell he would feel acutely uncomfortable being touched by a male Anglo-Saxon, even a doctor. No wonder Europeans conquered and colonized the whole world. Mawi didn't know on what devil's potion they were suckled. It certainly wasn't milk.

The doctor finished with Mawi and moved to the row of beds opposite. Felicidad drew back the curtains and followed with her clipboard.

She was soon at Mawi's side again. 'There's a gentleman in a dark suit to see you,' she said. 'You're quite a VIP.'

The gentleman in the dark suit had to walk the length of the ward to reach Mawi. There was something familiar in his looks and the way he moved. He had swept-back, pale brown hair, the face of a thirty-five- or forty-year-old, plump and unlined, but the prosperous belly of a man in his fifties. He carried a black leather bag. He glanced at the doctor, with a hint of deference towards a fellow-professional whose territory he had to cross, but at the same time with the air of a man who had the right to go wherever he pleased. The doctor was too busy to notice him. The gentleman approached Mawi on the side of the bed closer to the wall, perhaps so as not to be too near the next patient in the row.

'Good morning,' he said politely but with authority. 'My name is Paul Wickeham. I'm from the Home Office. Your wife's solicitor asked me to call on you without delay.'

Mr Wickeham's Spanish was impeccable. He spoke slowly and clearly with only the hint of an accent. He pulled up a chair and sat down as close to Mawi as dignity and status would allow.

'I've spoken to the prison governor,' he said. 'He told me what happened last night. How are you feeling?'

'I miss my wife,' Mawi replied. 'She may not know where I am. She's running out of money.'

'Her solicitor will have told her where you are. We'll contact the Chilean Embassy and ask them to make an advance. How are you feeling apart from that?'

'Better here than in the cell.'

'You're on remand. You should never have been put in the

same cell as convicted criminals.'

'But I was.'

Mr Wickeham looked embarrassed. 'All our prisons are under pressure, because of overcrowding. If it's any consolation, the three prisoners who assaulted you have been sent to the punishment block.'

'What does that mean?'

'It means a fortnight of solitary confinement. The prisoner is allowed no clothes and no books. He lives on a diet of bread and water and has only the floor to sit on.'

'What good does that do?'

'Hopefully it discourages convicts from assaulting their cell-mates.'

Mawi felt a flash of anger as he looked at this well-dressed gentleman who had probably never known anything more uncomfortable than an attack of indigestion after a large meal. 'What's the purpose of prison, *señor*?' he asked.

Mr Wickeham said nothing for a moment. His smooth forehead puckered into a frown. He seemed caught off guard. 'What would you say it was for?'

'Have you ever been inside a cell full of prisoners, *señor*? They live in their own shit, like pigs. They swim in one another's urine. They have nothing to do, nothing to look forward to, no light or fresh air, rotting food. Treat them like filth and they will behave like filth. Brutalize them, dehumanize them, and they will come out more corroded with hate than when they went in. What is prison for? For revenge. What do I say it *should* be for? The same as hospital: to cure the patients, to repair... to... rehabilitate the prisoners, turn their anger into energy, make them creators instead of destroyers, healers instead of hell-raisers. No wonder your prisons are overcrowded. How many of the inmates have been inside before? Eighty per cent? Ninety per cent? Three months behind bars and you're hooked for life.'

Mr Wickeham's expression had softened. There was respect

now in the way he looked at Mawi. 'You have a generous and mature attitude,' he said, 'considering what you went through last night.'

Mawi smiled for a moment. As he did so, he caught a flicker of recognition in Mr Wickeham's eyes.

'I've been through worse in Chile, *señor*,' he said.

A look of satisfaction appeared on Mr Wickeham's face: Mawi had brought them neatly to the nub of the matter, it seemed.

'You're from the Lake District, aren't you?' said the civil servant. 'How would you feel about going back there?'

'Araucanía is my home. Of course I want to go back there.'

'We don't want to keep you on remand in this country for a costly trial that would probably in any case end in your deportation. We would prefer to send you back now. You may not enjoy life in the cells but it costs us more than a room in a five-star hotel.'

'*Send* me back? To Chile? As a prisoner?'

'Officially, yes. It would be up to the Chilean authorities to make a decision. We would send a glowing conduct report. They might take no further action.'

It was either the cells in this country, with the sort of company he had had yesterday, thought Mawi, or prison in Chile, being tortured, then killed: the devil and the deep blue sea. At least in England he would eventually be reunited with Julieta.

'I think I would prefer to stay in England, *señor*.'

Mr Wickeham seemed put out. 'I'm not sure that you have any choice in the matter.'

'You mean you've decided to send me back?... Have you any idea what you would be sending me back to?... Since Salvador Allende's murder tens of thousands of honest, hard-working, innocent people have been shot, garrotted or thrown live into the quicksands, after being tortured or raped, for supporting a president who believed in justice, education and medical care for everyone, and racial equality. That's the régime you would be sending me back to. What if I asked for asylum? You couldn't refuse it. Not legally.'

Mr Wickeham was silent for a good few moments. His serious expression reminded Mawi of Father Lorencio's, the day he had prodded at the fabric of his friend's beliefs.

'The problem is that Chile is our ally in the current hostilities with Argentina. Offering you asylum would imply criticism of an ally's régime.'

'You're afraid of criticizing a criminal régime, ready to give it your support, for the sake of a few useless islands in the South Atlantic? Do you think this will make your country great again? How many billions is your little war with Argentina costing? Enough to provide work, medical care and an education for millions of South Americans. Your little country would be big again if it did that. The other rich countries would follow your example and poverty would soon be a thing of the past.'

Mr Wickeham was smiling sheepishly. His flimsy shelter of status and superiority was leaking badly. 'I'm afraid what you ask doesn't lie within my power,' he said. 'I'm only a servant of the Crown.'

'Everyone is always somebody else's servant,' Mawi replied. 'Does no one have the courage to step out of the shadows?'

Mr Wickham studied Mawi's face. He was smiling almost kindly now. 'I'm sure I've seen you before somewhere,' he said. 'I can't think where.'

Mawi stared back for a moment, then asked, 'Baker Street Station?'

A light appeared in Mr Wickeham's eyes. 'You were busking. I wanted to ask you what instrument you were playing.'

'I play the Mapuche flute, *señor*. We make them out of araucaria wood.'

'You're a talented musician. I used to play the violin. I never played as well as you.'

'You must start again, *señor*. Our gods speak to us through our music. Perhaps your gods will speak to you through yours and tell you how the poor people of Lima live and how they need your help.'

Mawi had at first seen the civil servant as one of the pillars of an oppressive power structure, as steely and rigid as the dragon and the moustached translator of the Marialabuena courtroom. Now he was starting to make out the human being behind the tie and starched collar. Mr Wickeham would perhaps have preferred the life of a violinist. He might be a victim like himself, of forces and pressures that were hard to resist. He didn't seem to mind being told about the squalor and demoralizing régime of his country's prisons and its antiquated quest for military glory. Perhaps he even agreed with Mawi but was prevented as a servant of the Crown from saying so.

Mr Wickeham got up. 'HMG will arrange for you to be put on a flight to Chile in the next few days. Your main international airline has conveniently laid on a service between London and Santiago. I will take personal responsibility for your good conduct report and will strongly recommend your release on arrival in Chile.'

He stepped towards the bed with a look and a handshake for the bereaved or terminally ill, repeated his promise to contact the Embassy and arrange an advance for Julieta, told Mawi what a gifted musician he was and that music was a comfort in times of trouble, and with a half-whispered 'Good luck!' donned his mantle of authority and strode across the ward to the door.

Mawi had known Julieta only a few weeks but his life was now inseparable from hers. He had had a life of his own before he met her but he didn't want it back. He would rather die than live without Julieta, even as a free man. The thought that he might not see her again appeared in all its starkness. He was desperate to make contact with her. How would he do it? Would Felicidad take a message to her? No, he couldn't ask her to travel all the way to King's Cross and back during the few hours she had between shifts. What if all the patients sent her on errands across England? Mawi closed his eyes and felt himself sink into the despair he had felt for three years in his early teens after the massacre that wiped out most of his community.

Maybe it would be best not to get in touch with Julieta, he thought. If she was going to lose her husband, might she not prefer to remember him slipping quietly away than dying in agony after days of torture? He would ask Felicidad, when she came with his broth and tea, if he could have a couple of sleeping-pills so that he could sleep during the afternoon. Same thing before lights out. He would store the pills in a sock or handkerchief. By the time he left hospital there would be enough for a fatal dose. Unless Julieta was on the flight to Santiago, Mawi would ask for a quarter-bottle of Rioja – two, if possible – and take one pill with each sip of wine.

'Cook likes a glass of red wine while she's working.' Felicidad's voice. 'She put a drop in your broth. Also in your orange juice: it will be like *sangría*.'

Mawi opened his eyes and saw Felicidad's face lit with smiles. She and another nurse were bringing the patients their lunch trays.

Like mist when the sun appears, Mawi's brooding thoughts began to evaporate. 'Are you going to spend your life working in a prison hospital?' he asked her.

'No, no, no. After England I'm going to the States. Nurses are better paid there. When I've saved enough, I'll go back to the Philippines. My parents will be growing old and I'll be able to buy them a comfortable bungalow. My brother needs help too. He was doing well, working in a factory, but he caught his arm in one of the machines. Now he's a street-vender. He can't afford a place to live, so he sleeps on his cart.'

If Mawi were a field of sunflowers, he would raise his many heads towards Felicidad. He was caught up in her hope and vitality. Felicidad was true to her name: Happiness. How could he think of taking his own life when she was giving hers to help her family?

As Mawi sipped his *sangría,* his thoughts turned to his ancestors: how would he face them if he had thrown away the life they gave him? 'We never ran away from danger,' they would say. 'We loved life but we died to save our land from the invaders.' Whatever happened to Mawi during the days and weeks to come, he must remember that he was a Mapuche, accept his trials with calmness and courage and use all his cunning and nerve to stay alive.

During the afternoon Felicidad came with a needle and syringe, and a quieter smile than before. 'I need your blood,' she told him.

'Has Cook run out of wine?'

'Half the patients in the ward have been through the same experience as you. They all have to have a blood test.'

Felicidad took a sample of Mawi's blood and put a plaster on his arm.

'We'll have the results in a week's time.'

'I'll be back in Chile before then.'

'I'll try and hurry things along. Otherwise you'll have to phone from Chile. I'll give you the hospital number. Better still, I'll give you the number of my digs and the times I'll be there.'

'What will my wife think if I start making long-distance calls to attractive girls from exotic Pacific islands? In any case, I'll probably be in gaol.'

'Ask your wife to phone. It's important.'

When Felicidad left the ward, the wind veered back to the north and Mawi's mood changed again. Even if he never had to use them, he would sleep more soundly knowing he had a stash of barbiturates knotted into his handkerchief.

44

Life was made up of millions of moments, good and bad, thought Mawi as he climbed in the twilight into the police van bound for the airport. The trick was to live in the moment, if it was a good one and even if it was one of your last, and not let regret for the past or fear of what might come distract you from the banks of blossom like pink and white clouds as you walked through the park under an azure sky, the stranger's greeting as you sat and played your flute, the taste of real coffee at the friendly Italian café after three hours' busking. Just now Mawi was concentrating his mind on the joy of feeling clean after his shower an hour or two ago, on the summery scent of the soap he had used, the freshness of his clothes and the half-chemical, half-herbal smell of the detergent they had been washed in, and he tried not to let other thoughts intrude.

Without any prompting from Mawi, Felicidad had asked the warders for his clothes, including his jeans, and washed them herself, so that they were now as clean as new. 'I couldn't let you fly to Chile in dirty clothes, could I?' she said with tears in her eyes as Mawi gave her a farewell hug.

Mawi avoided looking into Felicidad's face, so as not to become tearful himself. He had never imagined as he lay violated and bleeding on the floor of his cell that leaving prison less than a week later would be a wrench. It was the care we gave to others, and received from them, that made the difference between happiness and misery, he thought, and made the good moments longer and the bad moments fewer.

The van scrunched its way across the yard, paused for the gate to be opened, then left the crunch of gravel for the hum of tarmac. A black cloud filled the narrow strip of window near the roof of the van, and twilight turned to night; drops of rain distorted the view through the glass.

The good moment passed. Mawi's few sunny spring days with Julieta in London were over. They would never see those green mountains of the north together. England was – what was it Julieta called it when she came and saw him in the police cell? – the promised land that might have been.

Felicidad had hurried things on and was expecting the results of the blood test late today or early tomorrow morning. He was to phone her from the airport, if he got the chance. Would he be one of the seven lucky ones? Or the eighth?

During the past few days Mawi had felt the fear of death for the first time in his life. He felt it now, cold and wet under his arms, and like a cold black hole in his stomach. Shadows seemed to be closing in on him on all sides. One in every eight patients tested was found to be terminally ill. Even if he managed to outwit the Chilean army and police, no amount of guile would save him if the results of his blood test were positive. Felicidad's smile was no longer there to bring him courage. He slid off the bench on to the floor of the van and sat hugging his knees to his chest.

Mawi had spoken to his ancestors and heard their reply. To take one's life in the face of danger was a dishonour to oneself, one's family and the Mapuche people, but to rid oneself of a body that was incurably diseased and might bring disease to others was an act of courage. If Mawi evaded the authorities in Chile, he would devote his life to making Julieta happy, but if he was found to be terminally ill, he would be useless to her. He reached into his pocket and felt the sleeping-pills he had collected and knotted into his handkerchief. Ten of them: a fatal dose if taken in one go.

After half an hour or more of continuous driving on what must be dual carriageway, because of the sound of traffic overtaking but not passing in the opposite direction, the van slowed down, went round a roundabout, stopped for a red light, which Mawi could see reflected in one of the strips of window overhead, drove on slowly for five minutes, paused for a gate to open, whose flashing light was also reflected in the glass, advanced and stopped. The two policemen got out. Mawi got up off the floor of the van and sat on the bench. The rear doors were opened. Mawi climbed out.

Buildings that looked like office-blocks loomed on every side. Three other vehicles were parked nearby, all of them police-cars. Two men in blue suits, one wearing a broad red tie, the other a narrow orange one, got out of one of the cars and walked over to the van. The policemen barked at them. The men in blue barked back. A roar from somewhere behind the building was so monstruous that in a moment of panic Mawi imagined they were all about to be engulfed and swept away, together with the buildings, van and cars. The roar grew louder. A blinding white light appeared and an aeroplane the size of a ship rushed past just above their heads. Mawi covered his ears, and ducked. The four men, unflinching, paused in their conversation, waited till the noise subsided, then went on barking at one another. There was a smell of aviation exhaust, like paraffin wax. The men in suits indicated that Mawi was to go with them.

Inside the building a man in a dark grey suit sat on a high stool at a high desk in a space the size of a tennis-court. Behind him was a barrier of pale grey screens, with a gap between them leading to another area. The man at the desk, and Mawi and his two escorts, were the only people present.

'Passport,' said the man at the desk when Mawi was reined in in front of him. He solemnly examined José Luis Gutiérrez' passport, returned it to Mawi and waved him through.

In the centre of the next space a man in a white shirt and navy-blue trousers, which could have been a uniform or part of it, stood alone next to a long, low metal table.

Mawi felt droplets of sweat forming in his armpits. What were they going to do to him? Was this some kind of examination? He summoned his courage, walked to the table and prepared to lie down on it. His escorts stopped him.

'No baggage?' asked the man in shirt-sleeves. His face and voice were expressionless. A smile would have been unthinkable.

'Sólo mi flauta,' replied Mawi.

He had to put his flute-case on the table. The customs officer opened it, took out the flute, examined it and put it back in its case. Then he frisked Mawi.

The suited men escorted their charge towards a pair of double doors. They paused on the way, so that one of them could give Mawi his ticket and a card with writing on it.

'Bordinpas,' he said.

Mawi nodded and put the ticket and card in his pocket.

They went through the double doors into a hall full of people and chatter. Mawi stopped. He had been a prisoner for only a week but he felt dazed at his sudden return to a world of crowds and laughter and freedom of movement, like someone who raises his blind, having slept till midday, and is dazzled by the sunlight. The scene had an unreal quality, because he couldn't be part of it. He seemed to be part of it – he wasn't manacled or handcuffed – but an invisible chain tethered him to his two keepers.

Mawi thought he understood how the system worked. His two escorts were plain-clothes policemen, in mufti so as not to alarm the passengers by signalling to them that they might have been allocated a seat next to a man under arrest – a murderer or terrorist, perhaps. The uniformed policemen wandering about the hall served the purpose of reassuring the public in case of some emergency but were concentrated in this part of the airport to let Mawi know it was not worth his while to make a run for it. Within these limits he was free to roam – encouraged to do so, even. He could do the round of shops and cafés and use up his English money on coffee, cakes, a book, a cigar, a teddy bear. Wherever he went, his shadows would be at his side or his heels, like dark thoughts at the back of a condemned man's mind as he dines on roast beef and wine on the eve of his execution.

The smell of freshly ground coffee reached Mawi's nostrils. Coffee: once the drink of the poor man in the countries where it was grown, a gift from the gods to lighten his burden, now cultivated behind barbed wire and exported to Europeans and North Americans for their breakfast, lunch and dinner, and reimported at prices no poor man, and not even the well-to-do, could afford. Mawi headed for the nearest coffee bar. He offered coffee to his two men in blue, who shook their heads stonily, and ordered an espresso for himself.

A young woman passed, carrying two bags. Mawi noticed her too late to see her face. From behind she could have been Julieta: the same figure, the same graceful walk, the same wavy black hair. Even the clothes were right: Julieta's white cardigan and the navy-blue skirt she had bought in Camden. And the bags: were they the same bags Mawi had spent hours strapping to the backs of Pablo and Pedro?

Mawi left his coffee on the counter and went after the young woman. There was a clatter of stools as the two hounds sprang into action and took off in pursuit. A uniformed policeman stopped acting like everyone's favourite uncle and quick-marched to the middle of the hall to intercept the runaway. The young woman was just out of earshot, unless Mawi yelled, when the red tie appeared on his left, the orange on his right. The two men overtook him and stepped in front of him, so that he just stopped himself breaking his nose on a shoulder-blade. Mawi's escorts looked at him as if he were a homicidal stalker. Passengers who had stopped to stare walked on, wheeling their cases behind them.

'I thought I saw my wife,' he explained in Spanish. Did it matter if he was understood or not by these two granite-faced brutes who treated him like a steer on its way to the slaughterhouse?

Was the agony of being separated from Julieta affecting Mawi's mind? Would he see her in every young woman who went by, this one with Julieta's hair, that one with her walk, another with her clothes? Would he be like a man who has lost his leg but goes on feeling it as part of his body, until he falls over once too often and accepts that the leg has gone? Mawi remembered the phone call he had to make. He did a mime show for his guards, who marched him to a cubicle. He took a coin from his pocket and dialled one of the numbers on the piece of paper he was holding.

A female voice addressed the public over the tannoy. The woman sounded as if she were eating crisps. The two guards stepped towards Mawi. They seemed to have made sense of the announcement. One of them barked at him; the other took the receiver from his hand and hung it up. Time for the departure gate, Mawi guessed. He set off with his escorts along a corridor. After ten minutes they turned right along a second corridor. A quarter of an hour later they sank down one floor on a moving staircase, walked along a third corridor and arrived at Gate 13. Mawi wondered how the old and the lame managed the slog, especially if they had more than a flute to carry.

By the time Mawi and the two watch-dogs finished their trek, the passengers were already starting to go through the gate. Mawi looked about him, clutching at straws, placing his last coin on the outside chance of seeing Julieta. There was no sign of her. His hand went to the handkerchief in his pocket and the ten pills tied into it. Was it realistic to go on hoping? To wait for the aeroplane and the pain of not finding Julieta on board, or for Santiago, on the off chance of evading the police and army there, or for the results of the blood test, which could easily be his death sentence? Why not end it here? Was there a coffee bar anywhere near? Or just a fountain where he could get a drink of water?

Mawi's silent companions nudged him towards the gate. He took out his passport and boarding-pass but noticed that his guards were not producing any documents. Presumably they just flashed a little identity card at the airline reps as they passed through the barrier. Mawi's turn came. He showed his papers, went through and turned to wait for the two Dobermans. They had stepped aside from the queue and – was it possible? – they were not following him. Mawi was so relieved that he waved to them cheerily and called out '*¡Hasta luego!* See you later!', hoping that later stood for all eternity. The thought of not spending what might be his last hours sandwiched between those two cliff-faces made him forget his sleeping-pills for the present. This was one of the good moments, he thought, a moment to enjoy in spite of everything.

At the bottom of the gangway a bus was filling up with passengers. Two uniformed policemen stood on the pavement, one at either end of the bus, trying to look casual. Mawi got on board and the bus was soon weaving its way among parked airliners until it came to one with the Chilean flag painted on its fin. It was a big aeroplane but not as big as the Boeing 747 that had brought Mawi and Julieta to England.

'Rear door,' the young woman at the gate had told him. Why was the stewardess sending him back down the steps to the door at the front? X6 was the seat number on his boarding-card. That must surely be at the tail end.

A stewardess not much older than Mawi, with a mass of chestnut hair and large black eyes, welcomed him at the top of the front steps with a smile that wasn't glued on and seemed meant for him alone.

'I've got X6 on my card,' he said.

'Your seat's been changed to C2. Third row on the right.'

'But this is first class,' said Mawi, when he was inside the aircraft.

C2 was one of a pair of seats. C1, by the window, was already occupied. Mawi was wondering what to do with his flute when the young woman in C1 looked up at him.

'They didn't cut your hair short,' she said.

Moments later Mawi smelt orange-blossom and felt a pair of

arms round his neck and a cheek pressed against his.

'I've brought your bag with all your things,' said Julieta, her face buried in Mawi's shoulder, so that her voice was muffled. 'I've put it in the overhead locker.'

45

It had been a fine spring evening when Paul Wickeham had decided to walk home from Whitehall through Green Park, Hyde Park and Regent's Park. The downpour had come ten minutes before the end, just as he reached Regent's Park.

He pushed open the iron gate and stumbled exhausted up the path with his black briefcase to his porticoed Regency front-door. He would have a bath and a drink, then go out for a meal. He used to be a keen cook before the divorce. Now he couldn't be bothered. There was a smart Indian restaurant just round the corner in Park Road. He went there two or three times a week.

Wickeham left his briefcase on the elegantly backed, green and gold striped Chippendale chair in the hallway, and staggered up the three steps and through the arch into the dining-room, with its Georgian table, chairs and drinks cabinet, bequeathed to him with most of the other furniture by his parents when they had left Waynflete Manor in Hampshire for their celestial home, one within months of the other. Diana had taken some of the best pieces, collected with loving care and good taste by Sir Charles and Lady Joanna Wickeham over several decades, when she had left him for her scavenging actor, who in turn made off with them when he ditched Diana to prey on his next victim. Wickeham poured the last of the Macallan into a cut-glass tumbler, took a gulp and went through to what was once the scullery, where he stripped down to his underpants, removed the contents of his pockets and stuffed his jacket, trousers, shirt and socks into the trumble-drier. He collected his whisky from the drinks cabinet and puffed his way upstairs to the bathroom.

Wickeham couldn't get the Chilean boy off his mind. And off his conscience. He had had to carry out many an ethically questionable order in the course of his professional duties but this latest act of cynical officialdom weighed more than most. The boy was highly intelligent and a gifted musician. What would they do to him? Travelling with a false passport was not necessarily a serious offence. But he must have had a good reason to leave Chile. Nobody chose King's Cross for a honeymoon. Was he on the official list of Communist supporters? The Chilean authorities wouldn't be gentle when they got their hands on him.

'A trusty servant, that's what I am,' thought Wickeham as he ran his bath and visualized the icon hanging in an inner chamber of the secondary school he had attended, a nursery for future public servants, trusty as the Vicar of Bray most of them. He even had the same name as the founder of the school. 'Scarred for life,' he said aloud. 'Tarred, tattooed. A trusty bloody lackey, that's what I am. Wickeham the quiet intellectual – so quiet you can't hear him.' Politics was the natural home for power-hungry and untalented Etonians, he decided, the civil service for Wykehamists, who did their thinking for them and allowed them to believe that the ideas they blazoned forth in their parliamentary debates, and failed to understand, had been conceived in their own infertile minds.

'I need to lose weight,' Wickeham thought as he wallowed in the hot bath and contemplated his swollen feet. 'I'm not forty yet and I'm the shape of a barrel – with a tap that was never circumcised, because my parents were afraid I'd be taken for a Jew or Muslim in the baths at boarding-school and mutilated by the older boys.'

He reached for his glass and gulped his whisky. 'A Wykehamist? What's a Wykehamist?' he murmured. A Wykehamist was a time-server who changed course with every change of wind and tailored his principles to suit whichever master he happened to be serving, to protect his own six-figure income and his terrace house in Regent's Park or country mansion within commuting distance of Whitehall. Whatever the Wykehamist thought, he would probably not say. He excelled at lip-service but otherwise kept his lips discreetly closed – padlocked in the sacred painting in the holy of holies at the school – while his country's armed forces helped the Americans butcher defenceless women and children in countries across the world that threatened to turn Communist or put up their oil prices. A Wykehamist was a soft-spoken gentleman who would sign your death-warrant while nervously offering you another sherry and stuttering polite small talk about vintages and the weather; a spaniel who would lick one of his master's boots clean while being kicked with the other. Service was the word. Obedience. Time-serving, pen-pushing obedience. Doing whatever your superiors told you to, even when they were rotten to the marrow. And if it meant sending a sensitive, intelligent, talented Chilean boy back to his country in the middle of his honeymoon, perhaps to be tortured and killed, so be it: you were only doing your duty, serving Queen and Country, Pension and Promotion.

Wickeham had sometimes thought of cutting his own throat, preferably at a meeting of departmental heads, so that his blood would pump out all over the table, or of hanging himself with his old school tie, with its mismatch of red, blue and brown stripes, from the flag-pole outside the main entrance of the Home Office. Where would he find the courage, with his habit of mental and physical ease? His school had produced few suicides and fewer martyrs.

He reached out to the cork-top stool beside the bath, switched on the radio and had another gulp of whisky. Why were Radio Three broadcasting the last night of the Proms in May? Had the concerts been rescheduled this year? No, it must be a replay from last summer, probably at the request of the PM, to draw tears of nostalgia and whip up patriotism. *Land of Hope and Glory*: the song for grown-up schoolboys. It made Wickeham think of the nationalist rallies at Nürnberg and other towns in Germany in the 1930s.

He switched the radio off, covered himself in soap, splashed about like a hippopotamus to rinse it off, climbed out of the bath and dried himself vigorously, so that his body wobbled like a mountain of aspic.

Wickeham clambered back into his pants and padded downstairs to the tumble-drier, where he put on the rest of his clothes, which were now dry. He went through to the dining-room and broke the seal of a bottle of malt he had promised himself not to broach before the week-end. He was bound to finish it by Saturday. That meant he would have drunk more than two bottles in a week. He must cut down.

The diplomats had been doing a good job over the Falklands until the PM marched in backwards in her jackboots, hell-bent on war and a cheap victory at the next election, her braying right-wingers and the gutter press at her side, galvanizing the corpse of imperialism and fuelling her country's morbid pining for domination and military glory. The whole thing could have been settled over a few slices of Argentinian beef and a few bottles of their excellent wine: London would sell the islands to the Argentines, who would then lease them back to Britain. They would have the sovereignty they craved; the Falklanders would have a better life, with access to Argentinian shops, restaurants, doctors, hospitals, cultural events, wine, women, beaches and casinos. But no! They must be tied to Britain's apron-strings. So why not ship the lot of them to the Shetlands or the Orkneys, where they could live the life they were used to, rearing sheep and bonking their sisters and daughters, in pleasanter surroundings and a pleasanter climate, only an hour's flight from the capital of their beloved motherland?

Wickeham took his glass through to the drawing-room. The rain had stopped and the evening sun was staining the sky orange beyond the leafing sycamore at the bottom of the garden. He opened the French windows on to the terrace. The daffodils were massed in clumps around the trees, the faded petals hanging like little sodden yellow rags.

'At least Diana's left me the daffs she planted,' thought Wickeham. 'Even if this year's lot are finished. Like our relationship. Like this country. Like me, perhaps.'

He went to the hi-fi, slid in his cassette of Bach's concerto for two violins and returned to the window.

The Chilean boy had been right, he thought: the way to greatness today was to lead the fight against poverty and exploitation. If the PM were a stateswoman, instead of a Little Englander, she would let the Argentines have those God-forsaken islands, which Britain stole from them in the first place a hundred and fifty years ago, or rather seized from the North Americans, who had stolen them from Argentina. And instead of making enemies across Europe, friends with one of the world's most repulsive tyrants, and ingratiating herself with Uncle Sam, she would engage with her European neighbours and inspire them to join with her to change a world in which more than a billion people were undernourished and millions of children were dying every year of starvation and preventable diseases.

Wickeham became aware of the Bach concerto. How harsh our inner voice sounded, he thought, heard against the music of Bach. How futile politics and war and so-called public service were, compared with the works of the great composers! If Wickeham could write one piece to equal the least of the thousands written by Bach, he would feel he had achieved something in his life. 'You must start again, *señor*,' the boy had said to him. 'Our gods speak to us through our music. Perhaps your gods will speak to you through yours.' Wickeham would always remember the boy's words. Was it too late to start again? Did he have the guts to try?

The music came to an end. Wickeham was about to pour himself another whisky, rewind the cassette and play it again, but he didn't move from the spot. 'I've got to do something for that boy,' he said aloud. 'I can't just leave him to the mercy of those brutes.' He stood holding his empty glass, looking out at the trees with their half-open, pale green leaves. An idea was taking shape in his slightly fuddled mind. 'It might help him, coming from the top.'

Instead of making for the drinks cabinet, Wickeham went through the dining-room into the kitchen, where he rinsed his glass, turned on the cold tap and splashed water on to his face.

True service could sometimes mean breaking the rules, flouting the system, a supporter of Allende's had once told Wickeham, on a trip to England to try and make friends at the Foreign Office and spark a little interest in human rights there. If the hierarchy stood in the way of justice, integrity and freedom of expression, he said, you had to kick away the ladder, even at the risk of bringing it down on your own head.

'A letter purporting to come from the Home Secretary,' thought Wickeham. 'My career will be on the line all right if he ever gets to hear about it. The best I can hope for is a severe reprimand. No: the worst I can hope for is a reprimand. The best is to be out on my ear, so that I'm forced to make a fresh start.'

46

Seconds after the Boeing 320 had left the tarmac, it was lost in the folds of England's soiled mantle. The aeroplane climbed and climbed, through layer after layer of dirty whiteness caught once a second by the flashing lights at the wing-tips, sometimes with a low gap in between layers like one of the floors of a multi-storey car park. Julieta didn't know how so much vapour could be concentrated in one place: it was as if cloud and smoke had been sucked from the four corners of the earth to form a smeary, slush-spattered wedding-cake towering thousands of metres into the sky above the south of England.

For ten minutes the aircraft climbed through mountainous banks of cloud. Suddenly it broke surface and they were in bright moonlight under a black sky, skimming over an illusory snow-white landscape.

Julieta hadn't felt so elated since the day she and Mawi set foot on the Isla del Sol, not since their marriage night at Yucuma's. Mawi was out of prison and they were safely on their way to the Canary Islands. London, the dream that had become a nightmare, was behind them. Father Lorencio's saving hand had reached across continents and oceans and rescued them. Mercedes had carried Mawi and Julieta on her angel's wings out of England and would fly them over the heads of customs and immigration officers when they landed at Tenerife. Julieta had enough money to last them at least a fortnight, by which time they should be making a living from their teaching and playing. Things seemed to be going better than she had dared hope for.

Mercedes appeared. 'Would you like a glass of champagne?' she asked Mawi and Julieta. 'We offer one to all our first-class passengers.'

Julieta lifted her head from Mawi's shoulder, where she had been resting it ever since they sat down and fastened their seat-belts. They had hardly exchanged a word. Julieta had simply been enjoying Mawi as she would a bath after a difficult day: feeling him there, relaxing in his warmth.

Julieta nodded yes to the champagne for both of them, and Mercedes moved to the row behind.

Was Mawi as blissful as Julieta? He hadn't shown her any warmth – hadn't even held her hand. Then it dawned on her: he must be on the rack, imagining the flight was a brief respite before his delivery into the hands of the Chilean militarists, that these were his last few hours with his wife.

'You don't know and I should have told you,' Julieta said. 'It's the first thing I should have said. We've got something to celebrate with our champagne.' She lowered her voice, so as not to be overheard. 'We're not going to Chile. Mercedes is getting us off the plane and past the authorities at Tenerife.'

'Who's Mercedes?'

'The stewardess. Mercedes Aguila. It's thanks to her that we're sitting here together.'

'How did you meet her?'

'Father Lorencio. There's so much to tell you.'

Julieta began with her strange phone call to Santo Domingo, her despair, then her realization that Father Lorencio was directing her in code to a London number. She told Mawi about Mercedes, whose father had stayed in hiding at one of Father Lorencio's safe houses eight years ago while the rector persuaded a senior air force officer who attended mass at Santo Domingo to come to confession, so that he could study his mannerisms and voice, then phoned a small airport south of Santiago, posing as the bluff air commodore, and asked for a small aeroplane to be ready for use early the next day; about Mercedes' escape with her parents and sister from Chile in the borrowed single-engined aircraft, which her father flew along the Pacific coast all the way to the border with Peru at a height of no more than ten metres to avoid radar detection; about the airline set up by Mercedes' father in Peru, which started with five single-propeller planes and now had a fleet of fifty long-haul jets. Julieta told Mawi about Mercedes' visit, the five hundred pounds, the solicitor Señor Aguila found to try and prevent or delay Mawi's extradition and, when this failed, to arrange for him to be flown out of England by Aguila Airlines on the same flight as Julieta.

None of this had the transforming effect Julieta had hoped for: Mawi was still subdued. Julieta had never known him like this: tense, worried. What had happened to the calm, poised Mawi of ten days ago, the self-assured master of the Mapuche flute, to the eagle of the Andes, perched fearlessly, a bag in each hand, on the edge of a three-thousand-metre precipice? Julieta had never known anyone so relaxed when he was awake, so like a marmot when he was asleep. He had been his old self in front of the magistrates only a week ago. What had happened since?

'We'll be able to relax and enjoy our stay in the Canaries,' Julieta told him. 'Mercedes says they have the best climate in the world: warm and sunny almost every day of the year. The tourist season never stops: you'll be able to play every day if you want to in cafés and restaurants and at concerts, and I can teach the Spanish English and the English Spanish. We'll be able to swim and sail, climb the mountains, eat fresh seafood. It'll be a working holiday, until Papa relents and we can go back to Bolivia and the Isla del Sol.'

Mawi listened to Julieta but didn't respond. What she said failed to lift his spirits or kindle his enthusiasm. The soft light that always shone in his eyes had gone out. Had his love for her suddenly cooled? Was he tired of the company of this daughter of a Spanish Chilean? Did he long to be among his own people, with a good-hearted, unsophisticated Mapuche girl for a wife?

'I missed you,' Julieta told Mawi gently. When he didn't reply, she asked, 'Did you miss me?'

'Of course.'

She rested her head on his shoulder again.

'I knew you were running out of money,' he added. 'I was worried.'

Julieta remembered when Mawi would put his arm round her whenever she laid her head on his shoulder, hold her to him and press his cheek against the top of her head. Now there was no pressure in his arm, no cheek on her head. Just his worry about money.

After a minute or two she looked up and asked, 'You haven't gone off me?'

'Gone off you? No. Why?'

'I get the feeling you'd rather be in a seat the other side of the gangway from me.'

'I want to be near you. That's the problem.'

'Why is it a problem?'

'I don't want you to catch anything from me. Prisons are unhealthy places.'

Catch what? What did Mawi mean? He seemed perfectly healthy. The solicitor told her he had been moved into a comfortable dormitory because his cell was overcrowded but he hadn't said anything about Mawi being ill. He had lost weight, what weight there was to lose, but prisons were not places where you went to gorge yourself on fine food. Was it an upset of the mind he had, of self-image? Did he feel tainted by his few days behind bars?

Mercedes brought two glasses of champagne and two menus. Julieta and Mawi lowered their tray-holders. Julieta would like to have clinked glasses with him and drunk to the next stage of their ever-changing life together – to Mawi and Julieta in the Canary Islands – but this didn't seem the right moment. They sipped their drinks in silence and studied their menus. Mercedes took their order: chicken Marengo for Mawi, salmon for Julieta.

She would be patient, Julieta told herself. Prison must be a shock to the system, especially in a foreign country where you didn't speak the language. Leaving prison must be a shock too:

the sudden freedom and the feeling everyone was looking at you, as if you were sandwiched between two boards with *EX-CONVICT* printed on them, and avoiding you for fear of being robbed or murdered. She would give Mawi her quiet love and wait for him to unwind and his heart to unclench.

Mercedes brought them their slotted trays, designed so that half an avocado filled with prawn cocktail, several cuts of smoked salmon on a slice of pumpernickel, chicken and sauté potatoes, a quarter-bottle of dry white Chilean wine, a roll and butter, cheese, coleslaw and fruit salad could share their twenty by thirty centimetres like a large family in a small room but manage to look more compact than cramped.

Mawi started on his food like a wild animal in winter. Julieta had never seen him so hungry. No sooner was one piece of chicken in his mouth than a second was on its way. His hands were trembling with hunger. He was too impatient to spear the sauté potatoes with his fork: he ate them with his fingers..

'You're starving,' said Julieta. 'Didn't they give you any food in prison?'

'Only fluids,' Mawi replied. 'Doctor's orders.'

So he had been ill. Botulism? Listeriosis? That would explain the weight loss. But food-poisoning wasn't contagious: you caught it from food, not from other people. Perhaps there had been an outbreak of cholera or dysentery in the prison. Did people get cholera and dysentery in England? Whatever it was, he must be better, to judge by his appetite.

Julieta put her roll and butter and cheese on Mawi's tray. 'It's too much for me,' she said.

'They did some tests before I left prison. I have to phone in a couple of days for the results.'

'What are they looking for?'

'Microbes.'

Mawi started on his first roll and butter and cheese. Julieta didn't bother him with any more questions. Now that she knew what was worrying him, she would be able to try and keep his mind on other things.

Food finished and was followed by film. Just like home for most of the passengers, thought Julieta: supper, then gawp at the box. Mercedes' father's airline had escaped the stranglehold of the North American distributors and was showing a Spanish film about a bee-keeper. Not a promising subject, perhaps, but it wasn't long before Julieta was enthralled by this story of exile and migration. She glanced at Mawi, who was as absorbed in the film as she was. As absorbed as a bee-keeper in his quiet, careful work. Good! That meant he wasn't thinking about his medical tests. What a good bee-keeper Mawi would make, thought Julieta, with his nerve, his gentleness, patience and concentration. Perhaps when they got back to the Isla del Sol they would keep bees, and make honey for the children.

Julieta only half saw and understood the end of the film: waves of sleep kept breaking over her struggling mind and eyes and at last submerged them.

She was woken by the lights of Santa Cruz de Tenerife dazzling her as the aircraft banked for its approach to the island's northern airport. She looked at Mawi, with his gift for deep sleep, hoping to see him sunk in the same oblivion from which she had just surfaced, but Mawi was wide awake.

Mercedes paused beside them on her way from the cockpit. 'Wait on board till all the other Tenerife passengers have disembarked,' she said quietly. 'Then I'll tell you what to do.'

Two minutes later the jet touched down, roared and juddered and braked, and taxied to the airport. Mercedes' voice on the tannoy requested passengers not terminating their journey at Tenerife to remain seated. The plane came to a halt and the engines faded. Two sets of steps were wheeled to the two doors, fore and aft. Mercedes opened the door in front of Mawi and Julieta and gave a start.

A uniformed man, with the black butts of two pistols showing through their black leather holsters, stepped into the aeroplane.

'What's going on?' asked Mercedes.

'We have orders to examine the passports of all passengers leaving the aircraft,' he said.

'Can't you do it in the airport?'

'Our orders are to do it at the doors of the aircraft.'

Half a dozen passengers left by the door at the front, showing their passports as they went. Mercedes made her way through the cabin with a list. Five minutes later she was back.

'That's everybody,' she said, moving towards the *guardia* to see him out.

He didn't move. 'My orders are to wait here until the doors are closed.'

The cockpit door opened and another member of the crew emerged in his shirt-sleeves: the captain perhaps, with his grey hair and air of authority. 'What's going on?' he asked.

'This gentleman is examining the passports of passengers disembarking,' Mercedes explained.

'Isn't there anyone in passport control?'

'Extra security request from Santiago,' said the *guardia*.

The captain shrugged and disappeared back into the cockpit. Mercedes' characteristic smile had vanished; her face was tense.

The fuel lorry outside Julieta's window detached itself and retreated into the darkness. Mercedes gave the *guardia* a curt *buenas noches* as he turned and went down the steps. She closed and locked the door. The steps were wheeled away. The engines started to hum. The aircraft eased into motion and headed towards the runway for take-off.

There was still no smile on Mercedes' face as she made her way along the aisle, pausing beside Mawi and Julieta. 'We'll need a plan B for Santiago,' she said quietly.

47

'Reyes is losing his bottle,' thought Adolfo Cortez. Having pestered the army to go chasing after his daughter all over Chile and rescue her from the clutches of a rutting native, he had now stumbled on the thought that his slut of a girl might have had the hots for her Communist abductor after all, and that the best way of avoiding her undying hatred and his own isolation would be to redefine his family boundaries. If the daughter couldn't live without her Indian, then I'm terribly sorry Cortez old chap but there doesn't seem much point continuing your overtures to Julieta as I shall be forced to share my trough with the tom-cat of her choice. He hadn't said as much yet but his face and body language were like a notice-board for his thoughts.

Cortez had news for Reyes. He was just waiting for the right moment to throw it in his face. Nothing in the world would persuade him to marry that slag of a daughter of his, not just because she was some savage's left-overs but because she was now the daughter of a clown who couldn't keep his wife and had made himself the laughing-stock of Santiago. He had been obscene before but saved by his wife's grace and elegance. Now he was plain gross, and a buffoon with it.

If he had any dignity, he would turn his loss into a triumph and tell the world what a joy it was to be a free man, unsaddled by family cares. Instead, he shambled about in his increasingly crumpled suit, his tie askew, in a state of distraction, unable to express himself or take in what you said to him. He had no one to run his house, because the maid had gone too. No one to dominate, so that he could hold on to his illusion of authority. No one to get on his nerves. No one to shout at and manipulate. The fool had realized he needed his wife, even if he didn't love her. Now he was dead scared of losing his daughter too.

Reyes could have the girl back. He was welcome to her. But he wasn't getting the Indian. The elopement had cost the country a fortune, thanks to Reyes' friends in high places, and had made a fool of Cortez. Marriage to the Reyes girl would have brought him early promotion. Now he was at the back of the queue. The Indian would pay. With his nuts. Cortez would have them dried and made into golf-balls, ready for when higher rank made him eligible for the prestigious senior officers' club. He would get a thrill every time he teed up and whacked one of the balls with his driver.

It was five o'clock on a cool, misty morning. Adolfo Cortez and Franco Reyes were sitting in a military vehicle under a yellow street-light outside Arturo Merino Benítez Airport in Santiago, waiting for Flight 1317 from London. Cortez was in dress-uniform at the wheel of his officer's car, a khaki Ford imported from the United States, with a little Chilean flag apologetically replacing the Stars and Stripes at the front of the bonnet. An empty army bus was parked behind them: the soldiers had already taken up their positions in the airport.

'There are an awful lot of doors in this building,' said Reyes. 'You can't have a man on every one of them.'

Cortez had given up trying to control his impatience. 'Are you running this operation or am I?' he snapped.

'You told me that in the Canaries they had just two men, one at each door of the aeroplane. Why not here?'

'Because in the Canaries we wanted the deportee to stay on the plane. Here we want him off. There will be men on the doors of the aircraft and on every door between the aeroplane and here.'

'So long as they don't start firing their guns all over the place. I don't want Julieta killed.'

'My men are fully trained professionals,' hissed Cortez, almost spitting at Reyes.

'Are they the same men who missed the two of them at Putre, Tambo Quemado and Visviri?'

Cortez couldn't stand any more of this. It was bad enough having this walrus stranded at the far side of his office for a quarter of an hour or less, but to have him a few centimetres away in the passenger seat of a car for three hours at five o'clock in the morning was more than he could bear. Cortez got out, slammed the door and walked through the main entrance of the airport.

He saw two of his men in battledress, machine-guns at the ready, each at the bottom of a flight of steps. He nodded to them and made his way to the electronic arrivals board and watched the letters spin through the alphabet and the numbers whirl from zero to nine to give new times, places and flight numbers. Lima, Bogotá, Mexico City, London, La Paz, Buenos Aires.

London? Yes, there it was: Flight 1317. Cortez turned and gave his two men another nod, then walked unhurriedly out of the airport and back to the car. He took his walkie-talkie from his pocket and made sure it was switched on, with the volume turned up.

Cortez opened the driver's door a crack. 'Flight's coming in,' he barked. 'We should pick them up thirty or forty minutes from now.' He slammed the door again and paced up and down the pavement, tapping the revolver in his brown leather holster.

48

Until now, every difficulty Julieta had faced with Mawi had been a challenge, a stimulus to the adrenal glands triggering all her courage, ingenuity and determination. She had never till now felt the cold trickle of discouragement in her heart, thinning her blood and chilling her to the marrow. They had kept a step ahead of their pursuers but for the first time Julieta asked herself how long she could keep up this game of hide-and-seek with boots and uniforms, guns and guard-dogs, with vassals of an international system that favoured the rich and crushed the poor, built razor-wire fences instead of opening gates, created tension and insecurity instead of confidence and peace. Mawi and Julieta had been driven from Chile, Bolivia, Peru, England, and now the Canary Islands. She had been prepared to live like this for years, if necessary, seeing every difficulty as a challenge, so long as she had Mawi's support. But if Mawi went cold on her – stayed as cold as he had been for the past few hours – her motor would stop firing and her courage and determination would quickly drain away.

After Tenerife Julieta only dozed. In her exhausted but unsleeping mind she saw the country in which she grew up bathed in lurid yellow, the colour of disease, contagion, quarantine, of a society sick with tyranny, inhumanity and injustice. She longed to see her mother and Copihue again but in Bolivia or Peru, not in Chile. If armed officials were checking passports at Tenerife, Santiago Airport would be crawling with police and soldiers waiting to deliver Julieta into the clutches of her father, and Mawi into those of the torturers. Mercedes had said something about a plan B but hadn't come up with one. Julieta tossed and turned in her seat in the gloom of the emergency lighting. This was the longest night she had spent, with the airliner fleeing the sun westwards, made longer by her sleeplessness. It was already late morning in England but here, over the Amazonian jungle, there was no sign of dawn. With every half-hour that passed, her heart sank a little further. She glanced at Mawi in the hope of seeing a glimmer of his old self. His eyes were closed but she could tell he wasn't asleep. That made two of them.

The cockpit door opened. Mercedes came briskly out and hurried past Mawi and Julieta. A minute later she was back in the cockpit, then out again, carrying an oxygen cylinder. She flew down the aisle, quiet as a night-bird.

The grey-haired man with the air of authority came out of the cockpit and tried to look carefree as a country walker as he strode through the cabin clutching a large first-aid bag. 'He's the one who does the artificial respiration,' thought Julieta, who had volunteered for a first-aid course after leaving school. 'Mercedes has tried with her cylinder but oxygen is no use to someone who isn't breathing. Probably some poor old person whose heart couldn't stand the fifteen-hour journey.'

The aeroplane started its descent and the seat-belt lights came on. One of Mercedes' colleagues made an announcement saying they would be landing at Santiago in twenty minutes and asking passengers to fasten their seat-belts and make sure their seat-backs were in the upright position.

Julieta glanced at Mawi. His eyes were open now. She would like to have offered him some encouragement but couldn't think of anything to say. She couldn't bother Mercedes about plan B while there was a life in the balance further down the cabin.

They were already over Santiago, with the sunrise over Aconcagua, the white giant, flashing through the portholes like an orange strobe as the aircraft circled, when Mercedes and the captain reappeared. Was Julieta imagining it or did she see a look of relief on their faces? The captain walked smartly into the cockpit and closed the door. Mercedes did her rounds, making sure seat-belts were secure and seat-backs vertical, then followed the captain into the cockpit.

The airliner touched down and braked. The palms of Julieta's hands were clammy: the doors would be open in a few minutes and soldiers or policemen with machine-guns would be storming into the cabin. Had Mercedes been too busy nursing the sick passenger to think of a plan B?

The aircraft left the runway and taxied towards the terminal. The locker above Mawi and Julieta opened: Mercedes was beside them, taking out their bags and Mawi's flute.

'Bring your things,' she murmured.

Mawi and Julieta followed Mercedes to the area between the first-class compartment and the cockpit and in front of the forward door in and out of the aircraft. She drew the cabin curtain, so that they couldn't be seen by the other passengers.

'We've had a crisis with a diabetic girl,' she explained quickly but calmly, keeping her voice down. 'The captain gave her an injection but we didn't have enough insulin. We need to get her to hospital. We've by-passed air control and radioed my father. He's called a private ambulance company and offered the ambulance-men a month's extra salary to follow his instructions. To save time, the captain's going to stop the aircraft before we get to the terminal. Follow the girl down the steps and into the ambulance. Do what the driver tells you. Take care! *¡Hasta luego!*'

The aircraft gave a jolt as the captain turned the nose towards an unlit hangar several hundred metres short of the terminal, and another as he applied the brakes. The engines faded, with the same mournful sound as a dying siren. Mercedes picked up a telephone receiver and made an announcement over the tannoy requesting passengers to remain seated with their seat-belts fastened. A flight of steps appeared and thudded against the fuselage. A green Ford ambulance, with the bonnet of a car and the body of a van, drove round the nose of the airliner and pulled up at the foot of the steps. Mercedes threw a lever and swung the door open. A man in fluorescent overalls secured the handrail to a ring beside the door and disappeared down the steps. Two ambulance-men hurried to the rear doors of the ambulance and took out a stretcher.

Mercedes stood by the curtain, opening it to let the two men through and closing it after them. Mawi and Julieta pressed their backs against the plastic panelling to let the ambulance-men past when they returned with their stretcher. Julieta looked down at the diabetic girl, unconscious under the grey rug covering her arms and body, and caught her breath when she saw the face.

'I know her,' she whispered to Mawi. 'We were at school together. Raquel. The girl who always had bread and cheese instead of dessert at lunch.'

'Thank you, Raquel,' thought Julieta as Mercedes closed the curtains behind the stretcher. 'If Mawi and I get safely out of the airport, I'll buy you the biggest box of sugar-free chocolates you've ever seen.'

'Go now!' murmured Mercedes. 'Good luck!'

Julieta gave Mercedes a quick hug and started down the steps with Mawi. She glanced over her shoulder and saw that the terminal was hidden from view by the aircraft. Soldiers or police watching from the terminal wouldn't be able to see them.

The ambulance-men slid the stretcher on to a trolley in the middle of the ambulance. On either side was a bunk, and under it a rectangular metal chest the size of a coffin. The lids of the two chests were open.

'We use them for corpses,' the older and plumper of the two men said cheerfully, as he gave Raquel an injection and his tall young colleague closed the rear doors and put Mawi's and Julieta's luggage in a locker fastened to the partition dividing the sick-bay from the cab. 'There've been so many over the past few years. Most of the bodies we pick up these days are dead, what's left of them. They'd fall to pieces if we put them on the bunks. We load them like stewed chicken into the containers.'

Julieta felt the colour drain from her cheeks. 'You mean… we have to ride in the coffins?' she asked weakly.

'Don't worry!' the *ambulanciero* replied with a radiant smile. 'The refrigerator's switched off. They're quite clean: we've hosed out the blood. It's not for long: fifteen minutes at the most. Hop in!'

Mawi and Julieta did as they were told. The lid closed on Julieta. Her first impulse was to bang on it and ask to be let out but she clenched her fists and jaws, thought of Sister Thérèse and the missionary and asked them for a little of their courage to survive the next quarter of an hour. Julieta breathed for the first time and nearly vomited at the smell of disinfectant. 'I can't stand it,' she thought and pushed at the lid. It opened easily. She took a deep breath, then gently lowered the lid. 'I'll hold my breath for half a minute at a time,' she told herself, 'and open the lid a fraction to breathe. Fifteen minutes: that's thirty breaths.'

The engine sprang into life and the tyres squealed as the ambulance began its race to the hospital. A minute later the driver braked sharply and the ambulance came to a halt. Julieta heard one of the doors at the front bang and the rear doors open.

'Diabetic girl on the flight from London,' the ambulance-man was explaining, without the cheerful note of two minutes ago. 'She's unconscious. Needs insulin urgently.'

A pair of boots clattered on the metal floor of the ambulance. One of them kicked against Julieta's hiding-place. She gave a start and nearly kicked the metal chest herself. She eased a hand over her mouth and nose, to filter the smell of disinfectant when she breathed.

The rear doors banged shut, the engine revved, the siren started to wail and the career to the hospital resumed. The ambulance flew like a swallow through the streets of Santiago, weaving this way and that, slowed down for a few seconds, presumably for red lights, then rushed on, braking, accelerating, squealing round corners. At last the driver braked hard and pulled up.

'End of the road,' a voice called from overhead.

Julieta opened the lid of the chest and saw the older ambulance-man smiling at her cheerfully from the driver's seat through a little door in the partition.

'Grab your things from the locker,' he said. 'There's a red Beetle waiting for you, parked just behind us.'

'Thank you for everything,' said Julieta, smiling back when she and Mawi had climbed from the coffins, taken their luggage and were standing outside the rear doors. 'You're a couple of heroes.'

They closed the doors and the ambulance roared off.

'Just the driver,' Julieta murmured to Mawi as they made their way cautiously to the Volkswagen, which was facing away from them. 'I hope this isn't a trap. Do you think it's worth the risk?'

Julieta glanced at the doorways of the terrace-houses on both sides of the street, and at the other parked cars, then back at the Volkswagen. She glimpsed a beret and the back of a thin neck through the driver's window. A pair of long, thin hands rested on the steering-wheel.

Julieta knocked on the side window behind the driver's shoulder and opened the rear door a few centimetres. 'Are you waiting for friends of Mercedes?' she asked.

The head nodded but didn't turn. Julieta hesitated, then got into the car. Mawi climbed in beside her. The faceless driver started the engine and pulled away from the kerb. He drove unhurriedly but purposefully through the suburbs of Santiago, glancing in the rear-view mirror but not looking round or saying a word.

As the minutes passed, Julieta's unease grew. Why didn't he say something? She realized they had joined the national highway, heading south, and decided to try and break the silence.

'What's your name?' she asked. 'Where are you taking us?'

'I was keeping my eyes skinned for anyone tailing us,' the driver replied in a voice Julieta half-recognized. 'It seems safe now.'

He removed his beret and looked over his shoulder at his two passengers. For a few moments they failed to recognize the gaunt, bearded face. But when it broke into a smile they cried out in unison: 'Father Lorencio!'

Father Lorencio turned back to watch the road. 'Make yourselves comfortable,' he said. 'We have a seven-hundred-kilometre drive ahead of us.'

49

'I don't often lose my temper. Seldom even feel angry. I'm a good-humoured, easy-going sort, at work and at home, a good husband and a good father.' The fact that both his wife and his daughter had walked out on him hadn't altered Franco Reyes' opinion of himself: his wife's blood was contaminated, poor woman, and Julieta couldn't help being a bit Peruvian herself. Peruvians were a degenerate lot and needed to be licked into shape with lots of discipline and the occasional flogging. Reyes had always been too soft-hearted with his wife and daughter. 'I'm not steely enough. When I do occasionally lose my rag, it all comes out in a rush. Makes a bit of a mess. Maid has to clear up after me.' The master's last wobbly had cost him his wife.

Reyes was having the greatest difficulty holding on to his anger at this moment. He was gripping the handle on the passenger door so tightly that he had lost all sensation in his right hand. He would happily put his fist through the major's windscreen. The only thing that stopped him was the thought that army windscreens were made of reinforced glass. The blow would break every bone in his hand.

The two men were sitting in silence in the front of the army car. The major had been too cold pacing up and down the pavement, so he had got back inside, started the engine and turned on the heater. Reyes was fed up with having everything he said shot down by Cortez and now spoke only when spoken to, and then only in monosyllables. He had had enough of this young man's insolence and contempt. Thank God the arrogant twerp wasn't his son-in-law! He would poison Julieta's mind and turn her against her father for good. What had Reyes ever seen in the fellow? Julieta was right to run away. Why in God's name had he been soft-headed enough to send Cortez after her?

Reyes became conscious of the mechanism he had discovered

in his mind several days ago opening its valves and reducing the heat of his bile from a hard boil to a controlled simmer: the thought... the hope... the prayer that Julieta and her Indian would once again elude the army and make a fool of the haughty, priggish major. Not so long ago he would have prayed for the opposite. That was before Nicole left him. Before he felt the sting of public opprobrium. Before the manicured major allowed his mask to slip and began to show the contempt he had probably always felt for his prospective father-in-law. Now Reyes, arch-conservative and lover of all things sweet, had tasted the salt of rebellion and found it invigorating. Having been the cause of his daughter's flight and initiated the hunt for her and for the young man he had perhaps been a little hasty in vilifying, he now almost wished he could join them, for the pleasure of puncturing Cortez' conceit and cocking a snook at the flunkeys and society gossips of Santiago.

A wailing siren approached from behind and an ambulance rushed past with its blue light flashing.

'If they've shot my daughter,' thought Reyes, 'I'll geld this strutting peacock with my own hands.'

'They're overdue,' muttered Cortez.

Reyes' heart gave a leap: Major Tiddlywinks was getting worried. Was it possible— ? No, he mustn't even think the thought: it would be tempting fate.

The major switched the engine off and took out the key. He checked his walkie-talkie, then got out of the car, slammed the door and started pacing again.

'Little shit!' thought Reyes. 'Wants me to freeze to death. Or does he imagine I'd drive off in this heap of military scrap metal?'

He took a brown leather hip-flask from an inside jacket pocket and had several swigs of brandy. A wave of warmth quickly spread through his body and reached his fingertips and toes. The tension disappeared from his head and neck, and his stomach tingled and felt warm and comfortable. By the time

Cortez got back in the car, started the engine and turned on the blower, Reyes' mood had changed from angry frustration to carefree self-assurance.

'Missed them again, have you, you and your fully trained professionals?' he asked with a yawn. 'A couple of men, one at each door of the aircraft, would have done the trick.'

'Something you don't seem to have learnt in spite of your years, Señor Reyes,' hissed Cortez, 'is patience. Put you behind a parapet and you'd raise your head to see what was going on and have it blown off.'

Reyes was no longer at risk of losing control. 'I'm not so sure,' he replied cheerfully. 'After all, I've put up with your shrewishness and your sneers patiently for the past week or two. Your competence as a leader is for your senior officers, not for me, to judge. Just between you and me, though, having seen you on field duty, I wouldn't even trust you to empty my dustbin. Marry my daughter to you? To a neutered peacock? I'd rather have the Indian as my son-in-law. I'd rather marry her to a whole tribe of Indians than to a cack-handed majorette.' Reyes turned in his seat and looked Cortez square in the face. 'I like men to be men, not nancies.'

The blood had drained from the major's cheeks and his lips were trembling with fury. His hand was on his holster and his fingers were obviously itching to take out the revolver and blow Reyes' face off.

'Why don't you shoot me?' Reyes went on. 'That's obviously what you want to do. Trouble is, you wouldn't know how to use that thing. You don't even know how to use your own dick. You need a lieutenant to hold it for you, so they tell me. Don't bother to run me home. I'll wait for the next disabled driver to make a better job of it, and leave you to fiddle with your gear-stick. Or maybe I'll take a cab.'

Reyes got out of the car, slammed the door and strode off towards the taxi-rank, humming cheerily to himself.

50

Julieta was alone in the abandoned mountain village Father Lorencio had made his hide-out, sitting in the winter sunshine on a rock chiselled into a bench outside the little grey stone church in her woolly hat, gloves and poncho, surrounded by long grass and sunflowers that had dried on their stalks. Father Lorencio had gone to the village five kilometres away, which had a shop and a telephone, to buy provisions, make phone calls to collect addresses for his campaign, and hand a pile of letters, with a small fee and enough money for stamps, to the Trans-Continental bus-driver to be posted without fear of interception across the border in Argentina. Mawi had gone with him.

Julieta loved the peace of the place. There were no bangs or shouts – just the cries of birds and the sound of the wind through the empty houses and araucaria pines. The houses were single-storey and made of stone, with thatched roofs and floors of beaten earth. Julieta had felt safe as soon as she arrived in the village, mainly thanks to Father Lorencio, who had left Santo Domingo and made his home here in the simple presbytery he had come to with his books during vacations in his student days, but also because the place had a good energy. It had once been the home of farmers, herdsmen and weavers: peace-loving men and women watched over by both the Christian god and the local divinities as they themselves must have watched over the sheep, goats, llamas and alpacas that provided their milk, cheese, transport and clothing. Julieta had been in the ground-floor, often single-room, houses and found a loom, a sheep's horn made into a simple musical instrument for calling animals from pasture, and an alpaca jacket left hanging behind a door. She guessed the only wrong the village had ever known was done not by the inhabitants but by the soldiers who had evicted them when the village was commandeered by the army as a stronghold in one of the wars with Argentina.

Only today, alone here for the first time, did Julieta feel a vague sense of threat, of eyes watching from the trees or long grass. Was it her imagination or had she caught the merest whiff of cigarette smoke mixed for a moment with the smell of pine from the forest all around?

Mawi found the village depressing. It reminded him of his own village after the massacre in the streets of Temuco. More than half the community had been destroyed. Many of the reed houses were left empty and abandoned. Ever since, whenever Mawi saw an abandoned house, he remembered the massacre, and the bereavement and years of mourning that had followed.

Mawi had a phone call to make too, to the Filipino nurse who had brought a little friendship and hope into the stark lives of her prisoner patients. Mawi still hadn't said much more about the infection he might have picked up. The little he told Julieta last night alarmed her so much that she had hardly slept. For the two nights they had spent in Father Lorencio's village Mawi had insisted on separate beds. Julieta said it wasn't necessary, that she loved him, was his wife and was prepared to take the risk of catching whatever it was he thought he might have. Mawi had replied that the disease might cause the ruin of his mind and body and that, if she caught it from him, could do the same for her. If the tests proved positive, he said, it would be best if he missed his footing for the first time in his life, somewhere high in the mountains, on the edge of a thousand-metre precipice. Julieta begged him to talk to Father Lorencio about his possible illness and asked their friend to try and coax Mawi into sharing his worries with him. Father Lorencio agreed and said he would also make some phone calls to try and find out where Julieta's mother and Copihue were.

Julieta longed to introduce Mawi to her mother, once he was himself again. Three of the four people dearest to her were all beyond reach: Mawi, her mother, Copihue. Even with Father

Lorencio's friendship she felt painfully alone and kept trying to pray to her god for strength – not God any more but her god, the god she had been taught to pray to. Other Christians could believe in their monopoly of the supernal, if they wanted, but Mawi had taught Julieta humility. She had never met anyone with so good and pure a heart as Mawi's, yet most Christians would brand him a pagan. If he was fashioned in the image of his gods, then to Julieta's mind they had equal status in the heavens with her own god.

Her heart gave a leap. Here they were now, Father Lorencio and Mawi, climbing the steep, rocky path up the small of the back to the village hidden between these two great Andean shoulders. How would Father Lorencio manage when the snow came? With his usual quiet determination, no doubt, and with boots, sticks and wiry strength. How thin he was! Skeletal, with his green corduroy trousers held up by a length of rope slotted through the loops. Both of them emaciated. The two men closest to Julieta's heart – her two ex-prisoners – looked as though they had just walked on a diet of bread and water all the way from Siberia. Father Lorencio had said next to nothing about his arrest and imprisonment. He probably didn't want to make Mawi and Julieta feel they were to blame. He was much keener to hear about their adventures than speak about his own.

Mawi seemed to be talking nineteen to the dozen. Was it possible? He had been so silent lately. That must surely be a good sign. Yes, she could hear his voice now. What a torrent of words!

'*Empanadas de pino,*' announced Father Lorencio when he was within earshot. 'Accompanied by a wine from the best Chilean *pinot* and followed by real Brazilian coffee, courtesy of Julieta, and double measures of Glenfiddich, also thanks to Julieta. We'll drink to one another's continuing health and luck.'

Dear Father Lorencio! He was like a father to Mawi and Julieta, making an idyllic home for them in his humble presbytery and preparing delicious meals, sometimes out of next to nothing. He and Mawi were the ones who needed feeding up, not Julieta. She would disguise herself in Copihue's clothes, make a trip to the market in Temuco and fill her bag with the best fruit, vegetables, meat and fish she could find for Father Lorencio to work his magic on. She would insist on doing some of the cooking herself, while Father Lorencio relaxed with a glass of wine or Glenfiddich by the fire. She was not the daughter of a half-French mother for nothing.

Father Lorencio took the provisions into the presbytery and left Mawi and Julieta together. Julieta had to find the courage to ask the question. If only Mawi were relaxed and smiling, as she had prayed he would be. He looked different, certainly: not depressed any more. But still not himself.

Julieta found her voice. 'Did you phone?' she asked.

'My blood's not infected,' Mawi replied.

Julieta's impulse was to jump up and throw her arms round him but she stopped at the sight of the frown like a thunder-cloud on his face.

'Aren't you happy?' she asked. 'Relieved?'

'I'm angry,' he replied.

'With me?'

'Of course not with you.' There was a note of surprise in his voice, a grain of tenderness, crumb of comfort. He seemed about to say more but changed his mind. 'I'm going to play my flute.'

Julieta hadn't heard Mawi play since the fateful concert in Camden. It was good that he wanted to start again. Perhaps he would play the anger out of his system.

'Your mother and Copihue are in a hotel in Santiago,' said Father Lorencio, when Julieta had joined him in the presbytery to help prepare the meal. 'Perhaps we can arrange for them to move to Temuco, thirty kilometres from here. We must be careful not to lay a trail leading to you and Mawi. The authorities are smart enough to know that a mother will lead them to her child. Best if I bring her down in the car... Is that Mawi playing the flute? I heard a colony of herons the other day fighting off a predator. That's what it sounds like. Why? He used to play more gently.'

'There's a fire inside him, burning him up.'

'Fire was given to warm us, not destroy us.'

Father Lorencio poured a little of the paste into the frying-pan smoking on the wood-stove, waited a minute, turned the pancake and spooned in some of the mixture of raisins, olives, onion, peppers and chicken simmering in a little saucepan.

Julieta was sent to call Mawi. By the time she got back, the oil-lamps were lit, a fire was blazing in the stone fireplace, the sheets of perspex were firmly in place over the unglazed windows, the rough pine table was laid, the rolled *empanadas* were in a hot dish in the middle of it and the wine was *chambré*.

Mawi came in and they all sat down, wished each other *¡Que aproveche!* and helped themselves to the pancakes. Father Lorencio poured the wine. They were too hungry to talk as they each started on their first *empanada*.

Father Lorencio waited until Mawi had taken the edge off his appetite, then said to him, 'You play the flute better than ever but there was anger in your playing. What is it makes you angry?'

Mawi stopped eating and thought for a minute or more. At last he sipped his wine and replied: 'I was angry all the way through my teens. For seven years I was like a wounded animal. Instead of discovering the beauty and magic of the world, I discovered only its cruelty. Then I met Julieta. She gave me her love and I forgot my anger. My evening in the prison cell in England rekindled the fire and made me relive the outrage that had started it the day my community marched through the streets of Temuco. They were protesting peacefully against the discrimination suffered by my people. I was thirteen – nearly fourteen. I wanted to take part in the march but my parents told me I was too young and that, if I went, there would be no one to take the goats and llamas to pasture. So I spent the day on the mountain slopes with my best friend, minding the herd. While we were up there, the army came to our village and ransacked the houses in search of weapons, which they didn't find, as nobody had any. Half a dozen of my people, who had stayed at the settlement instead of going on the march, went to the senior officer to protest. He had them all shot. My friend and I got back to the village with the animals just after sunset and saw the twenty or more who had been killed on the streets of Temuco lined up on the grass ready for a Mapuche burial. We also saw the bodies of the six who had protested to the officer: two of them were my mother and father. My friend lost his parents too: they were among the marchers who were massacred. He drowned himself in the lake the next day.' Mawi sipped his wine. 'It's not the killing that makes me angry. The killing hurts, as if the bullets had torn into my own body – into my heart. The killing burns and brings sorrow but the injustice of the killing is like petrol thrown on a fire. If my people had been thieves and murderers, I would have felt their loss but seen some justice in their deaths. But the Mapuche like to live in peace, planting trees, looking after animals, to be in harmony with nature. They want to live according to their customs and feel at home in their own land, instead of being denied work and forced by their Hispanic overlords on to reservations.'

Mawi sipped his wine again. Father Lorencio refilled his glass.

'The injustice doesn't end at Temuco and in the mountains to the east, where we graze our animals, the forests and lakes to the south, where we grow our trees, and the ocean to the west, where we fish. Why did Julieta have to run away from home and escape with me from Chile? Because I'm what Hispanic people call an Indian. Why was I branded a kidnapper, instead of being recognized as Julieta's husband? Because I'm not Hispanic. The Mapuche are outcasts in their own land. And foreigners in other people's. In England I didn't look English enough, so they suspected me of being a spy and imprisoned me without a trial. In prison I told my three cell-mates I was Chilean, so they decided I was Argentinian. They overpowered me and undressed me. One after the other they raped me – raped me so that I bled all over the floor and had to be taken to the prison hospital. I was given blood tests for a sexually transmitted disease doctors say will soon be a worldwide epidemic. I could have been infected with it. My marriage would have been destroyed. Julieta and I would have had no children. Julieta would soon have been a widow.'

Mawi realized his hand had been rattling something in his jeans pocket. He took the object out to see what it was and found he was holding the little plastic salt-cellar he had kept from his tray on the aeroplane to put his sleeping-pills in. He turned and threw his pill-box into the hottest part of the fire, where the plastic sputtered and melted.

Father Lorencio and Julieta had been listening to Mawi without eating their food or sipping their wine. They were wide-eyed. Father Lorencio's mouth had dropped open.

'They deserve to be hanged, all three of them,' murmured Julieta.

'It would have been easy to kill them,' said Mawi.

Julieta looked at Mawi and at once thought of a jaguar, crouching, ready to spring, its eyes hard and bright, fixed on its prey.

'Easy. One of them gave me a demonstration of how to kill silently and quickly, without any weapons. I could have done it.'

'Why didn't you?' asked Julieta.

'Because I didn't want to spend the next thirty years in jail. I would have freed the three rats from their messed-up lives but been forced to live through the mess they had made of mine. As it is, they're crouching naked and alone in their punishment cells, with nothing to eat and nowhere to lie down, while I'm with the two people closest to me in front of a blazing fire, eating *empanadas* and drinking the best Chilean wine. But my anger's still there, smouldering, ready to burst into flames.'

There was a silence, then Father Lorencio said gently: 'Your anger is perfectly natural. It's a healthy assertion of your identity.' He filled the glasses and served everyone more *empanadas*. 'But anger is also dangerous. The danger is that it will lead to violence. Violence begets violence, endlessly, like a wheel that never stops turning, century after century, generation after generation. Anger is like petrol. Put a match to it and you will have a conflagration. Treat it with care, and it can be the fuel that drives you to achieve greatness. Anger is unreleased energy. Energy can be creative or destructive. The trick is to harness the anger from the wrongs we have suffered, as scientists harness nuclear power, so that it produces heat and light instead of wiping us all off the planet. Many of those who have done most for mankind have suffered wrong themselves and used their anger to help other victims of cruelty and injustice.'

'Are those the words of your gods?' Mawi asked.

Father Lorencio smiled. 'No, they're the words of yours. I've been studying the religion and philosophy of the Mapuche people.'

Mawi raised his head. There was a far-away look in his eyes, as if he were looking years into the past – as if a fragrance had brushed his sensory cells or he had opened a drawer and rediscovered a thing once treasured, then forgotten. Mawi's gods seemed to have spoken to him through Father Lorencio. His face gradually relaxed, like a flower opening, and became the face Julieta fell in love with, the face of the man she married.

'I'd like to take you both to my village,' he said. 'Before Julieta and I leave for the Isla del Sol.'

Father Lorencio gave him a worried look. 'It's too soon. The police and army may be looking for you – searching the length of Chile. You're safe as long as you stay in this hide-out and keep your head down.'

'Why should they look in a village they wiped off their map?' said Mawi. 'I only have two relatives there now: my sister and my uncle. They would want to welcome Julieta and make her part of the family. We could be married the Mapuche way.'

'Where is your home?' asked Father Lorencio.

'Twenty kilometres away. In the mountains east of Temuco, just near the frontier with Argentina.'

'There are no roads or paths from here. It means going west all the way back to the national highway, south to Temuco, then east. More like ninety kilometres.'

'I can find the way through the forest. Best on horseback but you can do it on foot. It's up and down because of the mountains – steep in places. Nothing dangerous or too difficult.'

Father Lorencio served the last three *empanadas* and drained the wine into the three glasses. 'I'll come with you,' he said. 'To see you married in front of your family.'

'Not just to see us married,' said Mawi. 'To perform the ceremony, if you agree.'

Mawi and Julieta sat Father Lorencio down in front of the fire with a large Glenfiddich, fetched water from the cistern, boiled a pot over the burning logs, made coffee and did the washing-up. They put on their ponchos, finished their coffee and, leaving Father Lorencio to write his letters, walked to the highest point of the village to watch the sun sink into the Pacific.

Mawi gave a slight sniff. Had he caught that whiff of cigarette smoke? He said nothing but looked round at the empty houses cupped among the snow-capped mountains. 'The Spanish always choose the most beautiful places for their atrocities,' he murmured. He didn't find the village depressing any more, he told Julieta. He saw it not as somewhere abandoned and decaying now but as a place to rebuild. 'Perhaps your mother and Copihue will come and live here,' he suggested to Julieta. 'We could restore one of the houses for them.'

Julieta gently put her arm through Mawi's.

'When we get to the Isla del Sol,' Mawi went on, 'I want to do for the Mapuche people what Father Lorencio is doing to expose the outrages of Pinochet and his junta. Telling the world is the best way. Better than bombs, revenge and murdering innocent men, women and children. I'll need your help: my Spanish writing is rusty and I don't know a word of English or French.'

'There's so much to be done in the world,' said Julieta. 'The Isla del Sol, Cuzco, the Mapuche people. If we each lived a thousand years, we'd still be only at the foot of the mountain.'

Mawi freed his arm from Julieta's, put it round her shoulders, held her to him and pressed his cheek against the top of her head. 'We will have children and grandchildren. A thousand years from now, when wars and hatred and unhappiness are a thing of the past, the children of our many generations of children will sit round their fires under the stars in these mountains and tell the story of their two ancestors of long ago. "It was with these two parents of our many generations of parents that greed and cruelty began to wither," they will say, "and the first flowers of our new era of peace and harmony appeared through the snow."'

51

Major Adolfo Cortez was sitting at one of the bars in the exclusive Santiago club he had recently joined, sipping soda-water with ice and a slice of lime from a cut-glass tumbler and watching a film on a screen that filled an end wall. Everywhere was burgundy plush and brass. The floor-tiles were hand-painted and imported all the way from Valencia. The waiters were in pristine, first-Communion white, with gold buttons and braiding.

The club was for off-duty soldiers and policemen *con gustos extraordinarios*. Having seen the waiting-list for membership, Cortez couldn't help thinking unusual tastes must be less unusual than usual ones. Most of the applicants were closet gays desperate to get out of the cupboard. Tradition counted for more than the law in the army and police force: the official punishment for homosexuality was dismissal; traditionally those caught were soused with petrol and set alight, or publicly flogged. In theory, a soldier received a lash from every member of his regiment; in practice, he was dead before he was half-way through his own division. The club had to be kept a close secret. Cortez had only just heard of it after ten years in the army. Applications had to be supported by the recommendations of three well-established members. Senior officers who were straight and got to hear of the Paraíso were paid large amounts of hush money. The club had its own secret police to discourage members from shopping either other members or the Paraíso itself.

Private rooms were reserved at the back for strapping creatures with heavily made-up faces and an abundance of nylon hair. They minced and swung their hips and made a bee-line for the gay end of the cocktail bar to collect their customers. Only in the safety of the private rooms, away from the tell-tale lenses of blackmailers, were the silver-spangled stilettos, fishnet stockings, nylon wigs and mini-skirts abandoned. Underneath it all were the body hair and stubbled chins of well-developed young men.

Other rooms were reserved for kosher females dressed in the uniform and boots of generals in the Chilean cavalry regiment, except that they wore no shirt or tie and their jackets were unbuttoned to reveal their breasts, which bounced as they provided their clients' preferred foreplay: ten minutes under the lash of a rhinoceros-hide whip.

Electric sex facilities were promised for the spring. Cortez had read the publicity leaflet. The hooker and his or her customer attached electrodes to their bodies. These wired into a machine plugged into the wall. Coition was punctuated by electric shocks, which racked the two partners at the same moment. The shocks became more frequent and intense and culminated in a high-voltage climax in which the couple were convulsed by a series of spasms that made their hair stand on end.

Cortez caught the barman's eye and ordered another seltzer.

The film show continued round the clock, seven days a week, three hundred and sixty-five days a year, like a flame burning under a triumphal arch, or totalitarian propaganda put out over public loudspeakers. The pictures, all of them documentary, were of men, women and children of non-European ethnicity being killed, beaten up or sexually assaulted. Some of the footage had been shot unofficially during operations by soldiers in one of the Latin American armies, then sold to clubs and video companies round the world. Much of it came from Africa.

Cortez had thought of trying out the electric sex facility when it became available. The shocks were intended to enhance the pleasure of sexual activity and make it more electrifying. For Cortez their purpose would not be to pepper up the sexual act but to take its place. He would persuade Lieutenant Görisch to come to the club as his guest, ply him with tequila, then take him to a back room and plug him in.

Cortez had considered a private room with one of the transvestites but, having heard their conversation at the bar, he had lost interest. These young men were nothing like Görisch. They had none of his *naïveté,* elegance and breeding. They were just interested in sodomy and money. If all you asked was to run your hands down their bodies, they would laugh in your face.

The body fluids of the back rooms were not for Cortez. He came to the club for the film show. The killings and beatings were an *apéritif.* The castrations and spayings were what he feasted on. They disgusted but thrilled him, as did the gang-banging of an adolescent Quechuan boy by six Hispanic soldiers. He had to put his ear-plugs in to deaden the screams. Why did the idiot film-makers bother with soundtracks? The agony was in the eyes. The screaming only reduced the impact.

The glory of the film was its ambiguity. One moment the mess of blood, tears and other body fluids was there in all its photographic reality. The next, as soon as the picture changed, the mess had gone. No smell. Nothing to clear up. The mess both was and wasn't.

Who was that at the end of the bar in the embraces of one of the stubbly, strapping transvestites? Cortez got up for a better look. 'I don't believe it,' he murmured. 'It's— it's Lieutenant Görisch. The— the tart! The— the— the swine!' He felt the pain in his gut blaze up into jealous fury and was on the point of marching over to the lieutenant to punch him in the face. With the self-discipline learnt from his German mother and grandfather he forced himself to sit down and suffer the fire. Assaulting a junior officer would achieve nothing but his own ruin – running the gauntlet of the regiment and being cashiered or killed. This was the punishment he would inflict on Görisch, not on himself, and he would thrill to see the agony in the young man's eyes when his beautiful body was shredded and minced beyond repair. He fumbled in his pocket for his miniature camera, to record the scene that would seal the lieutenant's fate.

'Hey! Hi there! Small world!'

The voice was familiar. It came from behind Cortez' right shoulder and was accompanied by a blast of stale breath and whisky fumes. Who did he know who spoke English with a slow drawl, made even slower by intoxication, so that every word was an expedition to the remotest regions of his skull?

Cortez turned his head. The broken nose; the copper hair and suit. 'Mr Gorringe! What a— what a pleasure!' He left the camera in his pocket.

'Call me Herman!'

'What brings you to the Paraíso?'

'Same as you, I guess: a little hooch and a little fun.'

Cortez winced: a little fun was not what he was having just at the moment. What were Görisch and his hooker up to now? Dancing? They were dancing the tango.

'You wanna whiskey?'

'No, thank you. I already have a drink.' The major floundered, trying to think of a reason for being at the club. Franco Reyes already had his suspicions. A word from Gorringe would confirm them. Reyes was on friendly terms with some of the senior officers. Cortez could find himself in a tight corner. 'I like to see what my men get up to in their spare time,' he explained at last.

'No kidding!' Gorringe tried to focus his eyes on the barman. 'Sonny! Scotch on the rocks.' He turned back to Cortez. 'You seen the broads here?'

'The what?'

'The broads. The dames. The hookers.' He leered at the major. 'Reckon I'd get a good tumble for my money?'

Cortez wondered if he should warn Gorringe that not all the hookers were dames and that he might get a shock if he took one of the stubbly ones to a back room for a tumble.

'You see that one over there, dressed like a Chilean general?' the Texan went on. 'She's driving me crazy with her black eyes and bouncing boobs.'

Cortez played along with Gorringe, feigning prurient interest, winking, sniggering, eyeing the hooker. The sight of the boobs revolted him: they should be removed and melted down to make tallow. He kept up the pretence while the North American told him about his failure of communication with the black-eyed broad, who spoke no English: she reckoned he wanted to be flogged by her, when in reality it was Gorringe who wanted to do the flogging. He longed to lay into her with a nine-thonged rhino-hide whip.

'Say! Whatever happened to those two kids I sent to you from Lima: the Red Indian and Reyes' daughter? Did you ever find them?'

Cortez shook his head. 'Still looking. Reyes' wife left him. He's changed his tune: daughter can have her Indian so long as she comes home to Daddy. Daddy can have his daughter, if he can find her. I want the Indian.'

Gorringe struggled to get something straight in his fuddled mind. 'Pardon me asking. If the father's fixed it with the Indian, why are you still looking for him?'

The question put Cortez on the spot. He had to think quickly. 'The two of them went to London. The Indian was detained on suspicion of spying for Argentina. If he spies for Argentina in London, he'll do the same in Chile.'

'A Commie spying for Argentina? The generals there are more Fascist than Mussolini. The White House loves them.'

The wheels of Cortez' ingenuity were spinning hard. The CIA man was no push-over, even when drunk. He needed convincing. 'He spies for the Commies in Chile and the Fascist generals in Argentina.'

'You don't say! Where d'you reckon he is, your spy?'

Cortez shrugged. 'We've checked with London. He was put on a flight there and stayed on board at the fuelling stop in Tenerife. He must be in this country. He somehow gave us the slip at the airport. Santiago's a big place.'

'He's not going to hang around Santiago and risk being seen by people he knows. Where's his home?'

'Araucanía. He's a Mapuche. He was sounding off about it in London. We've offered a reward to the local birdwatchers' societies if they come up with a lead.'

'That's where he'll go... My men are having a quiet time right now, waiting to protect a US mining corporation due to bulldoze a fishing village on the coast north of Santiago. They could do with a little bird-watching themselves. If you need help tracking down your Commie, just say the word.'

The major's pain vanished. Lieutenant Görisch disappeared from his thoughts. Cortez had just landed a prize catch he hadn't even been angling for. He knew quite well that the Mapuche wasn't a spy. He also knew that the army had spent a fortune on the search and would happily call it quits and turn their resources to more important matters. The pursuit had become a matter between the Mapuche and himself. Cortez had been humiliated sexually and professionally. He had a score to settle with the Indian – and with Reyes for changing his colours. Gorringe had a legendary reputation for moving through forest unheard and unseen, locating unwanted persons and disposing of them in the blink of an eye. His men had nothing to do. What better cure for boredom than a little clean-up operation in Araucanía?

52

Mawi, Julieta and Father Lorencio began their trek to the Mapuche village before sunrise, while frost was still coating the grass and pine-needles like icing-sugar, and mist was hanging thick as spun glass in the valleys and hollows. Any eyes awake among the trees or in the long grass would be sightless in the mist and half-light. The three travellers walked wrapped in their ponchos, their haversacks strapped to their backs, their heads and ears protected by their *chullos*, their hands thrust inside their alpaca gloves.

Mawi never hesitated or slackened his pace, reading every rock and bush as if it were printed on a map, avoiding patches of snow so as not to leave tracks, keeping to the trees as he led the way up slopes, and hiding in the mist as he shepherded his two companions across valleys. Every half an hour or so he deviated sharply to the left or right for ten minutes, to confuse anyone who might be following them.

After about three hours the climbs became shorter and less steep and the descents longer and gentler. They reached a ridge after an uphill stretch and saw a pale orange crescent peeping at them over the mountains to the east. The sun rose quickly and gained in brightness and strength as it sucked the mist out of the concavities, throwing long shadows westwards. Mawi made frequent detours now, so as to keep to the shelter of the trees. He had seen and heard nothing suspicious, and yet his sixth sense told him they were being watched – stalked perhaps. By an animal? By a human? He couldn't tell.

After another hour they found themselves on the tree-covered shore of an emerald-green lake enclosed within four snow-capped mountains. On the grassy southern shore were a dozen large windowless huts made entirely of thatch, looking perhaps to a newcomer more like the roofs of houses than homes in themselves. The three travellers had arrived at the Mapuche settlement where Mawi was born.

They were greeted at the edge of the village by a pale brown nanny-goat, who nuzzled each of them in turn, then led the way bleating to the centremost hut, sending three chickens squawking out of the way with a butt from her hornless head as she went. Smoke rose like a blue reed from an opening in the thatch.

'There's no one about,' said Julieta.

'The village used to bustle with life,' Mawi replied.

A girl of about sixteen in a red and brown skirt, with a thick black plait down to her waist, appeared in the doorway of the *ruka*. She stared at Mawi for a few moments, her eyes opened wide and she ran into the trees behind the settlement.

'What a beautiful girl!' said Julieta.

'That must be my sister. She always used to run away like that when people arrived. That's how I know her. She's very shy. Afraid of crying if it's people she knows and hasn't seen for a long time. She was nine or ten when I left. I wouldn't recognize her now if I met her in the street.'

'She has the same face as you.'

A man stepped out of the hut. He was in his forties, with a fringe like Mawi's but with grey hair at the temples. His trousers and smock were made of beige alpaca, with a grey, white and black design, and his ankle-length slippers of llama wool.

'This is my uncle,' said Mawi. *'Mari-mari, Malle.'*

The two men embraced.

'How did you get on in Santiago?' asked Mawi's uncle with no show of emotion, as if his nephew had been on a shopping trip for a few days, instead of away for six years.

'I've brought my wife to meet you.'

Mawi introduced Julieta, who kissed her uncle by marriage on both cheeks. Then he introduced Father Lorencio, their friend who had been to gaol on their account. 'Without Father Lorencio I wouldn't be married and I wouldn't be here. I would be in prison in Santiago, or dead.'

Mawi's uncle took Father Lorencio's hand with the composure and detachment of someone who had seen too much to be easily surprised or moved.

'Is there no one else here?' Mawi asked, as he walked beside his uncle, who didn't welcome the three arrivals into his home at first but led them along the lake.

'They've left to try and find work in Temuco. Trading with the Mapuche is discouraged by the régime. Slaughtering us only increases our resistance. They've found a subtler way to try and wipe out our people: they call it deculturalization, or identity-bleaching. Your sister and I are the only two left here. We've restored your parents' *ruka*. We hoped you would come back and live there.'

Mawi and his uncle, followed by Julieta and Father Lorencio, arrived at a *ruka* that had recently been rethatched. Mawi stopped dead. This was his home and birthplace, once as familiar as his mother's face, now restored and hardly recognizable. The garden alone was as he remembered it. It was the only one of the homes to be set in a garden. There was no fence. In the summer and autumn the neighbours used to be free to help themselves to peaches, nectarines and grapes, or sit in the shade of the jacaranda, surrounded by giant scarlet copihues, breathing in the scent of the fruit.

Malle led the way inside. A fire danced and crackled on the beaten earth floor in the middle of the *ruka*. The air was thick with the fragrance of burning pine-wood but there was no smell from the smoke, which was drawn as if through an invisible chimney in a straight line to an opening in the cone at the top of the hut. A cooking-pot and grill hung from an iron framework over the fire. Near the kitchen area stood a new-made pine dresser, table and chairs. Behind the dresser were the sleeping-quarters: a double bed for parents-to-be and two single beds for children, all with fresh pine bedsteads and newly woven alpaca covers with a Mapuche design representing family life. Under the beds, at a safe distance from the fire, the floor was covered with matting, still smelling of the straw from which it had recently been made. Oil-lamps stood on the dining-table and on the little pine table beside the double bed.

'Everything's brand-new,' said Mawi, who was unable to hide the dismay in his voice.

'The soldiers took all your parents' furniture. Don't you remember?' his uncle replied. 'Your sister made the matting and bed-covers. I made the furniture. This *ruka* is for you and Julieta. Lamngen's been sleeping here but she's not fussy. Sometimes she sleeps with the animals.'

Julieta held on to Mawi's arm with both her hands as they walked back behind Malle and Father Lorencio to the hut in the middle of the village. 'You've been away for so long,' she said. 'If you want to live at home for a while, the Isla del Sol can wait.'

Mawi freed his arm and put it round Julieta's shoulders. 'The battle for the Mapuche people has to be fought not locally or with blood and tears but across the world with words. When it's won, and when the trees we plant on the Isla del Sol have taken root, that will be the time to come home.'

Julieta seemed relieved. 'If only we could stop being fugitives,' she said thoughtfully. 'Two innocent people for ever on the run. What sort of a world is it where love's a capital offence?'

As they drew near to the *ruka,* the smell of freshly ground coffee reached their nostrils. The palates and stomachs of the three early walkers cried out for mugs of real coffee, hot and strong.

'It's sent to us from Brazil by one of our community working on a plantation there,' Mawi's uncle told his three companions.

The inside of his *ruka* followed the same pattern as the one they had just seen. The difference was that it looked more lived in: the furniture had been made three generations ago; Mawi remembered his grandmother ladling soup from the cauldron over the fire; ponchos hung on pegs behind the front-door.

Today the ladle was held by Mawi's sister. She didn't look up when her brother and the two strangers came in, but went on spooning boiling water from the cauldron into a battered tin coffee-pot, as if she made coffee for them every day.

'Good smell of coffee,' Mawi said to his sister. Like her he was happy to let his six-year absence disappear through the roof with the smoke from the pine-wood fire. 'Your sister-in-law loves real coffee. Don't you, Julieta?'

Lamngen glanced up at Julieta and gave her a shy smile – still a child's smile, in spite of the death and sorrow she had known. Julieta smiled back.

The three men sat down at the table. Julieta served the coffee Lamngen was pouring into mugs, then helped her remove the cauldron and replace it with the grill. A mixture of buckwheat flour, yeast and goat's milk was spooned into a frying-pan and a minute later an aroma like baking bread merged with the smell of burning pine and filled the *ruka*. Julieta took the pancakes to the table as they were made. The two young women sat down with theirs and helped themselves to wild berry jam. Lamngen ate her breakfast without a word and was back at the grill before the others had taken their first mouthful.

Malle drained his coffee, took his poncho from behind the door and slipped it over his head and shoulders. 'There are no shops in our village,' he explained to the two newcomers. 'We do as the animals do: we catch our own food.'

'I'll come with you' said Father Lorencio, following his host out of the *ruka*.

'My uncle doesn't take a rod,' Mawi told Julieta, as they sat drinking their coffee. 'He talks and sings to the fish, then catches them with his bare hands.'

Lamngen left the grill and went over to Julieta. 'Do you want to see the animals?' she asked in her quiet, low-pitched voice.

Julieta smiled and nodded.

They all finished their coffee, then Mawi left his wife and sister together and set off with a mixture of enthusiasm and pain to revisit some of his childhood haunts: pain, because it was in this now peaceful setting among the mountains and trees that his parents, grandparents, cousins and friends were murdered; enthusiasm, because his roots were here among the araucaria pines. He drew his strength from the same earth as they did. He climbed, listening to their quiet roar, until he reached the snow on the slopes of the mountain nearest the village. Once this had been the highest mountain in the world, reaching up almost as far as the sun. Today it seemed very modest compared with the peaks he had seen near Santiago and in Bolivia and Peru.

As Mawi climbed, he seemed to hear faint voices carried to him on the wind soughing through the pines. He stopped, closed his eyes and listened intently. After a few minutes he thought he could understand what they were saying. They were blessing him and Julieta and their journey to the Isla del Sol, but also calling them home. The waving arms he saw when he closed his eyes seemed to be beckoning to him and Julieta. Were these his ancestors? Mawi felt sure they were. What he saw was not a vision of decay and decrepitude: corpses disinterred and galvanized. The figures he made out were only partly embodied, as if seen through a mist, but he could tell that he was looking at them at the prime of life, not at its end. They made him think of people from the recent past. Who? Where? Not in Chile or England. Where was it? Then he remembered: the group of fisher-folk Julieta had seen on the Isla del Sol. Mawi had the same feeling now that he had had when he and Julieta rounded the north-west corner of the island: of peace, hope, serenity. 'We will cherish you,' the voices carried to him on the wind through the pines seemed to say.

Mawi's wife, sister, uncle and friend were waiting for him when he got back to the village. Father Lorencio was ready to bless Julieta's and Mawi's marriage according to Mapuche customs.

The simple ceremony took place on an area of sacred ground at the lakeside near a massive rock that was beyond all human strength to move but lighter than a hair on the head of Mother Earth, a rock whose face in the morning was that of the Sun God, in the evening of the God of Thunder and Rain. The Mapuche had no temples. Mother Earth and the gods of sunshine and fertility were best honoured in the open. Apart from Father Lorencio, Julieta, Mawi and his sister and uncle, the wedding-party included two white horses grazing on one side of the sacred area and a donkey and an alpaca on the other. All the animals were drawn to the group of humans out of curiosity. Most curious of all was the goat that had welcomed Mawi and the two newcomers to the village. Lamngen had to put a collar round her neck and keep hold of her to curb her excitement.

'We have come together on the shores of the emerald lake in a corner of the world loved and made beautiful by the gods,' Father Lorencio began when the goat had stopped bleating, 'to celebrate the marriage of a young man and a young woman whose love has given them the strength to foil and triumph over prejudice and coercion not just in Chile but in other parts of South America and in Europe.

'This is the marriage of two people identical in the strength of their love but very different in their backgrounds. Julieta is of European descent, as I am. Mawi is the son of a people whose wisdom, love of peace, and harmony with nature are founded on thousands of years of tradition and history. Thanks to his intelligence and goodness of heart he embodies all that is admirable in his people, community and family. Julieta's struggle has been the more bitter because events have placed her own father on the side of prejudice and coercion and she has had to escape from him to be free to share her life with the man she loves. This is why her family are not with us to join in our celebration.

'Julieta and I would like to feel proud of all our ancestors, as the Mapuche do of theirs, but there has been too much to be ashamed of in the European colonization of this continent. If there had been more marriages like Mawi's and Julieta's over the centuries, the history of South America during the past five hundred years might have been one of peace and fruitful co-operation instead of destruction, occupation, greed, cruelty and repression.

'This is the marriage between a young Christian woman whose gentleness and joy are in the image of the great teacher of two thousand years ago who gave his name to her religion, and Ñankomawizantu Suyifiwenuchaw, Eagle of the Mountains, Joy of the Gods, who is true to the name given him at his birth. Mawi is a blessing from your ancestors. Thank them now for sending him to be your brother and nephew and ask them to bless his marriage to Julieta.'

Mawi's uncle and sister took it in turns to pour out a stream of words in Mapudungun.

'Turn your faces towards Volcán Tronador and ask your god of thunder and rain to bless Mother Earth with fertility.'

All five of them turned to the south. Mawi added his voice to his uncle's and sister's prayer.

'Now raise your hands westwards to the Sun God and ask him for warmth and light to make the trees and plants grow.'

Five pairs of hands were raised to the west. The Mapuche prayed aloud to the Sun God.

'Now let us kneel and ask Mother Earth to bless next season with a rich harvest of fruit and grain.'

When the prayer was finished, they all stood. Mawi's sister placed an ornately carved metal necklace representing fertility round Julieta's neck and his uncle crowned him with a married man's headband. Mawi produced his flute from under his poncho, his uncle picked up the guitar he had brought with him, and the two men played while Lamngen filled the air with singing as warm and rich as her Brazilian coffee.

Back at the *ruka* she lit the oil-lamps while her uncle laid the five large trout he had caught on the grill over the fire.

'You and your sister are alike in looks,' Julieta told Mawi as they took off their ponchos and sat down with Father Lorencio at the table, which was lit by soft lamplight. 'In character too in some ways, but Lamngen is more impulsive than you are. You were more like her when you were angry at what you and your family and village have suffered.'

Lamngen put glasses on the table and poured everyone a drink from a jug of goat's milk and herbs mixed with nectar taken from the village beehive earlier in the year. She brought trenchers, cutlery and a wooden bowl with new potatoes boiled in their skins and sat down next to her brother.

'Julieta told me about Pablo and Pedro,' she said quietly when Julieta and Father Lorencio were talking and she could be heard only by Mawi. 'She wants to live surrounded by animals. It's the first time she's milked a goat. She got more out of her than I've ever done. I took her to see our donkey and the alpaca and then we rode two of the horses round the lake. She rides well. She's not afraid of horses or of falling off, like some town people.'

Malle took the five trout from the grill, laid them on a slab of pine-wood and brought them to the table. He put a fish on everyone's trencher, his niece served the potatoes, and they began their wedding-feast.

The sun was setting when they stepped out of the *ruka* after the meal. Malle suggested they observe the Mapuche custom dating back to the Spanish invasion of patrolling the borders before nightfall.

'It's a custom we share with wild geese, swans, herons. The difference is that instead of wings we use horses. Before the invaders came, we had never seen a horse. We stole theirs, learnt how to ride and were soon better horsemen than the Spaniards. They call us the Apache of South America. Once the whole of this part of the continent belonged to us. As the Spanish closed in, the more necessary it became to protect our land. Thanks to our horses and organization and knowledge of the land, it took the Spaniards more than three hundred years to conquer us.'

Mawi and his uncle and sister rounded up five horses: two greys, two blacks and a piebald. The white horses went to the newly-weds, Father Lorencio chose the piebald and Lamngen and Malle took the two black Arabs.

The territory allotted by the State to this Mapuche community consisted of the square formed by the four mountains enclosing the lake. As night was falling, Malle decided to confine the ride to a path through the trees encircling the lake a stone's throw from the shore. They said little as they rode, Julieta and Father Lorencio because they were under the spell of the orange sky, the emerald lake and the biggest full moon Father Lorencio had ever seen, rising above the trees and filling almost all the sky between two of the four snow-covered mountain-tops, the three Mapuche because this custom was more than symbolic. Spanish Chileans boasted that they had conquered the Mapuche people a century ago but this didn't stop them periodically raiding indigenous communities and committing atrocities. The Mapuche needed to keep alert.

'It's so quiet you can hear the water-drops turning to frost,' Father Lorencio said softly to Julieta.

Mawi and his uncle glanced at each other. Not a rustle, not a bird-call. It was too quiet: the silence of nature holding her breath, listening, of the jungle when the birds and insects have glimpsed a slithering and crawling of well-camouflaged scales through the rampant vegetation.

The orange afterglow had disappeared in the west when they got back to the village. The moon had risen and no longer filled the southern sky, though it was still bigger than any moon Father Lorencio had seen till today. Its face had lost its blush and cast a pale blue light, bright enough to read by, or for enemy eyes to see by, over the village, lake and trees.

The newly-weds followed tradition and invited the rest of the village – now only its two inhabitants and one visitor – to drink maté made with maize and dried peaches in their *ruka*. Lamngen had had the foresight to leave the ingredients on the dresser. She lit the oil-lamps, blew on the embers and put twigs and three new logs on the fire. While the fire was burning up, she took a pail and went to the village well for water. Mawi and his uncle were sitting on stools playing their instruments when she got back. She joined in, singing, as she heated the water in the cauldron over the fire. When the maté was made, Julieta took cups to Mawi and their guests, keeping one for herself. No sooner had Julieta sat down than she was up again, dancing with her husband, while everyone sang, Malle played the guitar and Lamngen and Father Lorencio clapped. Next Mawi danced with his sister, then his uncle danced with Julieta while Mawi played the flute. When all three men had danced with both young women, Lamngen took an oil-lamp, led the way to the large bed at the far end of the *ruka* and put the lamp on the little table. The two pillows were covered with the laurel- and olive-leaves, holly, rose-hips and winter azalea she had picked for her brother and sister-in-law. Mawi's uncle went on playing and he and his niece and Father Lorencio kept singing while one by one they melted out of the lamplight of the *ruka* into the moonlight outside, leaving the newly-weds alone. The playing and singing continued, growing fainter as the three people dear to Mawi and Julieta became part of the night.

Till tonight there had been an element of stolen pleasure in Mawi's and Julieta's love-making. Though they were married in the eyes of Julieta's gods a few days after they met, there had been something incomplete about the ceremony. Marriage needed to be seen not just by the gods but by the world. The Mapuche world on the banks of the emerald lake might have shrunk to only two but for Mawi today's wedding-guests had numbered thousands: generation after generation celebrating the survival and continuity of their family. Julieta had sensed their presence too, she told Mawi. She had felt it in the many hundreds of years of tradition that lay behind the ritual, in the devotion Mawi and his surviving family showed their ancestors, and in the love and respect with which his uncle and sister had welcomed the newcomer whose womb might soon carry the seed of the next generation. Mawi and Julieta made love with passion and seriousness, knowing they might soon be parents and that their children would be new growth in soil recently scorched with the same pitiless European fire that had first swept through the indigenous people of South America nearly five hundred years ago. This was the *ruka* in which he was born and where he had lived with his parents. The birth of his own children would go a little way towards avenging their deaths.

Julieta's naked body lay half across Mawi's. She had fallen asleep with her face burrowing under his chin and her hair draped across his chest. Mawi liked to sleep on his side but not if it meant disturbing Julieta and losing the bliss of having his neck warmed by her breath and his chest by her hair. 'I've never felt so happy in my life,' Julieta told him before she fell asleep. The words played in his memory like a lullaby as he was carried over the moonlit water to unconsciousness.

He was woken by a throbbing sound. It was faint and far away but in this silence even the hooting of an owl sounded like an explosion in a louder world. At first Mawi thought the noise was made by an animal or bird. His next thought made his heart thump: a motor boat? No: why would anyone bring a motor boat to a remote lake in the middle of the mountains? The throbbing got quickly louder and nearer. Mawi's heart thumped twice as hard when he realized what it was.

Julieta sat bolt upright as the helicopter nearly took the cone off the top of the *ruka,* making the whole structure creak and all the crockery rattle.

'We'd better get dressed,' said Mawi.

They were no sooner in their clothes than there was a knocking on the door. Father Lorencio came in, fully dressed.

'We must head back to my village while it's still dark,' he said. 'I've spoken to your uncle. He says we're to take three of the horses.'

'The chances are they already know about the abandoned village,' Mawi replied. 'That's probably where they picked up our trail. I had a feeling we were being followed. Better to get to the border and into Argentina. We'll be safe there.'

'The mountains and forests will be crawling with armed men.'

'I know every bush and rock. They won't see us. We'll keep to the trees south of the road.'

'What about Lamngen and Malle? Are we going to leave them to the mercy of the police and soldiers?'

'They know what to do. They'll put all the valuables in the *ruka* they use for storing hay, keep two horses saddled and listen out for helicopters and the alarm calls of birds. At the first sign of danger they'll gallop off into the forest.'

'I'll be a handicap to your uncle and sister if I stay,' said Father Lorencio, 'and I'll slow you both down if I come with you.'

'Come on!' Mawi interrupted. 'We must get going. There's no time to lose.'

They all three ran with their haversacks to the other side of the village, where they found three horses ready for them but no sign of the dark, shy girl who must have saddled them.

'Take the two blacks,' said Father Lorencio, recovering his breath. 'They won't be so easy to spot in the dark. Don't wait for me: I won't be far behind. If we get separated, find an inn at Moquehue, on the Argentinian side, and I'll join you there.'

Mawi and Julieta mounted the two black horses. Moments later they were galloping through the trees at the edge of the lake, which was jet-black now instead of emerald, and gashed from end to end by moonlight. They geed up their mounts and were soon lost from view as they began their twenty-minute dash to the border.

53

Father Lorencio left the village at dawn, haversack on back, binoculars round his neck, astride the piebald he had made friends with last night. Malle went with him on one of the greys as far as the unpaved road from Melipeuco to the border and Moquehue. Father Lorencio would look as conspicuous as possible until he was spotted, then behave as suspiciously as he could so that he was followed: anything to draw attention away from Mawi and Julieta. He had his passport, so he could cross the border at the frontier-post and wouldn't have to crawl under barbed wire.

In spite of the crisis, and the cold clawing at his face and pinching his fingers and toes, Father Lorencio was conscious of the pale greens and yellows of dawn as they turned slowly to orange, and of his empty stomach and whetted taste buds as he remembered yesterday's freshly ground Brazilian coffee and buckwheat pancakes with wild berry jam. He patted Piebald, who whinnied softly.

As the horse ambled along the road, Father Lorencio caught sight of someone walking towards him. The figure drew nearer and he saw that it was a man in camouflage fatigues carrying an automatic. He was about two metres tall, with blond hair under his peaked cap, and could only be a North American. On any other day Father Lorencio would carry on along the road towards the frontier-post and wish the armed man *¡Buenos días!* as he passed, and an early journey home. Today he had to arouse all the suspicion he could. He pulled on his right rein, nudged his knees into Piebald's flanks and, looking his most furtive and fugitive, disappeared with her into the undergrowth south of the road.

Piebald read Father Lorencio's mind better than any human could. Moments ago she had been half asleep, basking in the early morning sunshine, stumbling over bumps and stones. Now she was wide awake, alert, eyes rolling, each scanning a hemisphere, treading lightly and carefully. Well rehearsed in danger, thought Father Lorencio. He patted her neck again and wondered how many Mapuche owed her their lives.

Father Lorencio heard a whistle three hundred metres behind him. Piebald heard it too, stopped behind a wall of leaves under a tree whose branches brushed the ground, and flared her nostrils. A signal to other Marines prowling somewhere among the trees? Father Lorencio did nothing, leaving it to his mount to make the right decision. Piebald did nothing either: only waited.

A movement caught his eye a hundred metres to his left. He glimpsed another bulky figure, camouflaged and with a machine-gun, moving stealthily through the trees from the direction of the frontier.

Whoever planned this operation, thought Father Lorencio, had guessed that if Mawi and Julieta were at the village, they would have been jolted awake by the helicopter flying over and would very likely be heading for the border. Men had been landed at the frontier, had spread out and were combing the forest westwards from the barbed wire towards the emerald lake. The operation had been carefully thought out. By someone in a position to enlist the help of the US Marines. It had the hallmark of an army officer Father Lorencio knew only too well: Major Adolfo Cortez, the killer who ingratiated himself with God. 'I'm only doing my duty, Lord.'

Mawi knew every square centimetre of this country. He had the ears of a hare and the eyes of a condor. He moved quieter than an owl could fly, knew how to use shadow, the shade of trees and dark backgrounds so as not to be seen. Father Lorencio could have searched for ten years and found no trace of him. But Cortez' men were not stumbling, bumbling bookworms. They were trained in tactics, strategy and stealth and outnumbered Mawi and Julieta, perhaps by ten or fifteen to one.

Father Lorencio had no experience of military operations but he reckoned Cortez wouldn't move all his men west towards the lake and settlement. He would have deployed a second line along the border. In this case they would stretch several kilometres maybe, but not all the way to Cape Horn. All Mawi and Julieta had to do was lie low until the moving line of Marines were past on their way to the village, head south till the line of men along the frontier stopped, then turn east and scramble through the barbed wire to Argentina.

The most useful thing Father Lorencio could do, if his theory was correct, was to head for the armed man nearest the frontier-post and create a diversion, in the hope that the others would hear their comrade's whistle and come running north, so letting Mawi and Julieta cross the frontier south of this point unseen.

No sooner had Father Lorencio's thought taken flight than Piebald responded to it, as if by telepathy. She edged forward, peered through the leaves, saw no sign of the second armed man, and broke cover without a sound. With no prompting from her rider – no nudging of heels or pulling of reins – she set off without hesitating, making her way purposefully among the bushes and trees.

The first rays of the sun were lighting the wicks of the Chile pines. The smell of warm cones and needles filled Father Lorencio's nostrils and made him long to wallow in a hot, pine-scented bath. He could soon tell from the direction of the sunlight that they were heading east and slightly to the north: exactly where he would expect the first of the men lining the frontier south of the road to be positioned.

Piebald stopped, then took several steps sideways until she was in the shade of a monkey-puzzle tree. Moments later Father Lorencio saw what the horse had seen: the blackened face and the camouflage jacket and trousers, barely visible against the background of branches and leaves. How was he going to attract the Marine's attention without at the same time attracting a volley of machine-gun fire? Once again Piebald had the answer: she made a sound half-way between a whinny and a neigh. The Marine tensed, took a whistle from his breast-pocket and blew it, then raised his automatic.

Mission accomplished. The others would come running as planned, thought Father Lorencio, and if Mawi and Julieta were anywhere near the frontier, the way would be clear for them to get through the fence without being arrested or shot. But Father Lorencio hadn't thought of everything: what were he and Piebald going to do now that Cortez' men had been alerted? He would prefer not to play the bird-watcher to a group of cynical killers, for his own sake and for Mawi's and Julieta's: whether Cortez' men greeted him with bullets or handcuffs, he would be *hors de combat* in case his two friends needed help. Father Lorencio hadn't smoked for years but had a sudden longing for a cigarette. Or better still a Cuban cheroot. He picked a leaf from the laurel-tree Piebald was using for cover, pinched it and breathed in the herbal fragrance.

He should learn to trust his mount, he thought. Piebald stepped carefully backwards until she had the trunk of the monkey-puzzle between herself and the armed man. She waited for him to look to his left at the sound of one of his fellow-Marines approaching, then turned and, keeping out of the sunlight, slipped away as light as a deer through the forest.

Father Lorencio heard barking in the distance and was about to pull on the reins when Piebald stopped. A buck? No: that was the bark of a dog. His heart was in his mouth: Cortez had brought dogs as well as men. He should have thought of that. If they once picked up Mawi's scent, he would never be able to shake them off. He listened: the barking was coming from the south-west, from several dogs, but he couldn't tell how far away it was or if it was getting louder or quieter.

The most important thing now was to know what was going on, Father Lorencio thought: to see without being seen. He had

had glimpses through the trees of a mountain rising out of the forest to the south. If he and Piebald climbed at least part of the way up, they might get some kind of view among the trees below.

He was about to nudge Piebald back into motion when he heard horses' hooves approaching at a gallop. Were Mawi and Julieta making a dash for the border now that the line of men had passed on its way to the village? It was too risky. Why didn't they keep going south? The two black horses appeared between the trees a hundred metres ahead, heading not east, but west towards the lake. Piebald's ears were twitching with excitement. Father Lorencio knew she longed to greet them but had been too well trained to neigh when her human friends' safety depended on silence. The two horses galloped across a glade. 'They've got no riders,' he said aloud. Was this a signal of some kind to Mawi's sister and uncle? His own instructions were to send Piebald back to the village with a piece of white cloth tied to her saddle if all was well, without the cloth if things had gone wrong. Father Lorencio had seen no flashes of white as the two horses sped past. Were Mawi and Julieta in trouble? Then it dawned on him. This might not be a signal. Mawi may have decided to send the two blacks home in the hope the dogs had picked up the horses' scent, not his and Julieta's, and would set off in pursuit, leaving the frontier clear of dogs. The dogs would arrive at the village before the men and give Lamngen and Malle plenty of time to escape.

He waited and listened. The sound of the horses' hooves faded into the distance. He was expecting a pack of Alsatians to come racing after the horses but two minutes went by and not a single dog appeared. The barking hadn't stopped but it didn't seem to be getting louder and nearer or fainter and further away. 'I don't like it, Piebald,' he murmured, throwing away the laurel-leaf. He nudged his mount, and they set off for the mountain.

Twenty minutes later they had climbed three hundred metres and come to a clearing on the mountainside. From here Father Lorencio had a good view through his binoculars north, east and south. He could see the corrugated roof of the frontier-post to the north. Looking east, he had glimpses through the trees, in spite of the dazzling sun, of the barbed-wire fence separating Mawi and Julieta from Argentina and safety. It was when he looked south that his heart missed a beat. There was no way Mawi and Julieta could follow the frontier south: the forest rose gently to an escarpment. The escarpment curved, so that Father Lorencio could see a sheer drop of four or five hundred metres. The trees thinned out as the land rose to the cliff-edge and he saw that the frontier fence was being renewed and that a stretch about a kilometre in length from the escarpment northwards had been made impenetrable with rolls of barbed wire.

There was no point Father Lorencio moving till he could see men or dogs, or even Mawi and Julieta, and get an idea of what was happening. He hadn't long to wait. He scanned the forest again through his binoculars. At the foot of the mountain on the south side – the side of the escarpment – a glade twenty metres wide stretched about two hundred metres north and south. If you were heading east towards the border, you could either skirt round the open space, to avoid breaking cover, or you could take the risk, if you were in a hurry, and cut straight across it. A movement in the bottom right-hand corner of Father Lorencio's field of vision caught his eye. He saw two figures dash across the glade and recognized Mawi and Julieta. They obviously didn't know about the new stretch of barbed wire along the border and were heading straight for it. They were close enough to hear if he shouted to them but, if he did shout, others might hear too.

Father Lorencio became conscious of the dogs again. The barking was louder and coming from the west, from the direction of the lake and village. If Mawi's plan in sending the horses home had been to distract the dogs, it didn't seem to have worked: the dogs were heading east, and the trail they were following wasn't the horses', by the sound of it, but Mawi's and Julieta's.

Father Lorencio wiped the perspiration from his forehead and looked through the glasses again. The sun was high enough now for him to be able to glimpse the barbed-wire fence to the east without being dazzled. What he saw in the gaps between the trees made his heart race: the men along the frontier, who had hurried north in response to their comrade's whistle, were now returning to their posts. Mawi and Julieta would have to hurry if they were to head north themselves and find a stretch of fence they could cross without meeting them. Time and space were running out on Mawi and Julieta. There was no way of escape south, because of the escarpment. The way east through the fence was getting narrower every second. If they went west, they would run into Cortez' men and their dogs. The way Father Lorencio had come, from the north, was still open, as far as he knew, but it would take them within view of the frontier-post.

Father Lorencio glimpsed Mawi and Julieta again through his binoculars. What were they doing? They were heading south-east to where the reinforced fence met the escarpment. Mawi must be remembering where he crossed years ago. He still couldn't have seen the rolls of barbed wire. They would get to the frontier and turn north but wouldn't have time to get to the old stretch of fence before meeting Cortez' men. Father Lorencio must hurry to them and tell them to head due east to the old fence as fast as they could. He didn't care about his own safety. He would rather be shot himself than see Mawi captured or killed.

Piebald was already starting down the mountain when Cortez' men began to arrive from the direction of the lake and village to the west. Their dogs were on leads now and had stopped barking. The first two men were being led by a bloodhound, which was following Mawi's and Julieta's scent without hesitation across the glade towards the new section of fence. The next two were two hundred metres behind, with an Alsatian. Instead of following the pair with the bloodhound, they continued straight on towards the point where the old and new fences met. Two more pairs of men, also with Alsatians, followed the second pair at intervals, forming the base of a triangle running north-east and south-west. The meeting-point between the fence and the escarpment was at the apex of the triangle.

Father Lorencio's face and body were soaked in perspiration, as much from fear for Mawi and Julieta as from the heat. His two friends were now well and truly cornered. The only thing he could do to help was as before to try and act as a decoy to draw the men away from them. This would be easier without the dogs: Cortez and his Marines were more likely to be led by the bloodhound and Alsatians than come charging over at the sight of a strange man waving and shouting.

The line of men turned south-east towards the escarpment and moved slowly three hundred metres behind the pair with the bloodhound, so that the triangle and the gaps between the pairs of men gradually became smaller. Father Lorencio dismounted, to be less conspicuous, and continued his descent on foot, half-walking, half-running. Piebald followed, with no need of a halter. If only she could talk, he would heed every word she said. The ground levelled out, then climbed gently towards the escarpment. Father Lorencio tore through the trees, with Piebald close behind, and only slowed down when he caught sight of one of the pairs of men with Alsatians. 'I've got to be near enough to be heard if I shout,' he told himself, 'but not so close that they know they're being tailed.'

The trees were thinning out and Father Lorencio had to take special care not to be seen. For the past few minutes he had been walking stealthily but continuously. Now he made a dash to the shade of a tree, paused to look all around, then made a dash to the next tree. During one of his dashes he caught a glimpse of the point where the old fence joined the new. The last of the Marines deployed along the border was back at his post there. Mawi and Julieta were cut off from the frontier. There were fewer than a hundred metres now between the pairs of men advancing towards the escarpment. The only cover was the odd tree and a few bushes. Escape for Mawi and Julieta out of this triangle of barbed wire, precipice and armed men had become impossible. 'If only I had a gun,' thought Father Lorencio, 'a few bullets over the heads of the Marines would soon send them running and give Mawi and Julieta a crack to squeeze through.'

The two men with the bloodhound were near the escarpment. They were not wearing caps, like the men behind them, and instead of machine-guns they had holsters with revolvers. One was thin and of medium height, the other thick-set, with copper-coloured hair. Father Lorencio recognized the chiselled features of Adolfo Cortez but not the man in charge of the bloodhound.

All the men were near the cliff-edge now. Where were Mawi and Julieta? There was nowhere left for them to hide. Unless they were behind the low bushes right on the edge of the precipice, ready to throw themselves off rather than surrender to the forces of coercion and injustice. It was this thought that made Father Lorencio take action when he saw the bloodhound sniffing its way towards the bushes. He jumped up and grabbed the dry branch above his head. The branch broke off with a loud crack. All the men turned and looked in his direction. A figure rose from behind the cliff-edge bushes with the speed and silence of a jaguar. An arm was thrown round Cortez' face and the forefinger of the other hand was pressed into his throat. The major made not a sound. Even the copper-haired man next to him didn't realize what had happened.

'Put down your weapons, all of you!' Mawi called out.

The men about-turned, as if in response to a command. Even the dogs were too surprised to bark and snarl.

'I can kill Major Cortez by moving one finger,' said Mawi. 'I don't want to kill him because I don't like to take life. Put down your weapons and the major will be unharmed.'

The copper-haired man took the revolver from his holster and laid it on the grass. The other six men put down their automatics.

'There has been a misunderstanding,' Mawi went on. 'You are pursuing me because you think I kidnapped Julieta Reyes. I didn't. Julieta left Santiago with me of her own free will. We were married before we left in a Christian church. Yesterday we were married according to Mapuche customs. Julieta will confirm what I say. There are witnesses to support us. I want to release you, Major Cortez, but first you must give your word that you will let me and Julieta return in peace to our village a few kilometres from here. Nod your head to make your promise.'

Cortez nodded his head. Mawi released him. Cortez took the revolver from his holster, turned and took aim.

'The rat!' thought Father Lorencio. 'He's going to break his promise and arrest Mawi.'

Major Adolfo Cortez closed his index-finger round the trigger. The gun seemed to explode in his hand. The bullet tore into Mawi's body.

There was a gasp from one of the two Chilean-looking men in Cortez' company. '*Comandante*, you promised—'

'Silence!' barked the major.

Blood began to pump from Mawi's chest. The first gush splattered on to Cortez' pristine camouflage jacket. He cried out in disgust, turned away from his comrades and vomited.

'What's happened?' Julieta blurted out as she scrambled up from behind the bushes at the edge of the cliff. She saw Mawi's blood pumping from him and caught her breath, but neither gasped nor screamed.

Mawi collapsed on to the grass at the edge of the cliff. His head and one of his arms hung over the precipice.

Julieta's first impulse was to go to him but she stopped short. She looked at Cortez as he wiped his mouth with a previously spotless handkerchief. Her expression was not of anger but of disbelief. 'You gave your word,' she said. She appeared almost puzzled. Human life was perfectible, she seemed about to say. Why make a hell when with so little effort each one of us could help to create a paradise?

Cortez replaced the handkerchief in the breast-pocket of his camouflage jacket. 'Pepe!' His voice rang out, part command, part sneer.

'Yes, *comandante*?' Pepe still sounded shocked and confused, like a child who has just watched his father slam a fist into his mother's face.

'Remove the ring from the Indian's finger and give it to me. If it's stuck, cut off the finger.'

'No!' Julieta cried out. 'I'll get the ring. Take the wretched thing! I never wanted it in the first place.'

Cortez looked into Julieta's eyes and seemed to exult at the extra pain he was inflicting on her.

Julieta took off her poncho, rolled it up, knelt and tried to staunch the pumping blood. It was as hopeless as trying to bail out a rowing-boat in a heavy storm. She took Mawi's hand and tried to get the ring off. It wouldn't move.

A beefy Marine stepped towards Julieta. His eyes were aglint with desire. 'This is the same broad we drove across Peru,' he said to the copper-haired man with the bloodhound. 'No ban on her this time, chief? With her Indian gone she's got to be desperate for it. We'll be doing her a favour.' He unzipped his trousers.

'No!' yelled Father Lorencio, leaving the shade of his tree and advancing into the sunlight, so that everyone could see him. 'You've already murdered an innocent man who meant more to this girl than her own life. Are you going to compound evil with evil? Do you want to have bad dreams and consciences for the rest of your lives and an old age racked with guilt and foul memories?'

Father Lorencio couldn't go on. What he saw left him speechless. He uttered something between a cry and a groan and sank to his knees.

As he did so, he heard a rushing behind him and saw a shadow several metres wide in front and to his right moving quickly towards the escarpment. The sky above him was black for a few moments and air rushed through his hair and into his ears as the condor swooped over his head. Two seconds later it skimmed the heads of Cortez and his men, who all ducked and turned to watch the massive bird fly out beyond the precipice. When their heads tilted down and their eyes scanned the cliff-top, the quarry they had been stalking and had netted had vanished. It was as if the condor had caught hold of Mawi and Julieta as it passed and swept them up from the earth beyond the reach of human cruelty. Pepe crossed himself: had God made him witness to a miracle?

If Pepe and his comrades hadn't been looking behind them at Father Lorencio, they might have seen Julieta take Mawi's hand in both hers, lower herself over the edge of the precipice, let her feet hang and the weight of her body drag Mawi's after her. If Pepe looked over the edge of the cliff now, he might still be able to see two distant figures, hand in hand, revolving slowly like the sails of a windmill as they plunged earthwards.

What they saw instead was the condor lifted by thermals, carried by the wind eastwards towards the sun, its wings held still, the feathers at the tips fluttering like pennants. Its shadow grew, became fainter and eventually disappeared. The bird was soon no more than a speck in the sun, as if melting into it. Mawi and Julieta were carried on those wings, it seemed to Father Lorencio as he watched the bird disappear – carried into the arms of their father, the Sun, to circle the earth with him and descend as light and warmth on the island to which they had longed to return.

A helicopter drummed on the sky not far off. Father Lorencio became conscious of two armed men approaching from the cliff-top. He just had the presence of mind to turn, so as to speed Piebald on her way to the village. But Piebald had already gone: Father Lorencio glimpsed her white tail as she disappeared among the pines at a gallop.

54

Arrest, followed by an uncomfortable journey, then prison, was getting to be a way of life for Father Lorencio. Last time it had been the police; this time it was the army. There was little to choose between the thuggery of one and the brutality of the other. He preferred the transport offered by the police, especially when there was a long journey to be made. The wooden slats, smelly feet and drooling dogs were the same in both. The difference lay in the exposure to fresh air: an eight-hundred-kilometre ride in the middle of winter in a police bus would have been less gruelling than the same journey on an army truck with flapping canvas sides and an open back. Father Lorencio had expected to travel if not in comfort, at least quickly, by air, but the helicopter had turned out to be a bubble of a thing only big enough for the pilot, Cortez and his copper-haired partner in crime.

The cold and the bumps were not uppermost in Father Lorencio's mind. Nor was the prospect of prison and torture. He wished they had been: they would have been less painful than the images of Mawi and Julieta that crowded into his head however hard he tried to keep them out, and the sense of loss that came in gusts and filled his heart. He could imagine what it must be like to lose an arm or a leg – the same constant throbbing; the feeling that the limb was still there, while knowing that it had gone – or, worse still, to lose a child, or two children.

In spite of himself he kept reliving the experiences that had defined his two young protégés for him and nurtured his growing affection for them. He remembered the taciturn boy who had come to him from among the poor and homeless of Santiago, from a life cleaning shoes by day and sleeping in the park on the banks of the River Mapocho at night. He remembered how the boy had burst into flower one day, astonished him with his wisdom and intelligence, and involuntarily begun the conversion of his would-be converter. Father Lorencio thought of the wealthy family who had attended mass at Santo Domingo and the daughter who had come to confession regularly, though she never had any sins to confess. He remembered his alarm at the girl's love for his Mapuche protégé, until he realized she was ready to give up her privileged existence and marry and make her life with the boy. He had seen Julieta's single-mindedness and courage in the face of her father's opposition. He remembered her vitality, Mawi's coolness and clear head, their love and consideration for each other, their fearlessness.

Father Lorencio's involvement in his two young friends' destiny dated from his decision to marry them. For years he had been risking his rectorship, freedom and life, fox-like, behind a hedge of artifice. With Mawi and Julieta risk grew to recklessness. He had broken cover and been caught, though he had later contrived his release. He had no regrets. He would have given his life to save Mawi's and Julieta's. During his days at Santo Domingo he had felt compassion for those he saved from persecution. Mawi and Julieta had taught him a deeper love.

Father Lorencio thought also of the ease with which men like Cortez and the US Marines with him took other people's lives or outraged their bodies, minds and feelings. They treated human beings like cattle while they lived, and carcasses when they died. No piece of machinery was so complex and beautifully constructed as the human mind and body but they were thrown away as dismissively as fast food wrapping or empty cigarette lighters by the likes of Cortez and his men. Sex was no longer an expression of the deepest intimacy, based on friendship and trust, but something to be torn from victims, causing them pain and anguish and bringing no satisfaction to the aggressor. If only Cortez and his kind were exceptional and their behaviour the result of some unusual mental disorder or social dystrophy, but it seemed to Father Lorencio that nearly half the population of the world – the male half – suffered from a psychosis that manifested itself in distrust, fear, hatred, violence and destruction. One half of humankind was addicted to destroying what the other half – the female half – created. Father Lorencio didn't know what the answer was. For centuries idealists had been calling for love, a change of heart and the rest of it. There was no sign of any progress. We were no further on than cavemen. Science on the other hand was knocking at heaven's gates somewhere on the bounds of the universe. Maybe the time had come for medical science to intervene and try and rid humanity of the chronic disease of the male mind and the appalling behavioural symptoms that went with it.

Father Lorencio was overcome by a weariness of the body and spirit as he sat shivering on the slatted bench, with a Marine either side of him and nowhere to rest his back. The road was smooth and straight and he would have slept if he could, but how could you sleep sitting bolt upright on a hard bench with cold air blowing up your back, down your neck and in your ear?

He wanted to be with Mawi and Julieta. He longed for it, for something he knew was impossible, because his two friends had left this world: a world of army officers, marines and policemen, with their guns and dogs. Father Lorencio was tired of it – tired of lighting pinpoints of light in all the darkness, only to have them extinguished by men like Cortez. Was there a way of being with Mawi and Julieta, or rather of not being without them? If he caught pneumonia or pleurisy on this twelve-hour lorry journey, could he not refuse all medicine, sink into unconsciousness and be ferried gently to the other side? Not suicide exactly: more like euthanasia. Mawi had gone to his ancestors and taken Julieta with him. Would there be a place on the next boat for a loyal friend?

Would his life have been well lived if he left it now? He had saved the lives of hundreds of Chileans whose only crime had been to vote for a champion of human rights and social justice. He had enjoyed some of the good things of life: not marriage and fatherhood, because of the Church's unnatural ruling on clerical celibacy, but friendship, good food and wine, the pursuit of knowledge, a love of music, painting and literature. Not a bad balance-sheet.

What if he were to ask his friends what they thought?

Father Lorencio closed his eyes, concentrated very hard on Mawi and Julieta and asked them: 'Have I spent long enough on this side? What do you say? Shall I cross the water and join you?'

The reply came so quickly that it took him by surprise. 'Leave the world?' Julieta seemed to say. 'You, Father? You, who devote your life to others and give hope to everyone you meet? You must stay in the world for as long as you can. Don't underestimate the good you do. Every one of your good acts sends out ripples further than you can see. We will still be waiting for you when your life at last runs out.'

Mawi answered next. 'We left before Julieta could even begin what she felt called to do – her work on the Isla del Sol. The flame we lit will die if it isn't passed on. Our immortality depends on you, Father. Begin the work Julieta and I should have begun, pass the flame on when you can go no further, and thanks to you we will all three live on and meet again in the thoughts and words of those who come after us.'

Father Lorencio opened his eyes. Mawi and Julieta had lifted his spirits. He didn't notice the cold any more and the bench felt less hard.

The two young Chilean-looking soldiers were sitting together opposite Father Lorencio, sandwiched between two US Marines, both of whom were sound asleep in spite of the discomfort. Pepe, the one who had had the courage to speak out against his commanding officer's outrage, smiled gently at Father Lorencio. What kind eyes the boy had! What possessed a gentle soul like that to choose thuggery for a career, Father Lorencio wondered. Forced into it by poverty, perhaps, or by an autocratic father. He smiled back at the soldier.

55

Franco Reyes sat at his desk at home, waiting for the phone to ring. The clutter had disappeared from his desktop: papers had been filed, biscuit wrappers thrown away, empty plates and glasses taken to the kitchen – much to the dismay of the flies – and pens and pencils put in drawers.

Reyes was all bluster, boasting, grossness, lack of self-discipline, self-indulgence. This was how people saw him. It was the side of his nature that had prevailed for the past twenty years. There had been a time when he showed a different face to the world, the face of a man who would have to succeed on his own merits, as he had no useful family connections, a face of steely determination, ambition and shrewdness. He would not have become one of the senior men at the Ministry of Internal Affairs without steel, drive and hard work. His bluster, boasting, self-indulgence, buffoonery even, had been cultivated to mask the still less attractive spectacle of a man on the make: a covering of flab for the professional bone that had helped him keep a step ahead of his rivals and wrong-foot them when they weren't looking. With time the mask had become more familiar than the face it was hiding. After twenty years Reyes had almost forgotten what his own face looked like.

Since Julieta's death Reyes had been concentrating his will and energy on putting steel back in his character. He had forced himself to stop blustering and boasting. Ranting had given way to controlled passion. Everything he said sounded cold, rational and to the point, but his voice sometimes cracked like thin ice as he said it, one fist nearly crushed the telephone receiver and the other was clenched as if to drive his questions and demands home straight into the solar plexus of whoever he was talking to. Franco Reyes wanted answers and he wanted action. His daughter had been killed. He wanted to know why, how and on whose orders. If Julieta had been the victim of an army operation, he wanted the officer in charge court-martialled and shot. He would go on badgering, asking questions and making demands until he got what he wanted. He had already spoken to the President's secretary. He would keep phoning till she stopped talking about words in ears and knuckles rapped and started collaring the President.

Reyes had changed his eating and drinking habits. He had suppressed his taste for sweets, cakes and sugary drinks and taught himself to feel ill at the thought of the Café O'Higgins with its mountains of whipped cream. He drank his coffee black now, without sugar. The fridge was empty. He seldom had a proper meal. If he noticed he was hungry and saw ready-made sandwiches for sale, he might stop and buy one. He hadn't exchanged self-indulgence for asceticism so much as redirected his appetites. His craving now was for whisky, though not enough to cloud his judgement or slur his speech during working hours. He had switched from cigars to cigarettes: Turkish, because he didn't like Virginian tobacco. Not more than ten a day. Not yet.

Franco Reyes' appearance had altered. His once ruddy cheeks had turned sallow. The skin hung on his face like the shirt from his shoulders, which had fitted perfectly before but was now several sizes too big. Reyes' walk was different: he padded restlessly, instead of shambling, and had developed a stoop. He needed a haircut. Strangers would take him for an orchestral conductor, perhaps, but not for a senior member of the Chilean bureaucracy, where a military appearance was required, even when there was no uniform to go with it.

The telephone rang. Reyes answered it.

'*Buenas tardes*, Franco. Felipe here. Foreign Ministry.'

Felipe Sánchez? This wasn't the call Reyes was expecting. '*Buenas tardes*, Minister,' he said.

'We've just had a letter from the British Home Office that we thought might interest you. From their Home Secretary. One of his subordinates interviewed the young Mapuche who lost his life with your poor daughter. It describes him as a highly intelligent and responsible young man, with a deep love of his country, his fellow human beings and his wife. He was spending his honeymoon in England but looked forward to returning to his country, the letter says. Unfortunately there was an irregularity in his travel papers. Because of Britain's friendship with Chile, the Home Secretary felt obliged to hand him over to the British Foreign Office for an early flight back to Santiago.'

'His wife? His honeymoon? He was my daughter's husband?'

'Doesn't sound much like a kidnapper or terrorist to me.'

'And yet he was killed. My daughter wasn't a terrorist either. She was killed too. What's going on, Minister? Are the army going to wipe out the entire population of Chile?'

'Forgive me, Franco, but I've heard that not many days ago you were urging the army to go after your daughter and the young man you called her kidnapper.'

'To go after her, not to kill her. She died in highly suspicious circumstances. I've had a letter too, Minister. There's a witness being held in the military prison. Seems to have been a hiker or a bird-watcher. Looks as though they locked him up for no better reason than that he saw what happened and might blab. He must have talked one of the guards into letting him have pen and paper and smuggling his letter out. The letter spoke of US Marines and cold-blooded murder. It suggested the officer in charge was acting on his own authority and hadn't been sent to Araucanía on a mission. I tried to visit the witness in prison. They said I needed the written authority of a senior officer. I'm expecting a phone call today to tell me if I have the authority. It's like trying to get an audience with the Pope. They cover up for one another, Minister, these army officers.'

'I'm seeing the President at a meeting in an hour's time. Would you like me to ask for his authority for you? It would override everyone else's.'

Would Reyes like the President's authority? Would he like the goose that laid golden eggs? He thanked Felipe Sánchez in a voice that betrayed as little feeling as he could manage. He had learnt that the less effusively you thanked people for their kindnesses, the more they would do for you, in the hope of giving better satisfaction next time.

Sánchez was right, Reyes decided when he had put down the receiver, poured himself a Glenlivet and lit a cigarette. 'I was too hasty,' he thought as he paced up and down the room with his drink in one hand and the cigarette in the other. 'I should have waited before sending that reptile and his soldiers after her. And I should have trusted Julieta's judgement. The boy who died would have made her happy. Cortez, who is without heart or blood, would not.' Reyes was almost sure Cortez was behind the killing of the young couple but he didn't like to say so to Sánchez, to avoid making his struggle for justice look like a vendetta.

Reyes put down his glass and picked up a little photo of Julieta at the age of sixteen. He had found it in a drawer and it now stood in a leather frame on his desk. 'All that vitality, intelligence and beauty,' he murmured. 'Twenty years my daughter. Now gone. Forgive me, Julieta.' He blinked away his tears. 'The rest of my life will be devoted to making amends.' He replaced the photo on the desk, took a handkerchief from his trouser pocket and blew his nose.

The phone rang again. He put away the handkerchief and picked up the receiver.

'Reyes.'

'Colonel Santa Cruz de Valladolid here. Not good news, I'm afraid, Señor Reyes. I can't find anyone to authorize a visit to the prisoner you want to interview. I've done my best for you.'

The little swine hadn't lifted a finger, thought Reyes. They were worse than the Mafia, these army officers. 'Very kind of you, *Señor Coronel*. Thank you for all your efforts. Nothing more to be done, I suppose. Short of a letter from the President.'

Colonel Santa Cruz liked the joke and guffawed. 'Yes, that would do the trick.'

'Just the trick I intend to play,' thought Reyes as he replaced the receiver. 'And I'll bring my lawyer as a witness, so that no one can accuse me of inventing what the prisoner says.'

Reyes was not expecting any more calls, so he poured himself another whisky: a large one.

56

'Buenos días, señor.'

Father Lorencio woke with a start, threw back his grey army blanket and sat on the edge of the bed in his shirt and underpants. His mattress was covered in stains inherited from generations of recusant soldiers but they no longer made him squeamish.

'It's unlike me to oversleep,' he said. Talking half to himself he went on: 'Must be yesterday's meeting with Reyes and telling him Julieta's story from beginning to end. They say sharing your joys and sorrows is cathartic.' He got up, put on his green corduroy trousers, sighed and said to his warder: 'Reyes seems to be getting to know his own daughter at last, now that it's too late.'

Pepe put the tray with the prisoner's breakfast of maize porridge and a glass of water on the wooden table cemented into the floor in a corner of the cell.

'I'm to take you to the shower-room when you've had your breakfast,' he told Father Lorencio. 'You can help yourself to a change of clothes from your bag, if you want. Then they're driving you to the airport.'

'To drop me without a parachute or life-belt in the middle of the ocean and save themselves the trouble and expense of keeping me behind bars?'

'You're a free man, *señor*. Thanks to Julieta Reyes' father. Thanks to the President, who gave the order for your release.'

'I'm honoured,' replied Father Lorencio. He would rather share a bed with Stalin or Hitler than owe a debt of gratitude to the President. 'But why the airport?'

'Señor Reyes wants to meet his son-in-law's family. He wants you to be his guide.'

Father Lorencio nodded. The last thing he felt like was a jaunt to the Lake District in the company of Franco Reyes. He longed for his mountain retreat, solitude and a winter spent writing letters to the four corners of the earth. He was not filled with the same elation he had felt at the end of his first spell behind bars. That was for several weeks; this had been for only a few days. How could he even begin to feel elated about anything, having just lost his two closest friends?

'Were they very special, *señor*?'

'Julieta and Mawi?' Father Lorencio nodded again, picked up his bowl and spoon and started to eat, standing up.

'I'd like to hear their story.'

'You must hear it. Everyone in Chile must hear it. Everyone in the world. But stories take time to tell and you're packing me off to the airport.'

Father Lorencio finished his breakfast, had his shower and put on clean clothes. As he walked with his rucksack between two rows of cells towards the fifty-centimetre-thick rocket-proof steel door, a man's voice called out: 'Father Lorencio!' The voice was familiar but he couldn't place it at first. One of his former confessants? He stopped and peered through the bars of the nearest cell. Standing at the door, looking out through the grille, was Major Adolfo Cortez. Father Lorencio stepped back in a moment of revulsion at finding himself so close to Mawi's and Julieta's murderer, to a man now in his early middle age who had devoted his years as a young adult, the years of love and joy, to the planned torture and killing, often successful, of hundreds – perhaps thousands – of his fellow-humans. The two men stared at each other without speaking. Was one of Chile's cruellest gaolers himself behind bars at last? For how long? How could justice be done by the very generals and colonels who ordered the torture and killings?

'I have a confession to make, Father,' said Cortez. 'Will you hear it, then give me your blessing?'

This was like listening to a whining child, thought Father

Lorencio. His revulsion and anger surged up in him, against Cortez but also against the hundreds and thousands like him over the centuries – from bishops, generals and emperors down – who had used Christian ritual as a licence for their barbarities and so perverted and made a mockery of a religion that at its simplest and best safeguarded the purity of heart of a girl like Julieta.

Lorencio waited for the fire inside him to cool and turn to rock before replying. 'My faith is not the same as yours, Major Cortez,' he said at last, quietly but with uncharacteristic sternness. 'My faith is not the faith of torturers and killers, who are pardoned so that they can return without shame to their atrocities; of Europeans, who have gone about the world seizing land that doesn't belong to them and slaughtering millions of indigenous inhabitants, all in the name of their convenient god, so that they can grow rich in his honour and so that any survivors after their massacres can understand the meaning of bondage and humiliation. Bless and confess you? As if your felonies were no more than the pranks of a delinquent child? Your crimes are not venial. They are monstruous. If your god can content himself with a few moments' contrition before absolving you, then he's no god of mine and I can't act in his name. There's nothing I can do for you. Find another confessor to be your nursemaid, or take responsibility for your own actions and face your god alone. The truth is what you need, not sentiment and comfortable deceit. Choose deceit, and you will die for all eternity. Face the truth, and you have a long journey ahead, with perhaps a wintry rebirth at the end. That's all the blessing I can give you.'

Father Lorencio – or plain Lorencio, as he preferred to be called now that Mawi and Julieta were not there to invest the word with a special meaning – walked to the steel door, which Pepe opened for him. He clasped his gentle warder's hand in both his own and got into the back of the waiting jeep, which sped him away to Arturo Merino Benítez Airport.

Franco Reyes was waiting at the gate for Lorencio. At first the two men were tongue-tied in each other's company. What more did they have to say to each other? It had all been said yesterday. Lorencio struggled to get his mountain retreat out of his thoughts and overcome his resistance to revisiting the emerald lake so soon after the death of his friends. He and Reyes waited at the barrier in silence. Their clothes hung as loosely as those of scare-crows and they both needed a haircut. They looked more like two out-of-work musicians than a senior apparatchik and a former rector of one of Santiago's most prestigious congregations.

'It was good of you to arrange my release so quickly,' Lorencio said, when they had shown their boarding-passes and were walking down the ramp.

'Least I could do for you,' Reyes replied.

Lorencio got the feeling Julieta's father wanted to show his gratitude but was in danger of being engulfed in his emotions as he reached into the forgotten places of his heart. His breathing became audible and he started to sound like a furnace overheating.

'You were like a father to my daughter and son-in-law,' he said. 'More of a father than I was.'

Lorencio's own heart went out to Reyes. The poor man was stumbling against the inadequacy of words to express his strong feelings. Lorencio decided to lower the temperature by talking to Reyes about the Mapuche people. He had made a study of their religion and customs, and what he had read was still fresh in his memory.

While they crossed the tarmac and boarded the aeroplane, Reyes listened attentively as Lorencio told him about the Mapuche tradition of community life, the democratic election of community elders every year, the making of most decisions by a majority of elders, and of others by a majority of the whole community. Not a yawn from Reyes on the ninety-minute flight to Temuco as Lorencio described the Mapuche religion, which had never involved the sacrifice of humans or animals and whose simple purpose was to thank the sun, the rain and the earth for making human life possible and providing food, and to ask them to continue for the generations to come. In the taxi from the airport to the point on the dirt road nearest the emerald lake, Lorencio told his pupil about the Mapuche respect for nature, their principle of never felling a tree without planting a new one, the care they showed their animals, and their mainly vegetarian diet of herbs, fruit, berries and grain, with only a few lives lost among the fish and wild fowl to satisfy their needs.

The taxi pulled up and the two passengers climbed out of the back. Lorencio put on his poncho, Reyes his overcoat. Lorencio was silent as they walked through the trees to the lake, in the hope the peace and beauty of the surroundings would work their magic on Julieta's father and help him forget that his daughter had died nearby.

He grew apprehensive as they got nearer the village. Would Mawi's sister and uncle already know about his death? The return of the three horses without white in their bridles on the day he died would have told them that all was not well.

There was no goat to welcome Lorencio and Reyes when they reached the village, and no sign of Mawi's sister. A barely visible wisp of smoke rose from the central *ruka*. They paused outside the door, then Lorencio knocked gently. There was no reply. He opened the door a crack and saw Mawi's uncle at the table with a knife in his hand and an oil-lamp beside him, working at a block of wood.

'May we come in?' he asked quietly.

Malle looked up. 'I'm sorry. I didn't notice you. Come in! Father Lorencio, isn't it?'

'Lorencio. With someone who wants to meet you. His name is Franco Reyes.'

The two men came in, closed the door and sat down at the

table. Malle went to the kitchen area, put wood on the fire, swung the cauldron over the flames, poured coffee-beans into the wooden grinder and turned the handle. A comforting aroma soon filled the *ruka*.

Reyes breathed in sharply. Lorencio looked round and saw that he was studying the wood-carving on the table. 'What a fine-looking boy!' Reyes murmured as he handed the carving to Lorencio. The faces of Mawi and Julieta looked out at him from the block of wood. They seemed to live and see and breathe behind their wooden faces. Mawi's uncle had caught all of Julieta's vitality and Mawi's serenity.

Malle saw Lorencio studying the carving as he poured boiling water into the battered tin pot. He sat down at the table and was quiet for a minute at least. Then he said: 'We saw blood at the cliff edge but we couldn't find their bodies.'

After a few seconds Lorencio replied gently: 'They fell into the gorge.'

'We spent all day searching at the bottom of the cliff. Not a trace. If vultures had found them, they would have left the bones.'

'Removed in the army helicopter, perhaps,' Lorencio suggested.

'Why bother? It's into remote gorges like that that the army throw the bodies of their victims.'

After another silence Lorencio asked: 'How is Lamngen?'

'She spends all her time with the animals now. Mostly with the horses. She brings the goat in at night to sleep in the *ruka* with her.'

He got up to fetch the coffee-pot. As he did so, the door opened and Lamngen slipped in. She didn't say a word but went to the kitchen area and brought four mugs to the table. Her uncle poured the coffee. She took her mug into the shadows and stood sipping from it.

Reyes blinked, took his handkerchief from his trouser pocket and blew his nose. The wood-carving of Julieta's face and the mention of her missing body had obviously stirred his grief.

'I haven't introduced myself properly,' he said, putting away his handkerchief and trying to iron out the wrinkles in his voice. 'I'm Julieta's father. Lorencio has been telling me about Mawi and about the customs and way of life of the Mapuche people. Not only will I miss my daughter for the rest of my days...' Reyes' voice broke again. He cleared his throat and went on. '...But I will also always regret my family not being united with yours and with your people.' He sipped his coffee. 'Because of my work, I meet a lot of senior figures in the Government, civil servants, bishops and so on. Also ambassadors and politicians from other countries. After what Lorencio has told me, I will take every opportunity to set Mapuche society up as a model of communal life. I will do my best to persuade colleagues to join me in a campaign for the civil and human rights that have so often been denied you. I have no heir now and I am separated from my wife...' Reyes paused again to keep his emotions in check. '...I would like to regard your community as my family and to help revitalize it in whatever ways I can: by helping you sell your produce and works of art, for example, and encouraging those who have left to return.' He turned to Malle. 'I have something to ask of you. I've been admiring your skill as a wood-carver. I would like to commission another carving on a larger scale of your nephew and my daughter. I see the Archbishop of Santiago from time to time and will ask him to place your work in the Cathedral. Mawi and Julieta loved each other. Let their marriage be an example to Chile and every other country and a vision of a world where two races can live side by side in harmony, like members of a single family.'

Malle got up, went over to Reyes and shook his hand. After more coffee he took him on a tour of the village, while Lorencio and Lamngen stayed in the *ruka*.

'It will be good if some of your community resettle,' said

Lorencio. 'You won't be so much alone.'

'Will Señor Reyes also pay for my brother and parents to come back?' replied Lamngen.

She heard her uncle calling her and went to help him saddle four horses.

The two Mapuche accompanied Lorencio and Julieta's father through the sighing pine-trees to the waiting taxi. The driver woke with a start and scrambled from the back seat, where he had been lying stretched out. Lamngen's uncle and Franco Reyes dismounted, shook hands and embraced.

'Aren't you coming in the taxi?' Reyes asked with a hint of anxiety when he saw Lorencio still in his saddle. He seemed to have the same need for company that Lorencio had for solitude.

Lorencio smiled kindly. 'I live only twenty kilometres away,' he replied. 'The quickest way is across country.'

'Take the horse,' Malle said to him. 'She'll find her own way back.'

The four bereaved went their own ways, Julieta's father westwards in his taxi, the two Mapuche south on their greys, Lorencio north on Piebald.

Lorencio was lost in his thoughts all the way to the abandoned village. When he arrived, he couldn't remember if he had guided Piebald there or if she had somehow found her own way. He was pleased to have her with him to relieve the melancholy of returning alone to a home he had so recently shared with Mawi and Julieta.

Lorencio left the mare untethered and took his bag indoors. He lit the fire and oil-lamps, filled the kettle from the cistern and hung it over the logs. He went back outside, tore some thatch from the eaves of the presbytery and took it to Piebald.

'I have no hay,' he told her, 'but I've brought you some of my roof for your supper.'

Piebald ate her fill of Lorencio's roof and was led into one of the abandoned huts for the night. Lorencio returned to the warm of the presbytery and poured himself a whisky.

The next morning he went into Piebald's hut with more thatch in his arms and a tin in one of his hands.

'You must get back to your village,' he told her as he led her outside after her breakfast. 'They will be missing you.' He opened his tin. 'This will give you extra energy for the journey.' He fed sugar-lumps into the horse's mouth. 'We did our best, didn't we, you and I?' He gave her one more lump of sugar. 'We did our best to save them… Goodbye, my friend.'

He patted Piebald's rump. She cantered off into the trees.

57

It was the middle of the night in the vast shanty-town of El Salvador on the outskirts of Lima. The population of four hundred thousand were sleeping their shallow, uneasy sleep behind cardboard walls on cardboard beds under cardboard roofs. What little food they had was kept not in refrigerators but in cardboard boxes: no protection against sharp-toothed rodents, who like the refugees from the Andes had colonized the dusty hills in their millions. The only sounds, apart from those of human sleep – a snore or a rasp of breath here, a gabble of sleep-talk there – were the pattering and gnawing of corpulent rats and mice and the barking of dogs at well-fleshed cats, or the shadows of cats, moving silently as ghosts in the moonlight. Flimsy walls and knotted rags would have allowed easy pickings for thieves, but theft was rare in this cardboard metropolis of starving paupers.

A single oil-lamp burnt in the Comedor Paraíso above the table of planks and trestles, which was covered in empty glasses, mugs and Cristal bottles. There was an empty wine-bottle and a half-drunk bottle of brandy: the remains of the traveller's presents, bought while he waited at Santiago Airport for the flight to Lima.

Lorencio was sound asleep, his arms folded on the table, his head resting on them. He looked like an old wino more than half-seas-over in the middle of all these bottles, but his two beers, two glasses of wine and tot of brandy had been spread over half a day. Since mid-afternoon he had been reliving the last weeks of Mawi's and Julieta's lives, and a critical period in his own life, with only a two-hour break to prepare supper for another group of children and grandchildren, feed them and give them their reading and writing lesson. It wasn't drinking but story-telling, and his involvement in the story, that had exhausted him.

The visitor was standing in the doorway of the *comedor* in his shirt-sleeves on this warm April night, listening to ocean rollers breaking on the other side of a shanty-covered mound of dust, ready to inhale deeply whenever a wave of salty air cooled his face and neck, and breathing lightly between draughts to avoid the ripples of smell from rotting food and human and animal excreta. He couldn't help ducking whenever a meteor streaked overhead. He was a million light-years closer to the stars here than he had ever been in England.

The traveller felt reborn, having taken early retirement. No more suits and waistcoats, no more tube journeys, no more kowtowing to superiors he didn't respect. He had lost twenty kilos, given up smoking and cut down on haircuts. He still drank wine and spirits but in moderation.

All these things increased his sense of well-being. A deeper satisfaction came with the knowledge that he had begun to grow in mind and character, having been pollarded forty-odd years ago. Now he was himself for the first time in his life, doing what he wanted to do instead of what he was told to do, pursuing his own aims instead of other people's, playing Bach and Mozart every night instead of knocking himself out with whisky. He had even spent a day busking outside the Home Office in London to raise money for a school in some tormented corner of Africa.

The traveller felt sad to hear about Mawi – sad and guilty. He had come to South America to see him but had arrived twenty years too late. And yet, he thought, though Mawi and Julieta had left this world two decades ago, they continued to give life to others. Death, where is thy sting?

Lorencio was another source of life and positive energy. 'I gave up thought for action,' he had told his guest. 'Once I was a priest, blessing the poor from the comfort of Santo Domingo. Now I'm a chef in a shanty-town, providing food for them.'

The visitor had lost the contempt he had felt for most of his fellow human beings. The people of the Andes, and those in sympathy with them, had breathed on the embers of his youthful vision of a social order based on brotherhood and equality taking root perhaps in some Arcadian corner of the world and growing year by year until its branches encompassed the earth. He would make South America his home and get to know the Andeans, discover their artistic riches – their sculpture, ceramics and ornately woven textiles, their architecture and music – and study their history from the days of the great Tiahuanaco civilization that had begun more than one and a half thousand years before Christ to the massive Inca Empire destroyed in the first half of the sixteenth century through the treachery of Francisco Pizarro and his band of Spanish thugs.

The visitor looked round at Lorencio. He wasn't sure what to do. Should he wake his host, see him to his bed, take his farewell and go? El Salvador was miles from the centre. The nearest bus-stop was more than half an hour's walk away. There were no buses at night and the area was off the map so far as taxis were concerned. He had been warned against coming here alone even by day. Venture out in El Salvador at night and you were certain to be mugged, murdered or kidnapped, so the rest of Lima said.

Why wake a man who was already asleep, only to make him go and sleep somewhere else? The visitor removed the empty bottles from the table, to make Lorencio look less like the sot he wasn't, washed the glasses in the oil-drum full of water, and rinsed and dried them. He poured himself another measure from the brandy bottle as a nightcap, turned the oil-lamp down low and returned to the doorway to sip his drink.

The moon was still white and bright in the black sky, but the black had taken on a navy-blue look and the dirt road, dark brown a few minutes ago, was now touched with orange. The traveller looked east along the road and saw what looked like a conflagration in the mountains – a volcano silently erupting or a mine exploding without a sound. The sun was rising behind the Andes, over the Isla del Sol, for its daily journey across the Pacific coast, out over the ocean, round the world and back to the Andes.

The brandy took its effect. The visitor was overwhelmed by a towering roller of fatigue that nearly made his knees buckle. He finished his drink, washed and dried the glass, closed the door, sat down at the table, rested his head on his arms and fell asleep within seconds.

He was woken by the sound of women laughing. For a moment he imagined he was on the Isla del Sol among the fisherfolk from Lorencio's tale. When he raised his head and opened his eyes, he was dazzled at first by the bright daylight, so that the two women standing in front of him seemed to become incarnated out of light as he looked at them. One was a tall, thin woman of about his own age, with fine features, a half-Indian, half-European face, grey hair tied neatly into a bun and a denim trouser suit that managed to look chic although it was intended for cleaning and cooking. The only blemish in her appearance was the scar on her left cheek. Her companion was in jeans and a red smock and was younger – about forty – with the gentleness of expression, the large black eyes, lustrous black hair and brown skin that characterized the indigenous people of the Andes.

'Have you been debauching my Lorencio with wine and brandy?' asked the older woman, laughing.

'Only enough to fuel him for the twelve-hour story he was telling me about two remarkable young people.'

The two women stared at the stranger for a few seconds, then disappeared inside the two boxes they had put on the table to unpack. One contained cartons of milk, the other sacks of maize. The older woman put the cartons in buckets she filled from the cistern outside. The younger woman poured the cereal into a cauldron.

The visitor got up and apologized for his untidy appearance. 'Perhaps I should introduce myself,' he said. 'My name is Paul Wickeham. I arrived in South America a few days ago from

London.'

The older woman dried her hands and responded with a firm handshake. 'My name is Nicole,' she said. 'This is my adopted daughter, Copihue.'

Wickeham said nothing for a few seconds. Then he murmured: 'Nicole and Copihue. I know who you are. You're Julieta's mother, and you...' He looked at Copihue and hesitated.

'Julieta was like a sister,' Copihue said quietly. She added water and milk to the cauldron and lit the gas.

'We have to lay the table for the children's breakfast,' Nicole said softly. 'We'd better move Lorencio to his bedroom.'

Lorencio was already waking, with the sound of conversation and the rattling of utensils. 'The thing is,' he said, slurring his words sleepily, 'I feel closer to Christ, living as a layman among the poor, than I ever did as a cleric administering to the rich.'

'Another two hours before you have to start on lunch,' Nicole told him gently. 'Go to your bed and get some more rest.'

Lorencio got up with the ease of a young man.

Wickeham held out his hand to him. 'I may be gone before you wake,' he said. 'Thank you for everything you told me yesterday and last night. And thank you... for your goodness and courage. People like you and Mawi and Julieta are... are a light in a dark world.'

Lorencio smiled and shook Wickeham's hand in both his own. 'The *comedor*'s a grain of sand,' he said. 'But if every one of us contributed a grain of sand, we could build dykes and banks high enough to hold back the greed of the rich and stop it engulfing the poor.'

Wickeham caught a glimpse of Lorencio's bedroom as he disappeared through the bead curtain: a mattress on the earth floor; a plank on two trestles to form a desk; an up-ended wooden crate for a chair; an oil-lamp. Nothing more.

'I never asked Lorencio what happened to Cortez and Gorringe,' Wickeham said as he picked up his bag and the violin-case that he now called his cat's coffin.

'Adolfo Cortez and Herman Gorringe?' Nicole replied, her lip curling as if she had opened one of her cartons and sniffed sour milk. 'Cortez should have been sentenced to life imprisonment but he has influential relatives: he was released after a few weeks and soon promoted to colonel. He started to show an interest in politics. Pinochet, who has never been one for democratic elections, appointed him heir to the presidency. Cortez was photographed with a young man in a night-club, naked and engrossed in some kind of erotic activity involving electrical plugs and sockets. He was promptly cashiered. Pinochet disinherited him. He now lives in the luxurious seaside villa left to him by his grandfather, surrounded by marble and alabaster statues of Ancient Greek youths: reproductions, of course, but the marble and alabaster are genuine.'

Nicole started moving plastic mugs from the shelf above the cooker to the table.

'And Gorringe?'

'Mayor of a town in Texas. Someone I know found his picture in a local paper there. He was grinning and being mobbed by a crowd of adoring children. His nickname is 'Daddy': 'Daddy' Gorringe.'

'What about your husband and Mawi's uncle and sister?'

Nicole unloaded porridge bowls from a tray on to the table.

'My husband was as good as his word. He revived the lakeside community, bought all their products and resold as many as he could. Whatever his faults, he was a generous and dependable man. He paid for Mawi's sister to go to university. She's now Head of the newly founded Department of Mapuche Studies at one of the universities in Santiago. She founded the department herself, with financial backing from my husband. He set up a trust not long before he died. Interest from investments goes to the lakeside community and to the university department he helped to create.'

'And you? You prefer to stay in South America after what happened? You don't want to return to France?'

'France? France lost its attraction for me when my grandmother died. I left at the time of Algeria, when the French were arresting Algerians without charge and torturing them.'

'Does Peru have a better record than France for unlawful arrest and torture?'

'No, but it has several million inhabitants who are so poor that many of them starve to death: poverty-stricken thanks to European and North American exploitation. I am half Peruvian. My place is in Peru.'

Nicole paused in her work and stood facing Wickeham.

'When will all this poverty end, Señor Wickeham? The world is full of El Salvadors. I never realized it until my daughter pointed it out to me. When Julieta was twelve, she told me that if God granted her ten million years, she wouldn't rest till she had provided food, a roof, clothes, medicine and a school for all the underprivileged children in the world.'

Nicole took spoons from a shoe-box and laid them on the table, one for every bowl and mug. Copihue had her porridge on the simmer.

Wickeham put down his bag and violin-case. 'Do you ever need an extra pair of hands?' he asked.

'Extra hands, extra food, extra money for equipment. The State does nothing for its poor.'

Wickeham held up his forearms. 'This pair is at your service, whenever you need them.'

He shook the two women by the hand, picked up his bag and case and stepped out of the *comedor* into the tropical sun. He turned east for the half-hour walk along the yellow dirt road between the rows of cardboard shacks to the buses, humming the theme of the Bach violin partita he was relearning after more than forty years. He felt as safe as if he were walking through Regent's Park.

Wickeham would study the way of life of the Andeans. He would come back and help at the *comedor*. The seed for a possible third project dropped into his thoughts. Lorencio's story mustn't be forgotten. Could he be persuaded to write it down? If not, Paul Wickeham would offer to write it for him for all the world to read.

'As the rocks are to the sea,' he murmured as he walked, 'so is our love to their memory.'

50% or more of the author's royalties are used to fund medical and educational projects in the countries in which his novels are set. By buying this book you have helped an Andean weavers' guild to train some of the ablest villagers in the Cuzco area of Peru to read and write first in their own language, Quechua, then in Spanish, and to teach what they have learnt to other adults and to the children of their communities.

Aïsha's Jihad

Robert Southam

A major Western power and its allies are threatening to invade a Middle Eastern country, without the sanction of the United Nations. In an English country town a teenage brother and sister, refugees since early childhood from Palestine, live with their mother below the poverty line and struggle for social acceptance and an education that will allow their talents to flower. The bombs start to fall. Ali and Aïsha demand to know about the outrages to their father and grandparents that drove their mother from Palestine. The crisis polarizes the passions of the two teenagers: one turns to peace, the other to a more desperate solution.

The violence of war and the more subtle violence of unequal educational opportunities at home are ingeniously interwoven in this novel full of poignancy and humour, in which we see how the decisions of leaders at national and international level can influence personal relationships and individual lives.

Aïsha's Jihad received enthusiastic notices in England, Scotland, Switzerland and France, and on BBC Radio. The novel is as relevant today as when it was written. It has been enjoyed not only by adults but also by younger readers, who identify with the teenage protagonists: it was chosen as a set book for secondary schools in Switzerland.

At Roundfire we publish great stories. We lean towards the spiritual and thought-provoking. But whether it's literary or popular, a gentle tale or a pulsating thriller, the connecting theme in all Roundfire fiction titles is that once you pick them up you won't want to put them down.